C000133161

Talking Work

Talking Work

An Oral History

Trevor Blackwell and
Jeremy Seabrook

faber and faber

First published in 1996
by Faber and Faber Limited
3 Queen Square London WC1N 3AU

Photoset by Datix International Limited, Bungay, Suffolk
Printed in England by Clays Ltd, St Ives plc

All rights reserved

© Trevor Blackwell and Jeremy Seabrook, 1996

Trevor Blackwell and Jeremy Seabrook are hereby identified
as authors of this work in accordance with Section 77
of the Copyright, Designs and Patents Act 1988

A CIP record for this book is available
from the British Library

ISBN 0–571–14306–7

10 9 8 7 6 5 4 3 2 1

This boundless region, the region of *le boulot*, the job, *il rusco* –
of daily work, in other words – is less known than the Antarctic,
and through a sad and mysterious phenomenon, it happens that
the people who talk most, and loudest, about it are the very
ones who have never travelled through it. To exalt labour, in
official ceremonies an insidious rhetoric is displayed, based on
the consideration that a eulogy or a medal costs much less than
a pay raise, and they are also more fruitful. There also exists a
rhetoric on the opposite side, however, not cynical, but
profoundly stupid, which tends to denigrate labour, to depict it
as base, as if labour, our own or others', were something we
could do without, not only in Utopia, but here, today; as if
anyone who knows how to work were, by definition, a servant,
and as if, on the contrary, someone who doesn't know how to
work, or knows little, or doesn't want to, were for that very
reason a free man. It is sadly true that many jobs are not
loveable, but it is harmful to come into the field charged with
preconceived hatred. He who does this sentences himself, for
life, to hating not only work, but also himself and the world.

Primo Levi, *The Wrench*

Contents

Contents

Introduction

Everybody knows who the working class used to be. The troubling question is, who are they now?

People feel comfortable with the working class as long as it remains an historical concept. It is easy to visualize grainy newsreel images of men in flat caps framed against the black wheel of a pithead; chimneys with the smoke bending to the prevailing wind; a maze of redbrick streets, a factory on one corner, a pub on the other; the youth gathered around the white light coming from the chip shop; feet tramping to the rhythm of the factory siren; rows of female operatives in headscarves, working in unison and smiling hesitantly at the photographer; women on their doorsteps, elbow cupped in one hand, the other hand under the chin, watching or waiting.

Where do we find the contemporary equivalent of such images? Perhaps in the shopping centre – a group of young men carrying green and gold cylinders of lager, parading the transnational logos on their uniform of long-tongued sneakers and particoloured jackets. Perhaps on the rubberized floor of Luton airport on a Saturday afternoon in August – people camped on leatherette seats surrounded by a pyramid of maroon or navy-blue cases and hold-alls, the children chasing around a debris of paper cups and spilt coffee. Perhaps in the post office, where the long queues shift from one foot to the other, and older women waiting for their pension exchange censorious glances over the younger women who can afford to smoke even though they're on benefit. Perhaps at the supermarket checkout, young hands, a ring on each finger, passing every item over the electronic eye that registers a bleep of satisfaction as it records the price.

Why does this second set of images appear so insubstantial compared with the first? Of course, images from the past appear to have a superior reality. They are fixed, irreversible. The selection has already been made for us by the work of photographers and cameramen. It is against this fixed and familiar iconography that we confront the teeming confusion of the present, with its plethora of vivid and jarring images. The present is fluid, impalpable, but the past is, perversely, more solid.

Or was the life of people then as full of rich and diverse activity, which is now denied by the archaic postures in which they must come to us? Surely, their lives were as mysterious, as hard to grasp as ours seem to us? Or has something really changed, that makes our experience radically less comprehensible?

Whatever the working class was, or is now, it is always about work. This truism needs to be re-emphasized because the importance of work sometimes appears to have been marginalized by the superiority of buying over doing in the busy consumer societies of the world. It seems to us that we can best get to the heart of these puzzling, and sometimes disturbing, questions about class by listening to people's own accounts of their labour.

The interviews presented here span the whole of the twentieth century. For some of the early ones, we have drawn upon existing oral material, particularly from the rich and growing collection at the National Sound Archive; but as far as possible, we have recorded living memory. Clearly such material cannot be exhaustive, nor can it hope to document the epic changes that have occurred in every branch of industry. We have talked to people who had a story to tell, and through those stories we can glimpse, often obliquely, some of the social patternings which shape individual lives.

Does work make a class? Do changes in work cause changes in class? How important is making and doing in the formation of human identities? It may be that such fundamental questions cannot be approached directly. But as we listen to these people telling their lives, we hear voices and sounds which are not theirs alone, but which express the power of wider technological changes and the social upheavals that always come with them. The fateful consequences of these dislocations can be heard sometimes in an aside, an undertone, a wistful remark, a sudden afterthought . . . What would my life have been like, if my father had not taken me out of school on the Friday to go down the pit on the following Monday? . . . What indeed? But how could it have been different, things being what they were?

We have structured the book so that voices from the past interrogate the present, and voices from the present pursue their own uneasy dialogue with the past. And whatever breaks and disruptions occur in the work people do, the changing experience nevertheless raises questions that are hauntingly, poignantly familiar.

Acknowledgements

We would like to thank the following for their help in compiling this book: Ian Turner and Pat Ashford at Harlow College; Carole Hussan of Harlow Council; Ken Hancock of the National Union of Mineworkers; Steve Platt of the *New Statesman and Society*; and Adele Davis. We are grateful to Raphael Samuel for discussing with us some of the themes in the book, to Annette Rayner for help with the interviewing; and special thanks to Dr Robert Perks at the National Sound Archive for permission to publish material in the Oral History Collection. Most of all, we would like to thank all the people who agreed to talk to us, and shared with us their experience of work and life.

Acknowledgement is also due to Basil Blackwell and Victor Gollancz for permission to use previously published material.

TREVOR BLACKWELL

JEREMY SEABROOK

London, May 1995

PART I

One

One of the most profound of technological changes this century occurred in the first quarter, when horsepower was superseded by motorized vehicles. The consequences of this for those whose employment had depended upon draught animals were catastrophic; but within a few years vast new areas of labour opened up in the manufacture and driving of cars, vans and trucks.

Harry Price (*born 1890*): *coachman and omnibus driver, Hammersmith*

I was the eldest of a family of seven children. I was strong, healthy and fit, and when I was fourteen I wanted to work. We lived in Fulham, and I walked to Hammersmith with the aim of getting a job. You left school one day and got work the next. You expected to.

I went to Palmer's, a big store in Hammersmith, where they had about twenty horses, and they had two market vans which did the big markets – Billingsgate, Covent Garden and Smithfield meat market. I saw a 'boy wanted' sign, so I goes straight in and saw one of the chiefs. He says, 'Can you get up in the morning?' I said, 'Yes.' He said, 'All right. Go round the corner to the stables and you'll see the carman.' He said, 'How old are you?' I said 'Eighteen.' I was just fourteen. They offered me fourteen shillings a week on the strength of that.

This was on a big pair-horse van. We used to go to market every morning. The carman took a liking to me. After I'd been there only a few months, one day he said, 'Here, come on, up on the dicky.' He put the safety strap round me, and said, 'Come on, that's the way you hold the reins', and he taught me how to drive. He really made a coachman of me. So when I was fifteen – nineteen to them – they said, 'You don't want a van-boy job, you want a carman job.' So I was made the single-horse carman ... at a guinea a week ... right away. One morning, I'm coming home from Smithfield market, and I had a horse down. There was a breakman as I was passing Lyons – that's a man who used to break in all the young horses – and I asked him to help me. Luckily the pole never broke. This fellow came out, gave me a hand. He was made foreman at

Cadby Hall, Kensington. I was thinking, Well what I'm doing isn't much of a job. Some mornings I had to get to Covent Garden at two in the morning. I never got breakfast till eleven, and some nights I didn't get home till ten. I thought I'd be doing myself some good if I got a coachman's job at Lyons, because they paid twenty-eight shillings a week. They had twenty-five or thirty horse vans.

This was 1908. I went to Cadby Hall, and this fellow who was foreman there came out and said, 'What do you want, son?' 'To be frank, I want a job.' He said, 'Right you are, jump up on that pair; the boy will tell you the way to the shops you have to go to.' He took me on straight away. I've been lucky. I've never been out of work, I've always landed in the right job.

After some time at that I went to the Fire Brigade. I walked into the Kingsland Road station. In the Fire Brigade, the First Coachman was the senior and the Second beneath him. I started as Second Coachman, and became Senior Supplementary Coachman after about nine months. As coachman, it was your duty to look after the horses; you didn't do any fire-fighting. I was thinking of going on the buses, because buses were all the go then. In fact, the Fire Brigade was losing men to the London General Omnibus Company. I was a single man and courting; one day off every fifteen days. That's a long time when you're courting. If I hadn't been courting, I'd never have left the Fire Brigade, because it really was the job for me. I loved the excitement, the men you were with were always close together. Most men in the Fire Brigade had been seamen. You heard stories of the rough sea life, of storms and near escapes.

When I was Second Coachman, I was responsible for organization. I didn't go out much, because I took care of the horses. They were contracted from Thomas Tilling and other dealers; every week they came and delivered the chaff and the straw, all your tools for looking after the animals. The horses were rented, never owned by the LCC.

To become a fireman, they had three months in drill class. If you went to a big fire, there was always a refreshment van came up, and in those days, in winter, it was always Bovril. And of course, if you were on the life-saving appliance, you always unhooked your horses. There would always be a crowd round the horses, admiring them. You drove them by word of mouth. You've got to get them galloping in rhythm so your appliance is straight. There were many hazards, because the roads were uneven and full of holes. It's very skilled work.

When they started motorizing, it was the coachmen first of all they used to train, the juniors first, because they were more adaptable. They trained for six months – three theory and three practical. I wondered whether to; then I thought, no, the London General Omnibus Company is *the* job.

The money was great – £3 a week; up to twelve hours a day, some days maybe eight or nine; you were paid mileage. They didn't want to accept my resignation from the Fire Brigade. 'No son,' they said, 'this is your job.' And that's how I always felt. I didn't mind the discipline, I enjoyed it. I think the majority of the lads did.

When you were on duty, at night, you were only out of bed if you were riding the horse-escape, the life-saving appliance. If you were riding the steamer, you could go to bed. Of course, directly the bells go, you're out. So you always laid your trousers down by the side of the bed, with the flaps open, and your jackboots beside them. That made it easier. If you had twenty-four hours' leave, you'd never leave your trousers out. That way, when the bells went, you always jumped out of bed, you were trained to it. Then you thought hello, no trousers, and then you crept back into bed: you knew you were on leave ... When you were on duty, you always left everything ready so you could just jump into your trousers and boots and down the pole.

There's so much difference in the job now. It's an expert's job really. In my days, it was a case of 'There's a fire there', you go with the idea of saving lives, overcoming the fire. But look at what it entails now. It's so mechanical, isn't it? There's so much grading – leading fireman, sub-officer, station officer. In my time the coachman's job was simply to drive the horses safely to the fire; once you got there, you didn't do anything but look after the horses. When you got back from the fire, it didn't matter what time of day or night it was, if it was wet or muddy – the horses had to be cleaned before they were put away. They had to be cleaned properly, you had to wash down the legs, dry them properly. You had all the tools to do the job – you had the sponge, the leather; and you always had to put everything away tidily afterwards. Same thing with whoever was driving the steamer – it had to be cleaned. Its appearance was important because it was all brass.

A coachman was a coachman. Seven in the morning clean the stables, eight till nine breakfast and polish your helmet. If you were riding the life-saving appliance, you were not allowed to take your tunic off; you used to ease your tunic, undo your belt; but you always laid on the trestles; you weren't allowed in the billiard room. You had to remain in a state of readiness. A coachman was a coachman, and a fireman was a fireman. You never got promotion from coachman's post, only up the ladder from Second Coachman to First Coachman. The pay of the First Coachman was 31s 6d.

I joined the Bus Company in 1913. The unions were just being founded then. There were many restrictions at that time. If you were running, say, five minutes early, you'd get booked. You'd have to see the Superintendent. That might mean one day off, seeing him, and he might say, 'Three days' suspension', according to how many men he's got outside the gate waiting for your job. You paid for all your own accidents that you were held to be to blame for – up to £2 at two shillings a week. A man might be unlucky over the course of a few months, perhaps a couple or three little touches. So by the time he's paid off one £2, there's another one hanging up behind the door for him. Of course, you were out in all weathers, because you weren't covered – only a little apron in front of you. In winter it was hard. The money was good. Then you got the covered-in tops, and then the front.

We were called up in August 1914. I'd joined the Mechanical Transport Special Reserve. The company had to take girls on as conductors, because so many had gone into the Army. The first thing the union said was 'If you take girls on, the job they are doing is the same as the men, you have to pay them the man's rate.' And they did; no arguments. The bus company got unionized very quickly. By the time I was demobbed in May 1919, the bus workers were doing a 48-hour week.

I would have liked to stay a fireman. I could have become a coachman-fireman as they called it at the time of motorization. I couldn't drive till I went to the Omnibus Company. In those days the LGOC had no training school at all. They had their instructors at the garages. When I went for the job I was in my coachman's uniform, and of course they grabbed you straight away, because they knew you'd passed the LCC medical test. 'What do you want, fireman?' 'I want a job.' There's a crowd there, hundreds of men after jobs. 'Fill in this form.' I had eight hours' leave: by the end of it I had the job. I went to the Grosvenor Road HQ; then I was sent to see a doctor; then back to Grosvenor Road. Then to Spring Gardens, near Trafalgar Square, for a licence. In those days you only had to apply to get it. Then I came back. 'When can you leave London Fire Brigade? As soon as you do that, here's a letter to take to the Superintendent at Turnham Green garage. Get an instructor to take you out.' So you report next day. They have two learners' buses. You go up for the test at Scotland Yard two weeks later and pass.

When I'd passed I was sent to Forest Gate garage. You go out with another driver on the front of the bus to show you the road. The very next day, you're out on your own. They've just started a new service, the Number 40, from Forest Gate to the Elephant. The first time out, I run into a tram. It's done the bus in. They have to tow the bus back to the garage. It looks like I'll be going back to the Fire Brigade. I had to go and see the Superintendent. 'Now,' he said, 'you're not in the London Fire

Brigade, you're in the London General Omnibus Company . . . Come back tomorrow.' I lose a day. Sign on next morning, and I never had any trouble since.

I went in the union as soon as I came back from the Army; and I've never been out of it since.

But you never recapture the excitement of the Fire Brigade. If there's a fire and one of your colleagues is in trouble, they're there, there's never any argument about it. I loved the thrill of the job, the cheerfulness of the lads you were with. There was something in the shared position, in living close together, that you don't get elsewhere. Most had been Merchant Navy men. The job got a grip on you. Like fire – if it was a chimney fire, it was a washout, you just had your horses to clean. But if you're going to a fire, and you see someone sitting on the window ledge with the flames all around them, that's a different job, that's excitement and challenge.

I was nearly five years with the Army Transport Service Corps. They asked for volunteers to go over to the Machine Gun Corps. I was keen and joined. I gained the Military Medal in March 1919. I didn't talk about it, it's not the kind of thing you tell people. The Bus Company knew, because I used to head the London busmen to the Cenotaph every year. There were so many men walking about with ribbons on which they were not entitled to. I'm proud of my medals, but I don't want to let people know I have them.

I was the oldest in the family. I only had an ordinary education. My mother and father were out of this world; you couldn't want for better parents. My mother used to run a small laundry at the washtub. My father was on the buildings. They used to come off the buildings in the winter and go in the gas works; that was a recognized seasonal thing.

I didn't leave the buses till I was seventy. I couldn't stay any longer because I was holding up promotion. I was still active and I wanted a job, so I went in a uniform again to do the job I'm doing now. I'm working at Regent Street, as a doorman with a furrier's, a little light job. I'm only nearly eighty-seven; I've been doing this seventeen years. I used to say to my old Dad, 'I've never had the sack yet.' He said, 'Son, it's an honour; anybody can leave a job, it takes a good man to get the sack.'

I wanted something where I'd be made for life: I thought either the police, the fire, the post office, the LCC or the trams. Of them, the fire and police were pensionable. So it was one of these two. I didn't like the attitude of the police. It doesn't seem to be me, if I find a bloke drunk, to scoop him up and arrest him. If I could help him, take him home, I'd be happy to do it. No, that wasn't my job. So it had to be the Fire Brigade . . . I never had a day out of work all my life.

5

Two

The coming of the twentieth century changed little for many working women, particularly for those who were employed in industry and who — virtually all of them — were still expected to carry out an onerous, unending round of domestic labour too. Many people, no matter how hard they worked, were unable to procure an adequate living for themselves and their families; and the testimony of a few such lives is all that remains — an uncelebrated, scandalous heroism, the poignant words of those long-dead.

Ada Carey (*born 1902*): *boot and shoe worker, Northampton*

My mother was seeing my two brothers off to the Sunday School treat in July 1902, when she suddenly had to go home. I was being born.

I was born in a house in Narrow Toe Lane, and the outlook wasn't very rosy. The same night, my father came home, his job finished. On the day I was christened, my mother was asked by somebody comfortably off to let them adopt me, because they had no children of their own. I'm glad she refused.

The only help they got was a ticket from the relieving officer for a bit of grocery. They couldn't pay the rent, so we kept having to move where landlords couldn't find us. The winters were the worst, because my father was an outdoor worker, on the roads. Although we lived in a boot and shoe town, we never had new shoes, always second-hand, always too big or too small. Mother would get a little house in bad condition, and do it up. For a few weeks, while my father's work lasted, we would be fed better, but his work was casual, so it lasted a month or two if we were lucky.

Mother was always at the washtub. She went to scrub and wash for others for two shillings a day, and she would come home at eleven at night, on the last tram. You could get things from the shops late at night then — a halfpenny packet of tea, a penny-worth of sugar — boil the kettle on the fire and at least you'd got tea. We only saw cow's milk when somebody was ill. She would buy a rabbit for sixpence, with pot vegetables and dumplings. My brother would go and get stale pastries from the shop — rolls, bits of pork pie, egg custard, all broke up, but it was like a Christmas stocking to us.

One Christmas when father was out of work, we were classed as the poor and needy, and were given a ticket for a Christmas hamper which had to be collected from the Town Hall. My sister handed in the ticket, and we got a cake, an orange and a new penny. I loved the walk back, clutching our little gift under our arm, and holding the new penny tight in our hand. It wasn't that being poor was unhappy all the time; it's just that the bad times stung harder. We got our clothes from a Good Samaritan society; but you were branded as being poor, because all the clothes had a big round stamp like a vaccination mark. You couldn't wash it out. That was so you shouldn't sell it. Being sensitive, I tried to hide these marks when I hung my coat up at school; but when I went to put it on, it always seemed to have moved so the marks were showing. Girls and boys had the same boots, with five holes punched in the top.

My mother had another baby. The house was too small, so off we went with a hand-truck, one street away. Mother was very ill, and we were fed by charity. Father worked regularly for a time, and the rent could be paid. But then there was a big strike; they turned the music hall into a place where children went to get a cup of tea and a bread roll with jam. You had to hold it tight, or somebody would have it out of your hand.

We had to get a cheaper house – if you could call it a house. It was a shelter, no more. It was infested with rats, and the toilet in the yard was shared. You often had to wait a long time outside, because the old man we shared it with fell asleep inside. I daren't go into this house if nobody was there because of the rats. The food had to be hung up in bags on the doors. One Sunday morning, we got up for breakfast, and the rats had eaten the middle out of the cottage loaves that were in a bag hung on the door at the top of the underground kitchen. My father set a cage trap, and next morning there were five grey rats. Us kiddies wanted to keep them in the cage as pets, but that was out of the question.

My mother had another baby. The midwife was upstairs washing the baby, and suddenly the chair leg came through the ceiling, leaving a big hole. While mother was in bed, we could sit downstairs and talk to her through the hole.

Things were reasonable for eighteen months, but then there was another spell of no work, and my eldest brother became sick. He was a TB suspect. There were nine of us in the family by now, and no money coming in. If we were given a halfpenny, we didn't spend it on sweets – we went to a shop at the corner of Scarletwell Street and bought a halfpenny worth of cold rice pudding or bread pudding. We got jealous of our sick brother, because he got better things than we did. My brother said, 'I wish I was bad so I could have egg custards.' One day, we went home from school, and the house had no doors or windows. The landlord had taken them off because we couldn't pay the rent arrears.

My mother was a clean, hardworking woman, but that didn't bring in money. The landlord put all our bits and pieces in the street, and we had no home. The neighbours were decent. They took care of our wordly possessions – didn't amount to much – and we kiddies were taken in by different neighbours. After a week, my mother found a house that we shared with a man who had lost his wife; he was old, but clever enough to charge my mother the rent for the whole house. The four boys had one bedroom, and Dad and Mother and the three girls the other. That was my mother's twelfth move.

My oldest sister couldn't do much work, because she lost all the fingers on her left hand when she was two. She looked after the house while mother went out to work. I was nine years old by now, and one of my brothers had started work. My mother worked all the time, cleaning, charring, scrubbing. The only break she had was when she had babies.

The man we shared the house with used to call me into his room, to do his errands. I was frightened of him; I'd fetch his things, put them on the table and run out. He used to call me back, and mother made me go. He gave me a halfpenny and held my hand, and I had to pull away from him. One day, he pulled me into his room when mother was at work. I knew he meant bad, but I daren't tell mother. She was good-living and brought up very straight. Eventually, he went to live with his daughter, and we became tenants of the house.

We began to live more comfortably. We never had much furniture, but home was always clean. The children helped to keep it clean. The floor was plain boards, no lino. We ate better, and although clothes were still second-hand, they were clean.

When war broke out, there were many soldiers in the town, and there was plenty of work. I got my first job – at a shop at the top of our street, which was also a café; they had thirty soldiers billeted for meals. My job was to lay tables, wash up and wait at table, as well as serve in the shop, between times going to school. I got 1s 6d a week and my food. I had to be up at six in the morning to help with the breakfast. I went at dinner time and when school was over. I was sometimes kept there till eleven at night, because I also did some washing for them.

As the war went on, things became scarce. You had to go and queue for sugar or butter or margarine. This meant almost every family had to have someone whose job it was to go and stand in queues whenever there was a supply of whatever came into the shops. White bread disappeared.

My eldest brother enlisted at seventeen, because his pals had been called up. He was fighting in the trenches in France, and was gassed and wounded before he was eighteen. Mother tried to stop him from going, but she couldn't. In 1918, there was a bad flu epidemic. My sister, who was twenty-three, died. My mother never got over this loss. I was working full time by then in a factory for 3s 6d a week, and another brother was working, which was a good thing, because father had to stop with chest trouble. He drew ten shillings a week sick benefit.

After the war, unemployment was worse. If there was a job going, there would be a crowd of people going for it. In the factories, conditions were not good. You didn't dare raise your eyes from your work, you were not allowed to talk. We had a very stately forewoman, and she fascinated me by the way she walked up and down the room. She gave me the sack because I watched her. She said I couldn't be doing my work while I was watching her. So I was on the march for another job.

I tried everything in the next few years. I was nurse in a mental hospital, and then I went in service. I went for an interview in a very large house. The woman was elderly and walked with a stick. She said she had been without help for some time. There was a kitchen range, rusty and very dirty. My mother asked how many staff there were, and she said the maid was supposed to do it all. My mother said, 'You want a slave, not a maid', and she wouldn't let any child of hers take all that on. For refusing that, my bit of unemployment money was stopped.

My next job was in a leather-dressing factory, putting black dope on skins. I was rather small for my age and I couldn't reach the tables, so they gave me a box to stand on. I turned up for work in a starched white pinafore, and before the day was over I slipped off the box, with the black dope all over me. Later, I was put on a machine glazing the skins. This was a good job. But one of the skins had a hole in it, and the machine pulled my hand with the skin into the machinery. I had a smashed finger, and was unable to work for three months. I went back to a lighter job. Most of us in the factory were young girls. We used to go out into the toilets, and one day, two or three of us were there, learning a new dance called the Valeta. The foreman sent one of the staff to fetch us in. She told the truth about what we were doing, and he told us we could dance right out of the factory – he was giving us the sack.

I went to another shoe factory, on piece-work, where you had to work really hard before you made a decent wage. I'd started going steady. Then mother was taken ill, and the doctor said she – the main breadwinner –

9

would not work again. She had been kept going, like so many women, by willpower alone. She had cancer, and had struggled with it for two years. She wouldn't lay up, but kept on her feet. Now all my money had to go into the house. My oldest brother was married; the next one was a regular soldier, about to go to Hong Kong. There were six of us at home – father on the sick, mother with cancer. I was in a boot factory, and so was my brother; and two of them were still at school. We managed. I made my own clothes and also clothes for the rest of the family. Although I was courting, my time was spent doing housework at night and preparing the next day's dinner. Father would cook it once I'd got it ready.

In the end, my mother had to give up and take to her bed; so I had to nurse mother, look after the house and go to work. Father kept an eye on her during the day, but he was sick himself. I had to get to work on time – if you were a minute late, you were locked out for half an hour, and had to stand outside the factory gate. Mother spent six months in bed. I used to sleep on a couch beside the bed, so I could attend to her in the night. My mother died during that August Bank holiday. She had had no pleasure in her life, only hardship and hard work. She died owing nobody anything, and her total wealth was three half-crowns.

I was left in charge of the smaller family: a sick father, a brother just started work, two at school and 7s 6d. I promised mother I would look after them, and I did. My fellow was one of the best. When we got married, that was another poor affair. I took a house on the other side of the street, at double the rent. My husband was quite prepared to take on all the family. But first, I wanted to get a good home together; there was nothing in mother's house worth having. I covered the floors of the new house with lino. I bought cheap material and made curtains. I had saved up for bedroom furniture while we were courting; and I furnished the living-room on hire purchase. There was no wedding reception, no honeymoon; but a decent house to go to with the family.

I never had a lot of money, but my husband earned regularly in the factory, and now another sister started work. I had to leave my job when I married: that was the rule at the time. So I got another job – this time, at an outdoor closing room [where uppers are stitched to the soles of shoes]. That meant you collected the work from the factory and did the closing at home. Trouble was, holiday time you got no money at all; so after each holiday you were behind, and it took until the next holiday to pay off what you owed, and so it started all over again. It was like chasing your own shadow.

I fell for a baby soon after I was married. I hadn't allowed for that in my budget. I told nobody. I kept on working at home; and when I wasn't doing the shoe work, I was sewing and knitting for the baby. I worked right up to the time. Nobody knew I was having a baby; when I was bad, they wanted to know what was wrong. Even with the baby, I could still do shoe work at home.

I had a letter from my brother in Hong Kong, saying he had finished his service abroad and was leaving on the next boat. But the next I heard was a letter from the Home Office. I thought it was from him, but it read: 'We regret to announce the death of your brother.' His officer wrote me, saying he had had an accident, and had died of cerebral haemorrhage. He was twenty-three.

We had rats in the house. In spite of the rat-catcher coming, they couldn't put an end to it, because they were sewer rats coming from a broken pipe in the ground. This time I was given a council house, with a nice garden, but we were one bedroom short, so my sister had to leave us. She went to live with my husband's mother, as she was courting his brother.

She didn't like it, and came back to us. The Council said we were overcrowded, because I had my second baby, and my sister and her husband were there, making nine of us in all. So we moved to a bigger house, which was more expensive. My sister's husband fell out of work, so their total income was thirty-two shillings. Work was bad, everybody on short time. I had an accident and fractured my foot and leg. My father was still an invalid, receiving ten shillings a week, and he gave me eight shillings of this for his keep. But he was a man of twenty stone, and when he was taken ill we thought he had a minor cold. He went to bed on the Monday and died on the Friday. He was buried within a week of being ill. He had suffered with his chest for years. There was no time to order wreaths or anything, so my husband's mother fetched all the flowers, and we sat and made one long cross of flowers on the Sunday, the best we could do.

I had to take a cheaper place, so we moved back into a privately rented house. After a few months, the landlord came and said he was selling the house, and he would give me first offer. I didn't have two shillings to my name – how could I think of buying a house? If you kept yourself clean and respectable, it gave people the idea that you had money. So we moved again. I think one thing working people always dreamed of was being secure, not having to flit all the time.

My sister and her husband got a house and moved out. I suppose I always remained the centre of the family, because my oldest brother parted from his wife, and he came back home.

All this happened before I was twenty-five. Since then, I worked, boot and shoe, sometimes at home, sometimes in the factory. Our life was work, we knew that. We didn't expect anything else. We started out with nothing, and we finished up with not much more. It was our life. The thing that made it bearable was that we had each other. My husband was a good one; he died eight years ago.

Three

Much work for women emerged from the unpaid caring role which has always been considered 'women's work'. When this labour first figured in the public sphere, it had to be tightly controlled and disciplined, in an almost militaristic way. This was possibly because women who entered nursing were performing intimate services for strangers, including men, and the only other women who did that were prostitutes; so one major reason for the tight discipline was doubtless in the interests of differentiating them from less respectable social functions.

Mrs Kemp (*born 1899*): *nurse, Portsmouth*

My mother was trained as a nurse to deal with infectious diseases. She had worked in Salford, but after her marriage she never practised again, although she used to sit in with sick neighbours from time to time. My father worked in Portsmouth dockyard. There were eight children, five younger than me. I had to care for my smaller brothers and sisters, because when her last baby was born my mother lost her sight. In 1915, at the age of sixteen, I was at home looking after the younger children, while my mother had her baby. I knew nothing about how babies were born: girls didn't in those days.

For five years I helped look after the baby, and then, when he was five, I applied to be a probationary nurse at St Mary's Hospital in Portsmouth. One of my older sisters had trained as a nurse there. You had to have a secondary school education to get in. Life was very strict in the hospital. You were interviewed by the Board of Guardians, with Matron sitting in: she weighed about twenty stone, and the Board sat with black hats and white beards. I had to take a written test as well. I lived near the hospital, so when I started, in my off-duty times I used to go home to do some ironing, cooking, or ice the Christmas cake.

I started my training in January 1919. I was to be twenty-one in the June although you were supposed to be twenty-one when you started. I was overawed by this great big ward. The Sister on the ward had also trained my sister. My sister was clever and rather reserved, and she got the reputation for being snooty. They took it out on me. I gave as good as I got. I must have been a handful. I'd never left home before, and I'd spent all my life with younger children. I'd never really come up against discipline.

You had to live in. No nurse got married or lived out. I'll never forget. I was told my uniform was on the bed in the tiny room I lived in. I couldn't stop laughing, because the dress I had was blue and white striped, with a tight bodice, and it went right down to my ankles, and right up to the neck and down to the wrists. On top, I had to put a big apron that went over the head, all straps and belts. And the cap! I had very long hair, down to my waist, so it was a problem getting all this hair under the cap. I always refer to my entrance as sweeping into the ward with this long dress on. You see, when you went into the men's wards, you weren't supposed to bend over because the men might see your ankles.

I was put on this same Sister's ward, and she was a battle-axe. I went straight on duty. On my first day, I reported at six in the morning, and was on the ward by seven. Sister sent me to work behind the screens with a second-year nurse. She was doing a patient. Of course, we had had no instruction – you didn't do any pre-nursing training at all, you just had to take your chance and pick it up from the people you worked with.

I was helping with a patient and the nurse said, 'Go and get a back-tray.' So I ran off to the kitchen and came back with this big black tray. She said, 'Did you do what I asked you?' I said, 'Yes.' 'Well, where is it?' 'Under the bed.' It was the back-tray for doing the backs. Nobody told you anything: you just had to be alert and learn as you went along.

I started in a female surgical ward; and I had my first glimpse of people dying and being laid out. They were mostly what we would call geriatrics today. It was a sixty-bed ward, with two side wards with a dozen beds in each, and a little ward for patients who were not expected to recover. There was a Sister, a staff nurse, a third-year nurse and two or three probationers, all at the beck and call of the whole lot. There was a recognized time for giving out the bedpans. I used to take it to them if they called for it. I got into no end of trouble for doing that or giving them a glass of water between times. From there I went to the male wards. A lot of the patients were from the workhouse: ulcerated legs – they were just old; stomach troubles – some smoked too much and coughed a lot. They had been transferred from the workhouse when they became too ill to stay there.

We had lectures from the Medical Superintendent. We worked on the wards from eight in the morning till eight at night, with two hours off in the afternoon. That is, you had two hours if you were lucky, if you didn't have to report to Matron because you'd broken a thermometer or something. If you wanted to go into town, even a ride on the tram was a great excitement. I couldn't even afford the penny for the tram ride. You just walked everywhere.

We used to all wear corridor capes that belonged to the hospital. Our outdoor wear we had to provide – the cape alone cost six guineas; our navy-blue suit also cost six guineas; and we were supposed to provide that out of a monthly salary of £3 ... Of that I gave my mother £1 ... We got into debt; we had to buy our own books; I once paid two guineas for a book on surgery which didn't even interest me. We had our lecture books given to us by the hospital, but that was all.

Life was hectic. You had your lectures and you had to write them up. The Assistant Matron would find something she wanted taken up to the wards upstairs, and she would leave it on the table outside the messroom door in the nurses' home. And if you dared to go up to the ward without taking whatever she had left on the table, she would ring up and say, 'I'm sorry, Sister, but Nurse So-and-so's memory and intelligence are getting much worse.' She was very sarcastic. You were niggled at all the time, all the petty rules. If Matron was walking down the corridor, you stood to one side while she sailed by. And you never spoke to the Sister on the ward. You never spoke to the Medical Superintendent or the doctors. We occasionally organized a little dance on the top corridor; and Matron sat there resplendent, while we danced with each other, because, of course, no men were allowed in there.

We had some Welsh girls there who objected to the food. It was after the war, and we had mutton which was terrible. This mutton came up regular. One morning, we had eggs for breakfast which were black inside. On the ward where I was, we had a pen and ink artist, and I went in that morning, and I called out, 'Good morning' – I always did that, although nobody else did. He said to me, 'How was it this morning?' I said, 'Black eggs, hard bread.' Later he gave me a drawing he'd done, of an egg sitting in a cup, all black, holding its tummy with its little hands and saying, 'Oh I do feel bad today.' I couldn't resist it. I put it on the notice board outside the messroom. Matron's maid spotted me doing it, so I was for Matron's office, being told once again that I was nothing like my sister.

After working all night, we would go out and play tennis; how we had the energy to do it with all the lifting, twelve hours of work, I'll never know. Most of the nurses came from Ireland or Wales. The Welsh girls were miners' daughters, they were agitators; the Irish girls had been brought over by priests. Once, at the instigation of one of the Welsh girls, we got up a round robin complaining about the food. Matron had us all there in the sitting-room. Nobody would split on who'd started it.

Life was hard, but we had a lot of fun. The discipline was terrible. A Sister would stand at the end of the ward, and you had to pull all the beds out to sweep behind them. This particular Sister would stand at the end of the ward, and call out to you by name, and make some rude remark in front of all the patients. I got my own back on her. In the water-room, where the dirty linen had to be sorted, they had a stand-pipe with a big brass handle that you had to clean. I was cleaning it one day, and in reflection I saw the Sister standing watching me, waiting for the doctors to do their rounds. I just pushed the lever, so the water shot right out and hit her best white cap. She couldn't say it wasn't an accident, because she had no idea I could see her reflection.

The making of beds was absolutely rigid: how patients ever got any comfort in them I'll never know, because they were not very good bedclothes to start with – hard, heavy quilts, stiff blankets. You had to fold them at the corners, and the corners had to be corners, with nothing hanging out. The ward was inspected: all the patients' brushes and combs and soap and flannels – talk about military, it was worse than that. Then you had to do their hair and clean their teeth, lots of things no nurse would consider doing today. You had cleaning as well, you see. There were no ward maids. The only outside help was on the maternity wards, where girls used to have to scrub the place. There was no paid staff to do cleaning. We had to do the meals too – we were more hungry than the patients. They got mince, not much of it, because food was scarce. At home, too, we had to queue for bread, potatoes, everything; you couldn't get meat at all.

We used to have to peel the potatoes, because they had been cooked in their jackets. You couldn't say anything to the Sister – you had to be careful what you said. Even the staff nurses, they were only two years older than we probationers were, but didn't they give themselves airs when they got their bit of lace on!

I wouldn't have made a good theatre nurse, doing all the donkey work in operations. I was on nights, and you'd be called up to help out at any time. The first time I went into theatre, two nurses walked out. I thought, What's the matter with them? They couldn't stand the smell of the anaesthetic. We had to attend operations when we were off duty too. They wouldn't care whether you were on duty or not. You had to attend.

Lectures were in the afternoon, also in your time off. The Medical Superintendent gave lectures, while Matron sat there chaperoning us. They never told us anything practical, how to get a patient ready for theatre. I wasn't very interested. I'm very practical. I wanted to nurse people, get them well, see them get well. I wasn't too interested in drugs or operations or maternity. I just wanted to be a nurse. Not many were like that. When I look back, our training was not the best. We had to keep up to a certain standard. Third-year students were encouraged to stay on as Sisters; some hospitals didn't do that.

On a twelve-hour night duty, we had a bamboo hamper, which contained our own cup and plate, a small flask of tea, a little sugar, a small cup of margarine, some bully-beef and potato, and a bit of bread. It's no wonder we were all anaemic. When the Spanish flu came there were twenty of us, and two died. I was on a baby ward at the time, feeding a child, and I collapsed over the bed. Matron came and said, 'Come along, you can't do that.' When she got no response, she realized what had happened. We were nursed in a side ward. One nurse used to complain all the time; she was very gaunt. We thought she was just a complainer, but she was so desperate that one day she decided to end it all. She took some morphine. We stopped laughing then; they had to tip strong coffee into her, to make her sick. She left soon after and died of cancer. When we applied to become nurses, we had to have a medical. It was a bit perfunctory – if you weren't flat-footed you were in. Then they tried to make you flat-footed by the ward shoes you had!

A lot of the young women had to leave, they never finished the training. I've known nurses whose mothers waited on them hand and foot, and I've seen them sat there crying because they couldn't boil an egg or make a decent cup of tea. They never finished.

I finished my training in 1922, but I didn't get my certificate till two years later. Then there was a ceremony, with the Board of Guardians. By that time, I was a wife and mother. The testimonial given me by the Medical Superintendent had been done in my sister's name.

We were all much of a muchness, there were no Lady Janes. There were girls who thought they'd like to be dressed up as nurses and go out on the streets, chat the boys up, you know. There were a lot like that – they didn't last. There were dedicated ones. I'm afraid I was rather dedicated. Matron once had me in the office and told me I mustn't be an individual nurse. She felt I gave too much attention to each one. I used to make a fuss of them if they weren't too good. In fact, one of the men, he'd been there years, in a wheelchair, he used to call me Smiler. I used to chat and joke with him, I wasn't always very careful about what I did say some of the time. It used to be a bit of fun when Sister wasn't there.

Instead of being in and out of hospital like it is now, some had been there more than twenty years. This chap in the wheelchair was allowed out, wheeled himself out. One day he took Lysol in the park. He couldn't stand it. Terrible death. Somebody else took prussic acid.

My attitude to the patients was to try to do them a bit of good, feeling sorry for them. Some nurses used to go down the ward, forget the patients had names. 'Come on now Gran, come on Dad.' I used to go up and say to them, 'Hello, how are you, is there anything you want? Don't ask me to put your false teeth in, because I hate doing that' . . . I got on all right there, but I would never have risen high in the nursing world. The boss types got on. Both my elder and younger sister were inclined to be like that. I had five boys, but I could never boss them.

The patients were all workhouse people. They weren't used to kid-glove treatment, they were used to the rough way of doing things. Once I was on maternity, and there were a couple of women, about to give birth, and they were on the floor polishing. They were in the side ward, the illegitimates. I said to the Sister, 'Do you think it's right, do you think those girls ought to be doing that in their condition?' 'Do them good,' she said, 'they won't come back a second time if they know they've got to do that. Anyway, it'll help their babies to come.' Oh hard. Hard. I couldn't be like that.

The hospital was set out in three blocks, with long corridors connecting them. The consumptive wards were at the top. The baby ward never had less than sixty cots; there was a blue-baby ward as a side ward. Next to that was the block for mentally disturbed patients. It was nothing to see them wandering in in the night, and then we'd have to get the attendant up to get them back in their ward. There was a male attendant who bathed the men patients, but on the wards all the nurses were female.

I did put a man's trousers on back to front once. Sister said, 'Nurse, you can get So-and-so up today.' I thought, I expect the male attendant will come in. But he was so excited, he got out of bed; so I helped put his trousers on. Workhouse pants had these flaps at the front. I put them on back to front . . . I was happier on the men's wards, because a lot of the women were catty – they'd whisper to Sister.

Off duty, we used to race around the grounds, go cycling, play tennis. We walked for miles . . . We had one day off per month. That started at 10 a.m., although you might well be lined up outside Matron's office for some offence at that time. And you had to be back by 10 p.m. The gates were shut then. We were too artful – we used the fire escape. One night, I got all the nurses to give me their ration of bully-beef and potatoes, and cooked them up in a proper meal. I got this big frying-pan and fried it all up. I heard a noise outside: two attendants from the block where the mental patients lived were outside. They could smell the cooking and came to see what it was. They came into the kitchen. The Night Sister always used to hum as she came down the corridor. I heard her humming; she was coming this way; she would see the attendants unless we did something drastic. They got outside her office window, and hung by their hands so she wouldn't see them. They were clinging to the window sill while she talked sweet nothings. If we'd been caught, we would all have been sacked.

My younger sister also became a nurse. She trained at King's College Hospital in London. There's only the two of us left now out of the eight. My daughter trained in the Children's Hospital in Southampton. She's now in the US, married to a doctor's son, and working for the Emergency Squad, rescuing people from automobile accidents and so on.

My first and only boyfriend was my husband. He was a policeman, and we were married thirty years. Some girls got into bother, with sailors on South Parade pier. I took a job in Devon, but things got bad at home, so I came back and worked in a hospital at Gosport. I had six children in nine years. My husband earned £10 a month, and that's what I brought them up on. I used to help the neighbours with deliveries when their children were born. I have five boys and a girl. The oldest, he went in the Army when he was fifteen. He was in Italy for four years in the war, and finished up staff sergeant. The second and third both got scholarships to private schools, to what was known as a 'gentlemen's sons' school'. They both did well. The fourth joined the RAF, the fifth became a policeman . . . At one time, all eight of us were in uniform – when I went back to nursing in the war.

I belonged to the Nursing Guild, it was a Church of England thing. The hospital had the cheek to put a box out when we went to collect our wages which was so small you could hardly see it, and they told us we were expected to put so much in there for somebody's home for nurses.

I didn't get any training later. Both my sisters became SRNs. I just wanted to be a nurse, and I've been one ever since.

Four

The miners have an almost mythical place in the history of industrial labour in Britain. In the early industrial era they were regarded with fear, as being wild and violent, perhaps by association with working underground, in the earth – something elemental. They later came to be the mainstay of the labour movement and, over time, people's perception of miners was transformed so that they came to take on a heroic quality, as the indispensability of their labour and the dangerous conditions under which they worked were recognized. Later, there was an attempt to demonize them once more, particularly during the strikes of the 1970s and the long strike of 1984–5, so that the wheel appeared to have turned full circle. This was in anticipation of the severe reduction in the coal industry, so that now it employs only a few tens of thousands of people. The number employed in mining and quarrying in Britain just after the First World War was almost 1.25 million. By 1951, the number had fallen to about 680,000. Today, there are less than 25,000. There is no doubt that the miners were once regarded as potentially a very radical, even revolutionary, force; now, with their political neutralization, it is possible to be elegiac about the broken communities and ruined solidarities.

George Mather (*born 1910*): *coal-miner, Lancashire*

I left school in 1923. I had to go to the education officer to receive 'marks' for good attendance, which enabled you to leave school at thirteen; otherwise you couldn't leave till you were fourteen. These marks had to be submitted to the employer.

When I got these, I had to go to Worsley Meynes colliery to sign on for a job. I was duly taken on and told to be at the lamp room at 5.45 the next morning. You had to fend for yourself. Training was unheard of. They just pushed a lamp into your hand, and then you made your own progress.

The first day, I was to accompany a deputy on a weekly travelling inspection to an old disused colliery which had closed down in 1921. It was a nerve-racking experience. It took up to four hours of the shift. The wage for my first shift was 2s 2d, with one penny stopped for lamp oil. There was a 3d a day rise every six months. A normal working week was five days, from 7 a.m. to 2 p.m. By the time I was fourteen I had been upgraded in a sense, because my father had taken me working on the coalface. From that day until the pit closed I never saw any wage: all that was earned was accredited on one wage ticket, which my father drew.

The mine where I worked was about 3 feet 6 inches, and all the coal was gotten by hand. There was very little mechanization at that time. We were paid 4s 1½d a ton. These mines were worked on what was called 'longwall'. The main heading was always kept ahead, so that every so often a side road was struck off on either side. This distance always corresponded with the work place of the rearmost which had reached the boundary. As each work place progressed, day-wagers, called 'day-tallers', packed the waste by what were called 'stud packs', a block about four or five yards square. The material for this was obtained by blowing part of the roof down. The rearmost place had as far as two or three hundred yards to bring the loaded tubs to the main haulers' road.

Although work started at seven, it meant being down the pit by six o'clock, and travelling about a mile to your place of work. In most places, you were almost on your knees, and you had to carry your lamp, can of water, tommy tin, and maybe four pick blades that had to be taken up every day to be sharpened; and about once a week, two drills which you used for shot-firing purposes. Most days you never had time to eat your food. It was very seldom that we came up before 4.30 p.m. When time and labour were reckoned up, a day-taller, whose wage was 7s 7d, was better off than us. It took ten or twelve hours to earn a seven-hour wage.

Now this coal had to be clean – no dirt in it. The company had random checks on each tally. The company weighman would tell the man's check-weighman when he was having the man's tub checked – that is, overturned and cleaned. All the dirt that was picked up from this tub would be the man's average dirt deduction. It was bad luck if you had a dirty tub. At that time, safety regulations were not particularly stringent and there were many accidents. Explosions were a hazard. There were several serious ones during my life in the pit, and I was in one myself, too – Maypole pit, for example, when fifty-eight men and boys were killed, Gresford, near Wrexham, where 265 were killed, Edge Green where thirty-two lost their lives (my father and I were in that). Dust disease was another potential killer. It was only in the 1940s that this was accepted as a compensation claim.

These working places were called 'higher side' and 'lower side'. The lower side was harder to work, and the control of the air was difficult, but you always had one point in your favour – there was little or no gas there.

It was the higher side working where the gas accumulated, and this is what made it prone to explode, as at Edge Green. Fire was another hazard. Most of these were caused by internal combustion, and were commonly known as 'gob fires'. When these occur, it means sealing off the mine by packing the intake and return roads with sandbags. This is a very dangerous job, and has to be done systematically so that the amount of air inside and outside the seal is evenly matched. If this does not correspond, there is a likelihood of the seals blowing. This occurred at Gresford, and killed several men who were working on them.

Wages remained low in the pits – at the time of the General Strike in '26, a collier on day wage had 7s 11d and a day-taller 7s 9d a shift. But after twenty-six weeks of strike, the colliers had to agree to the coal-owners' terms. This meant a cut in wages and a half-hour extra on the working day. Each man had 2d a day drop, and the terms of agreement were day-to-day contract. This meant that the coal-owners could give you a day's notice when you went down, then when you came up you were finished. This happened to us at Worsley Meynes in 1928. They simply cut the winding ropes and let the cages go down as soon as all the men were out. The coal we had hewed and filled was still down, and owing us.

In the thirties, with millions on the dole, the means test was introduced. This meant that if a man had drawn his allotted amount of dole (156 days), his family circumstances were considered, and each member of the family had to contribute; married sons or daughters had to contribute so much to a father or mother. There were spies everywhere, people telling tales on you because of jealousy, thinking you were getting something they should have. If you were seen picking a bag of coal, there was always someone to report you as saying that you were selling it. Anyone with a truck full of old timber ran a good chance of somebody reporting he had started a firewood business.

There were people employed by the dole known as means-test men. When they were in the neighbourhood, news went out on the grapevine. It was not unusual when you signed on the dole for them to give you a green card – that meant a job in the offing. You had no option, you had to go; and to prove you had been, you had to get the manager's signature on the card before you left.

At the few pits that were employing, it was common for the under-manager to be besieged by anything up to a hundred men waiting in the pit-yard for a job.

One incident I was involved in was at Crompton's pit, where a man named Ellis Smith was underlooker. I had gone out there one Monday, and with fifty or more men I waited until almost five o'clock to see about a job.

As soon as he was spotted, there was a mad rush towards him, each one trying to get his word in first for the job. He picked the likely ones out, and told the rest to go home. I was one of those picked. We then had to line up again, whilst he ran his hands over us, feeling our arms and legs, to see how strong we were. Finally, he selected two others and myself; he took us into the office, took our names. By this time, we thought we were sure of a job. He then told us to come out on the following Saturday morning, and he would fix us up. Imagine our surprise when we got there. There were about fifty of us, and all had had the same going over that we had. After a sergeant-major's parade, he finally picked three of us.

In the thirties, we were on short time – three days a week. That meant signing on the dole each day you were off. The Friday we had to go to the employment exchange to draw our dole money; when we arrived at the exchange on those Friday nights, we had to fall in line behind a queue with maybe two thousand people in front of us. Many's the time we were there till ten; and then we had to go again next day because they'd run out of funds until the banks opened on Saturday morning.

During twenty-six weeks when you were entitled to unemployment pay, the authorities tried every means to discredit a man by sending him out to some place of employment in the hope that he would be accepted. These were atrocious jobs that employers found difficult to fill, jobs below union rates or in bad working conditions. If you refused, your unemployment pay was stopped for six weeks. Then you had to apply for what was known as UAB – Unemployment Assistance Benefit. Applying for this was the most degrading and humiliating experience I ever came across.

The people who worked at these places appeared to take exception to your predicament and often ridiculed you almost to breaking point. They wanted all the details of your relatives – who they worked for, how much they earned, if they or you had any savings, how much you paid in life assurance on all relatives. Could they contribute to your income? They gave you a long form to take home, full of embarrassing questions to get filled in. Just fancy – going to a distant relative whom you had had no connection with for years, and asking him to fill in details of where he worked, how much pay, any savings, how much he spent on tobacco or beer.

This system was still operating in 1946. Because of injury and complications over the compensation, I had to apply for assistance. I'd had no money for six weeks. Food was still rationed. I had to apply at the local Board, which was the workhouse. After several unnecessary visits, I was granted a food voucher for 7s 6d. It didn't cover the cost even of our weekly ration. As this was grudgingly handed over to you, before a panel of local council officials, you were advised to use it carefully and not to forget it was the public's money you were spending.

Hospitals and infirmaries were the same; my widowed mother had to be taken to hospital. Her widow's pension was kept by the authorities for her keep, and they practically ordered me to contribute four shillings a week towards the cost of maintenance.

Special clerks were appointed by the UAB to visit people who were in receipt of assistance. When he was in the neighbourhood, people were very resentful; the word spread about – 'The means-test man is about.' A majority of them seemed to gain satisfaction by humiliating you as much as possible. They were feared, because if they saw a member of the family doing something out of the ordinary – picking a bag of coal on the slag tip, digging somebody's garden, they assumed you were getting paid for it and not notifying the authorities. Your allowance could be stopped without warning.

Fear was used as a weapon, even at the cinema – there were a few front-row seats which cost twopence. In order to have this enjoyment, people had to wait until the lights went down before they entered, because the man who was in charge of the local Board Relief had a habit of sitting in the balcony seats where he could see each person who entered these front seats. If he saw them, people knew their allowance would be reduced next time they went for it.

One man, when he want to draw his means-test money, found it had been disallowed. When he asked why, he was told he had been reported as working. He was flabbergasted. He was then informed that he had been seen selling firewood on a hand-cart. He asked what day. When told, he said, 'Selling firewood? That was my furniture, I was flitting to another house.'

Five

A single industry became a whole culture; the division of labour within it an enclosed world, unintelligible to those outside, but which to those involved gave meaning and purpose. Shoemakers have traditionally been radical and fiercely independent: it was only well into the nineteenth century that boot and shoe production became integrated within the factory. It is difficult now to evoke the self-contained quality of the shoemaking culture in Northampton, which remained more or less intact until the Second World War: the distinctive sensibility of the boot and shoe people was dour, pessimistic, parochial. They were distrustful of outsiders, mean – but at the same time egalitarian and sceptical, disinclined to believe anything they were told, awkward and perverse. Everything about the streets, with the pub and factory on opposite corners, suggested an austere and puritanical existence: even their pleasures – playing darts, growing sour apples and rhubarb on their allotments – were scarcely joyful.

Len Greenham (*born 1914): morocco-grainer, Northampton*

I'd done forty-nine years at one place, forty-six years as a grainer. I finished the rest of my working life on a spraying machine, which was entirely unnatural to me, being a hand-grainer.

As a boy of fourteen, when I started work, things were bad and we were doing only three days a week. My elder brother got me a job at Pearce's where he was working . . . I well remember the man who taught me my job, Reg Canning, he was that much older than me. He was a very fast grainer, and I became more or less the same as him.

I started at Pearce's in 1928, and began to learn my job as leather-finisher. In those days the finishing of leather was a very skilled job, a very hard job. I was principally concerned with morocco-graining. Morocco goats were the only skins that could do a morocco grain. You put the grain, you lift the grain, and you grain it after the preparation of the skin. This was done by dyeing and glazing; before glazing it was tooth-rolled into a cross-section to make the grain smaller. Then the skins were dipped in a big tub of water and left to ferment overnight, and then we grained them eight ways. After graining them, you hooked them in a very hot stove, about 140 deg., and when they were dry, you laid them on a bench for the leather to absorb the damp air again up to a certain point, which we called turning out and running up. Then the skins would be pasted on the flesh with a paste. These skins were sent to other areas – Walsall was the main one – and in 1939 we had a subsidiary in America, and a lot of leather went there.

Also, besides graining goats, we had 'skyvers', which was a very skilled process: you had to learn to grain very thin skins, which were shaved right down practically to the grain, and they were used for making bibles and prayer-books, speciality work.

Light-skinned leather would be finished with egg albumen and milk. You would sponge this on the grain, and then you would lay them grain to grain, and after that, start on the driest ones again, and then you would grain them two ways, three ways, and then you would brush them, and hang them up a dozen at a time. Then you'd go back and brush again, and they would finish up like this wallet I have here made in 1935, and it still has the grain on it. I gave it to my wife later on, she still uses it. That was the era of milk and egg albumen for the light-coloured skins, and for the black skins we used to go along to the butcher's and get blood . . . They used to shine like diamonds when they'd been brushed. It was a very hard job. Many a time I've come home, had my tea and laid on the sofa to recuperate, because it exhausted the stomach muscles. You didn't have to smoke too much, because it made a difference to your stamina, but being a sportsman I ran and played cricket and rugby, so I was pretty fit.

You had to be fit. In summer, it was a very hot atmosphere, when you went into this stove to get these skins down – there was no electric fans or anything. Hard-grained moroccos they called them. You made handbags, from what were called bag goats – that was a stouter substance – and these, along with wallets, were expensive in those days. It was the pride of a woman when she bought her clothes, especially in the middle classes, to have these expensive morocco handbags. They were a sort of class symbol. Unfortunately towards the end of the thirties, they turned over to the new cellulose mixture that was used on the skins. It certainly took the brushing job away from you, but it wasn't quite as brilliant. In the early days the cellulose was such a nasty-smelling substance that you felt bad, you had to drink milk to counteract this, and later it became law that you had to have milk when you were spraying this mixture on the skins, and then the cellulose went right through the process of graining. It didn't make any difference to the graining except for the fact that it covered up slightly some of the small scratches or casualty marks on the skin, which were fluffed, to make it more smooth, and the cellulose gave it a coat . . . which an ordinary old-fashioned preparation for leathers couldn't hide.

They had only the best skins in those days, and the best came from Madras in India. Indian goats were the principal source of supply. And when I went there in '41, '42, I saw these goats running about. I also ate them as part of our menu in various parts of Bengal and Burma. I visited the hog market in Calcutta, where I used to take some of these goatskins back to the squadron. They used to do tooling of these skins, and with me being in the leather trade, they sent me because of that knowledge. I wrote to my director at Pearce's, saying having been a morocco-grainer, I've seen the process from the source of supply to the end product.

When the war came, it was a luxury trade, and we couldn't get the skins from India. We had to go on other work till I went in the Forces.

After the war, I was the one chosen to start up the department again. Before the war there had been sixteen of us; after the war it came up to four of us, and eventually by 1974–5 I was the last. They had to stop producing because of the cost of the material, which is the skin in its raw state, later bought from Nigeria, a different kind of goat. With technical knowledge in the industry they were able to produce something not as good as a Madras goat, but good enough.

You could strike a match on morocco leather. When I first went into the industry, my grandfather, who was a hand-shaver, would have thought it a sad tale that after all those years of this trade and skill, acquired from older people of many years' knowledge, it can't be passed on to anyone else. But the financial situation of the firm dictated to them that they had to stop this graining, and the production of goats too. Leather which nowadays would cost pounds per square foot was only pence when we started; and the quality in the old days was super.

My job was eventually taken over by printing machines, which use inferior leather. They made very good copies on machines made in the US and Germany, and they told us the result looked as good on the finished article, but of course this was not so . . . In the last few months of my working life, I was asked by the directors if I would grain and finish some morocco goats to put on their boardroom table and chairs. I said I'd do this job, and I went back about three months after I'd retired, and I grained these skins for the directors, and at a later date I saw them on the chairs and tables. They were the last skins I produced as a morocco-grainer.

When I was in Belfast in 1940, I went into a store to buy my wife a birthday handbag. I said, 'Can I look at some morocco bags?' and the girl brought these bags that were printed. They weren't even what we called 'printed' moroccos. I said, 'Well, my job is morocco-grainer – you fetch the manager, you're selling stuff under a false name.'

After the war, when the job became profitable again, we used to send a lot of stuff to the Pacific coast of America and to New York. The American agents came to us, and during discussions they said the best-quality work was sent to Canada, and the inferior stuff done in America; these bags were made in the ghettos of New York by refugees.

It's very disconcerting to see these skills go. My father was a hand-finisher in the boot and shoe trade. He used to finish hand-sewn shoes, and as a boy I used to go and sit with him. He used to say that even those factories that were supposed to make first-class shoes, the quality had gone. It wasn't like the high-quality shoes of Randalls, because they were connected with the Queen's shoemakers.

When you retire, you are naturally drawn to leather shops; and when you feel this leather, it's like a blind man feeling his way on something you've offered him, and because your fingers tell you more than your eyes tell, it's degrading to feel these things after the quality stuff over the years. Of course, one had to accept that the people who bought it were moneyed people; but of course this is the same in all walks of life. My father-in-law worked in service for Libby's and Tate and Lyle people, and he said to me that you have to accept discipline, which we don't have now. You had to behave yourself in those days, or you'd be out; and there'd be men waiting outside, and out of those men waiting outside there'd always be one who'd work for less than the others. That was life in the thirties . . .

When it came that you finished your time, you had to join the union. You had to join, but work was so scarce that we had a tough four or five years; the union was specifically for hard-grain and finishers. Then that started to shrink, the number of morocco-grainers was reduced, so we became the Amalgamated Leatherworkers Trade Union. The first treasurer of ALTU was my Uncle Joe, who was banished from this town, and he had to go to Kettering to work because of his union activities.

Little by little work increased, although the money didn't. We had to do so many feet of skins per day and per week; you would be paid according to the footage you'd done . . . When you'd finished your work, you'd have to go on some other job, padding some skins or brushing some goats. Boots the chemists used to buy a lot of these handbags at one time. Some days there was work, then you might not work for a week or a fortnight. You had to be careful as well, mind what you said. We were more or less called bolshies, because we belonged to this union. The other unions were hostile to us. We had to fight so hard to get a living wage. We would never have had the audacity to ask for the increases they later demanded, because at that time you had to provide the finished article at a price that was relative to the selling price. This is not so today – it appears that's gone out of fashion.

But it's a sad story. The last two years of my working life I earned more money on a secondary job, and I hated every second of it, and I was glad when I took my smock off and retired. I was on a spraying machine that sprayed all kinds of leather, calf and buffalo calf and goat and everything. They eventually had a new machine in from America which would do so many thousands of feet in an hour, where you took a week to do it.

I hated standing on the end of a machine, after I'd spent my life in a rhythm which I had had to learn, and which was the rhythm of the body: you went one shank, two shank, across the belly of the skin, from the neck to the butt, and from the butt to the neck. Then you hooked these things up, and after you'd done it, you looked at it and you thought, Well, isn't that lovely. And it was lovely, because right up to the war the quality of the goatskins was super . . . I always instilled into my wife and daughter that there is no substitute for real quality.

As a boy we went into a village in the country, where my father was foreman over hand-sewn boots and shoes and mountaineering boots. I remember visiting these men in their houses, and it was a common sight to see men in caps and trilby hats with the aprons rolled up, with their sprig-bags of shoes which they'd made, taking them back to the factory.

I'm a Northampton man and proud to be so. We went into the country for a time, but came back later to the town. I remember the soldiers in the First World War billeted in Victoria Road chapel, and they used to give us these hard biscuits as children. When we went on the train back to the village on Saturday nights, we would see all the wounded men lying on stretchers waiting to be taken to Barry Road School, a temporary hospital.

We lived in the village till I was fifteen. I remember the great strike. We went with our pram wheels to get wood from Clifford Hill spinneys, and I remember putting our arms through the railings at the station to nick a bit of coal. We always walked to town, about seven miles.

My grandfather, my father, my uncle and elder brother – we were all in the leather trade. My grandfather told me how he used to hand-shave the leather; it's now done a hundred times faster by mostly foreign machinery. But this was our life. It is essential that some of this is kept to show people, in this sub-quality age, that we made articles that would outlast anything made today.

What's gone out of life is the quality of things that you buy. I think it stems from the root cause that people have no pride in their work. They're not skilled people today. We had to do seven years' apprenticeship, buy our own corks, buy the sponges and the brushes. You got a percentage of full wage when you were twenty-one, not till you were twenty-three did you get full money; and you still had to buy the tools of your trade. It's gone now, and it only returns in very small-scale specialized work, such as my directors sitting on their morocco chairs, putting their papers on the tables . . . But at least there's something still there after you . . . The young people leave no trace of themselves in the world.

Six: The Steelworkers

Within all the staple industries of the 'classical' industrial era – from ship-building to textiles, shoe-making to coal-mining – there was a complicated division of labour and a subtle hierarchy of posts, even within what was referred to as 'manual labour' – a system of status and skill that an outsider would scarcely notice. Thus the general idea of 'steelworkers' concealed a nuanced stratification of labour. The steel industry, like all the major core industries of Britain, has been subject to continuous technological change, which the workers have usually perceived as a process of transfer of skills from human beings to the machine.

Robert Gladen (*born 1927*), *Middlesbrough*

My father was a sample-passer in the steel industry, at the Britannia Works in Middlesbrough. He fought in the First World War and died in 1945. He took me to the works when I was fifteen, and I started at Dorman Long's as a charge-wheeler in 1942. In 1966 I became a sample-passer like my father.

My father never talked about work. He would go to the club – he never told my mother anything about it. She knew what job he had, but she never knew his wages. All she had to do was have a clean pinny on on Friday when he came in; that way, he was happy, she was happy.

I left school at fourteen. I worked in factories, I worked for a tea and jam importer. I delivered lemonade around Middlesbrough. I got a job on a farm. But then, the next thing I knew, I was at Dorman Long's.

My first impression of the works was that it was like Guy Fawkes night. It was very hot and humid, and all sparks everywhere. A charge-wheeler filled pans of limestone for the furnace, and was odd-job man for the First Hand. You had to keep the materials, check the wagons, make sure there was the right amount of scrap for the furnace.

The workers were all big strong men, all six foot tall it seemed. They would always help you if you were in trouble. If you were a sample-passer's son, they made a scapegoat of you. It was hard work. They wore flannel shirt, black cap, safety boots, blue glasses and a sweat towel. The foreman was the First Hand, he was in charge of his furnace and his furnace crew.

I walked to work, which was one mile away. We all met up at a black bridge at 5.30 in the morning, so that you all walked in together at the same time . . . It was very humid in there, there was little ventilation, the plates on the floor were hot, you got lime on your clothes. You could make tea in a tin cabin which the workers built; there was a seat which was a plank on a pile of bricks. You went to the toilet wherever you could – at the back of the wagons, anywhere.

The First Hands were all good melters, but they were mostly illiterate. They'd ask you to fill in the columns on the information board, and they'd give you a cigarette at the end of the shift. We got paid on Friday. £1 0s 5d was my first wage.

You learned to drink there. Eventually you would sup about fourteen pints a day – eight in the afternoon, six at night. You soon sweated it out again. They'd go into a pub at two o'clock after a shift and order four pints at a time. The first two they'd drink straight down. You felt very fit after a shift. It was hard, enjoyable work. It was like body-building, shovelling for eight hours a day. You didn't feel tired; you stayed nice and slim.

The First Hand would work until he was seventy years old. The promotion line was very slow. I would fettle the furnace with the First Hand, if the Second and Third Hands were busy elsewhere. After it was empty of steel and slag, you had to fettle the banks, back wall and breast. The steel in the furnace used to make holes in the lining which you had to cover with gravel. You'd lift up the door, stand four or five feet away, and shovel this gravel in to fill the holes. It was hot work. The most you could bear it because of the heat was five minutes at a time. You did it in relays, man after man, until the furnace was fettled. It took one and a half hours.

If you were a pan-filler, you had eight pans of lime, six of stone. You started putting it into the furnace, lime and stone, and then filled the pans for the next charge. It was a continuous job.

You worked six till two, or two till ten; the nightshift was 9.30 to 6.30. You'd get to work at nine, to let your mate go off to the pub for a few pints. The pubs closed at ten. That was your life. You'd eat, sleep, get up, work, go to pub, with football on Saturday. There was little night life in Middlesbrough. You might go to the pictures. Pubs and beer were the main recreation. You never sat all night in the same pub. You'd go to eight or nine pubs a night. I lived at home until I was thirty-two. I courted for four years. In the first day at work, I joined the union.

During the war morale was high. We worked as a team, got on well together. Today it's not the same. It was hard work and I enjoyed it.

During the war, in air raids, everybody would go to the shelters except some of the Second Hands, who stayed to black out the glare of the furnaces. The shelters were cold and dark, sometimes full of water. You'd stay there sometimes six or seven hours, shivering.

There were quite a few accidents. There were no safety officers. People got burns, they got jammed in cranes. I got a couple of burns – you expected it, playing about with molten metal, but you looked after your mates and yourself. In World War Two there was a girl crane driver who was crushed. She got into the gantry when coming down; the changing crane squashed her. There was no safety clothing, only asbestos hood and coat, leather apron for shutting the manganese into the ladle. Manganese was very heavy, and there were splashes off the steel.

The first time you see a furnace tapped, it is very exciting, but you soon get used to it. You open the top hole, and the steel comes with a roar. You hear the roar before you see the flame. You turn your back, and the flame shoots past you; the steel follows ... All the sparklers and crackers, it makes November the Fifth very boring after you've worked in a steelworks.

The Britannia Works was closed in 1953. We were transferred to Lackenby Works, a new plant. The furnaces were very big – 360 tons after 60 tons at Britannia. But at Lackenby it was all new, new clocks, all small levers, dials indicating temperature, gas, air check. There was nothing like that at Britannia. Some of the First Hands who were illiterate, they packed up the job then. They couldn't cope. New tilting furnaces were built. You still relied on your skills; the older men didn't rely on the clocks and dials, they went by eyesight. An experienced First Hand used to take the temperature only about every two hours, using a thermo-couple and a glass tube that went from zero to 1800 degrees. You shoved the thermo-couple into the steel, and read the recording, say 1610 deg. The tapping temperature was 1620. In the old days with no thermo-couple, they judged the temperature by the colour of the slag. The browner the slag, the cooler the steel. As the slag got whiter and whiter it was hotter. They had a twenty-foot rod, which they dipped into the steel. If the rod was straight it was OK, but if it came out jagged, the steel was too hot. They would take a spoon of steel, pour it out, and if it left a skull in the lip, you had the right temperature; if not, you had no temperature. The 'skull in the lip' meant the right temperature.

Lackenby was open-hearth. The people working with you changed. You still had First, Second, Third and Fourth Hands, but they did away with the box-filler, whose job had been to get the material for the furnace. That was all done by machine then. When they charged, the box-filler's job was to keep everything tidy. The hands then had to do it; they didn't want to.

Discipline was not so good, people fell out over it. With oxygen-fed steelmaking, the tapping time was cut to six hours, where it had been twelve hours before. Less scrap was used and there was not so much mess.

I became a First Hand at Lackenby. The sample-passer was the god. At work, they were abrupt, but in the pub just like anybody else. At work, they would sit themselves in the cabin until the First Hand sent for them, until the furnace was ready to tap. What the sample-passer said, you did. In the early days, the sample-passer had the power to hire and fire. It was rare for anybody to be sacked, except occasionally, for bad timekeeping. The sample-passers were very fair – they would always listen to you, help you. You could get sacked for fighting at work, for coming in with too much beer, but it was rare.

Steelmaking was a twelve-month-a-year job. You used to pile it on the 'prairie', there was always a lot of stock. Christmas and New Year, some people always had to work. It never closed down. People took their holidays at different times. We went to Blackpool, Yarmouth; later we went abroad.

Eventually I became a sample-passer in 1966. I was picked out by management. I felt big. I was over the moon. It wasn't the power, it wasn't the money. It was an achievement. That's what I wanted to be, because that is what my father was. That was as far as I wanted to go. My ambition was to be what my father was.

Being a sample-passer was different from what it had been in my father's day. The skill had gone out of melting. It was skilled work in my father's day, semi-skilled in mine. Computers, clocks and gauges had all come in. It took the art out of steelmaking. It became boring. No challenge. Originally, it was you against the furnace. The equipment had taken the skill out of it.

You had big responsibility. You had to make sure that five furnaces and mixers were fully manned, check the charging cranes and machinery. Then you'd inspect the furnaces. Check your manganese and the coal you wanted. You had to tap the furnace, inspect it when empty before it was charged, then give it back to the First Hand. It was an interesting job; you had to make different qualities of steel – high-carbon, low-carbon – and all that involved variations in the proportions of material.

The manager didn't like the sample-passer talking to the vessel crew. On the first day I got a message – Would I go to the office. I was told, 'Next time I come into the plant, I don't want to see you in the cabin talking to the vessel crew. Also, wear a suit and tie.' I did as they said. I wore a tie from nine till five, then took it off.

In 1971 I was vessel foreman at BOS, when the plant opened – a sort of glorified sample-passer. The open hearth came to an end then. I felt sad. After Lackenby closed down, they kept some furnaces open for a few months. I was asked if I'd like to go down and see the last tap on the furnace. I was that cut up, I wouldn't go to see it.

It was a challenge – each charge, each tap was different, it was you and the steel. You were like fighting the furnace. It was the boss, you were the boss. One minute it would give itself up, and the next minute you would give yourself up ... You had to get everything right, the sulphur and the phos. One vessel would react differently from another.

My first impression of the BOS system – I didn't like it ... It was a dirty process, a dirty place, too small. I didn't enjoy it. I felt like the old hands from Britannia had felt when Lackenby opened. All those who'd been through the open hearths felt like it. They say you can't teach an old dog new tricks. To me, it wasn't steelmaking. The art had gone out of it.

When I first started, it took twelve to sixteen hours to charge a furnace and tap it; then it went to twelve hours, then six hours, and then finally twenty minutes. The skill had gone. When you look at the technology – the computer can't do the work until you feed the information in. It's only as good as the knowledge we put in it. We had a computer, nothing in it. We had to do everything on a manual basis, then log it on a log sheet. Everything we did went down on this sheet – ten tons of lime, manganese, the time we put it in, time of starting and finishing, the temperature. Then it would print out the analysis. The information was only stored up in the computer ... It had to use our brains, but it could do it quicker ... It's too quick, it's too dirty. There was pride in the open-hearth plant.

Today it's rubbish steel. The art and the soul are finished. Technology took over. I retired in April 1989, after forty-seven years' service. I enjoy retirement. I finished up a vessel foreman. I was happy to retire. Young people take no interest in work now ... They have the wrong attitude today. Discipline is nil. They don't work, they only go for the money. I'm proud to have been a sample-passer like my father. The sample-passer, he was a god, but he didn't use his power. The day I became a sample-passer was the greatest day of my life, apart from getting married. I met my wife in 1959. We met in a pub. That was the main recreation – pictures, pubs. I drank a lot. You had to, the amount of liquid you lost. It ruined my stomach. Drinking broke a lot of marriages up. Women used to chat more, the men did the drinking while they talked about work. I used to come home at 4.30, go down to the club by about 6.30 ... I've got bronchitis now. The fumes in the BOS plant gave me spots on my lungs. I get short of breath. I have to be careful, digging or gardening.

There was only one strike and that was in 1980, at Lackenby open hearth. There were a lot of grumbles, but you couldn't stop work until every furnace was empty. Union meetings were a farce – 'beer talks louder than words'. There was no need for unions in the steel industry. The strike lasted thirteen weeks. You always lose money. We were just getting comfortable, our house nicely furnished. Our nest-egg in the bank all went. Only the union people wanted the strike. It was nonsense.

My son wants to be what I was. He has been in the industry for eight years. When I retired, I said, 'I've finished. I don't want to hear anything about the steel industry, unless you've got something funny to tell me. I want to forget about the works.' When I got married I said, 'When I leave the works, it's finished. I want to leave work at work.'

Stanley Hullock (*born 1913*), *Workington*

When workers appear in the news, it is usually because there has been a strike, or some industrial dispute; in other words, when they are not working. This has made it easier to overlook the relentless physicality of manual labour, particularly in the earlier part of the century. Stanley Hullock evokes something of the overwhelming intensity of the workplace, the heat and the danger of the steelworks.

I left school at fifteen, worked two years in a butcher's shop. I went to the steelworks as a mould-life observer when I was seventeen. That meant recording the life of an ingot mould. I had to write a form for each cast made – that was the life of the mould. That was in the old Bessemer hydraulic shop. There were three converters, twenty tons per converter. The ladles were carried on a ram; the three converters were built in a circle and the centre-pin was a ram, or a ladle carrier, and four pitside bogeys that held the mould into which the cast was to be made.

One set of moulds was cast each time a ladle was filled. Having cast the mould, they were stripped with ingot eyes, which was a piece of metal sunk into the head of a cast while molten and then set. It was then pulled out of the mould, put on a little bogey and weighed, and then it went to the soaking pits and to the rolling mills.

At the interview for the job, I was just asked, 'Can you do figures?' That was just to keep an eye on each mould as it was cast, and look at the number of ingots: that was the life for that mould. I was at the old Bessemer for two or three years, and then went to the new Bessemer plant. There were two converters driven by electricity. Wind passed through the tweers, air went through the metal, which burned out the carbon, manganese, silicon and sulphur.

My first impression going into the old Bessemer was one of shock. I'd never seen a steelworks before I went there. I came to enjoy my life there, though. The new Bessemer was different. There were bogeys on railway lines. The converters were straight in front. I was still on mould-life observing, and I wanted to advance, because I was getting nowhere. I went to the union and the management, and they said I could go on to the slag bogey, which was a raise. The slag bogey was a bogey having the metal blown in the converter to its finish; 'finish' meant the carbon and manganese content was 0.4 carbon – that was the lowest point of carbon content. You had to watch a 30-foot flame, and you'd know by looking at that flame the temperature of it; you had to know how to cool it down or how to warm it up. To warm it up, you put silicon iron in – to cool, you put cold scrap, added from skips, tipped down a chute into the converter as it was going ... The blower had to know when he looked at that flame when it came to the end point, leaving 0.4 carbon in the content of the metal. Then the heat was turned down; you had a ladle underneath ready to accept the metal. And the metal depended on whether it was making rail steel or rimming steel; if rimming steel, the extra analysis was added by 30-pound paper bags of solid manganese chips. They knew the content of the manganese they were putting in, and that built up the analysis required for that metal in that ladle when it was cast into its mould. The ladle was taken away, lifted by crane, then cast in the moulds.

The rail steel needed a high quality of carbon and manganese. A great quantity was needed to bring it up to the quality, so it was put in a 'spiegel', then into a little 5- to 6-ton ladle. It was poured into the converter before the converter was tipped into the ladle. There was no great reaction, because the metals were the same temperature. If there had been a difference in temperature, you'd've got a reaction. Rail steel was poured into the mould; having cast the mould the ladle was taken away, tipped to tip out any slag that was left on top of the metal. Then the ladle was put into the slag pan and a new pot placed beneath the ladle where the metal ran out – a brick pot with a stopper ready for the cast. Having got shot of the ladle ready for another cast, the moulds were taken away on this wagon. They were stripped by a stripper crane, a crane that took the mould off the solid metal left. Then it was taken to the mill, to the soaking pits, so that the metal was uniform temperature. Soaking made the metal consistent, otherwise the outside could be cooled and the inside still molten. After so many hours, it was brought into the rolls, where it was squeezed into rails, billers, slabs, sleeper plates and so on.

We wore ordinary clothes, old clothes. There was no protective clothing. You wore heavy boots, not shoes, because if there were any splashes or sparks, the sparks would go into your foot with ordinary shoes. We did eight-hour shifts, six to two, two to ten and ten to six. You clocked in each shift outside the steel plant; you put the card in the clock, pulled a lever and the card was stamped.

I didn't join the union straight away. I wasn't interested in unions in those days. It was a long time before I joined. I didn't need it till I got older. In fact I never had to use it. I was one of the blue-eyed boys, as you might say. I got on well with management. Most of the men were great, marvellous fellows. Occasionally, a foreman might be aggressive. That's life.

When I became blower in the new Bessemer, I rose in the ranks to scrap-loading – that is, loading the skips to go into the converter when it was blowing, when the blower signalled that he wanted it. First they wanted a 'boxman' – that is, assistant to the blower. They picked me as assistant boxman at first, then boxman. Then management came and said, 'How about a spot of blowing?' I'd watched the flame many times, so I said, 'All right, I'll see what I can do.' 'Fair enough. We'll give you ten weeks.' So for ten weeks I was on different shifts, watching the blower. A blower will not tell you what you're looking for. He can't tell you, you've got to learn it yourself. You've got to look at that flame, know what you're looking for and find it. Once you start finding it, it's a piece of cake. But you've got to know what you're looking for.

I achieved it, I was a spare blower for some time, then I'd've got to be a regular blower as he retired. I was to take his job. I did fourteen weeks on my own. I didn't make any mistakes, the metal was OK; then they said, 'What about it, Stan?' I said I didn't want to be a regular blower. 'Why?' I said, 'Coming up those steps, I could brain my head against that wall.' It was getting to me. I couldn't take the responsibility. I found out I couldn't take it. I was twenty-six.

So I went to the pitside as an observer. I had to observe the amount of aluminium added to the casting, how it was stripped, how long it took to strip, and how long it was in the moulds; were there any scars on the strip side? – when you take an ingot out of a mould, you don't always get a clear strip, sometimes you get a bad mould with a bit of scrap in it. I had to record the times and the quality of the metal and the quantity of aluminium added to take out the oxides.

I walked to work. There was a cabin to eat in at the old Bessemer; it was rat-infested, under the box, all hydraulic, with a lot of water. In the new Bessemer, the cabins were more respectable. In the old, you had to eat while you were doing your job. There was no knocking-off time, it was a continuous process. For the toilets, you had to go on the shore, there was a shed with a plank across. There were no washing facilities. Later, after the war, they built an area in the mill where you could have a shower. Most didn't bother.

In the Bessemer, there were fifty men in the blowing shop doing various jobs; labourers who cleaned the slag off the floor. Slag came over the lip of the ladle, and that had to be cleaned up before the next heat went into the converter. Spiegels were melted in cupolas, which were adjacent to the vessels. There were two mixermen; the mixer was where you stored the metal that came from the blast furnace – that's molten metal. It came to the Bessemer in 25-ton ladles, it was poured into the mixer; then you had to take your samples out of the mixer, because you didn't know exactly what analysis had been missed. Then there was a 100-ton crane, and a 15-ton crane on one track, then a 30-ton stripper on another track, like a T-joint. I had a go on the 100-ton crane, putting my ladle of metal into the mixer.

Between charging and tapping, you'd put a heat in, put the wind on, blow for twenty minutes, then it would be cast, and teemed after about ten minutes – about half an hour per cast. The quicker you got through it, the more bonus you got, because you were paid on production. Sometimes, if everything went smooth, you'd get a big number of blows, and get good pay for the day. If there was a breakdown – the cranes or something went wrong – it would hold the job back and you'd get less blows. Sometimes you had to wait for iron if the blast furnace broke down. If you didn't produce the ingots you didn't get the money. The average was six, or twenty-eight casts per shift.

I left the Bessemer then and went on another job, to the mill. You had to wait in line for promotion. You can't jump from one place to another. There's ladlemen, pitmen, vesselmen – they took the plug off and replaced it with a new plug, or put a new tweer in. My younger brother was a vesselman.

Before the war, the chimneys behind each converter were open; the flames from the converters went up the chimneys. They could see the reflection of those flames as far away as Penrith on a clear night, and you could see the reflection of them on the clouds. They had to cover those in for the war. The flame had to be killed.

I was in a reserved occupation, being in steel. I was transferred from Workington to Chapel Bank when I went into the electric arc-furnace. With the arc-furnace, scrap metal is put into the body of the furnace. It is a circular furnace, with a spout at the front to pour, and a gap and a door at the back to feed. They used to feed cold scrap into the arc-furnace. There were so many men senior to me on the arc-furnace, there wasn't room for me. So they put me on what they called a 'soaking furnace'. They used to put the ingots on a brick trolley, pull them by a crane or rope into this furnace, and shut the doors down; and you had to let them get to a certain temperature, but you hadn't to drop the temperature too quickly, because that would spoil the metal. That was a twelve-hour shift. I had a little furnace by the side, and had to lower the temperature slowly.

Then they were opening five arc-furnaces. I got a job as Third Hand. There are three on each furnace, a melter and Second and Third Hand. The Third was a labourer. You had to feed your furnace, or bring the material for it to be fed – limestone, silicon, metal. You had to lift the trap door, and throw in the material. There's a lid on the furnace with three electrodes going into it. You're putting cold scrap in, and burning and melting this scrap by the electrodes going through the roof. When you'd got your bath built, then you'd so much limestone put in for slag, and you put a skin of slag on top of the bath – comes also from the impurities in the scrap, car scrap, that made a slag. When you'd got your bath melted, you had to take a sample which you'd put on a big spoon; you'd put this spoon in and pour into a little mould to find the analysis. When you got your analysis back, you'd find out if you needed silicon iron in it to bring it up to the temperature.

It was the same as the Bessemer, except that Bessemer was blowing it, putting air through – in the arc it was melted by electricity. Then you lift the door, see what your slag was like, slag your spoon, take the sample, pour it in your sample pot, send it to the laboratories. When your result came, you knew then what analysis you had in your iron – how much silicon, carbon, manganese you had . . . whereas in the Bessemer, when you were blowing a heat your sample didn't come until you'd teemed it.

The Second Hand took the samples. The First Hand told him what to do. He was the boss-man, responsible for charging.

Then they put a Siemens furnace next to it. I was Second Hand there. I enjoyed myself on that, I knew every nook and cranny, every bolt and nut on the Siemens furnace. Then a third was put up, a Siemens, and I got to be First Hand. I had fellows beneath me old enough to be my father. I had to dish the orders out. It was great, but a responsible job. You had to know what you were playing at.

The heat was terrific. I had a sweat-rag on. I used to bite the end of my scarf in my mouth. I had green glasses on, with a big pad round my nose, so when I looked into the furnace I didn't get my nose burnt. You had a rag to keep you from burning your face – in the Bessemer, you had nothing of that. We were given bottles of 'sweat-water'; I don't know what it contained, but you used to get it from the ambulance station; and they gave us halibut oil tablets too.

The work on the electric arc-furnace was physically easier. In the arc-furnace you're shovelling, but you have a big instrument panel, you controlled your power from the panel. You had to make sure you didn't overmelt, overheat the metal. If you overmelt, you add slag on – you have a reflection on the brick roof, with the three holes for the electrodes – you'd melt your brickwork. A certain amount of brickwork would then be removed.

You fettled the furnace at weekends, and repairs were carried out then. When the furnace was empty and the slag drained out, you'd a wooden rabble, or a block of wood on a long iron bar. If there were any holes or worn parts holding metal, you had to rub them out with your 'wood'; then you had to fill the holes with a kind of brick lining, and rabble it in, so that the furnace would be capable of carrying its full load next time. If there was a big hole, you had to bring your electrodes down and burn it in. The melter was responsible for fettling the furnace.

I can't remember any strikes. Yes, there was – one – it started in the morning, but was settled by the time the afternoon shift started.

With the Bessemer, you relied on your eyesight; with the arc-furnace you relied on instruments. After I left as a blower and went as pitside observer, they started to use instruments for blowing. By that time I was in the labs, a job 'pickling', etching billets in hydrochloric acid. I had a small lab with two tanks, extractors and so forth, and I was decked out in boots, leggings, jacket, safety helmet, safety cape and respirator, because of the acid. I was putting six-inch billet samples into acid for a certain length of time, boiled with steam jets to heat the acid. Then I took them out, dried them with compressed air; then you could see if the piping was separated from the billet; if so, you had to take another sample, and so on until it was correct.

I achieved my ambition, more than my ambition – I reached what I was capable of doing. I was able eventually to put a grinding-wheel on a piece of metal and to read the sparks, to judge the manganese or carbon content of that metal. I could read the sparks. If somebody had sent the wrong metal to a firm I had to go down with my grinder and my electric gear, and put my grinder on these billets or reels, or whatever they were, and read that spark to see if it was the right content. The colour and strength of the sparks told you; a high manganese spark was different from that of high carbon. The manganese was bright red colour.

I was never depressed about work; only when I was blowing, I learned I couldn't take the responsibility for fifty men and for the steel they produced. I'd have been a wreck within six months if I'd accepted that.

Accidents? Not so many. I've seen a 100-ton ladle, sixty tons of metal in it, the brakes give way, and it just gradually lowered on to the floor and didn't splash a drop ... Once a shackle bolt broke on a ladle, and there were two men working beneath, splashed by the metal. Two got a bellyful; one died straight away, the other nine weeks later. When they took him to the hospital, the nurse who received him was his wife who was working there.

One fellow, a bagman, tipped the bags into the ladle. There was a trapper on a chute above, like a box with an open bottom, and they used to trap the solid lumps which used to go into the bath on the way down. And this fellow was walking underneath, and I shouted – I swore at him – to make him get out of the way. He said, 'Don't you ever come and swear at me again, because if you do, I'll leather you one.' I said, 'Next time I'll let it drop on your head. Don't worry, I won't shout at you.'

In the old Bessemer, there was sparks flying everywhere; you had to watch which way the sparks were flying before you ran. It was an awkward spot for a labourer to work in, but for anybody with a given position, you just had to go to your position – pitman, pitside observer, mould-life observer. The only danger was with the converters going up or coming down. If you were in line when it was coming down or going up, you'd get riddled with sparks or burnt to death. A big flame used to fly right out from the nose of the converter.

There were plenty of characters at the works, although no dangerous pranks on the shopfloor. In the cabins, one of the welders used to sing opera. There was another fellow who used to get his old man out and whirl it around; he was reckoned to have a large-sized one.

But on the whole it was a good life. I was married in 1934. We had to, my wife was having a baby . . . We used to bike down by the railway, and we'd arranged to meet two lasses. One of them never turned up, she sent her friend instead, and she was the one I courted. We courted a long time before we made a slip, and that was it. There was no pressure from anybody – you just accepted it. In fact, they didn't know she was expecting till she had it.

My first wife died in the doctor's surgery. We had one daughter, and she now has two boys in their twenties – one works in the steelworks, the other is unemployed. I've a good'un this time though. I'd seen her around, and after I retired at sixty-two, we got together. We've been nine years together now.

I enjoyed life as a steelworker. The young people who came into the works didn't care the same as we used to. They're not as keen to go to work. When I started in the Bessemer, men used to come out at six in the morning, standing idle to see if there was any vacancies. Half a dozen men would be waiting there, perhaps one or two taken on; those not taken on would come back at two for the next shift, and then back for the night shift. That's how hard it was to get work. They'd be taken on labouring, cleaning up, lifting slag.

I left in 1975. I took redundancy . . . I left in good grace. During the day now, I don't do anything. I have to get some weight off. I don't have any ill effects from my working life.

I'm disappointed that it's gone. There are too many out of work. It's a pity there's not someone younger to carry on what I was doing. I saw the last converter taken from Workington, the shell. My brother was the last vesselman to take a plug off the last vessel that blew before it was closed down. It was going to a museum in Sheffield. I went to see it off.

I enjoyed life. All of it. I was in favour. I was a worker. I accepted it and did my job. But now, the people I see, mostly ex-steelworkers, we never talk about the old days, unless someone dies. My grandson who works in the rolling mill, he drives pushers. There's not the same keenness we had to go to work. They'd rather have a shift off than a shift on. After retirement I took tours, visitors, around the steelworks.

In the night time, it was more spectacular than anything you'd ever seen, a Bessemer converter turning up or down . . . The slag bank was like a mountain. They're trying to get rid of that. It's like a big hill covered in grass, like Everest. The slag used to hit the sea with a big splash – it poured into the sea with a bang and then cracked up. But on a good clear night, the works used to light up the sky.

Edna McDonald (*born 1921*), *Workington*

Until recently – the last two decades – women gained access to the traditional male-dominated areas of work only at times of emergency; and that, for the most part, meant war. After both world wars, women were compelled to return to the family, or at least to occupations not regarded as a male monopoly.

My maiden name was Edna Moon. I was born in November 1921 in Workington, down by the docks. There's nothing at all there now.

Both my grandfathers worked in the steelworks. My father was on the finishing engine, and he died when he was nearly fifty. Mother had never worked outside the home. The steelworks were good to her: she only got ten shillings pension, because you didn't get a full pension if your husband died under fifty. The steelworks gave her a job cleaning the offices, so she wouldn't be destitute. She did that till she died. They looked after the widows the best they could. She'd go in the morning at five, and half past seven she came home; then another two hours at night.

If there'd been better work anywhere else, the men wouldn't have gone to the steelworks, but it's like the miners – there was mines round here and steel, so you were either a miner or a steelworker and that was it. There was nothing in between.

I left school when I was fourteen and started work at fifteen. I went to Morecambe to work at a dentist's house. In them days the Labour Exchange got you the jobs. I'd never left home before, and I went there as a maid, as a slave really. I was a real slave. I had to do everything – ironed, washed, cleaned, polished. Everything but cook, I was too young to cook. She had a cook. I wasn't happy at all there. I used to send five shillings a week home to my parents, and used to keep three shilling for myself. I saved a shilling a week; the other two went on the pictures, and I used to roller-skate with my friend around Morecambe promenade. This was in the winter when all the visitors had gone; we used to enjoy ourselves there. But I got so unhappy, after nine months my Mam came and took me home. The missis wasn't very nice to me. You were working all the time – I got maybe one Sunday off in a month, one night in the week. It was work, work all the time, very hard work.

My auntie was working in Blackpool as a waitress in a café on the promenade, and she took me there to work for a while. You did everything in those days; you weren't qualified for anything at all, but you learned your profession by doing it – practice – you really did. Then I went to live and work in a golf club in Wakefield.

The war started when I was eighteen. I'd gone to Keswick as a waitress in a private hotel there. You got a lot of gentlemen farmers; at Blackpool you got shilling tips, at Keswick the farmers used to leave you ten shillings. It was more high-class waiting in the hotels at Keswick. When we had our meals, the housekeeper was at the top of the table, with the chauffeur. After the housekeeper and the chauffeur the dining-room waitresses came next, then the pantry-maids and the chamber-maids, and the kitchen-maid was very low down. You all sat in your own place; everything was in its place, nobody stepped out of line, and nobody did anybody else's job. The real gentry, they were very good to you, they didn't look down on you at all, they always used to speak to you.

When the war started I went home, and of course all the men had gone away, and they wanted people for the steelworks. My father came home and said, 'They're going to start women on at the steelworks'; so I said, 'Right, I'll have a go there.'

The first morning we went in, we were twenty years old, only young

44

girls. In those days you wore turbans round your heads, and we put our best jumpers on, and had our clogs all covered, and all our make-up on, lipstick, the lot. Eight of us started that morning, and my father, up in his cabin, he's seeing these eight girls coming along the railbank, and there was a wooden bridge went over the road you see, and he said we looked like a football team. There was more make-up on our faces than anything, but by the time we went off at four o'clock we were like coal-miners. Because in them days it wasn't clean, there was a lot of blue dust used to fly around, it got in your eyes, on your skin, it got everywhere. We went back home covered in this dirt – it nearly broke our hearts, because we thought we were pretty when we went out, but when we came back . . . There was no showers, you didn't get a wash or anything, you walked home in all your dirt.

My first impression – I was terrified. It was all these ingots coming along and big saws cutting them and sparks flying everywhere, and the noise! Really terrifying, until I got used to it, and then I started to use sign language. I'm a very good lip-reader – that's a good job, because I'm pretty deaf nowadays. If my father hadn't been there . . . I felt safe though, because I knew he was there. When we put our fingers in our mouths, it meant I want something to eat, and you put your fingers to your eyes and looked and pointed, and that was to tell someone what you wanted. There was a sign to tell someone off, and everything.

I started off 'running cards'. That was cards coming from the soaking pits, and it said what ingot was being taken out of the soaking pit; a big crane would come and lift it out and push it on to the cogging rock, and then it started coming through the mill. We would get these cards, then run through the mill down the railbank to the bottom, and give these cards to let the railbank know what was coming through. That was a low job; you worked your way up.

We were in a union. You had to be in a union, because it was very dangerous down there, and you had to be covered. There was no facilities at all. We used to go in the men's cabin. You were on your job the whole eight hours. Everything was moving, you couldn't leave your job. If you wanted to go to the toilet, you might get someone just to hold it while you ran there and back. You had your bait alongside you, and you just ate it as you worked, with your flask of tea. No facilities – we were just women in a men's environment and we had to adjust ourselves to that.

The men weren't very keen at all when we started. In fact, they voted against it, but they couldn't do anything about it; there was a war on, and there was no men to do the jobs. We showed them we could do it as good as them. They all thought it was a huge joke. The men were older than us;

there were men in their forties that hadn't gone to the war. To us they were old men. In them days a man of forty was a middle-aged man. We were just teenagers, and they didn't think we could do it at all. It was hard work, but we did it.

There was a lot going on between the older men and the young girls. Of course, an older man will always think, Oh great, because of these younger women fancying him. A few of them got really serious, but none of them ever left their wives.

I got moved into the railbank, and when the big ingots came through, at the very end, after they'd been through the rolling mill, been through the finishing, they came down to the saws, down a long roller, and then there's a big saw that used to cut them into strips. We had to sit on like pulleys and push these rails on to long banks, where the men used to inspect them when they got cooler; and these pulleys pushed them over, outside, so they could put them on the engines to take them wherever they were going to, to the factories, for the war effort.

There was no comfort at all. It was very hot and very dirty. I don't know if it had anything to do with it, but at that time a lot of the girls were starting to get married. There was eight of us, and before we left we were having babies; and seven of us lost our babies – only one girl managed to keep hers. And we said it was with the weight, the strain of pulling heavy levers to push the ingots through. In them days, when you were having a baby and the war was on, you couldn't go to the doctor for three months, because the doctor wouldn't have anything to do with you. Then she might give you a certificate to say you're allowed to leave work, but till then you weren't allowed to leave because there was a war on. But by the time three months had come, with all this heavy work, the damage was done. Through pulling these heavy levers, and the heat. You were working alongside the ingots, you'd only a bit of a tin sheet to sit on, you were absolutely roasting, burnt to death really.

When I got in the rolling mill, I got the 'back roughing', and from that I moved to 'front roughing', and that was as high as we were allowed to go. We weren't allowed to go on the cogging. We had to learn as we went on, there was nobody to teach us, they'd all gone to the war. These jobs we did, we just prayed to God we did it right. As the weeks went on, you saw the next job you were being moved up to, and you used to watch how it was done. We used to get salt tablets because we used to sweat that much; and we got a milky drink. We had to take that. That was the law.

The steel that we used to roll used to go to make into shells and they used to put the gunpowder in at the munitions factory. They had a lot of illnesses there. I had a friend, she was never the same woman, she went old and yellow, but you never found out what it was. In them days everything was secret in the munitions factory. They wouldn't say if it was poison, the stuff they were working with. It was the same with us, we used to breathe in all the steel dust into our lungs and it got in our eyes. I remember my father going to Carlisle to get his eyes cleaned out; he said they lifted his eyes out of their sockets and he could feel this blue steel running out of his eyes as they were cleaning them. It was amazing we didn't die, the stuff we breathed in . . . And a lot of us were deaf in the steelworks. You didn't wear things over your ears for noise . . . We never had any compensation. We just took it. As long as you were making a bit of money, you never thought of the consequences.

In the morning, we used to meet up at a corner and go in together. In them days you could walk around without being frightened in the dark; there were a lot of people around at that time of the morning. There was the miners coming home from work, or going to work, and the steelmen were coming off shift. So at six o'clock in the morning it was really noisy along here, there was more people out than at any other time of day.

When you got to work, you clocked in, took your coat off and sat down. As you came in, the person on the shift before you would say so-and-so and so-and-so, and you just took over. There was no training at all. If you were sharp, you got promoted.

None of the men used bad language while we were there. My dad told me, the men all came together and said, 'Now there's girls coming to work here, and bad language is out.' If they used bad language in front of us, it was instant dismissal. It was really one big happy family to tell the truth, because you were all in the shift together, the men looked upon us as their daughters, and they looked after us, they wouldn't let us be molested by anybody, they were very protective. You never saw the management. They were upstairs, faceless men, you never saw them.

My future husband was already working on the railbank when I went down. He fancied me, but was too shy to ask for a date, so one of his mates came round. I know it sounds corny, but it's what was done in them days. He came and said, 'John wants to know if he can take you to the Carnegie, the pictures.' And I said, 'Which is him?' And he showed me and I says, 'Oh I don't know, I'll have to ask me Dad.' So I did, I said to him, 'There's a John McDonald wanting to take me to the pictures. Do you know him? What's he like?' 'Cause I was me Dad's girl. I don't think he was all that happy really, but he said, 'Well, I haven't heard nothing about him.' So this mate came back and said, 'Have you made your mind up?' and I said, 'Yeah, I'll go'; and that's how I met him. He went after a while, he volunteered for the Army. He didn't have to go, because he was exempt, being on the steelworks, but they went because it was war, and they wanted to fight for their country. I wasn't really interested in him as a boyfriend. He was a very shy man, and I was his first girlfriend, I'd had other boyfriends. To me, he wasn't the man I wanted, he wasn't world-wise enough for me at the time, so it was quite a time before I started to feel anything toward him – more a long friendship really, but we got married before the war ended.

I used to like night shifts better than anything. It was all right, once you got used to it. My father was a bad sleeper when he was on nights, and everything had to be quiet in the house – no radio or nothing, the kids had to be quiet. When I was on night shifts I slept like a log. Something about nights I liked; I used to get tired between two and three, but once three o'clock came, I was all right. The lighting in the mill wouldn't be allowed now. You had to watch where you were going – it wasn't tidy, there was all sorts lying about, bits of ingots – and you could break your ankle. My husband took me back years after and it was spotless – you could eat your dinner off the ground.

I always wore clogs. I polished them every day, blacking them. Used to buy them with toecaps on, so they'd look nice. Some of us wore rubber clogs, corkers they called them, with steel corkers, and when they wore down the shoeman put new corks on, like a horse. Sometimes we wore them for going out in – fancy ones, with rubber round. They were comfortable and warm. They were good for your feet and all. Only one thing about it, you used to kick your ankles, and always had sore ankles on the bone when you kicked them as you walked. We used to kick our corkers and make sparks along the ground, that was one of our pastimes as we were going to work.

Morning shift I didn't like, because of getting up early. Of course, you could go to a dance at night, but you knew you had to get up at about quarter to five. I liked to give myself plenty of time to get myself pulled together. Some of the girls used to get up at quarter to six, and be flying down the road for six o'clock, but I was never like that.

I lost a baby – she died when she was ten months old. I was rushed to hospital after five months with haemorrhaging. But in them days I wasn't allowed out of bed, I'd to lay on my back for two months; twice I went into labour, twice I was taken down, but she didn't come, so they gave me an injection to keep her back till I was seven months, to give her a better chance. They said if I could stay over the seven months, there was a chance she'd be all right. When she was born she was only two pounds, a bag of sugar; and she went down to a pound and a half. There was no incubators in those days, so they just put them in an ordinary baby's cot with hot

48

water bottles all round. People came with special milk for her. There was rationing then, and you couldn't get things – you were only allowed two ounces of this, two ounces of that. I couldn't feed her, she was too small to be fed, so they put it out on the radio at work; and people kept bringing condensed milk into the hospital for her, so the nurses could feed her. Everybody rallied round. Anyroad, I got her home when she was three months old, and she was five pounds in weight, and she died when she was ten months old. She never had a chance, really. But the others who lost their babies, they died before, they were miscarriages. There was nothing said at the time, but we've all talked since – we've said that there must have been something for all of us who worked at the steelworks to lose our babies.

Women didn't have maternity leave. I didn't go back. I don't think anyone stayed, they all left after having babies. We'd been there four years, and the men started to dribble back, so they didn't want the women.

I enjoyed working, I had a good time. We had some bad times as well, it was hard work – but it was fun. You didn't wash. You went in, you got on with your job. You just worked for eight hours. Only when the mill broke down or something, then you got a bit of a break. There was a cold tap on a stand for a drink of water. You used the men's toilets. They didn't cater for women.

We really had no choice. It was part of the war. There wasn't anything else really. Unless you went into service, or canteen work in the mines. That's all there was. There were no big shops, anything like that. I started for about twenty-five shillings a week, and when I left I was getting £4.50; that was top wage, same as the men were taking home.

My grandson worked at the steelworks till about six months ago, until they paid him off. He used to work on the railbank, so I knew what he was talking about; but he was only on contract all the time, two-month contracts. He stayed there two years before they paid him off, but he was always on edge because every time the two months was up – were they going to give him another two? That went on for two years.

When John came back from the war he went back to the steel, and he used to sit and talk about this and that, and I knew what he was talking about because I'd done it, and that was good. He used to come home sometimes and he'd had a rough day – he would complain about someone, maybe who'd stopped the mill. He used to take out his frustration at home, and I used to understand, so I'd say, 'Yeah, well, they were wrong and you were right, love, weren't you . . .'. And it helped.

You knew when the mill had stopped working. You used to lie in bed and say, 'Oh something's gone wrong with the mill', because the sound wasn't there. You got to know the sounds, the working of the machinery; and when the wind was blowing and it was a quiet night, you could hear everything that was going on, you could follow it in your mind. I missed that when the steelworks closed down. Missed it all, yes. I missed the horns blowing. It was as if the clocks'd stopped. I know they were only horns, but it was very reassuring. Yeah, I enjoyed it. I had a good life. Can't complain at all.

After the war, Edna stopped working for a while. Her husband came back and they had a baby. They were forced to live with her parents, which caused some difficulties, and they separated. She was about to get a divorce, when the Council gave her a house, and she agreed to give her marriage a second chance. 'We got back together and we had a happy married life, a marvellous married life. I'm just sorry I lost him, that's all. We had thirteen good years together in this house.' Her husband worked his way up at the steelworks to shift inspector, a foreman's job. He retired at fifty-nine and died in 1989.

Selwyn Morris (*born 1923*), *Splott, Cardiff*

Whether or not there ever was a 'working-class culture' has become a matter for academic debate. What is sure is that the testimony of people from all over Britain converges around certain specific recollections on the nature of work and the communities that served the pit, the works or the factory. There is a powerful sense of the sameness of life in the community that evolved in the neighbourhood of the specific workplace, whether this was a mill in Blackburn, a foundry in Walsall, a shipyard in Glasgow or a steelworks in South Wales.

Splott was a steelworkers' area; almost everyone in the street worked in the Dowlais Works.

My father was a blast-furnaceman, a pipe-fitter. Where he worked, it was not unusual for a heavy escape of gas to occur. They would get them into the works ambulance, take them home. When it happened to my father, he'd take a couple of days off, till it was out of his system. He was paid for those two days. They were good but hard employers – they wanted their poundsworth. In his later years the work was too much for him, he went to another part of the works as a fitter's mate. He stayed there till he died, in his sixties. Like everybody else in Splott, he had a hard life. They were tired men.

When I started work, he said, 'Do you want a job? Go and see Mr Moses.' He was the one who would take you on; he never said no – the turnover of labour was terrific. I was a small fellow, and I got a job as a sample-carrier. Shift work. I took the samples from the furnace to the laboratory. I carried them on a shovel from the melting shop. Mind you, if I put the shovel down to talk to anybody, they'd disappear; I'd get to the lab and they'd play heck. But they were a good bunch of lads. Everybody helped everybody else. It was an enjoyment to go to work.

I wanted to get on, so I approached the manager. He said, 'Turn up at the mill tomorrow.' All the lads went there. My father was there and also an uncle. As a youngster, if my father wasn't home for his meal, my mother made him a box of food and I was the carrier. I'd go to the gate and they knew me there, so I'd take his food in. So the mill was known to me before I started. It was a very happy place. If you were sat for any reason at lunchtime, they'd spot it if you didn't have a sandwich – food was all sandwiches then – there was one appeared in front of you.

I had one brother and one sister, Beryl; she lived with my auntie who had no children. My father was unemployed in the Depression, so my mother took in washing. We had some relatives who were well off, she did housework there, and that was the income we had. My father would be wandering the docks, looking for work. They were desperate, but kept their sense of humour. My father was going round with his mate looking for work. He said, 'I bet this next chap says yes.' So he went into the factory and said, 'Is that right you don't have any vacancies?' 'Yes, that's right.' 'See,' he said, 'I told you he'd say yes.'

Everything helped. I'd go down to the foreshore, there was so much coal tipped there that the incoming tide washed it all up. There were thousands of wagons. I'd pick a bag of coal, and I'd got a bit of a bike, I'd push it home. But you didn't put all the coal in your own house. There'd be Mrs So-and-so down the street, so you'd put some in there. It was the same with food. Those who had allotments, they'd always be taking a bag of something to other people. They wouldn't say anything, they'd just take it – potatoes, cabbages. Nobody ever took money for it. They all had nothing. We had nothing but we shared it. That was Splott.

Most blast-furnacemen were Irish – my father was one of the few Welshmen. They worked twelve-hour shifts in his time, twenty-four hours at the weekend change-over. They were big, huge men. Big drinkers, too, flagons of beer.

Opposite the works was the Lord Wimborne pub, and the Bomb and Dagger Club. Shirley Bassey lived near. She used to sing there. Singing, jokes. Great days. One Sunday dinner-time, this tramp came in. No one knew him. Everybody was giving turns. He said, 'I'll drink a pint without the glass touching my lips or my hands.' 'You can't do that.' 'I can. You fill up and see.' So somebody filled his pint up. He had slippers on his feet. He took them off, put one on each hand, and lifted the glass, poured it down his throat. He was right – it didn't touch his lips or his hands.

The coke ovens were in a lane just behind the Bomb and Dagger. It was dirty living so close to the works. The windows were covered with dust. If there was a breakdown at the works, they wouldn't be able to contain the dust. The washing was covered in it. My sister and her friend once marched down to the works, went into the general office and told the manager off for discharging all this dust.

When you were on days, you started at eight, then the hooter went at 4.30. Waiting for the hooter, we'd be hiding behind stacks of bricks, one foot ready to leave. As the hooter went, we'd all go together – two hundred men would suddenly appear out of the blue. One minute you wouldn't see anybody; the next, there we were.

During the war, the mill went on two shifts because of the air raids. The air raid warnings would go, and all production was stopped because of the lighting. This went on for four or five months. Then the night shift was cut altogether. We were told either we could leave, or go labouring on the site by day. It meant a drop in wages. I went labouring, but after that went to a factory making bomb casings. I wanted to be called up. I joined the Fleet Air Arm, although I wanted the Navy. I was trained fusing up bombs in Lancashire, trained as hammerer. Then I went on the *Colossus* aircraft-carrier, Gibraltar and Alexandria. I enjoyed it. I finished up in Australia. We picked up some British POWs – poor fellows, they were skeletons. It would make you cry, they were all bone, that's all they were. When we got to Trincomalee, I was dropped off, because they were picking up another load. At Trinco, I met a guy from Splott in the canteen.

I didn't want to go back to the steelworks after the war. I went to the Labour Exchange, and got a job. Aircraft were being put back to normal, ready for sale. I went to St Athan's as a hammerer. I couldn't get on there. I lasted six months. We used to go to the toilets for a smoke, in turns. One day, there was one guy who had already been for a smoke. When I walked to the toilets, he walked in behind me. Behind him, the guy in charge came in and said, 'You', pointing at me, 'get out.' I said, 'I just want a smoke, I've just come in. You know the system.' 'You've been in here twenty minutes.' I hadn't. I said, 'I'll come when my cigarette is finished.' I came out. He said, 'You're on a charge. Go and see the station commander.' I couldn't believe it. I said, 'I'm not in the services now.' He said, 'You are on this site.' I had to go up there. It was do this, do that, do the other. I said, 'I won't be doing any of that.' 'You will.' 'I won't', I said. 'I don't know what the bus service is like, but I'm getting the next one out of here.'

So I went back to the steelworks next day. They were always looking for men. I started at the bottom. Steelworker isn't a trained man. You just went in. 'What do I do?' 'Here's a shovel, there's the slag.' I was shovelling it into the wagons. Labouring. I was happy for a while, on days; every day, including Sundays. I had enough of that. I went on preparing the ladles, cleaning them out. You had to go down in the ladle, drills punched it out, and then you had to clean it out ready to hold more metal. It was an apprenticeship, if you like.

I joined the union as soon as I started. I didn't have to be told . . . The Secretary worked in the melting shop. He gave me a book and pen to collect the subs from the pitside area. It wasn't easy to collect subs, unless you caught them on pay-day. Some would get behind. I used to say, 'If there's an accident, we can do nothing for you if you're behind.' One guy paid every half-year. I used to stand outside the office on pay-day, so they couldn't say they hadn't seen me on shift. Eventually, deductions were made at source.

At union meetings we discussed conditions of work, wage negotiations. The melters were the top men; then the pitside area, the casting area, labourers, assembly men. They were all individual units. You couldn't negotiate a round figure to suit everybody. If you had a genuine case to argue, change of work practice or something, we always asked for more than we'd get – ask for £1 and know you'd get ten shillings. The manager would sit opposite with the personnel representative. We always asked for more, but eventually you would get down to basics. He'd say, 'I'll go away and think about it'; and it was the same with us. You don't jump at an offer. You arrange another meeting. It depended on who you were dealing with. Some called a spade a spade. But I have dealt with those who approached it with a you'll-get-nothing-out-of-me attitude.

The conditions in the melting shop were very bad. The dust was terrific. I don't see how they could control it – they had no dust extractors. It was very noisy, but how can you stop it? . . . they did their best. They were open-hearth furnaces, seven of them, six always working, belching out smoke – how else do you melt the bloody scrap? It was damned hard, dirty work in the melting shop. When they fettled a furnace – there was a hole in the furnace and they had to fettle it – men with shovels would keep going for hours. Those lads, they earned their money.

When I worked in the pitside area, those ladles held 110 tons of metal. We'd run out of ladles, the brick wall might have gone, and the brickies would strip it – that would take two or three days. We'd be out of ladles, but the furnace never stopped blasting. So the teemer and assistant teemers queued up to get this ladle right. It was black-hot, an hour before it had

had over a hundred ton of metal in it. They'd put the ladder down and the ladder would catch fire. A man would go down there for two minutes, something over his head, do a bit then come back up, and someone else went down. But they never failed. They could've refused to go down, but they never did. There were no grumbles, they had pride . . . Four men would go down into the ladle – I've seen them – put the nozzle in the hole, get this 'ganny' as we called it to fill it all up. I'd go in there and I'd be out in two minutes. But *they* would go in there, it meant nothing to them – marvellous men, hard men. They were very hard men; whether that's good or bad I don't know.

They'd finish a shift's work and go to the pub or club and they'd drink eight pints off like that, without exaggeration. Lou Jenkins, he was Branch Secretary for many years. He drank two pints to our one. If there were eight of us, and we went to buy a round, we'd always call nine pints. That's the sort of drinkers they were. They worked hard and drank hard. There was one man who never drank. 'Silly devils,' he used to say. They were bloody good men. They looked after me as Branch Secretary. They knew I'd done my best. I never had to fight them.

We did wear special clothing, heat-resistant trousers and jacket. They still use them at Llanwern. Initially, we had nothing, just an ordinary jacket – you wore your oldest clothes. You couldn't do anything else with them.

There were a lot of accidents. At one time the Branch Secretary dealt with them. The firm's solicitors were in London, they'd come and investigate if necessary. I was thirty years as Branch Secretary, I went into the hospitals and got them to fill out the form when they were fit to. One poor fellow, a ladle of metal came across the shop on an overhead crane towards the teeming bay, and he's going up the steps, and he slipped; the crane driver couldn't see him, went over him. I think he lived a few days. There was nothing we could do. The union solicitor also took on community settlements. There was a little girl knocked down by a van – they took that on.

At one time, there was about eighty accidents on the books. I only had one accident. Management denied responsibility. Where the ladles were situated, it was over a pit, and you had to go down into the pit to clean it out, to shovel the rubble and brickwork out to the outside of the ladle to be barrowed away. I went down there – the steps were six inches wide – and I and others had often complained. I broke my leg. I won the case, because the steps should by law be at least ten inches wide. We won most compensation cases.

I have to say I overdone it. If one of my members was in trouble, the wife would say, 'We're going to So-and-so's.' 'No we're not.' 'Oh?' 'No,

Billy So-and-so, I got to go and see him.' I always put the union first, which was wrong. I should have controlled myself. She tells me to this day, and she was right. I loved it. I was a fool. I used to be there before the accident happened.

They introduced new methods of melting. At first, G furnace held three hundred tons, the smallest fixed furnaces held a hundred tons. They didn't tilt. It took G furnace twelve hours from tap to tap, ten hours the smaller ones. With improvements later, oxygen injection, it took six hours.

We had a job to do and we did it. When the ladle was hot we could have said, 'We'll wait a couple of hours.' But our lads weren't built that way. Our lives were working in the industry. We put up with the circumstances. They weren't imposed on us deliberately. 'Come on lads', and we'd get that ladle done.

If I had to start off in it right away, I'd be scared to death, but you're all built into it from when you started. When you start, you don't go near the ingots or hot metal – you start on the ground floor, cleaning up. The teemer would say one day, 'I've got one short, do you want a shift?' He wouldn't give you a lot to do – there's twelve in a crew, and they were good to you. You'd go down the ladder with him a few times before you went on your own. They were willing to help you. Great people.

They were determined to close East Moors. They gave four years' notice; we managed to extend that. We set up a works council, had monthly meetings. We were not going to lose, but by God the writing was on the wall. Things got so bad, people were saying, 'Give me redundancy, let's go', and management were giving it. My advice was 'Don't go. If we're going to close – which we're not – we'll get a better deal.' A lot of the lads had jobs to go to. One man held the assembly bay together, no one left until he was ready to go. Then he left, and it fell apart. I couldn't forgive him for that. They deserted us, done a bloody deal. If he'd been open, I'd've accepted that.

We set up a coke and cement business on the site to get funds in to fight closure. We'd buy coke from the ovens, cement from whoever supplied the works, and sold it cheaper than the lads could get it outside. Management went along with us.

I felt sick as a pig during closure. 'We will win this fight,' we said. We worked damned hard. We went to lobby the Labour Party at Blackpool, we were in London once a week. Jim Callaghan was good to us. Neil Kinnock advised us to close down the works for a week. He said, 'In less than a week everyone will want to talk with you.' We didn't have the following by that time. The lads wouldn't have done it. If we'd had the following, I would've been delighted to do so. But we were beat. It was a fact of life.

We campaigned night and day. I went to the last shift. This ladle had to be teemed, there were hundreds of people there. We saw the last cast teemed. After it was over, we said, 'Where do we go now?' We went to the club – I'd never seen the club so full in all my life.

I extended my time, doing odd jobs. The terms of closure were very good, but we could've done better. I knew I was on a loser. Good as we were on production, there was a shortage of orders, and our costs of production was too high. We couldn't carry on. We could've modernized a few years earlier. Callaghan had plans drawn up – that was the way we were going – but events overtook us. He lost the election. Jim Callaghan worked hard on our behalf, but he was a loser, like me.

I worked for the contractors demolishing East Moors. I had to earn a living somehow. Then I got a job with another contractor, getting out all the machines that could be sold; other demolition jobs, including a power station at Bristol. East Moors was demolished by blasting. There were a lot of chimneys. They got an old blast-furnaceman to blast the blast-furnaces. Later, I was offered a job in the London docks for the company, bringing in scrap, shipping it out . . . I wouldn't work away from home.

I don't think I could get along with the steel industry of today, such as Allied Steel – a hundred ton in half an hour. Loaded up in big containers, in thirty-five minutes they get their metal. I don't think I could've done that. But I'm getting on now, I guess in those days if they'd had that sort of furnace we could have done it. But we were brought up different. They still work hard, though.

I can see East Moors site and it doesn't hurt me in the slightest. What hurts me is not the area where the works stood – there's units there, not many working, just a few hundred, which is good. What hurts me is, in the process they pulled Splott down. About twenty rows of houses in that area where I was born, and they've destroyed it, they've ripped the bloody lot down. We fought that at the time. My family had to move out. My mother had said she would never leave there other than in a coffin; and that is what she left in. That's all destroyed. We were what I call real people. Today the area is wasted. I can never get over that. My sister wouldn't budge. She died in the house.

They took a big slice out of a marvellous community. They'll never replace it. The people there would see no one go without. The spirit was there. I was used to that all my life. No one went short. The women knew when anybody was having a baby, didn't wait to be asked. There was one lady, she was automatically walking down the street when the baby was due. They knew.

Seven

The growth in self-employment has been a significant feature of the past twenty years; there are now 3.2 million people classified as self-employed.* However, this process is ambiguous. For one thing, it is not always a question of self-employment in the sense of people creating their own jobs. Rather, it is that it often places them in the position of subcontractors, with all that that implies for taking responsibility for their own conditions of labour, insurance, and so on. Many small businesses are short-lived; there is a constant turnover. Many self-employed people, especially homeworkers, are working casually, part-time, and long hours – often for a modest income. Much of this has come about because of the decline in 'jobs for life', the inability of 'secure' companies to ensure continuity of employment for a large workforce.

Terry Hamlyn (*born 1935*): *painter and decorator, west London*

Originally an industrial worker, Terry Hamlyn became self-employed in the 1960s, at a time when this was still regarded as a slightly foolish, if adventurous, thing to do. He now lives in Kingston on Thames.

My father was a long-distance lorry driver. He worked for various companies, including Mayhew's flour mills at Battersea, owned by J. Arthur Rank. He used to load the lorry with sacks of flour. The building was a kind of warehouse, three storeys high. He had to climb a ladder outside the building, and come down with every sack of flour, fifteen tons' load in a day. He had his shoes built up, so that the weight wouldn't damage his instep. Then he'd drive to the coast, deliver to bakers' shops.

On the day before he was married he went to J. Arthur Rank, who was manager, and he said he'd like the Saturday off. 'Why?' 'Well, to get married.' 'You can have the morning off, but I want you back in the

---

* *Of a total of 28.2 million employed, December 1993.*

afternoon.' So that was how he spent his wedding day, loading bags of flour.

During the war, he drove for a company delivering ammunition all over the country. It was a reserved occupation, so he didn't have to join up. He took me with him sometimes. I have vivid memories of it, an eight-wheeler lorry, the engine inside the cab. It was covered with a blanket, and I sat on it. I used to steer the lorry while he filled his pipe. Later, he drove articulated lorries, Scammells. There was more room in those cabs. One day, he was driving it empty, going back to the depot in Kentish Town. He stopped near Regent's Park. He said, 'Here, you take it.' I was twelve. I knew how to drive from being with him and watching him. I started it up. There was a left turn into Primrose Hill. He told me to get into the middle of the road. I was doing what he told me. 'OK, now straighten up.' I saw a police car coming the other way. I said, 'What shall I do?' He said, 'Look old.' He had nerves of steel. The police car drove straight past us. My Dad was never out of work.

In the house where we lived, there was no running water. No electricity. You had to carry the zinc bath up- and downstairs full of water on bath nights. There was an outside toilet. After the war, my mother and father separated, but I was always close to my father. I had two sisters, both younger than me. One worked as a secretary at the Queen's Ice Rink. Her husband became the managing-director and she was his secretary. Then they broke up, but she carried on with the same job, taking dictation from him while they were getting divorced.

I left school at fifteen. There was no such thing as careers advice, no discussion of what we wanted to do. You looked at the labour market and took anything you could fit into. I got my first job through the Junior Labour Exchange. It was in Ravenscourt Park, under the arches – a lorry workshop. My job was to take the engines out of Bedford lorries, strip them down, drain them of all the sludge, then hose them with a high-pressure hose to see if there were any leaks. I used to get covered with grease and water and oil – it went right through my overalls, trousers, and ran down my legs.

At that time, most youngsters got jobs through their relatives or neighbours. You got taken on if somebody knew where there was something going. My uncle worked for Joe Lyons, at the Coventry Street Corner House. He was the rear-of-building manager. He knew the chief engineer there and got me an interview. I started in the electrical department. My job? Changing light-bulbs. I'd been getting thirty-three shillings a week at the first place, now I went up to four guineas. It was a better environment, a warm building, waitresses to have a joke and laugh with. There was a scheme for when you went sick. Changing light-bulbs was actually a full-time job. About forty a day would go; there were all these chandeliers and there was fluorescent lighting. There were two of us doing it. You had to carry step-ladders up and down the staircases, go and get stuff from suppliers, cable and so on. 'Lamping', we called it. Although we weren't supposed to do overtime under eighteen, we used to do it, setting up the spotlights in the evenings in the restaurants when they had dinner–dances. We got our meal thrown in – whatever the customers were eating. That was a privilege.

That lasted till I got my call-up papers. You had to do square-bashing, and then you were sent to your trade regiment. They asked what you wanted to do – radio mechanic, cipher operator – and if you passed the aptitude test, you more or less got what you asked for. I went to Ripon, where drivers and electricians were being trained. My job was to drive a three-ton vehicle, with charging equipment, a generator on a trailer behind. If there had been any fighting, we would have been attached to the infantry regiment, and set up the generators to light the tents and so on.

Then I was posted to the Horse Guards at Windsor, charging batteries for armoured cars. That was a cavalry regiment. I enjoyed being at Windsor. Sometimes we'd swim across the Thames in the evenings. We used to drill with the guards, who did everything twice as fast as the other regiment. After a few weeks, the CO came looking for me waving a piece of paper, saying, 'You shouldn't be here, they've been looking for you all over the place. You should be in Newton Abbot Training Camp, you're going abroad.'

My mother was very worried. It might have been Korea, Malaya, Kenya. The papers at that time were full of stories of 'terrorists' in the far-flung outposts of empire which we were still defending. It turned out I was being sent to the Gold Coast. Accra. I'd never heard of it. It was a shock. I thought it would be mud huts. As it happened, it was less different than I thought it was going to be. It was a brick-built camp, a row of rooms with a veranda, no glass in the windows, louvred shutters.

It was great. An adventure at no cost. It was the first time I ever went in an aircraft, a two-engined Viking. The flight took three days. I remember coming in over Gibraltar, seeing the rock orange-coloured in the setting sun. We had our first night in Africa in Mali, near Timbuktu. We had dinner on the veranda – and these insects, they were called goliath beetles, so big they would push sugar bowls across the table with their body.

When we got to Accra, I was put in charge of the Transport Section. I knew nothing about how to do it. I was made a sergeant, which was the lowest rank of any European; rank was manipulated so you could tell the Africans what to do. In fact Africans of the same rank, and even above you, were beneath you – they all called you 'sir'.

I got help from African NCOs. You couldn't ask too much, you mustn't be seen to be dependent on them. I was told off by the Commanding Officer. We had gone to an African wedding, an army wedding, and it was great. High life, dancing and drumming went on all night. We had a few drinks and joined in. Somebody spotted us. The CO said, 'Look, you mustn't fraternize with the natives. If you get too friendly they'll misbehave.'

I enjoyed my time there. We'd work till one, then go down to the beach, surf, swaying palms. It was all fairly lax. Sometimes the officers never showed up for guard duty at night, so we thought, Well, we'll take time off too. So you'd ring the African orderly sergeant and say, 'Take the guard', which they would do.

It was lovely there. I used to wonder why they wanted their freedom when we were in charge. Nkrumah was leading the anti-colonial struggle, but we couldn't understand why they wanted freedom, because we were having a good time. If we went to the cinema in town, of course the audiences were mixed, there was no apartheid like in South Africa; but when they played 'God Save the Queen' at the end, all the blacks would charge out. We didn't like it. We'd been indoctrinated, we were in the service of the Queen. That annoyed us. But that was the limit of anything we saw. There was no violence there.

After eighteen months, it was time to come home. That was an adventure. We'd refuelled at Kano, and looked out of the window and saw all the fuel coming out of the wings. They dropped 1,800 gallons of fuel, to make an emergency landing. There was a cracked cylinder. There were no fitters on board. They sent another engine in a Dakota, which broke down at Gibraltar. There was only the aircrew, two Africans and us. When the engine came, we all had to work through the night to install it. We were going on to Malta. Suddenly I looked down and saw the Sahara getting dangerously near. There was another cracked cylinder. We went to Tripoli, and eventually back to England. It took about two weeks altogether. When we landed, we were all tanned and relaxed – everybody here looked miserable. I wished I'd signed on. I was the only National Serviceman in the whole of the West African Command. They said I had to sign on, but I wouldn't.

After National Service, the firm that had employed you was obliged to take you back. I went back to the Corner House, and was offered the job doing what I'd done before. It didn't seem a very attractive prospect. There was a vacancy at a factory, Cadby Hall in Hammersmith, repairing forklift trucks. I stayed there about ten years, till 1964.

There was always a stigma in wearing overalls. In Cadby Hall, you were more highly thought of if you worked in the office, even though there was less pay. My mate who worked at Dagenham said that there were different toilets for the office and the shopfloor. Sometimes, even members of the same family living in the same house couldn't use the same toilets at work.

It was hard enough settling down after being in the Army. The comradeship was not there. I got fed up with being inside the same four walls. It was dirty work. In the early sixties, they sent in the time-and-motion people to assess our work. That created a lot of ill-feeling. To add to that, there was a strike over the use of non-union labour. The company refused to sack him. That was at the time when there was a lot of criticism of the ETU for being Communist. We used to say, 'We don't want Tory officials, do we?' We thought later that the strike was a put-up job. It was rigged by the firm to clear out all the people they wanted to get rid of, because there, people had jobs for life – it had got lax, we knew all the wrinkles. In fact, all the big companies were doing it at that time. When the strike was called, the shop steward was not a good orator, but the assistant shop steward was. He said, 'I won't be behind you, brothers, I'll be beside you.' We all charged out of the shop. What happened? Next day he went back to work as manager of the bakery department. He'd been paid to do it. It was the same elsewhere: they would provoke a strike because they wanted to rearrange the assembly lines.

I think that experience changed my view of the world. Till then, I'd always more or less accepted what I was told, but then I started to question things. When we went back to work, after four months, everything was in a mess. Management had tried to do repairs and maintain the machinery and vehicles. It wasn't a strike over money. We didn't want blacklegs. During the strike, a lot of people got other jobs. In fact, the Americans moved in on Joe Lyons. The tea-shops were a waste of time, people would sit there one hour, two hours, with just a cup of tea and a cake. In fact, people used to eat in the evenings, before going to theatre or cinema – solid traditional English things, fish and chips and puddings. That was all changed. The Corner Houses closed and opened up as Wimpy Bars. It was still run by Lyons, Empire Caterers. The London Steak Houses also opened about then; they've all gone now. It was part of the Americanization of our eating habits. It wasn't seen like that. People thought, Oh, this is more modern.

I got married in 1957. We lived in a bed-sitter in Holland Park. We had our first child there; then we had to leave, because they didn't allow babies in bed-sits. I was paying four guineas a week there, half my weekly wage.

We got a maisonette in Tooting. Then when I got the tools in 1958, I got more pay. Getting the tools meant you stopped being a mate and became an electrician. There were apprentices and then mates; mates could do the fitting, but it was not guaranteed that they'd get the tools. Their wages were better than apprentices', but apprentices were more or less guaranteed to get their tools. One of the electricians left, and they said, 'Can you do this?' I'd been doing it unpaid anyway. My wage went up to £12.

Working in the food industry, I used to think how unfair it was, when a sack of flour went up by twopence, each loaf of bread also went up by the same amount. I got to dislike going to work. It only takes one bloke to be miserable on a Monday morning, and it can affect the whole place. I was talking to my friend – we used to go to the pictures together – and he was working with his father-in-law, building. He'd been a typewriter salesman, but gave it up. I said I was leaving my job. He said, 'Why don't we work together, set up on our own account?' I decided to do it.

Lyons had been a big, protective place. All the blokes said, 'You'll be back.' They couldn't conceive there was anything outside the firm. For them, that was the limit of the world. 'Going to work outside' was the height of folly and insecurity.

Of course we started off with no work. We put cards in people's doors. We knew a guy who ran a property maintenance company. He asked us what we charged for this and that, and he gave us our first job. My mate used to phone every day, to see if anything had turned up. I said to him, 'Get your overalls on, we've got a job.'

Then nothing again. I'd spent my superannuation money, not realizing it was taxable. Her indoors wanted a washing-machine. In fact, we got no praise from our wives, either of us. It was always 'Where's your Rolls-Royce?' Self-employed people were supposed to be rich then. We paid ourselves £15 a week. We were scratching around for work. Then my mate's brother, who was in building, became a site agent in Folkestone. He asked if we'd do some painting. We went down in the freezing cold, before the building was even finished. I was following the plasterers around, this guy said, 'I've never been so close to a painter before.' We were living in a boarding house. We decided to split up, and I left him there and came home.

I knew other builders. I was always good at watching how people did things and then doing it. I'd worked to a thousandth of an inch on forklift trucks. I could point and paint. I was in the café, and this builder said, 'Can you plaster a ceiling?' I'd seen them smack it on, spread and polish. Plastering is a seven-year apprenticeship, or it was then. I can't do stick-and-rag, or cornices. But basically I was a self-taught electrician – all you had to know really was to keep up with the rules and regulations. I'm very adaptable, and pick things up very quickly.

I've been doing it for thirty years. I still feel young in myself although I'm sixty. I see blokes of my age who look twenty years older. My mate works in a factory, a jig-maker, making shapes for car parts, he's been in the same job all his life, stooping over a bench.

I've met a lot of different people. Worked in some terrible places. One old girl, her house was so dirty, she used to make tea and I'd pour it down the drain. There was another guy I used to work for, he was on the Pay Board at the time of the miners' strike, lived in a posh house in Wimbledon. He was a naturist, and he used to wander around the house with nothing on. His wife used to ask me to join them for a cup of tea on the lawn; she was dressed, he was starkers. This man had worked out a formula to help both Ted Heath and the miners to save face in 1974. He took it to Heath, who threw it out of the window.

One married woman in Streatham, she kept giving me the come-on, telling me she never got any loving. I was working there, and she kept on with these innuendoes. I couldn't sleep at night. She was married. I thought to myself, I could do it. In the end, I did. It got to me, though. I was dissatisfied with home, I got angry with her. I think this woman was asking other guys in. I thought, I'm being two-timed. Although I was two-timing my wife, I didn't want to be two-timed. They went away in the end, and that solved it.

Some people were ridiculously fussy, you daren't touch anything. There was one couple, civil servants. She was like Mrs Bucket in *Keeping up Appearances*. One day, they greeted me with serious long faces. 'Have you been washing out your paintbrushes in the bathroom hand-basin?' I hadn't. 'Why?' 'Come and look at this.' I looked and they had detected a tiny scratch, invisible. I couldn't believe they were being serious. Working there was a nightmare. I used to get into a cold sweat at night.

I used to sub off one guy – he was a little man, used to shout at people. One day I was late getting on the job, my car had run out of petrol. 'What time do you call this?' I said to him, 'I give you the price and I do the job. I'm not accountable for every minute.' I could've stayed in a factory if that was what I wanted. I said to him, 'You're like some big tart.'

Then I had no work. I worked for the Marine Society, which used to be the Seafarers' Education Society. I used to take boxes of books down to the docks for long journeys. I'd do anything. That's how I kept going. What I didn't know, I learned, I taught myself.

The longest I've been without work is three weeks. I never starved and never got rich. It's easier to work on your own now, because no job is safe.

I have no regrets. I don't think about it – like Mr Micawber, I wait for something to turn up.

Building, decorating, plumbing – it can take a day to switch from one to another, to get into the swing of it . . . I don't do central heating. Apart from that, no problem. When I hear government ministers going on about how we need more training, I get mad. It's like a creeping disease. You learn through doing, through being with skilled people when you're young. Now it's 'We can't give you a job because you're not qualified.' I always liked to find out how things are done. I'm fascinated by bridge-building, engineering. That is what being a good worker means – being interested.

More education, more training – it's an illusion. The government don't know what jobs are coming, they don't know what training is needed – it's all to disguise the fact of unemployment. My daughter in university wouldn't be there if there were jobs. I have four children. One daughter in Milton Keynes is a registered childminder. My second daughter was a nurse, now she has a baby. She became very disillusioned, went private nursing and hated it. She prefers the NHS. My son lives with a Dutch girl in Amsterdam, he's an airframe mechanic. He loves aircraft. He has the same feeling about making things work that I do. My youngest daughter is at university. She was designing ceramics. Her designs were a bit too complicated for pottery, so now she's doing a course designing fabrics. But she would prefer a job.

I don't want to retire, because I don't like sitting at home doing nothing. If I stayed at home, I'd deteriorate. I won't retire. Like my father, he never really retired. When he was an old man he used to clean cars. He died on the job when he was eighty-one. I hope I go like that. He used to ride an old commercial bike, with his brushes and leathers in a basket.

I've enjoyed my working life. I wouldn't give it up . . . I have a lot of interests. I love jazz. I'm going to a Stan Kenton weekend over the holiday. My wife tolerates it. Sometimes, I'm sitting in the working men's club where I go, and all these guys are talking about football. It's Gary Lineker this, Gazza that. They get really worked up. One night, I said to them, 'Here, hang on a minute. You're talking about these people as though you knew them. Does Gary Lineker know you? Does Gary Lineker care about you? Why are you wasting all this energy talking about people you don't know and never will know? For God's sake talk about something that matters.'

Eight

*One of the major growth areas in present-day work has been in transport:
because of the increasingly international division of labour goods are regularly
carried long distances, not merely across the country but across Europe and,
indeed, the world. Fewer and fewer of our needs are answered locally, but are
supplied by distant, unknown providers. The split between producers and
consumers has become almost total in the West.*

Gavin Webb (*born 1945*): *HGV driver, Hertfordshire*

*Gavin has just bought a flat in what was previously a council block in Hemel
Hempstead; on the edge of the town, the blocks have been upgraded and
provided with security doors. The living-room is spacious; on the walls are
Gavin's photographs, and his books. He has all the novels of Stephen King.
He is the oldest of five children, born to a carpenter and factory worker in
Watford.*

I started off as an apprentice electrician. I enjoyed it, but being an
apprentice was a form of cheap labour, and they weren't teaching me
anything. I persuaded my father to let me leave, and I became apprentice
in a factory as a capstan lathe operator. The factory made aircraft parts. I
wasn't taught much there either, but I'm very good at learning things from
observation. I've only to see something done a couple of times and I've got
it. I learned a lot there, but mostly self-taught. I was told there that if I
didn't like it, I could get out. I left two years before finishing the
apprenticeship. I disliked the smell of the oil which was used on the lathe;
the smell of it stuck to you and you stank of it even after you'd had a bath.

I did some electrical work with my uncle for a while. But as soon as I
passed my driving test, I knew what I wanted to do. In fact, when I went
to BSM driving school, they asked me if I'd ever driven before. They put
me in for my test after just six lessons, and I passed straight away.

To start with, I drove a small van – first for a grocer, doing deliveries,
then a greengrocer. Then I drove a lorry carrying building materials, all the

time moving up to a bigger vehicle. After that I went into general haulage. This was in 1969, at the time when HGV licences were first being issued. The government decided that if anybody had been working for a company for a minimum of six months, whatever vehicle, you would get the licence. There were a lot of fiddles – people claimed they had been driving trucks for a year or more, which they hadn't. I'd been driving for the guy I worked for for three years. There were three classes of licence – class three, four-wheeler, whatever weight; second-class, more than four wheels, but non-articulated; and first-class, artic. I got a second-class: if I'd had an artic. licence, the bloke I worked for knew I would be off. The first articulated trucks appeared in the early sixties; in the late sixties the big ones got going. The first artic. sleeper-cab was a Volvo 86; there are still some around – they're regarded as crap vehicles now, but then they were an innovation.

Next I worked for Cementation, based in Doncaster, a company which did foundations for big buildings. I mainly worked on office buildings in East London. When they were building multi-storey blocks, they used to lift the earth and drive a concrete pillar into the ground, and this had to be able to withstand the weight of the building that was planned. They used to place concrete weights on to these pillars to see what weight it could bear before building. I drove a Leyland Octopus – so called because of its eight wheels, and I carried these weights, which were anything from a few kilos up to six tons. This tested how far the piles had to be driven into the ground, and the diameter required; each was tested by a specific weight to test the stress. Big weights were lifted by crane, smaller ones on a metal pallet. I worked there for about five years.

Then I worked for a clothing company, picking up garments for C&A, which we distributed countrywide. You don't realize the weight of clothing. We picked them up by the hangers, and you could carry so many hangers on each finger. I could carry 150 garments on one hand. It kept you fit, running up- and downstairs, loading and unloading.

The image of the truck driver is of a fat slob who eats greasy breakfasts. Some were like that, if they were only driving; but people who have to load and unload are very fit and muscular. It is stressful work. The hours are supposed to be limited. In the sixties, you were allowed to work up to fifteen hours a day, and you could legally be driving for twelve of those; the rest of the time had to be something else, loading or unloading. In those days, we had to keep a logbook. In fact, if you were carrying perishable goods, you were allowed to do even more hours at the wheel. You can still work up to fifteen hours a day in the food trade, but the driving is now supposed to be limited to nine hours. The maximum without a break is four and a half hours. Many drivers are pressured into doing more.

Continental work is usually a question of going from A to B within a certain time. They pay you 'trip money' – that is to say, x pounds to go from here to Brussels or Rome. If you do it quicker than the allowed time, two days instead of three, you can do two trips a week. That is double the money; say, if it's £150 from London to Brussels, you can make £300 by going twice. It sounds like good money, but if you work out the actual hours you do to make that £150, it works out at about £1.50 an hour. It's not taxed, in the sense that you are self-employed. The last time I went to Sicily, some years ago, I got £275 for the trip, which took twelve days. I had two days' break, but the hourly rate was actually very low.

Some companies pay an hourly rate. The Wellcome Foundation do, for instance; they'll have two drivers in the truck so they can drive longer hours, and they'll put them up in hotels.

I stayed with the clothing firm for three years, then went into commercial recovery, going out to breakdowns. I had a small car-transporter or a breakdown truck. Sometimes, if an artic. vehicle had broken down, I'd have to tow it back. The articulated vehicle was 15 metres long, plus the 5 metres of my vehicle, which meant at least 20 metres. I was on twenty-four-hour call. We took it in turns, you could be called out day or night. Of course, some of the calls were trivial, or crazy things – people who'd run out of petrol. Originally, the company only charged for the gallon of petrol, but in the end they charged a call-out fine of £10. I was once called to a Danish Bacon vehicle overturned on the motorway. The police were there. They couldn't find the driver, and never did. The driver had gone and so had the cargo.

At the time of the dispute over seat-belts, there was a guy who crashed his Ferrari at Hendon; being fibreglass, the car blew up and was burnt out. The driver was not wearing a seat belt, and that saved his life.

There was a lot of pressure in that work. Once I went to a breakdown in Hackney. We used to take the drivers home. I said 'Where to?' He said, 'Truro.' Then on the way back they called me up, and expected me to do another job, after almost twenty-four hours on duty.

At that time, the government was running courses for those wanting to take the HGV licence; you were paid £20 a week for a two-week course. I got the artic. licence. The trouble was, when you first get the licence no one will employ you, because they won't trust you with your vehicle till you get experience. So you have to work for an agency. The agencies go round supplying drivers to companies as relief drivers for holidays and sickness. They would ask if you can do roping and sheeting. I learned not to tell them that I could do that, because if you're stuck with twenty tons of timber or fibre-board, trying to get a sheet over it that flies away in the wind, it isn't much fun.

The agency charged £6 an hour, of which I would get just over half. There was no guarantee of work, so you'd sign on with three or four agencies. If you were good and reliable, they'd offer you seven hours' pay a day even if you didn't get any work. Then you'd get a job lasting two hours and get paid for seven, and then get another, say three hours, from a different agency, with another seven hours' pay.

After that I worked for an aerial platform company – you know, those vehicles with a platform on a long retractable arm which they use for street lighting. I drove the biggest one in Europe, 150 feet high. It was used by the BBC at Mark Phillips' wedding to Princess Anne, and they used it in programmes like *It's a Knockout*.

I knew a guy who did a lot of driving to the Continent. He was stuck one day and asked me if I wanted to drive to Rome. The first time, I followed a driver in another truck – it was easy. The paperwork at Dover was very complicated then. Then I worked that route to Italy regularly. He would pay me so much for the road tolls and everything, give me a diesel card for use at Shell stations, and all the paperwork for customs and a green insurance card, which you need if you're outside the UK, and a *carnet*, a notebook, with leaves stamped at the borders of the countries you went through. If there was any error in that, you could be held up for days. You had to give backhanders to officials all the time – police, customs – 'diesel money' we called it. If you didn't give money, they'd say, 'Do you smoke?' and they knew you had your duty-free stuff, so you had to give that, cigarettes or whisky. Trucks aren't allowed to drive on Sunday unless you're carrying perishable goods, so you are fined if you're caught. If you're done for speeding, you pay the fine, but if it's for driving on a Sunday, the employer will pay. Sunday you weren't allowed to drive between 6 a.m. and 10 p.m. unless you were less than eight hours away from your port of embarkation.

I always used to go out on a Sunday, get a ticket for the boat, go through customs; if it was a valuable cargo or perishable stuff, you had to go into a special bay. Once I took a cargo of cigarettes and whisky to Rome airport for the duty-free. The customs at the Italian border took their share, then asked me which route I'd take. I told them one way and then took another, because if you took the route you said, they'd ring their colleagues along the line and they would stop you for their hand-out too. You'd get held up and your truck taken away. The police didn't actually do it, but they were in on it; it was the Mafia or whatever.

A lot of work I did was transporting antique furniture. The buyers

68

would come to the markets in London – Portobello Road, Jamaica Street – and we'd take it over. The buyers were waiting for us at the other end, and they'd pile it into a warehouse, or sell it off the back of the trailer to dealers. A lot of that went to Naples. They made a fortune; they'd buy up all these old pianos and wardrobes, cannibalize the wardrobes, rip out the workings of the piano, install an electronic organ, mirror glass above the keys, and turn it into a musical cocktail bar. They'd buy them for £200 and sell for £2,000.

Some of the material that's transported is absurd. I once took sixteen tons of eggs to Padova, where they were turned into egg powder for export, and the shells made into fertilizer. Eggs and such like had to be checked by a veterinary surgeon; he'd pick out a few and smell them, test for freshness. Then he'd take a tray of eggs; another would go to the border guard. Before we left England, we were always given something extra to pay off the officials.

I took glass bulbs to a factory in Piacenza just to have the filament put in, after which they were transported back to England. Brillo pads went to Padova, to have the soap put in. I took cans to Athens once, empty cans without lids, to be embossed with the Coca Cola logo; then they would be brought back to England. You brought back the consignment that the previous driver had taken. Some drivers took meat from Denmark which had to go to Italy before it entered England. Don't ask me why.

I slept in the cab. The bed in the truck was not good, so I bought a single mattress. I'd pick up hitch-hikers, mainly girls. One girl I picked up outside Paris, a French coloured girl, she stayed with me for seven nights, but she wouldn't sleep with me. That was all right. It was more or less understood that if you picked up women on their own, they'd have to get their knickers off as payment. You never forced them; it takes two to tango. Some drivers would say to them, 'Get your knickers off or get out.' I'd never do that. I was more at ease with women; I liked to talk to them. Men might nick things, or more likely, they'd ask your name, where you're going, what you've got on board, and then go off to sleep. Driving all hours, it was company I wanted. Sometimes you'd drive for hours, with only a short sleep. You'd stay awake if you had a girl in the cab. Of course, women were constantly in fear of being raped, so they would stay alert. They'd stay awake and they could be good company. A lot of guys thought they were God's gift . . . I'd pick up a hitch-hiker and if it happened, fair enough. I'd pull up, not because the tacho had run out, but because I was tired. I'd say to her, 'I'm sleeping now. Stay if you want to. If not, I'll see you in the morning.' I basically wanted people to chat to.

I had a CB and I'd use it to talk to other drivers, wind them up sometimes. I'd once got this woman in the cab, and I had her break into our conversation; and the guy kept asking her where she was, whether she'd meet up with him. He didn't twig that she was in my cabin. That was just a bit of fun.

The British drivers would help one another, if you had a puncture or breakdown. Italians would help and the Spanish drivers, and the Dutch. But not the French.

It's not really a lonely life. It's what you make of it. But if you need people around you, don't drive on the Continent. I'm a bit of a loner. I'm happy with my own company; I'm happy, just sitting in a pub with a drink. I like reading, which is useful, some of the long waits you have at frontiers. You'd be stopped at the borders for a four-hour minimum. You have an agent who does the paperwork. He'll say 'Four hours'. You go after four hours: 'Another hour'; then maybe another one.

Stress is part of the job, which you have to be able to deal with. If you can't cope, don't do the job. You have to do a certain amount of maintenance on the vehicle, check the pressure of the tyres, the tread, lights, radio, polish and clean it up. Do that while you're waiting. I had a little cooker and a gas bottle. I'd cook my own food most of the time. Some drivers carried food just for emergencies; like when there was snow on Mont Blanc, if it was bad, the snow chains wouldn't help, you had to wait for the snow plough to come. You had a night heater in the cab which ran on the diesel from the tank. I took food for emergencies, but also to save money – especially, bacon, milk, eggs – you could keep the bacon in a sealed packet in a bucket of water. I hit on the idea of a bottle of Bailey's to put in my coffee. Brew up inside the cab if it was raining, outside if it was dry. You could sometimes sit underneath the vehicle in the rain, brew up. You'd make a driver's stew: you know, the labels would come off the tins, you never quite knew what would be in it – it could be disgusting or wonderful – sardines, soup, beans, even custard.

I have fallen asleep driving on occasion. I've thought, Oh, I'll stop at the next service area. Then I'd come to the service area after that, and thought, I don't remember passing the other one. Where was I? I must've been asleep. Once I woke up as I was hitting the crash barrier on the motorway; I hit it at a sliding angle, fortunately, I bounced off.

The longest drive I ever did was from Prato outside Florence to Paris: twenty-four hours. I stopped just for coffee here and there. It was a fairly light load of shoes and fabric, and a new vehicle with a big engine: 350 horsepower. I hardly needed to change gear in it. A big Fiat – it was not so stressful as driving the older trucks. Outside Paris, I just crashed out. Slept six hours, then off again.

I do miss it now. It is a way of life; I loved meeting people. Once you left England you were your own boss. As long as you got the truck from A to B, the way you did it was up to you. There was a freedom there.

A lot of the drivers who worked on the Continent, their marriages broke up. When I came home, my ex-wife would ask me why I was so tired. I'd come home and fall asleep. It wasn't much fun for the women. After my marriage broke up, I lived with a girl. She went off with another driver. I'd said to him 'Go and have a cup of tea with her.' I got back after one trip, she said, 'It's finished, I'm going with him.'

It is a kind of wanderlust. A lot of men have it. I wanted to be a racing driver. This was the nearest thing I could get to it. I loved it. I love driving, movement, change.

I tried to get back with my wife. I stopped doing Continental work for a time. Then a guy asked me to pick up a truck in Toulon whose driver had been taken ill. He drove me down in his car. Then I started working for him. He was a bit of a cowboy. He once sent me with some flammable chemical material which I didn't know was on board. They wouldn't allow that stuff to go through the Mont Blanc tunnel because of the risk of fire. It was supposed to go via Ventimiglia, a much longer route that cost more in diesel. So I was held up over that.

A lot of illegal stuff was brought in on trucks. Once, there was a consignment of suede jackets from Italy. They weren't really suede: they'd just sprinkled some kind of dust on glue with which they'd coated the jackets. I signed for it, took it on board. We were given a jacket for our wife and children. Two weeks later, I realized this wasn't suede at all.

At other times, there'd be a consignment of bogus Omega watches in with the legitimate cargo. I found some virgin olive oil, preserved artichokes, and some figs soaked in orange liqueur and stuffed with almonds. They were wonderful. If you found illegal cargo on your load, it was fair game for you to take it. If contraband was found, you had to leave it in what they call the Queen's Locker. Drink and drugs come through illegally. I've known drivers themselves buy quantities of tobacco, King Edward cigars, which they would sell when they got home; they were so much cheaper there, they could still make a good profit.

The idea of the tachograph is a good one, to prevent people from overworking. But there are a number of ways it can be tampered with. You won't stop people breaking laws; they'll always find a way round restrictions if they feel they are against their interest. You do more than the legal hours on the Continent. Unless you have an accident, no one's bothered. If you do have one, then they throw the book at you. There are needles inside the tacho, one of which registers speed, the other mileage; the gap between each peak has to correspond, and they can then see if you haven't fiddled the speed. But you can put an elastic band on the needles which stops them from registering anything over 80 km an hour, which is the limit on the Continent; it's 60 mph in Britain, which is somewhat more. So you can do 100, 120 km an hour and it won't register. Or you can put a cigarette filter on the needle to prevent it from going too high. You can also bend the needle, but that is a bit too obvious.

The tacho works on an electronic basis; you can earth it and stop it, and make it do what you want it to do. You can fuse it and put a new tacho in; you can stop it on the dial that registers sleeping time, and carry on driving. The needle won't move. Then you use a legal tacho to show driving – far less than you've really done. You have to be careful of the mileage. You must work out exactly where you're going; it's a tedious business, but there are always ways round these restrictions. When the tacho was first introduced, the drivers were up in arms about the 'spy in the cab'. It is, but spies can change sides. It can be a help: if there is an accident, it will prove that you were not speeding, even if witnesses say the contrary.

I'd like to go back to Continental driving, but I wouldn't want all the hassle with the tacho.

Since 1987, I've been working for Golden West Foods, which employs about five hundred people. We're on the go day and night. I share a unit with a night driver. It's ironic, my day starts at any time between 2 and 6 a.m., and finishes in the early afternoon. The night driver starts at eleven in the morning. I get back, diesel up the vehicle, take it into the frozen, chilled or dry dock, according to the consignment of the night driver.

We deliver to McDonald's. Because of loading and unloading restrictions we have to work unsocial hours. There are three sorts of cargo. We carry the dry goods – the food cartons you see lying about the streets, the paperwork, and also the buns for the burgers, which are all made in Golden West bakeries. The chilled goods include milk, the shake bases, lettuce, tomatoes, cucumber, onions, sauces, cream portions, eggs, bacon etc. The frozen stuff is the meat products, chicken, pizza bases, muffins and doughnuts. Golden West are the sole supply company and transporters for McDonald's. McDonald's are sure of what they want. We have to deliver the goods at the approved temperature – frozen is minus 18 deg., chilled 2–4 deg., give or minus one degree. The driver has a temperature probe. We can be stopped by the Environmental Health authorities if there is any discrepancy.

Golden West's buns are exported too, to Madrid, Paris. We used to import sauces from Germany, but now there is a syrup and sauce plant in

Corby. Meat is supplied by a company in Milton Keynes. That must be their own subsidiary. Chickens come from Hereford. The English muffins are imported from Germany; doughnuts and fruit pies come from Peterborough.

The hamburgers really are a hundred per cent beef, but they may be bits of beef that you wouldn't fancy. It's all fit for human consumption.

McDonald's don't seem to build very accessible delivery areas; I guess they're built to look nice. We can't even get the delivery vans into the drive-thrus sometimes. I just have to take the appropriate stuff out of the trailer, and their workers do the rest. It's interesting work, sometimes tedious. It keeps me fit. It is heavy work. I ride a bike to work.

It's a job. I'm at an age where it'd be hard to get another one; because of my age and experience I got refused a lot of jobs, because I'm on top rates, and they'd rather pay less to a younger more inexperienced driver. There is no union where I work. There are things that could be improved. The equipment we have for moving goods inside the vehicles could be better; but it is being upgraded all the time. Every trailer now has a compartment for dry, chilled and frozen goods.

I'm on a forty-hour week. I get paid overtime any time before 6 a.m., and then after eight hours I'm back on overtime. So today I started at 4.15. I got overtime till six o'clock, then after 12.15 I'm back on overtime.

The wage is important to me, to help me to live and do what I want; to buy camera equipment, which is one of my great interests. I get satisfaction from driving. It was an achievement to pass the HGV test first time . . . I wish car drivers would realize what a lot of space a truck like mine needs to stop in – we need more room than they give us. My truck and trailer, empty, weigh eighteen tons; you can't stop in a short distance.

I think of myself as working-class. Yet I have a middle-class lifestyle. I don't like snobbery. The work I do is very individualistic, if you like. I enjoy it.

Nine

Technological change has always involved constant de-skilling and re-skilling of people. The problem is, they are not the same people. Those who witness the decay of an industry and the skills it provided them with can easily see this as a symbol of national decline, whereas those employed in the new industries obviously have no such perception. Just as the ending of the dominance of agriculture seemed to many people in the early industrial period a catastrophic development, so many have equally deplored the passing of the dominance of manufacture in Britain. There is always a tendency to universalize our experience; but it is only in the longer term that a more complete perspective on the meaning of change can be gained.

Bob Clark (*born 1944*): *engineer, Harlow*

I was taken on at fifteen as a trainee sheet metal worker at an electronics company. I was brought up in a small village just outside Epping, and I'd never actually seen a factory. Then, ten days after my fifteenth birthday, I started work – 1959 this would be. My mother had bought me a boiler-suit, which was much too big, and I went with a pack of sandwiches – I weighed about six and a half stone at the time, I think – on the early morning workers' special at quarter to seven.

When I arrived, I was shown to a position on these long wooden benches. There were about four or six sheet metal workers sat at each bench. There were power presses, and a lot of women working on drills. The foreman came up. He wore a suit, though all the other workers wore brown coat overalls. My first job was to wire-wool these aluminium chassis. He gave me a bundle of wire wool, and I had to go in a circular motion all over the aluminium to clean it. There were boxes of these chassis, and I was doing it for three days, going round and round with this wire wool. Then the foreman came up and said, 'How are you going, son?' I said, 'Well, sir, I'm a bit bored.' He looked me up and down, and his eyes widened. 'Bored,' he says, 'bored? What do you expect to do, make bloody battleships?' I can remember my eyes watering. I worked forty-six hours the first week, and my pay was £2 13 6d.

The blokes there were very good, and they took to me like their own son. I used to go and get their tea and their tools for them. The firm used to be in London before it moved to Harlow, and a lot of the workers had moved down with the firm, often in order to get houses. For those workers who hadn't moved, they ran a coach from Manor House, which used to pick me up outside Epping. Everyone tended to work very hard then. There was a bonus system, so there was a lot of competition to get the best bonus jobs. It could be very fiery, because Harlow wages were lower than London, and the bonuses were very important.

As an apprentice I went to Tottenham College for five years, and I did a course in sheet metal work. It was a very old-fashioned course that involved coppersmithing and tinsmithing. When I finished, I got top rate, but there were a number of top rates, so I went on the bottom top rate of £11 a week. They started organizing a union when I was about seventeen, and then things became fairer. We had these fantastic union meetings, where everyone had to turn up after work. The meeting was held in a community centre with a bar, so they could be very fiery. Anyone who didn't turn up was fined half-a-crown. We always discussed money and working conditions. There were a lot of work-to-rules, but as an apprentice you weren't allowed to participate in any industrial action.

It was heavy work, because they tended to use more steel then and there was more chassis work, all made by hand. We apprentices had to hold up the chassis while the men worked on them, sometimes for an hour or two. You used to get some of the bonus when the job was finished, but not much. Later, new technology took over the hard work, and I've been more involved in model and prototype work, so it's been more creative in a way.

But in the 1960s, work was very labour-intensive, and they were always wanting to recruit people. People themselves were different then – they were much more collective, and there were some marvellous characters on the shopfloor. Once a year we went on a beano to Southend. We'd load the boot of the coach with beer, and start out at eight or nine o'clock in the morning. We'd stop along the road, drink the beer out of the boot, and then go to the Half Way House, where we'd stop for some more drink, and then get back on the coach for Southend. By this time I'd be totally drunk. We'd spend the day in Southend, and the men would pick up women who were on beanos from their factories. In the evening the coach would drive back and stop at the Half Way House for a big rave-up. Just about everyone from the shopfloor would go on the beanos.

Then we used to have a big party at Christmas. We would organize a big turkey dinner in a private room behind a pub, and there'd be about forty sheet metal workers sitting down. Even the foreman, whom the majority hated, used to come. After the turkey and Christmas pud and crackers, a couple of men used to do turns – they'd sing or tell some jokes, play an instrument, or dress up in a funny way and do a turn. We saved up a shilling a week for it. And every Christmas the men had a whip-round for me, because I used to get their tea and their rolls.

It's totally different now. It started to fade away in the mid-1980s, it changed then. It's a number of things. People buying their council houses, new technology – it's hard to pinpoint one thing. The new technology means that there's not much skill required, you're only operating a machine. People have become disillusioned with the unions as well. A lot of skilled workers moved into office work, but I didn't, because I've always enjoyed working on the shopfloor – I liked the atmosphere.

You've got to remember that when I started working, there was a strict demarcation between shopfloor and office workers. On the shopfloor you had to work for seven years before you were entitled to any sick pay, whereas a young filing clerk got full sick pay as soon as they started. We got Christmas Day and Boxing Day, the factory closed down for two weeks in the summer, and that was it. The unions got these things changed in the 1970s, and conditions improved greatly. But the unions didn't maintain the status of the skilled men, and differentials got eroded. The skilled workers felt they were missing out, and they got very disillusioned. The skilled men lost their status, and many left the shopfloor in order to become draughts-men and production engineers or management. The shop stewards always seemed more interested in the semi-skilled workers.

Working conditions got much worse in the 1980s. I think the worst job I had was in 1983, when there was the first recession, and I was working in a small engineering firm. The employer realized that he could get any number of workers, and he really treated them badly. He used to intimidate them in front of other workers, shout at them. There was a young lad who I'd known from when we were both made redundant. He was a trained welder, and he'd welded a job and was filing it off the weld when the bloke who owned the firm came up, kicked the chair away from underneath him and said, 'You don't sit down here, you stand up and work.' The lad had no option but to take that treatment. He was young, he'd just got married, and there was no other work around. There was another guy there, and he reduced his hourly rate in front of everyone because, he said, he was working too slowly. Another guy had a nervous breakdown. He always walked to the firm from where he lived, and one day when he got to within fifty yards of the factory, his legs gave way and he couldn't walk any further – he just froze. He was off work for nine months. He's OK now.

He treated me OK, because of the work I was doing, but when that particular job was finished he tried to intimidate me too. He told me he wanted me to work faster, so I just told him where to stick his job, picked up my toolbox and walked out. I found then I couldn't get another job for over six months. But I'd done the right thing.

We've just had a lot of redundancies where I'm working now. They've made people redundant who've worked for the firm for twenty-five years and more. At the beginning, people seemed slightly dazed. It happened so quickly. They went to these meetings, and they set up an advice centre, and it was all over. In two weeks they'd all gone, the whole shop had disappeared.

I'd just come back from a week's holiday, and I was told to stand by my bench, and within the next hour and a half I'd be told. If I'd been picked to be made redundant, someone would come up to me and I'd have to follow them to the manager's office and be handed an envelope. That's what happened. Everyone stood in the shop, and the foreman came up and asked people, in alphabetical order, to follow him. They had to walk through three or four shops to the manager's office, where they were handed an envelope to tell them that their services were no longer required. They'd given one of the men a gold watch two weeks previously for working there thirty years. He was devastated. He threw the watch back at the manager and told him what he could do with it.

We had a party the last day. We went to the pub – about forty turned up. We had a good drink, and at the end of it there was a lot of hugging and a few tears. These were people who had come down to Harlow together, they'd got their first houses together, they'd invited each other to their children's weddings, they'd all gone on the beanos and the Christmas parties. Of course they'd had their arguments and their fights. But it was like a small community on the shopfloor, and now it's totally gone. It's like an era's finished. It's very cruel.

No one tried to resist the redundancies. The feeling is that no one had any option. There's no strength left. We did have large union meetings, but all the stewards could do was try to get people to volunteer, to save some of the other people who were going to be made redundant. All they could do was to argue for the best redundancy conditions possible.

The whole way management thinks of workers has changed. I suppose our firm has been one of the last bastions of the old shopfloor practices and comradeship. People aren't regarded as important any more. Previously, the management tried to keep the workers happy, but now everything is based on fear. What you hear now, if you do complain about anything, is

'You're lucky to have a job.' Whereas only five years ago you were told you could always knock on the door of the manager's office, now the manager wouldn't know who you were, and he wouldn't be interested in knowing. It makes you feel alone, it makes you feel that you can't make any contribution to the way the firm's being run. You just have to do what you're told.

Everyone's fearful for their job. We've still got good conditions that the unions negotiated over the years, but now, with a greatly reduced workforce, these conditions will be eroded. And there's nothing we can do about it. When I think of myself in five years' time, I think I'll be lucky if I have a job.

There's no longer a collective feeling on the shopfloor. Everyone is hanging on for their own jobs. People have been gagged. People are not getting made redundant because they don't work hard, or because they don't have the skills – they are being made redundant because they speak their minds. So you just keep your head down, you just stay clean. What I'd love is some little cottage industry, something I could make, create, and sell a few to make a living. I'd just like to be out of it. This isn't what I stayed on the shopfloor for, it's a different culture, a different feeling. It's got to the point now where you don't feel you can trust the person you're working next to, or at least it's best if you don't, put it that way. I've had some great experiences on the shopfloor. I doubt if I will in the future.

Ten

During the 1960s there was a considerable extension of work within the 'caring professions', associated with the expansion of the Welfare State, especially in health, education and administration. In spite of public rhetoric, the numbers employed in these categories have scarcely shrunk, although some of the services formerly carried out by public employees have been privatized. The introduction of what are called 'market disciplines' into what were formerly seen as public services has considerably modified the nature of the satisfaction derived from the work.

Celia Duerden (*born 1947*): *nurse, Blackburn*

I'm an enrolled nurse, doing community nursing on 'twilight'. It involves going round to people's homes and putting them to bed if they need help. They may be people who are young disabled, or with chronic illnesses like multiple sclerosis or strokes. We also do a lot of terminal care on twilight – patients who are dying from cancer. And we go to emergency patients – people who have got blocked catheters, or people whose carer has had an accident; or if people have had a 'pot' [plaster cast] put on, we make sure there's no swelling. It's a very varied job, and it's a very basic nursing job. There's no high tech in it whatsoever.

At fifteen, I had no idea of what I wanted to do. Looking back, it's a job I've really enjoyed doing, but at fifteen, I wouldn't have had a clue. I thought about teaching cookery – I was into cooking at the time – and I don't know why nursing came up. Seeing the nurses look after my Grandma when she was dying helped it come up, and I had two close friends who were training to be nurses.

The training was nice, and in our breaks we used to get jam and bread. It was an eye-opener. I remember the first morning I went on the ward, never having been on a ward before. We did eight weeks' basic training, but as soon as you started you were assigned to a ward on a Saturday morning. I couldn't even make my cap. We had cloth caps, which you had to make up into the shape, and I didn't know how to fold it, no one ever told you these things.

I was assigned to ward E-1. I'll never forget it. I had to be there for seven, and when I arrived I met this really black nurse, and I'd never really seen a black person before – we're talking about 1965 now. She knew I was new, and she was a bit unhelpful really. I thought, Oh God, I'm never going to make this. Just before I went home, they sent me to collect a patient from theatre. They sent *me*! I didn't even know which end of the trolley to stand at. The porter said, 'Hold her chin up', because you've got to keep the airway open. I thought, I'll never cope with this. But I loved it on E-1, it was a lovely ward. But it was right in, no messing.

The first time I got upset was when we had a lady in the ward that I really liked, and she had her breast off. That really upset me. Though I think it's easier not to get upset when you're younger. I find it much harder now. If they cry, I'm going to cry. When you're young it feels so far removed from you.

I remember being surprised at how people looked when they were dying. It wasn't what I'd imagined from television, where people gasp out pearls of wisdom. People just die. Their breathing alters and you can tell they're going. They gasp for air, then there's a period when they don't seem to be breathing, then they gasp again. It can last for a couple of hours. Then their fingers go blue, and the peripheral circulation packs up. There's a definite sequence. And they don't usually come out with 'Tell Harry I love him' – well, I've never known that.

A man upset me – Alan he was called. I was only nineteen when I nursed him. He had a brain tumour, and he went to Preston for treatment. When he came back he was a different person, and that really made me sad. I was on nights, and he had a white thing round his head, some sort of bandage. He died when I was there, and he was sat up, so we never noticed he'd died. It was awful, he was still sat up in the morning, and I didn't know he'd died. They'd left me in charge that night, and I remember going home in the morning ... I thought, This is ridiculous, changing insulin, people bleeding, drips, transfusions. I'd only been out of training for six months, I didn't know anything really. I was upset because he had died alone.

We used to lay people out. You would wash them down, and they might have had a bowel movement, so you would clean them all and give them a wash. Then you would pack the orifices, put their teeth in, and you would tie a bandage under their chin to keep their jaw up, and tie it on the top. If it was a man you would tie this round his penis, make a little bow, so that nothing would come out – people tend to drip and drop for a while even after they've died. Then you'd put a paper shroud on with a death card on the top of the shroud – name, religion and time of death – and then wrap them up in a sheet, like a mummy. Then a clean white sheet over the bed, with a second death card. Then they would go to the morgue. I don't think they do that nowadays.

Nursing children is quite hard, especially when they're very poorly. And dealing with the relatives is hard. You get through that with experience, and listening to other people, like the Sister, giving bad news. I found that hard. I still do. Perhaps that's why nurses are so well known for enjoying themselves. I think it is like when the war was on, and you were still all right. Nurses live life to the full, they certainly know what they're doing when they get out.

I'm also a Marie Curie nurse, where we nurse patients in their own homes who are dying of cancer in the terminal stages. We go in and give the night medication, change the colostomy bags, do what needs doing. Often you talk to the carer, or rather, they talk to you. They just pour out their hearts. They're absolutely shattered, and you think, You should be going to bed really. But they just want to talk. It's quite difficult, Marie Curie, it takes more out of me. There you are in someone's house, in the middle of the night, with this poor person. And sometimes I think, What the hell am I doing here? I look at them, and I read their notes. Sometimes I talk to them if they're with it. Then I take out my big flask of coffee to keep awake, and do my crosswords.

A lot of the people I visit are incontinent, and they can get very smelly, but their husbands or wives will still go to bed with them. You pack them up, the man or the lady up, and their partner will say, 'Just leave a bit of room for me.' I think, 'How can you sleep with them? – but they love them so much they don't care. I don't think we understand what it's like to be losing someone, you just want to hold on to them as long as you can. I'd like to think I could do it.

Things haven't changed much in my job, because I do very basic nursing. But there's more paperwork, and at our staff meetings where we used to discuss the patients and how we could make their lives easier, we now talk about cutting down on our mileages, or filling in the forms correctly, or how we aren't doing our statistics properly. Everything is pie charts and graphs. It's a waste of time. It's all to try and cut down on the money.

It's true, there was a lot of waste in the NHS, but now everything is completely cut back. Which is right in some ways, but I don't think all these market reforms can work. Nursing is too people-involved, so I don't think it could ever be run like a business. I don't like the way it's going.

There's a lot of administrators, and they're so keen to save money. And yet at the end of the financial year you'll see new chairs appearing, or carpets will appear, because they have to spend the money or it goes back. And yet, you can't get wipes to clean patients up, and people are buying paper towels out of their pensions. That's not right. They're allowed two pads a day if they're incontinent. It's crazy. They've cut back too much.

I think community nursing is the last bastion of nursing as it used to be. On the wards, it's much more high-tech, but what I do is like a cottage hospital. It's a nice job, a basic job. It's caring for people in their own homes in the best way you can, so they can get through. And community nurses are available 365 days of the year. We're a bit like the old Windmill Theatre – we never close.

I think of myself as working-class, because I do 'hands-on' nursing. I haven't gone up the ladder into management. And I think nursing is a fairly classless profession, in that anyone can start and rise up. It's not like being a barrister, where it helps a lot to have been to public school. I have been in houses where I thought, I don't think these people would let me through the door unless I was doing something for them. If they saw me otherwise, they wouldn't have the time of day for me. Not very often, but I have felt that occasionally. But I've never yet been to a house where they haven't said, 'I am glad to see you.' It's nice in that respect, that people think highly of you. As a nurse, you're very welcome wherever you go. I wouldn't change it really, and it's worked in well with the family life.

I enjoy talking to the patients, and obviously it's nice to see them get well. But really it's your colleagues. The people I've worked with have been a joy to me. I wouldn't have missed them. I've got my sense of humour out of nursing, and it's given me more confidence. I was a very scared, frightened eighteen-year-old really. It's a very maturing occupation. It also gives you a sense of your own mortality; it puts you in your place.

I think the main difference between my life and the life my parents lived is that I've had a choice. I don't think they had any choice at all. And now these days, kids don't have any choice about jobs either. I think we were a very lucky generation.

Eleven

The rise in the numbers of women in employment has been one of the most spectacular changes of the past twenty years, with the result that now women constitute almost 50 per cent of the labour force. In spite of the commitment to equality, women's wages remain at about three-quarters of the amount paid to men for similar work. There is still a tendency for women's work to be concentrated in subordinate caring roles, secretarial work, the service sector – hairdressing, retailing, waiting.

When women talk about their working life, it is easy to catch a glimpse of that vast submerged area of unpaid labour which is still the fate of a majority of women, and is taken for granted: the endless round of domestic chores, child-rearing and home-making.

Pauline Scott (*born 1946*): *PA to college principal, east London*

In my life I've done far more unpaid than paid work. I've thought about it, and I don't see how you could organize wages for housework: it would be like paying people to live their own lives.

My father was a factory worker. He worked for Decca in South London. The company was taken over by Racal, and he was made redundant not long before he was due to retire. He died within a year; losing his job was definitely a factor in his death. His life was his work. He had no hobbies, no interests outside of it. He used to be interested in athletics and football. He used to take me to White City as a child, to watch athletics. He played football for the firm – he was goalkeeper.

He worked a lathe, but he never talked about work. A lot of social life revolved around the company. Once they hired a cinema to show the Cup Final on a big screen. There were children's parties at Christmas. He would come home, his dinner would be on the table, he'd read the paper, listen to the radio, later watch TV, and that was it. On Saturdays there was always football. It's funny, I took my mother to Crystal Palace recently, and it was the first football game she'd ever been to. He had never taken her.

My father worked in Decca all his life. He and my Mum had met before the war, working in Venner's which was also an engineering factory; my mother was working on an engraving machine there. [She] worked as a cleaner for British Oxygen in the evenings after I was about eleven. My sister and I needed uniforms for secondary school; and she worked then till my father died. When he stopped work, he used to go with her, drive her in the car, wait for her. She was working at a solicitor's in Wimbledon at that time.

Nobody ever came to our house. We knew the neighbours, but no friends came. We rarely took any of our friends home. I passed the eleven-plus. I wasn't expected to, and everybody was surprised. I didn't go to the real grammar school, but to the 'grammar stream' at the secondary modern school. That was a class thing. Even there I realized that a lot of the girls were different from us – they had a house, a car, and we didn't. Till I went to secondary school, I more or less thought everybody was like us. [There] some girls had fathers who owned their own businesses, didn't work in factories. I had a friend whose father actually worked in the City, in an office. I'd never met people like that before.

I left school at sixteen. I did O-levels: I took five and passed four. In fact, I did shorthand, typing and book-keeping as well, which was not the academic stream; not because I couldn't – it was the class expectations again. Some girls did eight O-levels, they were expected to go to university. Someone came from the careers office, asked what I wanted to do. I said, 'I want to be a journalist.' I'd done well in English. 'Oh no, you can't do that.' 'Why not?' 'You'd have to go to university.' I knew my mother and father were struggling to keep me, and I couldn't stay on. It never even occurred to me that I might – it had never entered our discussions at all.

The shorthand and typing teacher told us there were jobs going at Sun Life Assurance Company. They were looking for typists. I went for an interview, got the job and was told to start at the Cannon Street branch. I had worked on Saturdays at Woolworth's, on the sweet counter in Tooting Broadway. But I'd never been to London alone before. It's funny, although I never entertained the idea of staying on at school, nor did I ever expect to work in a shop or factory. My sister left school at fifteen and went as an apprentice at a hairdresser's.

It was very proper at Sun Life then. I think it's shut down now. It was an old granite building, with a cage lift. I worked on the third floor. There was a glass door with 'Sun Life' engraved in gold on it, with a golden sun. There was a big room with partitioned rooms for the inspectors, the assistant manager and the manager. The chief clerk sat in a corner of the main room. It was Dickensian. The chief clerk was very magisterial; we

84

young girls worked for the insurance clerks, the older women worked for the inspectors. Relationships were very formal; everyone was Mr or Miss, the chief clerk presiding. We took turns making the tea, which we did in a corner behind these grey metal lockers. There was also a doll's-eye switchboard, which I learned to operate.

The regime of checking the work was very strict. I'd type a letter; the insurance clerk would scrutinize and initial it, then it went to the chief clerk to be checked for content and propriety; then he'd initial it, and then it would go to the manager to be signed.

I earned £6 a week. I liked it. I stayed two years, because our teacher had always said, 'Never stay in a job longer than eighteen months to two years, because by that time you'll have learned all you need to know.' There were so many jobs – you could pick them out of the *Evening Standard*.

I wanted to move on. I got transferred to Head Office in Cheapside. I hated it. It was a big open-plan office that took up the whole floor. I only stayed a few months, then got a job at a solicitor's in Great James Street. I wanted to be more than a shorthand typist, and there was more secretarial work there. I also got better pay. The man I worked for had never actually passed his exams as solicitor. He pushed people very hard. No one had stayed very long with him till I went there. He'd dictate for two or three hours in the morning, and I'd spend the rest of the day typing it up. He was very unpleasant – in his sixties, I suppose. I was eighteen. He was rather sadistic. He drove his secretaries to tears, and they all left.

I decided to leave, and went to a small engineering company near home. I was so bored; there was nobody else there, no one to talk to. I rang the solicitor's, and asked if they'd got another secretary yet. 'Can I come back?' I decided to stand up to him, and after that he was nice as pie. My feminist leanings go back a long way, although I never recognized it as such then. I stopped being a timid little thing. Once you recognize your skills, other people will, too. My present boss, although I'm working for him, I don't feel subservient. Working, you gain confidence. In fact, my boss now, he has no children, he lives with his girlfriend – in some ways he is immature. I'm not inferior to him, it's just that he earns twice as much as me. I'm not intimidated by people's position any more. I've learned, not so much through my job as through having kids I had to stand up for on my own.

I was married at twenty-one. He lived across the road from us. I'd still do it again, it's no good saying I wouldn't if I'd known. He was an apprentice engineer at another Decca factory. I met him when I was seventeen; he didn't finish his apprenticeship till after we were married. I stopped work because I was pregnant with Anthony fifteen months later.

My husband was just coming out of his apprenticeship. Apprentices always left when they finished; he got a job making baling machines at an engineering works, then he went to another place, where he met the woman who is now his second wife. My third child was then one year old.

We were together ten years. It was a struggle to survive at the beginning, when I had Anthony; we never had much money. On Friday I can remember going down the road with a shilling in my purse, enough to buy two tins of baby food, and nothing else till he came home with his wage packet. We didn't starve. That was the way we'd always lived – all families that depended on the weekly wage packet lived like that. He had a ramshackle car to get to work in.

When Anthony was one, I got a job at a solicitor's. My mother looked after Anthony; Terry, my husband, took him there each morning. I travelled up to the City. It was too much. My mother couldn't really cope – she used to put the dog in the playpen to separate him from Anthony. Then she had him two days a week, while I got a job on a building site in Harley Street, in a big house that was being done up. It was freezing cold. When Anthony was two, I worked in a travel agent's in Putney, a horrendous journey by bus. When you're young you have all this energy, but it's used up doing absurd things. Then I got another job nearer my mother's in an electronics firm, making alarms. I could go home on the bus with Anthony afterwards. I stopped work when I became pregnant with Gerald. That was when my real work started.

It was a relief to give up going out to work. I was very ill with my second pregnancy. I had no energy – getting through the day was hard. I had pre-eclamptic toxaemia, which meant that basically the baby was not getting the nourishment he needed through the placenta. I gained little weight, even lost it at times. When he was born he weighed 3 lb 4 oz; he had no sugar in his blood, he was blue. This wasn't diagnosed at the time. When I failed to gain weight, the doctor said, 'Oh, you're having a girl this time, they're smaller than boys.' I had high blood pressure. The night before he was born, they gave me morphine – my blood pressure was high, my heart and pulse racing. They said, 'The baby is in distress.' He was born quickly. They placed him in an incubator. I said, 'Is he all right?' All the other mothers had their babies. 'Can I see him?' 'No, you wouldn't want to see him as he is, he has all these tubes in him.' I made a fuss and got into a state, because I thought they had no right to keep him from me. They took me in a wheelchair. He did look like a little rat.

He couldn't come home for six weeks, until his weight had reached five pounds. The night he came home, Terry went to this club he belonged to, Scalectrix, model railways. I couldn't believe it. He never got involved with the kids at all. I know that working-class men traditionally left the women to get on with it, but this was even more than that. He might take Anthony to the park for an hour occasionally on Sundays, then say he'd done his bit. He still lived a life as though he was single. He said as much. That was what he intended to do. He just cleared off. I got so angry. Later, I found out he was with his girlfriends.

One night Anthony was ill. Terry told me he was going out with his mate Brian. I rang Brian and said, 'Is Terry there?' 'Oh, he's just gone.' I didn't twig. Brian said, 'He's just gone to meet another of his mates at this pub.' It still didn't dawn on me. I was so worried, I rang this pub. 'We're shut. We're closing up.' When he came in, I said, 'Where have you been?' He wasn't fazed at all, he said the car broke down. I didn't realize for ages.

It's funny, while I had been working I had gained confidence in myself. The job, the achievement of all that, was wiped out by Terry. I had to build it up all over again, and this time when he left me alone with the children. He left me once for a short time, and then came back when I was pregnant with Mark. Then he left for good. Mark was nearly three, Gerald five and Anthony eight.

The day-to-day living was just endless work. I took the two older ones to school, came back, took Mark to play school, came back and spent the morning washing – especially washing – cleaning, household jobs. Then went to get Mark at midday, feed him, take him shopping, an hour in the park, go to get the others at 3.30. The whole day was running around. The evenings were bleak when I'd put them to bed. I was morose then, sat staring at TV without watching, depressed; I'd do ironing in the evening. Once a week I'd visit a friend with the kids. Terry gave me enough to live on. I never felt poor, he carried on giving me the same money he had when he was living here. As he married and had children, so the money was reduced, but by then I was working again.

I got a job with the school meals at £15 a week. Mark had a day nursery place, and I went to pottery and dressmaking classes in the morning. I started doing patchwork; I've become very proficient at it since then. [*She brings out some of the intricate, exquisite work she has done; a labour that began in the long hours of waiting for and watching the children, work of extraordinary beauty and skill.*] I worked on dinners, served the meals, put out the tables. There were no kitchens on the premises, it came in big metal containers. I'd finish meals at 2.30, then help around the school for an hour till it was time to take the children home, doing odd jobs around the classrooms.

Looking back, I don't know how I did it all. I was divorced by then. There would be fleeting visits from Terry to the children at birthdays and

Christmas. I did housework in the evenings. It was relentless. You just did it; there was no point in stopping to think about it.

Then I got a job as copy-typist in the local college, term-time only, when Mark was five. The other women in the typing pool were very good – they allowed me to organize it so I had half-term off. I wasn't very well paid, and of course in the holiday period I received nothing. Terry still paid maintenance. He took it to court to get the payments reduced.

Then the PA to the Principal job came up. It was term-time only, but a full day. That meant [the children] would be on their own for an hour or so. There were phone calls almost every day – Mum, Gerald's done this or that. It was such a tension. The money from Terry decreased. But I never went on Social Security; they did have free meals and clothing grants, though. We lived fairly tight, nothing special. If they were deprived, it was only of their father. I felt sorry for Terry that he couldn't accept the consequences of the life he'd made, he couldn't accept responsibility. He ran away. Later, of course, he played the great I-am to the kids, and for a time they thought he was wonderful; by now I think they've all seen through him.

I think women are stronger because they don't run away. They stay. I felt, well, if I don't carry on, who will? I felt responsible for the children, because they don't ask to be born. I was the only one they could depend on, the only one standing between them and who knows what?

When Terry first went, I did think I wasn't strong enough to do it on my own. I felt angry; I wrote to him, saying he could have the children. One night, I got their clothes on, and called a cab. I was going to take them down there to him and leave them with him. The cab never came. It was a cold night. We stood waiting in the passageway. I rang again. 'The cab's on its way.' It never turned up. That was fate. If I had done it, it would have been traumatic for all of us. His girlfriend would certainly have done a bunk. But I felt I couldn't cope at times. I had some very low points. I cried a lot. I spent hours on the phone talking to a friend of mine who was very understanding.

As time went by, looking after the children became both easier and more exacting. I had to be mother and father to them. I learned to fix their bikes, mend punctures; I took them to Cubs and Scouts. I think I learned selflessness through it, I learned to put myself last. I had to be prepared to do anything; self-reliance; to fix anything or find someone who could. I've done things I never would have done if I'd not been left alone. You come out better and stronger in some ways.

I don't hate men; I just hate the way they've treated me. I hate men's perception of and treatment of women. I've lived in this flat since we were married, rented. The owner wanted us out because he was going to sell it. He put a lot of pressure on us. I learned to stand up to him. It's not a wonderful place, but we're still here. It's still the same. If I go to football, I'll get all excited and start chatting with whoever is next to me. If it's a man, he'll say, 'Are you on your own?' There's still that feeling that they see me as a poor little thing who needs a man.

I'm PA to the finance director of the college, and I'm also administrator to the team of the finance department. It stretches you, I like it; but nothing fazes me. It's second-nature. My work has given me self-confidence again, and has restored me to the level I was at before I married. I find women who have husbands are very different – their attitudes are more mundane, unthought-out, boring. A lot of them have no life outside their home and husband. My consciousness has changed. When I see things that are wrong, socially, morally, I'll do something about it. There were some kids fighting outside college the other day. They were anarchist types. They weren't doing any harm. Suddenly, about five police cars and twenty police came out, roughed them up, kicked them, shoved them into the van. I went to the police station and complained. They could have been my kids. They were released later without charge. I spoke to one of the senior officers. I said, 'I don't care what they've done, they don't deserve that kind of treatment.' I said there were a lot of us in the college who saw it. I was prepared to stand up for them.

I suppose being in an educational environment, the people I've met have changed me too. If I'd been in a small firm, where women just did the typing, I suppose I might have been different; although I don't know. It was like the Sarah Thornton case, the woman who was jailed for killing her husband after he had goaded and tormented her. I could relate to her through the same experiences, and I felt a horrible injustice had been done. I wasn't physically ill-treated by Terry, but mentally I was. That could've been me. I got so angry. I had been abused mentally, emotionally. And he had done it deliberately. He used to tell me it was all my fault, and I believed that for a long time. But a good deal of it was him: he had never been involved with the children. He used to say, 'I've got nothing here.' I said, 'Only three kids.' But he walked out on them. Of course he wasn't really wanted as a child. He lived with his Nan on the other side of the road from his parents, she brought him up. I think he got more involved with his second family. He has his own engineering company. He isn't stupid, he's well off, but I think deep down he's not a happy man.

But work has given me . . . self-esteem. Although it has been painful, I don't regret any of it.

Twelve

As we have noted, there has been a great loss of skills during the restructuring of the labour force in the past twenty-five years. It is not simply that industrial skills have gone, but many of the new jobs that have appeared do not demand any great dexterity or training. The fact that the increasing proportion of the workforce is female is often seen as representing an economic enfranchisement of women. And this is how, subjectively, it feels. They speak of their 'independence', having control over their own money. But much of the work is intermittent, casualized and unskilled. The idea that 'flexibility' in the labour force is a good thing is perhaps a tribute to the ability of women – certainly no new thing - to survive by being adaptable, emollient, compliant. Indeed, much of the rhetoric about 'training', 'equipping', 're-tooling' the workforce conceals an agenda on which flexibility itself is perhaps the greatest 'skill': that is, the ability to adapt to whatever whim the market summons people to. It is a strange kind of skill, one which is market-specific and of little use in any other area of experience. Much of the work is not necessarily either fulfilling or well paid. Indeed, the millions of new jobs created in the past generation have often been casual and ill rewarded. Then, when there is recession, they are abruptly wiped out. There are no benefits, no sick or holiday pay.

There is something else in this upsurge of service work. Many of the women performing it originally did so as a second income. But frequently, with the increase in marriage breakdown, they find they are the sole breadwinners for themselves and their children; and then the emancipation that 'the little job' once seemed to be, becomes a pitifully inadequate means of ensuring family survival.

Many women now in the labour force are actually victims of downward social mobility. The erasure of class-consciousness somewhat relieves the pain of this, but many find that status, expectations and standard of living are all removed from what they might once have expected.

Linda Forbes (*born 1949*): *print- and copy-shop assistant, north London.*

My father was an accountant, and I am the eldest of six children. My parents split up when I was fourteen. I had what was seen as 'a good education'. And I hated it. In later years, I think I came to understand why I hated it, and also that there were some good things in it. I think now the class system has disappeared because people are more affluent. But when I was at school, it was very much there. The stereotype of a respectable girls' school, where everybody was quite well off, was real; and they were not sympathetic to those who had no money. Not at all.

I can see the value of some of it now. Then, there was too much importance given to discipline – wearing hat and gloves and walking up the right-hand staircase and down the left-hand one. I thought it was a waste of time then. It was snobbish. They pushed you for the sake of the school, not for the sake of the girl herself. The school was geared to getting girls into university, the higher professions. I got a job in the civil service when I left at eighteen. In fact, I got the job quite independently of the school, but they announced it in assembly as though the credit was all theirs. I was angry.

I was in the typing pool at the Overseas Development department at Victoria. The wages were diabolical. You were supposed to sit there for years until you got promotion. I used to go out at lunchtime to various secretarial agencies. At that time, they would give you a big box of cards with vacancies advertised. You could more or less take your pick. I left the civil service after a year and went to work for the Autocycle Union, which organized TT races, motocross and scrambling events.

I'd always had a weekend job, which I continued even when I started work, since I was fifteen, at a newsagent's. My mother had no money, so I had to earn. I carried on with that, and in fact, while I was there I met my ex-husband; that is, he wasn't my ex-husband then, he was to become my husband, and later my ex. We got engaged. The owner of the shop had several newsagents all over South London. When we married, we had the opportunity to run one of these shops in Camberwell. There was a flat over the shop. We decided to have a go. I gave up my job with the British Autocycle Union, and we ran the shop until we later emigrated to Australia. (I was married at twenty, and by twenty-one we had emigrated.) The guy running the shops was a very bad businessman. He had bought four or five shops, but he wasted money on cars and women. We worked our guts out, we got the custom up, and he'd spend all the profits, so that he couldn't afford to buy fresh supplies or pay us a decent salary.

We went to Australia on the assisted passage scheme. For £10. I didn't want to go. Not at that time, anyway, but he made me. It was his decision and I had no choice. We had had an offer to manage another newsagent's business. I wasn't ready to leave my family, but my husband had a brother who lived in Perth. He said he needed to go. I wasn't very assertive then, I went along with what he said.

I don't regret it, and I didn't then, although I hated it when I got there. I didn't realize how much I'd miss my family. It's such a different way of life. As a matter of fact, I went for an office job and was told I was too old. At twenty-one – that must be a record. The youngsters there seem to be taught a wide range of office skills – book-keeping, filing, switchboard; they go into a job qualified for the lot, whereas here I'd done a specialized typing course. In this country, you were expected to learn the rest by experience.

I never had a lot of confidence. We stayed in Perth with my husband's brother. They were very close. I think the authorities were not very fair in not telling us how things really were, what to expect, after we were taking such a big step. You can't write home and say you've made a mistake. You have to put a brave face on it, and that makes it worse. In any case, we had no money to come back; we'd've had to pay our own fare, as well as the £10, which at that time – 1969 – was quite a bit. I feel now they were right to insist that people stay two years, because it takes that long to get integrated. If you stay for less time, you don't give it a fair chance.

He got a job, driving for a cement company. He worked seven days a week, a twelve- or fourteen-hour day. Everybody was like that; it's a disease with the Australians, work. They work to achieve that one step more. It's much more like that than it is here. You start with a block of land, you pay that off, then build a house, then a pool, get a new car; have two children on the way. Then when everything is OK, you buy a bigger block of land, build another house. It's a merry-go-round. In fact, some of the Southern Europeans – the Italians and Yugoslavs – buy the land, live in a rough shack, and then build their house with their own hands, brick by brick. Nobody thinks any the worse of them. There's no snobbery there.

At first I didn't work, but I got a job later in Fremantle Hospital, out of desperation really. I was cleaning. I worked on the children's ward, and stayed there six years. It wasn't seen as a low job there. I worked full-time, on shifts. I wouldn't do it in this country – the way you're treated, people look at you as if you're low life, cleaning here.

We bought our first house, and then I left work before my first baby was born. Even though I stayed at home for a year, I looked after a neighbour's children; and then I got a job at another hospital, part-time. Work was easy to get. I went round giving the menus to the patients, organizing the food. I was called 'cook', although I never did any cooking. I was in charge of the kitchen, supervising the staff. I stayed there three years.

Then my husband got a job with Mount Newman Mining Company. Mount Newman was a town of about eight thousand people, seven hundred miles north of Perth. He was driving big trucks that carried the iron ore from the mine. Later, he gave that up and drove a bus for them, fetching and taking personnel to and from work, driving visitors to the mine around. I stayed in Perth for six months while he was in lodgings. Then he got married accommodation, so we moved up there. We rented out our house in Perth. We stayed eight years.

It was a company town. Very isolated. Wages were high. Most went there with the idea of making a lot of money quickly, but certainly not to stay, not to settle. I didn't hate all of it. I made good friends. From a woman's point of view, though, it was diabolical, because the men were out working, and if they weren't working they were sleeping. It was made bearable because I had friends with young children who were in the same situation as I was. You had to get involved in something, otherwise you'd crack up. I used to play volleyball, badminton, do aerobics, play softball. My husband was involved in football refereeing and coaching.

It did put a strain on our relationship, but what went wrong would have gone wrong anyway, wherever we were. There was no 'normal' life – the children had to learn to be quiet because Daddy was sleeping at odd hours.

I got a job cleaning at the mine. In the offices. That was not a rewarding job. There's only so much you can do to clean up the red iron ore. The dust was everywhere, a film of it over everything. Dry and dusty. But it was good fun, the group of girls I worked with. I gave that up and got a job emptying the telephone boxes. I used to put the children in the back of my Suzuki and go on a fifty-mile radius around Mount Newman. There was never any danger. There, you never locked your car, you never locked the front door of your house.

But Mount Newman, there's nowhere you can go to get away from it. Only the bush. I hated it. I used to dread weekends, holidays, because you couldn't go anywhere. It was dirty, full of flies, hot – the temperature in summer could be 45 degrees. You'd drive miles and miles to a water hole; that was nice, icy-cold, clean water. But then my youngest was coming up to school age. Primary school was no problem, but senior school was. A lot of children went to Perth; they went to boarding school, and there were government grants to pay the air fares for the holidays. You paid the fees of course. I didn't like the idea. And then, if I was stuck at home without the children, my husband on shifts, it would have driven me mad. By this time, there were no prospects. Recession had hit Australia. Jobs were like gold dust.

I said to him, 'I can't stand it, what are we going to do?' We had sold the house in Perth two years earlier. I said, 'Why don't we buy another house in Perth? I'll live with the kids down there, while you stay here and work.' I thought I'd have more job opportunities there. But the question didn't arise, because unemployment had become a major problem by then. In the end, I gave him an ultimatum. I said, 'I've never really settled here. I want to go back.' Every four years or so I got this strong homesickness. I said to him, 'I'm not asking you to go, but I'm going. I can't spend the rest of my life being a housewife.'

He didn't agree. I put a lot of pressure on him. I said, 'I wouldn't ask you to do this, if I were the one working.' Life there is geared to men, and the women have to run round and adapt themselves to it. He wasn't at home much. He liked the bush, he loved to go out camping. I was only thirty. I'd've gone mental. I needed to do something for myself. You become a non-person, a wife and a mother – nothing beyond that. It leaves you so you can't talk to people. You lose confidence in yourself.

We came back at the end of 1983. Housing was the biggest problem. That and schools for the children. He got a job as a bus driver. I worked in a big shop in Croydon, Allders, a department store, then in the British Home Stores. Then I saw an ad for a part-time photocopy operator. It's supposed to be like working in a shop, but in fact it couldn't be more different. It's more than being a shop assistant. You have to be numerate, and quick, and able to talk to customers about printing and what their requirements are. I've learned about printing. I found the job fulfilling, especially in the early years, but the recession has changed all that. It's less of a challenge now, there's less to do. They've had to lay off staff. I like talking to people, I love it. Sometimes they can be awkward, shout at you, abuse you.

When we came back, our marriage broke up. I know he was resentful. In fact, he has had the opportunity to go back if he wanted to, but he chose not to. He is a very traditional-minded man, sexist – male and female roles are clear. He flourished in the Australian sexist society – very macho. The women go out with their husbands and they wait for the men to tell them when it's time to go home. I wouldn't say women accept it, not deep down, but they have to do it. I think being in Mount Newman, I'd say if there is any flaw in your relationship, it'll be exaggerated and made more extreme by being there. There were lots of affairs there. Women took the attitude if their husband wasn't interested, they'd soon find somebody else who wanted them.

94

Without work, I wouldn't survive. I say it's the money, but it is and it isn't. Even if I had enough money to live on without working, I'd still work. I need to do something. I need the social contact, I need to feel useful. If circumstances had been different, I would have chosen a career. But I had to get a job instead.

I think women have to be more creative, more flexible in their lives, more adaptable; that's why they make better workers than men. I think women are stronger than men. A lot of men are broken by unemployment. When we came back, my husband had never had any experience of being out of work, and for a short time he was unemployed. He was driving me insane. He couldn't cope. It wasn't that we lacked money, it's simply that he had no purpose, no security. I'm in a new relationship now that's been going on for over a year. He couldn't be more different from my husband. With him, we negotiate what we'll do, and we both give and take, and there's no resentment there.

I wouldn't change what I've done. I've no regrets. All the experiences I've had, I've gained something from them, even though, at times, they could have driven me mad.

Thirteen

While for those in traditional areas of labour the de-industrialization of the 1980s and 90s has represented pure loss, for others the 1980s and 90s have been a golden age, an opportunity to succeed beyond the wildest dreams of their parents. One reason why the contemporary working class is so difficult to locate is that many people have moved out of anything recognizable as a 'working-class' occupation. The debate about the effect of affluence on the working class is as old as the working class itself, but it was given a spectacular impetus during the 1980s.

John Vallance (*born 1953*) : *businessman, Chelmsford*

I was born in Muswell Hill, London. We lived in a flat which was very cramped accommodation – myself, my brother and sister and my parents. We had a shared toilet and bathroom, it was pretty grim. My father got a job as a milkman in Harlow, and two weeks after he started work he had a house, so we moved to Harlow. That would be 1961. My mother worked as a home help.

I got on quite well at school. I remember thinking, I'm not dim. The thing I liked most was technical drawing, and the only thing I could think to do when I left school was to be a draughtsman, which was quite a reasonable job to go looking for at the time.

So in 1968 I was offered a job as a trainee draughtsman, and I spent five years with a construction company. In fact, by the time I left that job I hadn't become a draughtsman, and I never went anywhere near a drawing-board again. It's easy to see how that happened. After the first six months on the drawing-board – which I found dreadfully boring – I spent the next four years on the shopfloor. I effectively did an apprenticeship. They had engineering workshops where they used to overhaul anything from a waterpump or a concrete-vibrating machine right up to cranes, JCB diggers and earth-scrapers. I learned a lot of welding and metal-cutting techniques, and became very good at fabrication work.

It was probably one of the best times of my life. I really did enjoy it. The comradeship was brilliant.

I went back into the drawing-office for six months, yet again got thoroughly bored, once again couldn't stop looking out of the window at everyone driving around on cranes and bulldozers, so I just decided I wanted to leave.

I got a job at ITT – they were manufacturers of electronic components – as a planning engineer. The biggest project I ever did – there was a chemical plant based down at Milford Haven that anodized aluminium, and I had to go down there, work out what it was all about and how it worked, and then prepare the premises for it up in Harlow. This meant designing a whole series of tanks, pipework and structures, so that the plant could be switched off, unbolted, shipped up, unloaded, bolted up, connected up, plumbed in and set to work within two weeks of shutting down. It took me about six months to plan that and get it ready, and in two weeks it was done and finished, and it worked. We're talking, even in those days, of a £60,000 contract, nowadays probably a million pounds.

I loved that, that made me feel really great. It never struck me that it wouldn't work. The thing about any engineering-type job is that it is something where people day in, day out, are making things happen. They have a lot of experience and a lot of skills that they have built up over the years. So all the things they do, in isolation, are not terribly difficult, and they've done them many times before. It was a brilliant experience.

After working for five years at ITT, I began to realize that it was the sort of company where your future prospects came about through people leaving or dying, and whilst you might be able to influence something about people leaving . . . One of the contractors who used to come in spoke to me one day and said, 'I hear you're looking for another job.' He offered me a job as the manager running his contract cleaning and painting business, because he wanted to spend more time developing his used-car sales business. It wasn't a wise decision, but as time's gone on, it was probably the best thing I could have done, because it got me out of ITT. The people I worked with there have no future, and they haven't had a future for years. They're well stuck.

At the time it felt like a bad move, and my self-esteem went down the pan. Having been on something of a pedestal in both my first two jobs – in my first job I was a class above the average apprentice, and in my second job I was the person who people used to see walking around, and soon after I'd been walking around, things would start to happen – and then to go into the contract cleaning and painting business, was to go into a very different class of work.

97

Among the people we employed were people who'd been inside for GBH. We had people who used to tell you a lot of things, but did actually the opposite. I'd never come across people who lied so much and who were unwilling to do a decent day's work, and it shook my confidence tremendously. I didn't like it at all. I could have sat down and cried. But I'm a worker, I always have been. That's just the way I am. I have the commitment, I do the job I'm paid to do. So I stuck with it, but after the first year I tried hard to get out.

After two and a half years, I got a job at a recruitment company in Bishop's Stortford, where I'd gone to do a quote for some painting. I was there for about eighteen months, and that was the first time I'd really come into contact with sales. And I realized there was something better than ITT – selling. At the recruitment company, I started to be overwhelmed by this feeling that selling is really what the vast majority of our existence is all about. It was like the penny dropped.

If you were to go to an average person and say, 'Describe a salesman to me', they would all think of a double-glazing salesman, or somebody who they love to hate. But go anywhere on a Saturday, with your wife and the children, and you come face to face with people selling. You go to any shop, it's full of people selling things. You go to a leisure centre, a swimming pool, you go to an amusement park – it's people selling you something. You sit down in your home and you're surrounded by things that you've bought. You watch television, and you may be watching BBC, but someone's paid a lot of money to buy that programme . . . I suddenly started to feel that buying and selling was my forte.

Eighteen months after I'd been in recruitment, I saw the job, the job I'd been looking for. The people who were most sought-after at the agency were design engineers and computer salespersons. They were top-class. Then I saw this advert for an engineer to work on installation of computer systems. I took one look at this and I thought, This is the job. That was the start of three and a half years of working for a computer company, where I became quite a confirmed salesperson, very passionate about my job, very dynamic. Until I was made redundant. The computer company had grown very very fast, it was very very dynamic, and when I joined it it was seven years old and turning over £25 million a year. But they'd started to build a fabulous building in Leeds which they'd tried to fund themselves, and they got into very serious cash-flow difficulties, and basically decided to wind up the company.

So I decided to have a go at doing it myself. I actually started my business with about three days' preparation. My first customers were people I'd already quoted for computer installation. I didn't have a business plan, I didn't have to borrow any money, I had no backers. I was in the middle of negotiating a deal for twelve and a half thousand pounds, and they said, 'No problem'. They let me have some money so I could buy the materials, and I went down to our local photocopying shop, bought some blank invoicing forms, typed in a company name which I'd dreamed up, and they wrote me out a cheque. That first job, I made £5,000 profit. Having started, I had the experience, and I had motivation – obviously I was very hungry. That was how the business started in 1985, and it was nine years old last week.

We haven't been without duff years, particularly two or three years ago, but it has been very successful. My salary in the first year went up from £9,000 to £28,000. Not only had I trebled my salary, but I was not having to explain my actions to anybody else. It was really quite good. Brilliant, in fact. Within six months I'd started to employ someone, and we now employ six full-time people, plus myself and my wife as directors, so that's eight, and we have three YTS persons. We now have a turnover of roughly £350,000 a year.

It is a success story, though I'm not complacent. I'm suffering from growing pains. The early years of running the business, it was easy to double your turnover, it was like falling off a log really. But now in order to grow even more I have to make a move to delegating a lot of power and responsibility. I'm finding that next step quite difficult, but I'm optimistic about it.

By twenty-three I was married and buying my own house, which was fairly uncommon in Harlow, because what we youngsters did, we got married, and six months later the Council provided us with a flat, and that's what happened to us. But almost from the day we moved in there, we had decided that we should be buying our own place. We saved to get a deposit for a house, but there wasn't really any low-cost housing in Harlow, so we put a deposit on a place in Witham, and when we got the plans through we didn't like the plans, so we ended up buying a semi-detached in Witham. This was really a jump for us – we'd expected to live in a terraced house or a cottage.

We didn't start having a family till we'd been married for ten years, so we had really quite a reasonable standard of living. We were both working, and we started to feel good about life. We liked owning our own property, we liked being in control of what we were doing and where we were going, and we started to mix a lot with people who were buying their own houses, and were very much in, I think, white-collar jobs.

I vote Conservative. When I was on the shopfloor I wasn't particularly political, but I was definitely one of the workers. But it didn't take me long to figure out that the general attitude of the unions was very negative. I thought the unions were much more confrontational than the management. I don't really know at what point my ideas started to change, there was nobody influencing me in particular, but my feelings swung to Conservative politics.

The magic thing that Mrs Thatcher's done, which has affected the quality of my life, and of most people's lives, is to deal with trade unionism. I think when we look back on the history of this country, trade unionism has stunted the development of the country, in terms of technology, in terms of attitude, and in terms of development of wealth. What Margaret Thatcher had was a vision, to say that this minority of people – I'm talking about the people who controlled trade unions – I think she felt that these people were responsible for that situation. A handful of people were able to manipulate people in such a way that their opinions were made to count for the minds and decisions of millions. She changed all that. I think that this is the single, most significant thing she's done. By creating union reform, she has provided the opportunity for lots of things to happen which couldn't happen before. It could be said that she crushed the unions, but I don't like to say that. She just removed the opportunity for the minority to manipulate others. And I think that's improved circumstances in all sorts of ways for everybody.

I worry about other people and their feelings and circumstances. I worry about us not being a caring society. I don't think Mrs Thatcher necessarily wanted to encourage selfishness, but I dare say that some of the things she's done have given the opportunity for those inclined to be selfish to be selfish. And I dare say that some Conservative policies have removed a lot of benefits from thoroughly decent, honest, hardworking people, who unfortunately have been dealt a very poor hand, and are not able to do much about their circumstances. If any political party in this country were able to provide a balance between opportunity and free enterprise, and still look after the people who were less fortunate, then I think that would be the greatest thing we could all hope for. I liked Neil Kinnock. I thought he was excellent. If he'd continued through with his vision he might well have created a Labour Party that people like me could vote for, believing that our future was assured, but that the other people we worry about, who haven't had such a good hand dealt to them, would be looked after.

I think things have changed so much that you can't categorize people nowadays. In the nineteenth century, there definitely was a ruling class and there definitely was a working class, and there was a tremendous gap between them. But in the 1990s, you obviously have some very rich people, but they are not necessarily the people with the power. There is obviously still a working class now, but their living standards are way beyond what they were. People nowadays get upset and think they're hard done by if they've only got one car and two videos. And they still create and moan.

I came from a working-class background, and I would still say I'm working-class really. I still have to work to earn a living. All the financial commitments I have – mortgage, schools fees, the standard of living I want to live to – I have to work very hard, at least five days, and often five and a half days a week, to achieve that. My working day is never less than nine hours, and very often twelve hours. I started work at 4.30 this morning.

The class thing doesn't apply anywhere near as much as it did. I think the thing that distinguishes people from other groups is their attitudes rather than their wealth, or what job they do. Attitude to life, and morality, and crime – that provides class.

Fourteen: In the Salon

One thing that remains constant through all the upheavals of labour in the twentieth century is the consolation of the companionship of fellow-workers: it was as true of the necessary solidarities of survival in the pits as it is of the more sociable environment of some of today's service sector employments.

Barbara (*late 30s*)

Busy afternoon in the hairdressing salon on the high street in Walthamstow. It is a bright, clean place, with tiled floor, motifs in black and white; black-bordered mirrors, flattering muted strip lighting; a series of wash-basins, where the customers lean back for a wash and shampoo before being attended to by the hairdressers. On the walls, photographs – all very attractive – of customers whose hair has been styled here. A separate counter sells gels, conditioners, shampoos, colourings, and so on. Hair has become a major employer of labour at the end of the twentieth century.

Barbara now works only two or three days a week. She has a young family, and works two days regularly, but is flexible when others are sick or on holiday.

I couldn't bear not to work. I love my children as much as any mother, but if you don't get out of the house sometimes, you have nothing to talk about. Here, I'm in touch with the world. I have my regulars. I prefer to do men's hair really – they're more appreciative, less critical.

Sometimes people come in with a magazine, a colour supplement or a copy of *Hello* or something, and they'll open it and say, 'I want to look like that.' They'll show you a glamorous picture of someone twenty years younger than they are, with thick lustrous hair. You think, My God, what kind of a fantasy are you living in? – but you don't say anything. You do your best. I always think of that saying about making a silk purse out of a sow's ear. But you never disagree. You say, 'Of course'. And you make some rough attempt, though even if you did get it like the model in the picture it would still look terrible. But you know, they're always satisfied.

You say, 'How's that?', and you get a mirror and show them, and they touch it at the back and move their head and smile at themselves. You haven't disturbed their fantasy. Then you know you've done your job properly.

Other people will come and tell you their troubles. I don't know, but they look on you as a sort of therapist. I think I know why it is: it's because you touch them, gently, not in a sexy way, but a bit like a nurse. Combing somebody's hair, massaging the scalp, it takes them back to childhood. They think you're their mother, and that makes them relax, and they will tell you things which they normally wouldn't mention, at least not to strangers. Men, too. I mean, they will start to tell you about their wife, and what she won't or can't do for them. I don't encourage that. Sometimes, customers you know well, they'll come in with another woman who you know is not their wife. People think they're invisible to us. It's strange, they're concerned about their looks, but they don't think we will recognize them. Some men will just sit down and tell you what they want and sit and read a paper. You respect that, if that's what they prefer.

But the women I'll listen to. I'm discreet, they know their secrets are safe. Sometimes a woman will come in and say, 'I want to make myself as sexy as I can, give me a real tarty hairdo', because their husband has been cheating on them, and they want to go out and find somebody else. They're full of anger, and the stories you hear! One woman told me her husband only wanted to watch her have sex with another man. He wouldn't touch her. I say, 'Oh yes', as though they were talking about the weather. Never show any surprise. It's very common for them to tell you their husband doesn't notice them any more, but his eyes are wandering as soon as they go out together. I think for some women having your hair done is a big consolation. It gives you the feeling that you're being rejuvenated. You're renewing yourself somehow, giving yourself another chance.

Then you get those who are always discontented. They want their hair a different colour, a different style; some will come in twice a week, they spend a fortune. They don't like themselves – you can tell them. They're really dissatisfied, and they think by changing a style they can change their lives. You really want to say to them, 'This isn't really what you need', but then I'd be doing myself out of business if I went round saying that.

Katrina (*late 20s*)

Katrina works full-time. She is unmarried, and is just filling in for a few months until she finds something more interesting. She has worked as a hairdresser on liners and in hotels. She did her training at an André Bernard salon in the West End. She doesn't like the up-market salons, because people are both bitchy and competitive. Here, the atmosphere is relaxed. She has spent time in Australia and South Africa. Hairdressing, she says, is a passport to anywhere: 'You can generally get work. Even in the recession, people don't stop having their hair done. In fact, if anything, they cheer themselves up by changing their image. It makes you feel good. That's why I feel that I'm doing a useful service for people.'

I worked for a time in a hotel in the West End. I didn't like that. The customers were very upper-crust. We weren't allowed to enter by the front door, we had to go round the back entrance, which I think in this day and age is absolutely ridiculous, and also insulting. It was rather an up-tight place, you had to be careful about what you said. I once dropped something and said, 'Oh shit', and this woman took it personally, and made such a fuss. I said to the manager of the salon, 'If she never hears anything worse than that in her lifetime, she's lucky.' I apologized profusely; I'd cut myself or something, I can't remember, and she graciously said she'd accept my apology. I could cheerfully have set fire to her hair. But most people are very nice. I've made some wonderful friends, all over the world.

It's much better to work like we do here. We're self-employed, and we sort of rent the space here. That is to say, the reputation of the salon, you pay for that. We have to provide all our own material – scissors, brushes, hair-driers, combs, cloths. We pay our own insurance stamp and tax. You have to get a good accountant, because there are a lot of things you can claim. We split fifty-fifty with the salon. It means that when you get quiet times, your earnings go down, but on the whole it gives you freedom. You're flexible. I mean, you can't come and go as you like, you have to arrange it with the other workers here, but everybody tries to make it easy for each other – if you've something special on and you want a day off, people will cover for you.

Of course, the other side of it is you get no benefits from being self-employed, you've no protection, you've no unemployment benefit, anything like that. My Dad used to work for the Council – he thought he had a job for life, till he was made redundant; but he still goes on about having no security. I say to him, 'My skill is my security.' I've got a good track record, I could work anywhere. It's just that I've been round the world twice, I've achieved a lot of the things I wanted to. I'd like to start my own salon, but you need capital for that, and I'm not very good at saving. I've been married, but it didn't last very long. He wanted to settle down, and I wanted to see the world. It's usually the other way round – the woman wants to settle, and the man is the rover. But I think you have to get as much out of life as you can, especially while you're young.

I can talk to people. I love it. You learn a lot about other people's lives; we have a laugh here, sometimes we say we're social workers dressed up as hairdressers. On Thursdays, there's a cheap day for old-age pensioners. You ought to hear them. Some of them tell you dirty stories. They say, 'At our age, we can say what we like, we know we're safe.' Even when they're very ill, having their hair done, you know it's their last outing, some people. They give up shopping for themselves before they'll give up having their hair done. We've got one old dear, she has a little electric chair thing that she goes along the pavement in. She parks it outside the door, we have to help her in. She says that coming here is the highlight of her week.

I'd like to have children, but I couldn't bear to give up my work. I don't think I'd be a very good mother. For a year or two, I'll carry on like this. I don't think of the future. I do know some older women in the business, and they get very tired – varicose veins from standing all the time, back pain from bending. I'll pack it up before I get to that stage, but for the moment I'm happy. My Dad is very proud of me secretly, although he seems to think hairdressing isn't a proper job, like emptying the bins was. Well, I'm still working and he isn't.

Jackie (15)

Jackie is doing work experience. She has another year to go at school. She works on Saturdays in the salon, washing hair and cleaning up. She would like to do hairdressing as a career, but not if it means going to college – 'It's too much like school.'

I want to leave school. It's boring. I hate the lessons, science and that. I can't stand it. It's three years at college. If I could get a job where I earn some money, be independent, that's what I want. There's isn't anything much for young people round here. My brother works in McDonald's . . . he gets £3.15 an hour, and he's only sixteen. That's not bad. Mind you, it's shifts and he comes home exhausted. He's working down Brixton, where he's the only white worker in the place – I think he'd rather work in a more mixed area. I wouldn't mind that. He gets free meals, but you get tired of hamburgers every day. I'm lucky to have this job on Saturday, it earns me a bit of money for clothes and things I want. What I want is to have my own money. I want to be able to have a good time while I'm young. I don't think about later – you only live once.

Fifteen

The sex-worker's story. Most people who make a living from sex are far removed from stereotypes. It is the everyday ordinariness of Jayne that strikes you first; nothing glamorous – it isn't even a very lucrative job.

Jayne (*born 1974*): *sex worker, Nottingham*

Saturday afternoon on an estate on the edge of a Midland town, bounded by a cornfield. A corner of green, where some children are playing. A man, stripped to the waist, is bending over a car engine; three women stand outside a front door, talking, enjoying the sunshine.

In the corner house, the curtains are drawn. Inside is Jayne, with her four-year-old son. There is a war film on TV, the colour faded where the sun is filtered through the closed curtains. Jayne is also nursing Dionne, a two-year-old with pale coffee-coloured skin, frizzy hair and dark eyes. She cries intermittently; wants a biscuit, a sweetie, her dummy. Jayne explains that the child is unhappy because her mother, Jayne's friend, is serving fourteen days in jail for soliciting. Jayne wears a white sweater and plain dark skirt, fleecy slippers. She moves to and fro with Dionne on her lap, trying to comfort her.

There is an oatmeal-coloured carpet, a table of smoked glass and tubular steel, a big vase of pampas grass and russet and ultramarine barley and oats. The window is open on to the green, and the curtain billows up in the breeze. Jayne's little boy comes to the window and asks to be lifted inside: this is the quickest way of getting into the house.

Jayne went into care when she was thirteen. Her mother and father didn't get on, and she, the fourth of five children, was the scapegoat; systematically punished by her father, physically abused and hit by him. Her father left the family while she was in care, and her mother moved away to another town to live with her boyfriend. Jayne went into this household, but ran away repeatedly. She was sent to a community school in Bath, and saw her mother only at weekends. She was pregnant at fifteen, and had to leave the school. She decided to keep the child, and the father said he would stay with her; but before he was born, he left her. She now realizes that she cared for him quite deeply. 'In fact', she says, 'he was the only man I've ever loved.'

She lived with her mother in a two-bedroomed flat, the mother's relationship with the boyfriend having finished by this time. But there, she and the baby had to share a room with her twelve-year-old sister, and the baby's crying kept her awake. She came back to Derby to live with her married sister. She couldn't get a council flat, because she was still under eighteen. Her sister was living with her boyfriend in a one-bedroomed flat, and when the sister became pregnant Jayne and her baby had to move out.

Jayne lived with her little boy in a series of hostels, in one of which the child got gastroenteritis and had to go to hospital. She stayed with a friend for a few days, and then went back into emergency accommodation. There she met a girl who told her how easy it was to make money. 'I never listened to her, but I put the idea at the back of my mind; filed it away, sort of thing.' She came to the present maisonette about two months later. There was no furniture, no cooker.

The Social gave me a grant for a cooker and a bed. There was no heating and it was January. My Mum helped a bit. That was when I went out on the street to try and get some money. There's a pub in the centre of town where a lot of girls go, but you get too well known there, so I do the street.

There is a block of flats, six storeys high, in the centre of town, built on the site of demolished streets. At the base there are garages and rubbish chutes, and a sort of concrete courtyard. The roads along three sides of these flats are where the girls go: discreet, not too well lighted, with enough shelter from the eyes of residents and police. But it is a bleak, cold place.

I was stuck here one night, and I hadn't a penny. No money, no food, nothing for heating. I couldn't shoplift because, well, I just couldn't. I'd borrowed money and paid it back. I thought maybe I should go out and try my luck.

I got someone to look after Greg, and then just went down there, to these flats. On the bus I thought, Oh I can't do it. I thought I'd have to have a drink first. I went in the pub, then when I came outside I thought, Well I've got to. So I went and saw there were plenty of cars moving round slowly. I didn't see any other girls. A car stopped and a man asked me if I was looking for business. I said yes. He said, 'Five pounds'; I said, 'All right'.

So I got in the car, and he parked on some waste ground and I done him in the car. I was more frightened of him than anything else. It turned out he was nice, and he gave me more than I asked – he gave me ten. It only took a few minutes. I was relieved. I thought, Great. So I did another one, and I went home with £20. I was surprised how easy it was. The next night, I went out again, stayed longer, got more money. I was in a terrible state, because I'd had the electricity cut off, and I was paying rent direct to Social; after that, I was left with £13 a week.

It wasn't long before Jayne was going out several nights a week. It seemed too good to last, and soon she was picked up by the police for the first time. She was cautioned, and for two weeks was so frightened that she didn't go out. But the money had become indispensable; hesitantly, she went back. 'The police are always driving round the flats, all night. Sometimes they follow the car you get into, and when the guy stops, the copper opens the door and says, "You're under arrest."' The second time Jayne was picked up, she was taken to the police station. Then she was really scared, and denied that she was soliciting.

If you're young and new, they lock you in the cell so you have to confess what you were doing. I was worried about my little boy. They said they were keeping me there all night. I was worried, so I said yes to everything – I was doing it – and they let me go. They said next time, it would go to court. This was at the time before they thought the men were guilty of anything. It was just us, the girls.

I carried on, and I wasn't caught again for a long time. Some nights, they watch you. You know they've seen you, and you think they're going to take you in. But they don't. Then I was picked up again and charged, and taken to court.

It was six weeks before the court hearing, and during that time Jayne was picked up several times more. They picked her up every other night.

Once you're known, they keep on. By the time it came to court, there were seven charges. You get reckless, you think, Oh well, the worst has happened. So you don't stop. I was fined £100, to pay at the rate of so much a week. Well you have no way of paying off that money, so you're back again. Then I was arrested a few more times, and got a two-year probation order. I had quite a nice probation officer, but he wanted me to tell him I was going to be a good girl, not do it any more. It's the only way I had of getting money, of living – well it's better than just the Social. It's not brilliant, but it's better than nothing. All the things my little boy wants, I'm not going to get them any other way. What else can I do? There's no jobs. I've got no training for anything, except what I do. I worked on the phone for a time, but couldn't pay the bill, so I was cut off. It was easier then, because I didn't have to go on the street. I could work during the day.

Jayne doesn't like to think about the future. If she looks too far ahead, she feels depressed. Just getting through the day takes all her energy and time. She hopes that something will happen – that is, that she will meet someone who will look after her. Yet she knows that is the ambition of most of the girls, and it is very difficult to achieve it.

The trouble is, meeting men like we do, it isn't easy to establish anything more permanent. They don't want a relationship, they want relief; sometimes relief from the relationship they've got already. You can't get to know them.

Jayne cannot imagine doing anything else. The life has become almost a compulsion for her. When she needs money, she just goes out and gets it. She hates being alone, and spends a lot of time either with her friend or with her Mum, who now lives on her own in the centre of town. Jayne has a brother at university, and a sister whose husband has his own business and who refuses to have anything to do with her. 'She found out what I done, and doesn't want to know me.'

I go out two or three nights a week, but never at weekends. There's no business at weekends. The men are all at home with their wives and children. What does make me mad is the men get away with it. The girls are only answering a need, a demand of the market. Why should we get blamed, as though it was us tempting the men from the straight and narrow? And why haven't the police got anything better to do, with all the crime and violence around?

All the time, Jayne has been nursing Dionne, who cries and throws her arms around, and asks for her mother. Jayne tells her that Mummy has had to go away for two weeks; but two weeks means nothing to the child. She grizzles a little, then sucks her dummy, then gets angry and hits out with her fists. 'Why should she be the one to pay? It isn't fair.'
    Jayne is far removed from any of the popular images of prostitution – a woman who goes to work on the bus, she says, doing a twilight shift in the sweetness industry.

Sixteen

*The decline in manufacturing in Britain has been filled by an enormous
expansion in the service sector over the past forty years. While manufacturing
work was being lost during the 1960s, 70s and 80s, 'real jobs' were invoked as
the alternative to maintaining labour-intensive industry that had become
uncompetitive. The change from manufacture to service is as profound as that
which, from the late eighteenth to the mid-nineteenth century, transformed
Britain from a primarily agricultural country to a manufacturing nation.
Indeed, this shift has had as profound an effect upon the sensibility of the
manufacturing working class as that imposed on the agricultural workers
nearly two hundred years ago.*

Alan McVie (*born 1969*): *union official, south London*

I left school at eighteen, and went to university to do Business Studies,
with the thought that this would get me a job at the end of the day.
University didn't work out, because I found what I was studying didn't
motivate me, so I left at the end of the first year – I was enjoying myself
too much. Then I was unemployed for a year. That was terrible. I actually
went to a sperm bank for extra money. I went up to Glasgow every single
week and got a tenner. In fact, I know a student whose grant was so
small that he had to go four times a week to get enough money to live
on. It was very depressing, not knowing what you were going to do with
your life.

Then a job came up at the local branch of a big store, as a stock-room
supervisor. I was desperate for a job, I needed the money, so I applied. I
remember they asked me this question at the interview: 'What would you
do if you disagreed with the manager?' I said, 'Well, I'd put my point of
view, but at the end of the day, the manager's there to manage, so I'd have
to capitulate.' Which was a blatant lie, but I knew what they wanted to
hear.

Initially, I worked as a stock-room supervisor for a year, and then when
they made the job redundant, I was offered a job in the record department.

I've always been interested in music, in fact I've got a huge record collection of my own, but I was really forced to take it.

I'd get up about eight o'clock, and my father would give me a lift in, and when I got in I'd go upstairs, have a coffee and a cigarette. I started smoking after about a year. I'd go downstairs about ten to nine, the doors would open at nine, and I would maybe do an order for seven-inch singles. On a Monday, the charts were changed, so you could see what singles were going up or down, and you'd put in an order, estimating what your sales would be. That was eventually done away with, and the tills do that now, so any skill you had has disappeared completely. You'd be serving customers at the same time, and at ten you'd be replaced by a part-time person, so you could have a tea-break and a moan. Then queues would form downstairs, because the staffing level was so strictly controlled. You were always trying to do more than one job at once.

After an hour for lunch you were very busy serving customers till about three o'clock, when it would die down a bit, and you'd have a fifteen-minute tea-break. Then the manager would come down towards the end of the afternoon and criticize you for not doing certain jobs – like not cleaning a cassette rack. At four you'd start to tidy up, shut about half past five and finish at twenty to six. It was quite a tiring old day. Have your dinner and go to sleep. I think it was the boredom of the job that made it tiring.

I worked there from 1987 to 1992, and it got worse. The management unilaterally took away the time and a half they used to pay part-time workers for working before nine or after six, and because we all realized what was happening we went along to a trade union meeting, where they wanted me to speak on their behalf. I'd actually joined USDAW previously. The organizer who addressed the meeting coerced me into becoming shop steward, and I was then shop steward for four years.

We began to get a reputation as a 'militant' store – though the company's definition of 'militant' was any store that stood up to what they wanted them to do. The crunch came when they wanted all the part-timers in on a Saturday evening for a store refurbishment, and many of them had to travel in from the surrounding villages. They only offered single time, and we said, 'No, we're not prepared to do that. It's unsocial hours, and we want time and a half.' The manager refused, and he told us, 'You're coming in, whether you like it or not.' But no one came in.

Two weeks after that I was told that I was going to be given a written warning if the standard in the record bar didn't improve, though there were no grounds for it at all. Then they switched me from the record bar to paint and shoelaces. I was on that for a year – it was murder, you have to go on the till for three or four hours on end. But my colleagues were very supportive. They knew what was going on, and they said, 'Don't let the bastards get you down.'

What I liked most about the work was the camaraderie amongst the employees. We had a fantastic relationship. We'd hide in boxes in the stock room, we had water fights, we had some great goings-on. That's the one aspect I missed when I left. They were fantastic people, there's no doubt about it, but the management never gave them any opportunity to use their real abilities.

Initially it was very difficult for me as shop steward to get support from the other workers, because it was so fragmented, and so many workers were part-time. I always took things collectively; I always argued that if an issue affected one person one day, it might well affect someone else the next. Gradually, over a year, the more people came to see that this was the right way to do things, the more they stuck together. The latent strength in a retail store is very great.

Nationally, union membership has fallen for a variety of reasons. The company have introduced a vast closure programme – casualization became very important to Woolworth's, and they did that. People get very frightened, there's fear at the end of the day.

Working people are under tremendous pressures – I'll give you an example. Last week I went to a branch in south London, where the shop steward had asked to see me. When I got there, she called the other women together – there were about eight of them – and they asked me a series of questions. The manager had taken away the seat at the till – he said they shouldn't have time to sit down. Was that right? – because they were aching from standing up all day. The manager had changed their hours without consulting them. 'Well,' he'd said, 'I'll listen to what you have to say, but you may as well know that my mind is made up.' Could he do that? They were planning to refurbish the store on a Saturday night, and they'd been told to come in without any overtime pay. Was that right?

No, I told them, no in each case. And I drafted out a statement of collective grievance, listing these points, and asked them to sign it and give it to the manager so I could come in and negotiate with him. The shop steward signed, then passed it to her colleagues. One signed. The others refused to sign, even though a few moments ago they had been full of grievances. 'I'm not signing,' said one, 'I need my job too much.' The shop steward was in despair. 'What's the use,' she said, 'when no one will back you up?' The women avoided each other's eyes. 'It won't change anything,' commented one. Another woman said, 'It didn't used to be like this in the union when I joined – we'd've done something about it then.'

I suggested that they sign the statement 'aggrieved workers', and Tipp-

Ex out the names. The relief on the face of the woman who had signed was visibly apparent. Whether the shop steward will dare to hand in the paper to the manager, I don't know. I think she will. I've talked to them about their rights, and the fact that if they didn't stand up to the bullying manager, it would get worse. I reminded them of the strength they had if they acted collectively. I told them I would fight vigorously on their behalf if only they would take this first step. But they were scared.

'If we do complain,' they said, 'the manager just says, "If you don't like it, you know what you can do. There's three million out there that would be glad of your job."' They pointed to a notice on the wall behind them, announcing that the company was running a competition for the politest store. The notice said that they'd failed the first test, because one of them had answered the phone with the words 'How can I help you?' This was not polite enough for the company's requirements. The sentence was 'How may I help you?' Underneath the notice, the manager had written 'You're not being polite enough, and I don't want anyone who is not polite working in my store.'

As I left, the shop steward turned to me and said, 'What kind of country is it where people are afraid to speak their own minds?'

My parents were brought up as Labour supporters and socialists. My grandfather was a conscientious objector in the First World War. He was imprisoned for it, and he never got a job afterwards. My father was also an active trade unionist, and I was brought up in a home where politics were talked about openly, and there was always a great sense of what was right and wrong. That was the way I was brought up. I've always felt very strongly that people aren't being given the opportunity to contribute what they can to society. This union job is my opportunity.

Seventeen

The boundary between employment and unemployment is increasingly shadowy. Although Mark is unemployed, he is a very busy man. The unofficial, or black, economy is difficult to quantify, but it is undoubtedly very extensive, and serves at least one very useful purpose: it cushions people against the harshest effects of unemployment and the declining value of benefits, and thus preserves a kind of social peace. Ironically, it has usurped one of the primary functions of the Welfare State. What we have here is a form of private, even secretive, enterprise, which reflects back to us a caricature of the rhetoric of self-help.

Mark Sheridan *(born 1962): unemployed, east London*

I was born in Smithfield Market, just by the hospital. My Mum used to work, packing in a cigarette factory, and my Dad's been a haulage driver all his life. I didn't do too bad at school, I got five CSEs, but I didn't have much idea what I wanted to do. I was so active being Jack-the-lad that I didn't stop and consider what it would be like later. I used to like being out with my mates, and doing what they did – birds, booze, drugs and cars – you name it, we did it. I used to love music as well, we had a band, that was good. I played in quite a few bands – I played drums – but we didn't have the patience, and no one had the go to keep it up, you know.

I didn't get on with my Mum. I had a rough spell with her, because I was always being out late, or disobeying her. So I was told to leave home, or to do something, so I joined the Army when I was seventeen, done three years. It was good, I really enjoyed it. Then when I came out of the Army I tried to get in touch with Mum, and she'd moved out to Enfield by then, so I got the address off her ex-governor and went to see her. But I couldn't move home, because she thought I should be independent after three years in the Army, so, basically, I hit the street. I just had a rough spell. That was when I started hitting the gay clubs, looking for anywhere I could put my head down. That was when you could earn a couple of bob. And there were some nice people, and I learned some experience as well.

I'll be honest with you, I enjoyed it. They looked after me as well at the time, so I thought, The least I can do is give them my body, it ain't a lot – which it ain't. I appreciated a roof over my head and something to eat. They give me a drink, smoke, and even give me a tenner when I go, to see I'm all right. And I thought, Yes, well, why not? It ain't as if I ain't seen it, or ain't got one myself. I didn't have no problems with that, no. I suppose I can say I'm more bisexual than homosexual. I like both worlds. I like to walk on the wire. I play on the fence, always have done.

I got molested when I was a youngster by a man in the toilet at a cinema. I'd gone with my kid brother to see *On the Buses* – that's how far back we're going – I'd be about eight at the time. Funny enough, I didn't scream or nothing, I think I was too scared to do anything, I just let him do it. Then when he done it, I reported it, because I was crying hard; but they never caught him. But since that day, I suppose, I was grateful in a way, because I weren't sure which way I was going anyway.

Five years that lasted, bumming around on the streets. Mind you, I did have some good friends. I met an old RAF man – God bless him, he died about five years ago – he looked after me for years.

Then I got a job. I was staying with this friend in Tottenham – he was working for a removal firm – and I went to see his governor, and he said, 'Yes, well you can work here, and you can sign on, but the wages aren't good.' So I said, 'Well it don't matter, as long as I can get my dole money on top of this I don't care.' So we sorted that out and I started. We was always on the thief, always nicking this, nicking that. If you did a removal, something will go missing. 'That weren't there, love.' Hundred quid for this, a hundred and fifty for that. A good day's wages, plus we were getting paid.

Then I got a room, a tramped-out place in Camden Town. One night I couldn't go back to the place, I dreaded it, so I goes raving up at Tottenham. Spends all my money and has to walk all the way back, and when I'm walking home I starts thumbing a lift, I'm shattered. Someone pulls up for me and says, 'How far you going?' So I says, 'Camden Town', and he says, 'Well I've got to go that way.' So he drops me off, and I says, 'Do you want to come in for coffee? I can't offer you anything else.' He goes 'Yes', so I bring him into this run-down derelict of a place, and he says, 'Not being horrible, but you live in this?' I says, 'It ain't too bad during the day, because with all the lights on, you can see everything.' So anyway, he laughs, and then he turns round and says, 'Come on, you ain't staying here tonight, come home with me.' So I thought, 'Yeh, why not. Take the option.' So I goes home with him, and he treats me with a couple of beers, we're smoking dope, and he introduces me to some friends the following day. So anyway, he give me a job with him for a while, window-cleaning. Then I started on my own, picked up a nice little business running in Camden Town. But when I gets into a pub, these two window-cleaners come in, and threaten to do my fucking knee-caps unless I get off their site. So that ended.

I thought, sod this – do agency work. I was a fork-truck driver, I was a packer, I was a security man, I was a bricklayer, I was a scaffolder, I was a carpenter, I was an electrician, I was a plumber. I just picked it up, learning from the people as I went along. I didn't have a clue about plumbing until someone said, 'Well, now, this is a U-bend, that's a normal straight pipe. What you do, you burn your wire so it gets bubbly, and it'll melt round, and then you just connect it.' And ever since, I've just looked, and I've done pretty well.

I get the dole, you've got to take what they give you – couldn't fucking survive without that, I need to take that, because my rent's being paid for out of that as well. If everything works out right, if it's the same week as my dole money, I could clear a hundred and fifty quid. But that's unusual, because that includes my girlfriend's money as well. That's still good money every fortnight, three hundred quid. And bits of work often come up. I often get someone phone me up and say, 'What you doing?'

I'd say it's been a happy life, at least since I joined the Army. When I came out of school it was a bit rough, but I did what I wanted to do. I made the mistakes, no one else could tell me, or whatever – it was my error. But before that it was a bit rough. My Mum and Dad were always fighting and arguing. My Dad would beat my Mum. He didn't touch me, but we used to have arguments. And my Mum and me were always having arguments as well, we were always at each other. Mums and elder sons, they always do. Nothing really serious, we just didn't get on. And I suppose it was having the pressure of me and my brother. And my old man fucking off after a while, and they got a divorce. So I thought, Do I stay or do I go? And I thought, Well, the way things are going, I might as well go. I wanted to take that chance. I wanted to be out all night when I was out with my mates, and in the end I got the fucking chance so I had to take it.

The one thing I regret is Mum and Dad splitting up. That was the biggest shock, and it shook the shit out of me really. I knew my Mum and Dad all them years, and then all of a sudden, my Dad was gone . . . And I thought, Well, I'm more or less the provider now. But I weren't. Because I wasn't the provider, and I didn't know what to do, I think that's what fucked me up.

I do see my Dad now, but I don't see him that often. He's more or less denied me, said he don't know me and my brother, because he's got another girlfriend now – well, his common-law wife – and they've got two girls. And I think that's what my old man really wanted, two girls, all them years ago. Because he took these two girls on and looked after them more than he's looked after me and my brother. I think that's a bit of a fucking sickener. Me and my old man had a good punch-up about nine years ago, so I got all that grievance out of the way with him. Since that day we had the punch-up, we've got on better. We don't see each other much, because we both understand, he's got his family life, I've got mine. My brother, he's different. He wants Dad to do this, do that. I say, 'Fucking do it on your own, lad, don't worry about him.'

In five years' time, I reckon I'll be pretty much where I am now. To tell you the truth, I haven't got much lined up, there's not much looking for people at my age now. Well, I'm thirty-three next year, so in five years' time I'll be thirty-seven, coming up to forty, and then I'll be taking my retirement. I don't know. The girlfriend's got a chance of a council house up in Derby, and I'll try and keep the flat down here going, so there'll be money coming in. Then I'll come down here, do my business, do my windows, my grass, my lawns, whatever, and anytime people want me down to do the work that specific week, I'll come down and stay.

I'm too used to working for myself, too independent, to start going back to work and getting someone telling me what to do and when to do it. At work, you get a lot of stubbornness and a lot of back-stabbing. It's like when I had a job at Sainsbury's. I came up from ticketing the old tins to assistant manager. After that, higher management were giving me more aggravation, more trouble, and I thought, No, that's it. And it was good money, but I just walked out.

Class? Middle, I suppose, really, with the income I get. Some weeks I'm really hard up. But I'd put myself somewhere between poor and medium. Some weeks it works, some weeks it doesn't. I'm always ducking and diving, always trying to find something to earn. It usually comes through.

Though things are getting worse with the job situation. We're going into Europe now, but this country wants to sit back instead of going forward. We're worrying about who's going to be the next fucking prime minister – there's so many other things to worry about. I mean, this country just ain't doing it. So that's why you're getting people like myself. We'll go out, we'll duck and dive, we'll do this, do that, we'll do anything we can to keep our heads above water. And we don't care how much it costs. Especially if you have a family, and you want to keep that.

And it's not that hard to duck and dive. It is harder in certain aspects now, like fraud, car theft and stolen goods – them three are pretty hot – but as far as other things like, I suppose, burglary and videos, that's all under the carpet, mainly. You get people come round, if they come round – they either confiscate the gear or the money, and then they don't say no more. Then you start selling again. They know you're going to do it. It's your way of life.

Politics and religion I don't talk about. I try to stay out of them conversations, they take me down too much. No one seems to know what the fucking hell's going on, so let them carry on, know what I mean?

The most important thing for me is staying alive. That's the main thing at the moment . . . I've been very lucky in these last six years. I had a girlfriend a couple of years ago, put me in hospital with concussion, stabbed me in the chest, give me five stitches, missed my jugular by about two inches. Got away from her, lost my kid. Forgot all that. Get into a fight a year ago in a pub. Missed my jugular again by two inches. Two inches and I would have been dead, gone in three minutes. I was a very lucky man there. And I thought, Yeh, I don't believe in religion, but I think someone's watching me upstairs, because I'm still here. I'm still alive.

Eighteen: Young Workers of Harlow

Harlow was designated a new town in 1947, one of a group of towns within fifty miles of London designed to take pressure off the capital and to provide a better environment for those living in congested areas of the city. Considerable efforts were made to decentralize industry, and many industrial companies located themselves in these places, where there was a ready supply of skilled labour. The towns were designed as vast public housing schemes: houses with adequate bathrooms, gardens – amenities that had been lacking in the city. They were seen by many of the families who moved there as a new beginning, evidence of commitment by government to a continuous process of improvement in the lives of the people. Their fate has, in many ways, become emblematic of the destiny of working people in the intervening period: much of the housing stock is now privately owned, and while many people have prospered, others, especially the young, have found themselves confronted by a future of unskilled labour or unemployment. The speakers on the following pages are all in their early twenties.

Graham McIsaac, *painter and decorator*

When we were almost ready to leave school, the careers officer came round and said, 'Well, what do you want to do when you leave?' First of all, I thought of bricklaying; then I decided against that because it was too heavy, too much lifting. And I thought decorating sounded fun, but I didn't take it all that seriously. Most of the time I was at school I thought, Well, I'm going to live the rest of my life on the dole. But it all went horribly wrong, and I got into decorating. My Dad was a bank manager, but I didn't want to follow in his footsteps because I saw what stress he went through. My Mum did secretarial work.

In June 1986, I started with a YTS scheme. There weren't many jobs about even then, and YTS seemed the easiest way out. I got day release to do a City & Guilds at Tottenham College in painting and decorating, so the YTS scheme worked well for me.

I worked for four years at BNR, a large company making optical fibres. I get up at six-thirty, get the bus in for about eight, and start off with a cup of tea. The factory is a horrible-looking place, with dome shapes on the roof, and loads of computer equipment. They always need one decorator at least – it's a never-ending job. The good thing is, no one is looking over your shoulder, you're just left in there, and you can sneak a few extra minutes for the breaks.

If you know what you're doing, it's not really hard work. The worst bit is the rubbing down, breathing all the dust. If you're sensible, you get a dust mask. The painting I don't mind, I've grown to like it over the years. It can be a bit tedious – painting that radiator for instance looks like a nightmare. But after you've finished a job, you look back at it and you think, I did that. I got a lot of satisfaction from painting old people's homes. Most of the old ladies are really sweet, and they make you cups of tea every ten minutes.

Now I'm working for the Herts and Essex Training Group, but I'm not too happy with the way things are going at the moment. Last Friday they told us that our company is being liquidated, and I'm facing redundancy in two weeks' time – though there may be some work left for some of us. I'm shocked and worried. I could be signing on the week after next, for all I know.

What I'd really like to do, though it's very impractical, is to play in a band. Me and my brother have got this band and we'd like to get it off the ground. Some of our mates play in Collapsed Lung, a hip-hop band which is getting very popular, and getting really good reviews in music papers. They said that if we're playing live by November, we could go and support them. But there's millions of bands that make a loss all the time. We'd have to be bloody good to get anywhere. You never know. But I wouldn't be unhappy to spend the rest of my life painting and decorating.

I think things are going pretty badly. I reckon that any government that gets in is going to muck things up one way or another. I voted for the Greens at the last election, a conscience vote. When I see big buildings and new roads being built, I don't see it as progress at all. No, it's regression as far as I'm concerned. But even if the Greens got in power, they'd muck other things up.

Harlow's a pretty boring town, apart from the Square, which is a venue for live bands. I do the DJ-ing down there – live music is still the best form of entertainment for me. Music is a very powerful influence on young people's politics, I think. It can definitely change people. There are lots of politically aware bands about now, mainly hip-hop. Bands like Manic Street Preachers and the Blackguards – they're an anti-Fascist band. But I don't see how anyone could be a Nazi anyway, so I don't think there's much point in having an anti-Fascist band. But Fascism is a threat in Germany, so maybe it could be here too.

I'm a vegan – I don't eat meat or dairy products, whereas my Mum and Dad do. I became a vegan when I was about twelve, because of the music I was listening to. I used to listen to a lot of punk music, and whatever you might think about punk, there were some very good ideas in it. Equality, including animals as well as people.

I don't really know what class I'd put myself into. It's very confusing. You see, my Mum and Dad are very much middle-class, so whether I like it or not, part of me is in that category. I'm a little bit working-class, because I'm not on £30,000 a year. I'm certainly doing a working-class job. But I'd like to think all class barriers can be brought down. The more equal everyone is, the better.

Some of my friends down the Square are into anarchy. They don't mean destruction or chaos – they mean a lifestyle without oppression. They have no faith in any government, so they wouldn't vote. Whoever's in power, it's a dead end. It's very sad. I don't know where we're going. Who knows? I'll tell you when we get there.

Shane Baptiste, *unemployed*

I left school in 1986, when I was fifteen, but while I was in the middle of my exams I actually had a part-time job in Sainsbury's, on the meat counter, stacking the shelves. When I began, I would start on Thursday evening at half past five, and I'd be working through till half ten. The evening would involve unloading the meat counters, cleaning down the huge freezer, and re-stocking it with the newer stock. You had to clean it thoroughly, because it was inspected before you were allowed to put the meat back in. That was fine, but then I had to go and get stock from the warehouses, and I had a lot of problems with the people working there. So I'd work down on the shopfloor cleaning rather than go into the warehouses.

First off, the trouble was just name-calling. It was stuff I felt very uncomfortable with, so I wouldn't go into the canteen to eat – I'd eat walking round the stores. Part of it was shyness and not being able to cope. I was very young, and I'd just thrown myself out into the big outside world. In the end, it led to my leaving. I just went upstairs and handed my notice in, and signed on unemployed.

It got really bad. For example, when you were loading from the freezer in the meat-packing room, you'd walk through the flap-doors and one of the guys would walk behind you and nudge you on purpose while you were holding heavy trays of frozen chickens, and you'd get pushed over. I was knocked over many times. And these guys were a lot bigger than me. But there were only a couple of them, whilst there were about five or six guys of my own age that didn't like what was going on, so I stuck with them. I tried to talk to them, but it made it worse, much worse. My first reaction was 'Why don't you just leave us alone?' But I didn't say that in the freezer, I said it in front of everyone, and I said, 'I'm going to report you.' Of course one of the group that was doing this was the highest one up in the section. This was late evening, and there were about eight of us working there, so I didn't really have the bottle to report it.

Whether or not you believe how dramatic it was, that was my first experience of work, and I've worked in places much worse than that since. My Dad got me a job at STC, electronics company, picking and packing components. I liked the job, but it came to the same factor when I had to go into the canteen. I'd walk in, and there'd be only a few seats left, they'd know you'd got to go and sit there, so they used to get up and walk out as you sat down. Tea-breaks were bad. I used to go to the toilet during tea-breaks, and stay there for fifteen minutes. I managed to last till the end of my contract, but it was a feeling of being degraded, walking into the canteen and knowing that people were talking about you. The women weren't so bad, it was the men – the young men particularly.

It made me so scared. Most of it isn't physical, it's the intimidation that you know you're going to get. I thought, If I shout out, something's going to happen to me anyway. So I shut my mouth, got on with my work, and prayed for the day when my contract would run out. I knew if I left, I would have to wait for thirteen weeks for unemployment pay.

By the end of 1991, I was suicidal, and on Christmas Eve I tried to take my own life, and it was only because of my younger brother that I pulled through. I've had counselling since then, so I'm over that now. But because of all my experiences I haven't worked since then – I'm not prepared to go out there.

At the moment, we're having trouble with gangs coming to our house and terrorizing us. I've had my unemployment benefit cut a number of times. When you fill in the form, it asks: 'What reasons would you not want to take a job for?' I tell them it's because of the bigotry I experience, and their own reaction is 'What, racism in Harlow? There's no such thing.' I've had that every time from the unemployment office. The unemployment people look upon you as a troublemaker. They say to me, 'There's bigotry towards many different kinds of people, people who are tall, people who are short, people who wear glasses – everybody experiences some sort of harassment.'

With the racist harassment you're told right from school that you're meant to accept it, and that this is the way things are. You've got to accept you're going to get trouble, and live with it. And I did that for years. But when you're actually physically assaulted ... Three weeks ago I was assaulted just outside my own street, and I was smacked with a bar and taken to hospital. I thought I was going to die. We've reported fourteen incidents of actual attack to the police – even our white friends have trouble. One of my friends works on the market, and a lot of the guys who are in organized racist groups work next to him. And if he gets found out that he's actually with us he'd be in deep trouble.

Harlow is a very racist town. It's mainly the youngsters – it's the kids who've left school and have nothing to do, or who for some reason just want to start trouble, and it's making our lives hell. And listening to my younger brothers, I think it's getting worse. It's a minority of white people who give us the trouble, but the others don't stop them. It's easier for them to say, 'Just be careful of yourself.' I've spoken to people who've seen the trouble that's been happening, and I've said to them, 'Will you help? Will you report it?' and they say, 'Well, no, because it's like interfering isn't it? It's between you and him.' And so they turn a blind eye.

All of this means I only go up to town every other Monday to sign on. My brother comes with me, and we dart up into town as fast as we can, through the woods, until we get to the Unemployment Centre, and then we run home. I've not been into the town centre since 1991. We're actually prisoners.

I think racism comes from a kind of power trip. White people want someone under them. They think their space is being invaded by someone who's not from this country. They think, You're taking over, you're taking our jobs, you're taking our women, you don't belong here, this is my place. I don't really want to see you here – go back home.

But where is my home? My home was invaded by Western civilization. Deep down, I can only see it getting worse. The school system is where it all begins. We sit at home sometimes talking about it at night. And you realize that this has been going on for hundreds of years, and it's even worse for some people. I think one day one of us is going to be attacked, and one of us is not going to pull through.

Emma Chapman, *receptionist*

I work over at Stansted airport for a taxi company. We do taxis to order, and we also do executive-class cars for the private jets that come in through the Business Terminal. It's a two-shift system. I do three lates, three earlies and three days off, and I work in the International Arrivals lounge.

Over at the airport, it's like one big family. I look forward to going to work, we all get on well. Even the managers there – well, they're not like managers, they come out with us, and we have a good time with them. It's brilliant. It's partly because you're working so close to each other. We've got a fax machine and a copier, so everyone comes to us. Then if we need to do some Wordperfect we go to someone else's office. It's just good.

At school I wanted to be a nurse in the Navy. My brother was in the Navy, and I wanted to be a nurse because when there were accidents in the family, I was the one who wasn't squeamish. I was never bothered about blood. I went to college and trained for it, but then they made a new law, that women had to go to sea, and I didn't want to go to sea, because there are a lot of bad vibes about women in the Navy – that they were harlots – and that put me off. And you had to go away for six months, and I didn't want to leave my Mum and Dad for that long, so I decided not to do it.

I was seventeen by then, and I didn't have a clue of what else I wanted to do, so I went to the Careers Office and said, 'What am I going to do?' She came up with a job in a small office working as a receptionist for a television cabling firm. I worked there for six months, and I loved it. I was the only girl in the office, and all the lads helped me in the first week I was there. I would have stayed there for yonks, but then I got made redundant after six months. I was very upset. One Friday morning, we were all in my office just having tea, and the boss came in and gave us all this letter. He said, 'You can either go now or next week.'

After that I couldn't find anything, and I was out of work for three months. It was horrendous. Because I was under eighteen, I didn't get that much money, so I couldn't pay Mum anything and I couldn't run my car. It was a bad time. My Mum and Dad supported me, and my brother used to slip me five pounds to go out. I used to get up in the morning and think, What am I going to do today? It gets you to that point where you can't be bothered to get out of bed. I was very low. I'd hate to be unemployed again.

After that a friend of my Mum's told me about a junior post at a solicitor's in the town. I went for an interview and started the next day. I went out for a meal to celebrate. I was there for about a year, and I enjoyed all the going to court – but the wages were about £2.50 an hour, and after a year I was still only taking home £300 a month, and I was eighteen then. But the people at work were really helpful and they kept pushing me into doing law, but I couldn't get a grant for it.

Then one of the solicitors helped me get a job at a computer firm that they had business contacts with. Now I was getting £7,000 a year. But I found it hard to work with these Pakistani men. They were going through their ritual thing of Ramadan, where they weren't allowed to eat. And they kept going past and spitting on the floor. They didn't treat me badly, it was just the way they did things. None of the men would talk to me, they thought women were nothing. All the men got the good work, and we girls got the rubbish jobs. Basically, I was just being paid to make the tea, and there's only so much you can take of doing that. I wanted to be working, to be doing something. Then this man at the end of my road told me about this job at the airport, and got me an application form. I got the job at £8,500 a year, and when I got my first wage I was so chuffed, and I didn't know what to do with all the money.

I get up at half past four, try and find the bathroom, get ready, put my uniform on, sort out my ID badge, and then I eat my toast as I drive to the airport, which takes me half an hour. When I get to the office, I put the kettle on, relieve the person who's been on the night before, talk though any problems, and find out if we've any early morning bookings. Then the drivers are standing in front of your desk, so you chat to them and allocate the morning jobs. Then we have the morning flights coming in, and there's a constant flow of people wanting taxis. You have to keep smiling, and never lose your temper, even though there are lots of people having a go at you. 'Your prices are terrible,' they say. The men are the worst, and they start pointing a finger at you and shouting – it's usually about money. You just have to keep smiling.

If I didn't work, I'd miss all the enjoyment, it's such a laugh. And the friendship. Also I'd miss not being busy – that's the thing that drove me crazy before.

If I were made redundant, I couldn't cope without the backing of my Mum and Dad. You're all right as long as you've got your health and you know that you're loved. I feel secure in my family. I live each day as it comes, and then at night Mum and Dad kiss me goodnight and, whoosh, I'm off.

I'm not really interested in politics, but I vote Labour. I think the Conservatives are just ruining this country. Apart from that, I don't follow much politics, I don't really get it.[*Laughs*] My Dad's heavy union so I avoid politics at home, because if I said, 'What do you think of that?' he'd lay into the whole lot and spend about three hours on it. I've never been in a union in any of my jobs. I would have joined if I could, because I think unions stand up for people.

I'm working-class. My Mum and Dad brought me up to be working-class. They said, 'You've got to stand up for what you believe in.'

Especially my Dad. He's been a bus driver for thirty-five years, and he's always been involved in the union. Money doesn't bother me that much. Yes, it's nice to have the good things and all that, but it's never bothered me that much. I've always been taught that you go out, you earn your money, and then you can stand on your own. I've never thought I was anything other than working-class.

At the moment everyone is so miserable. So many people are out of work now, and all the businesses are closing down. My boyfriend's unemployed, and sometimes, when I go up to town with him, I can't believe how long that dole queue gets. You see people from my age up to my Dad's age, queuing for their dole money. There are solicitors, people who've got good qualifications. They tell you to get a good education, go on to university, and then they put you in the dole queue. That's the first thing they should sort out. Everybody would feel better if that was sorted out. Even my brother in the Navy's worried, because they're making people redundant there. I mean, that's always been such a secure thing. You just don't know now.

Lance Carver, *dance student*

When I left school, I joined a two-year YTS in carpentry and joinery. I didn't finish it, because I didn't know whether I wanted to be in it or not. I've always been the sort of person who can't sit down at a desk – I've always been involved in jumping about and in sport. My Mum encouraged me to do the carpentry, and I liked the idea of being able to make something, whereas when you go into a factory you're just told what to do.

My next-door neighbour was heavily into martial arts, and he used to train with me, so I got into it from a very early age, about six I think. I've tried Chinese boxing, kung fu, karate, t'ai chi and judo. I liked being able to jump about and do my own thing. It gets things off your mind, and you also get to think you're better than some other people because you can push people around. Though I didn't, I was never a bully. I've been in plenty of fights, but I've never started one.

From there, I went with my friend to a club, and he used to train with this dancer – it helped him stretch and maintain his equilibrium. So I went to the dance club and I loved it, and then I went to do Saturday classes at the Playhouse. My Mum said, 'Oh, it's just another five-minute wonder.' But I really enjoyed it. The college where I study now is about fifteen boys and 235 girls. A lot of boys say to me, 'Oh, you're gay.' But I say, 'Well, think about it. Wouldn't you like going to a college with all those girls?' A lot of people are in work and they don't enjoy what they're doing, whereas

I'm doing something I really love. And it's a job where you get the opportunity to go round the world.

I've done some acting, I've been in a couple of McDonald's adverts, and I've done some small fashion shows. I've just come back from a luxury cruise which toured Miami, Jamaica, Mexico and Grand Cayman. I was dancing aboard the ship, two hours a night, and three hours of duties in the day. It's hard, working among people who are on holiday, because you see them having fun, and you're working, basically. And there were rules on the ship, where we weren't allowed to mix with the passengers, or dance in the disco. We weren't allowed to go into the casinos, or even sit on the chairs. And if you got caught in a cabin, you were sacked.

There were other people working on the ship from South America, Puerto Rico – people who didn't have work, so they'd go for anything that came up, no matter what the wages. They're normally the people who work below the ship, and it's only entertainers and people who work in the shops and casinos who are allowed up on top deck – the others have to stay below.

When I did the McDonald's advert, I felt like a star. Unfortunately, you don't see my face – it's an advert with a Chinese dragon introducing a new sauce, and it came out at Chinese New Year. We had to come into the shop inside this Chinese dragon and order. They didn't film it inside a studio, they actually filmed it in London, in a real live McDonald's, and they closed the shop down for two days. For the actual costume, it was a yellow dragon, and they had all these bells and Chinese slippers. There were lights everywhere and cameras and all the passers-by were peering in. It was great. Good money too. I was on £250 a day, and my friend, who you can see speaking through the dragon's mouth, got about four grand, which is brilliant.

I've got the pure blues since I came back from America. It's such a different world out there, so warm, and it makes everybody feel more warm and happy. Things are open much later, and it's so cheap. I loved it. I've got to get away. It sounds horrible, but everybody I know is pregnant, settling down, in Harlow, where they've been born, and they're only about twenty. They've all got married and got kids. It's not for me. I'd like to emigrate, to America or Canada. But it's hard – you've got to have something to get you over there. Being there is like watching the movies. I know it's not like that all the time, they get fed up with their own place too. But it's warm there and there's so much to do. I'm a weather man.

Being in Harlow, you know everyone, you see everyone, there's one pub, you go to that pub and you see the same old people. And the thing is, when you meet someone, if you meet someone new, everyone else knows your background and what you used to do, and they can say stuff that might embarrass you. Meeting people here, you don't get that sort of a buzz. They've known you, and that's you.

They say money's everything, and in a sense, it is. I'd like to be just well off, but not to be over-rich. Then it gets a bit like 'seen it, done it, had it'. I just want enough, perhaps a bit more than enough. I could be really well off with £250 a week, but a grand a week would do nicely. I know people in my line of work who are getting loads more than that. It's a matter of being in the right place at the right time.

As far as politics goes, they're all hypocrites. They're destroying the world, and it's getting worse and worse. It may sound silly, but my main fear is that the world will come to an end. My Mum's a Jehovah's Witness, and she talks about Armageddon, and if you read the real Bible, it says that no one will know the day or the time. What the scriptures say will happen is happening now – there's a lot of proof. I reckon it's going to happen soon. I fear that.

Andrew Hasty, *electrician*

I usually get up about seven, and then I can drive to the council depot in about ten minutes, where we start at eight. I tend to do the bigger jobs. Last job we did was rewiring the community centre. We'd go in, look at the job, see how much cable we needed, check what kind of fuse board they have, then we'd go down to the wholesalers, order the gear and get on with the job.

It's harder than people think. People see electricians turn up on the site with their tool pouch, and they think you've just got to strip a few cables and wire it in. But there's bending conduits, and carrying heavy drums, so that side of it can be a bit heavy. But it's varied, and some days it can be a doddle.

I don't like doing the same job every time, and on the Council you've got the rewires team, and all they do is just go from house to house for years. I don't like that. And sometimes the tenants can be very awkward. You'll go in there, and you'll be tidying up at the end of the job, and you say, 'Can I borrow the Hoover or the dustpan to clear up?' and they'll say, 'No, it's all right, I'll do it', and you'll go, and then they'll complain that you've left a mess. That happens quite often with people – I don't know why.

When I was at school I didn't have a clue what I wanted to do. It's the old story – you go through school, it gets nearer and nearer, and you think, There must be something I want to do! But I didn't. My Dad's a lecturer at Harlow College. He lectures in electrical installation, and he said, 'It's always handy to get a trade underneath your belt.' I came straight on to a council YTS scheme. The Council doubled the YTS money, up to about £50. That was for the first year, then I carried on for the full four years of my apprenticeship. I enjoyed learning, but I didn't like doing all the homework.

In our section, people are quite close – everyone gets on well with each other. We're all members of the social club, and we're always doing something together, like playing golf, and we've just started a monthly bowling club. If someone's leaving or having a birthday, we all get together and have a night out. There's darts, five-a-side, and eleven-a-side; we play the plumbers. A lot of my mates say they wouldn't work here without the social side of it.

At the moment with the recession, you just keep your head down and hope redundancies don't come your way. I know a couple of people who left about a year ago, and they've been struggling, out of work. So at the moment, the money's all right. You've got to look at it with the benefits – holiday pay, sick pay etc. Before, we used to get a lot of overtime, but with the cuts, that's gone completely. The Council had a policy of no redundancies, but in times like these, that's no good at all. Overall, there've been hundreds of redundancies. Luckily, we've had quite a few people in our department retire and go on their own, and they've also said that the apprentices coming out of their time won't be kept on. It's the next round that's going to be the worrying one – I'm not looking forward to that. If it comes, it comes. There's nothing you can do about it.

I've always wanted my own business, but I want to completely get away from electrical work. The only thing stopping me is I can't think of something to do, so if someone could come up with an idea for me, I'd be well chuffed. I mean, you're never going to be rich working for the Council, and you're never going to be successful. I want to be successful, I want to be comfortable in life, not to have to worry. I've always wanted enough money to look after my family, to look after my parents so they could have a happy retirement. And just not have to worry about financial things.

If I categorize myself, I'd have to call myself working-class. There's nothing to be ashamed of in that. I've got some rich friends who are stockbrokers and work in the City, and they'll have a dinner party or a barbecue, and when you go they're talking about their holidays in Tahiti and their £100,000 mortgage, and how they've got a pay rise of £50,000 this week, so you don't like to say, 'Well I've just put a new exhaust on my Ford this week' or 'I'm going on holiday to Minorca.' I'd like to have their money. It's mostly rich people who turn round and say you shouldn't worry about money. But it's a security thing. I'd just like to have a bit in the bank, because the way pensioners are treated in this country is shameful. But that's back to politics.

Clare Hickey, *telephone salesperson*

When I was at college, I wanted to be a drama teacher, but I was no good at maths, and maths is compulsory. I got so funny with maths, I just couldn't do it.

My first job was in Customs and Excise. There were about six of us altogether, and we were all on six-month contracts, but as soon as the six months were ended they chucked us all out. I was a telephonist and receptionist, but I didn't like it because of the bailiffs. I was working in VAT, and if you don't pay after the red bill, the bailiffs go round and clamp all the stuff in your business. They used to love doing it, and they talked about it all the time. I didn't like that.

Now I'm working for a magazine, and I get all the advertising. It's a magazine for residential homes for people over fifty. They're luxury mobile homes, really beautiful. There are over fourteen hundred parks that we cater for, and we distribute our magazine to them – it comes out every two months.

I get up at half seven, and it takes me about quarter of an hour to cycle to work. When I get to work, we usually have a chat about what we're going to do. First, I do the call-backs for the day, people who've called during the week that I need to get back to; and the people I've sent our media packs to, I give them a week, and then I ring them back. Then I have to get *Mobile Holiday Homes* magazine, which is our biggest competitor, and nick all their advertising. I ring the advertisers up and make them better offers. I spend most of my day ringing people up. I discuss the size of the adverts, get the copy in, type it all out, put it all in order, check it, and then send if off. I phone about fifty people a day at the moment. Our target for each day is £400 of sales.

That's basically what I do, but I think it's a bit dodgy there. Since Customs and Excise, I've done lots of casual jobs – cleaning jobs, bar work. The dole money is never enough, I only got £32.50 a week. Then I saw this job advertised at the Jobcentre. It said: '£100 a week basic, plus commission, and an hour's lunch-break.' Anyway, I went with Mark, he's eighteen, for the job. When we got there, they said I was working nine to five, three-quarters of an hour lunch-break, and £80 basic. What he does is, he pays us £80 a week by cheque – which just pays off my debts, I don't see that – and £20 in cash. Mark's well happy with it, because he lives at home, but I'm not. I was earning more than this when I was sixteen. They took us on for a trial month, and our next pay will be less, because they're going to take out our National Insurance and tax for the month, so I'll probably not get any money next Friday for working all week.

Yesterday, the boss was saying, 'Oh, it's very good, you're on contract now.' But he's only put us on one-month contracts. So I said to the boss, 'Have you ever heard of one-month contracts before? The least amount of time I've ever heard of is three months. Why is it only a one-month contract?' He just said, 'There's lots of reasons why. We're a new company, and we really need to work hard, and that's why.' I think the real reason is that he knows it's a buyer's market, and he can pick us up and drop us whenever he wants.

I get so annoyed, though. Everyone thinks that because he's the boss you should respect him and think he's brilliant, and that I should be grateful to him for giving me a job after being out of work for two years. I am pleased I have a job, I am going to work hard, I do want to get all my life sorted out and my debts paid, but I'm not stupid. He thinks we are, he really does. I think he's going to do a runner one of these days. He's kept the company going for two years, but it's a bit dodgy – but I'll keep working there because I need the money.

I was in about £560-worth of debt three weeks ago, and I've got it down now to £247. The debts are mainly rent, for me and my boyfriend. He's getting kicked out, and he hasn't paid anything. I've lived with him for ages, but he's gone really funny, and he won't pay any rent. He's got me in so much debt. The more and more we weren't sorting it out when I was on the dole, the more I just gave up with it all. And I was thinking, That's it, I'm going to get evicted, I'll get taken to court. I just gave up. I hate being in debt, it's the first time I've ever been in debt, and I've lived on my own since I was seventeen. In another six or seven weeks I'll have paid off my debt from the £80 cheque, I'll be clear, and I'll be back to normal. I can't wait for that – that's why I've got to work. That's why I'm working there. I don't think I'd be such a mug otherwise. And they've got us in a trap, because if we leave, then it's six months before we can get dole. And he knows that.

Since I've been seventeen, I've had to worry about money constantly. And I'm so fed up with it ... I can't remember the last time I went shopping for clothes. My friend Tracey bought me a new skirt and top to wear for my first day at work. When I was younger, work never seemed so important to me. I've never tried so hard, never wanted to work so much. All I want is to be normal. All I want is to have some money so I can go out with my friends, and have some money for food, toiletries, rent money and that. Because I'll be able to live on my wages once I've paid off my debts. Out of the £80 I'll have to pay £45 a week rent, then I've got £55 for myself, and £20 from my two cleaning jobs, so I'll have £75 a week. I don't think even my Mum has got £75 a week to spend on herself.

The good thing about being on the dole is that everybody's on the dole with you, so you don't get bored. Everybody used to come round to my flat all the time, because there are no Mums and Dads, and we used to have quite a good time. We used to go up to the pub on giro day – we'd go to the Jean Harlow, loads of us, it was only good at lunchtime. We used to have a really good time, and spend about £7 on beer and cigarettes. But you do get to spend a lot of time in pubs, because they're the only places to go where there are loads of people and anything is going on. I thought to myself, If this goes on, I'll be becoming an alcoholic, it's not good.

Most of my friends don't vote. Don't ask me why. Their parents never talked to them – it was always 'It's none of your business, it's private.' If they'd talked to them, they'd vote. But they say, 'It's all the same. Nothing will ever change.' That's their exact words. I go potty, I can't understand it.

I vote Labour, definitely. They're not going to change everything, everything's not going to get better, but they're not for the rich getting richer and the poor getting poorer. They're for levelling it off a bit. The way I'm living at the moment, I would be under the breadline, wouldn't I? And I'm only turned twenty. So many of my friends are the same and I can't understand why they don't do something about it. None of them will talk about it. They say, 'Oh no, don't talk about politics. Don't want to talk about this, don't want to talk about that.' I've got a few friends who know what's going on. I was so happy the first time I could vote. I don't think that they can even be bothered to go down there and vote.

I'm working-class – at the moment. When I lived with my parents I used to think they were middle-class, although they've got working-class views; they're actually middle-class because of the jobs they do and the house, and they've got a mortgage, and they go on holiday. I don't think that any more about me – I haven't got enough money for any of those things. The last time I went away on holiday was when I was at home. I've been to the Glastonbury Festival, sneaked in there, that was excellent. I suppose I'm working-class. I don't think my friends think they're anything.

I think everybody's just given up. They all think because there's been Maggie for so long, and now John Major, they really don't remember anything different. Everybody just thinks this is the way it is, and nothing's going to change . . . They've just accepted it. But I haven't.

132

Nineteen

Personal services now employ large numbers of people, mainly women. Much work that was previously the prerogative of local authorities has now been privatized. This opens up opportunities for young people, but low pay and low status may lead to poorly qualified people doing work that is both difficult and delicate; none more so than in the large numbers of private nursing homes, which have recruited many young women with negligible qualifications.

Tricia Duncan (*born 1977*): *care assistant, Leicester*

Tricia's experience is not unusual, but for her it has been a great success. She is now eighteen, and lives with her mother and her mother's boyfriend in a new town flat; a place landscaped into invisibility, on the edge of a motorway, and shielded from the superior private estate by a vigorous new growth of plane trees, rowan and white poplar. Tricia thinks she is lucky; almost none of those who left school when she did has work. 'They're on schemes, or at college, but they don't take it seriously. They don't see where it's leading to, so they just mess about, have a laugh.'

Tricia saw an advert in the local paper for an old people's home that was opening in the town. She applied, and was taken on as care assistant at £2.55 an hour. She is a vivacious and self-possessed young woman, and knows that she interviews well.

To tell the truth, when they said I could start on Monday, I was scared. The first few weeks were the most frightening thing that's ever happened to me. I could've walked out any time; but I thought, If I do, I'll never get another job. So I stuck it, and now I'm glad I have. It's given me more confidence. I quite like going to work now, but at the start I had nightmares about it.

I mean, I'd never seen old people. Well I'd seen them, but I've never had anything to do with them. My Nan doesn't seem old, she's about sixty. These people in the home, a lot of them were in their eighties and nineties. What do I know about people that age? I'd never even thought about it as a job.

I was interviewed on a Wednesday. On the Friday, I was shown round with two other girls. We all started more or less at the same time. Linda lasted a fortnight, the other girl left the same day. When I got there the first morning, there was just me and an older woman, Rose – she was very nice. If it hadn't been for her, I would never have stuck it. There was always a nurse on duty, but she wouldn't do the dirty jobs, you know, what we were supposed to do.

Because you're a girl, you're expected to know all about caring. Don't bother to give any training. Just do it. We had to get these twenty-three old people up, get them to the toilet, help those who needed dressing, get their breakfast. I'm not kidding, it was chaos in there. These old ladies stranded on the commode. Nobody had taught me how to lift them, how you're supposed to stand before you take the weight. Some of them couldn't do anything without help. It was heavy work, hard labour.

When we were shown round, we saw the dining arrangements, the rooms – they were very nice – the sitting-room; it was as if we were buying a house. They just show you all the nice features. This couple had bought it and converted it. It was their business. They were charging £275 a week; most of the people were getting paid for by DSS. It had all been done very smart, but with me, it didn't even sink in what it meant when they said it was a nursing home. That's really the last stop. You know what I mean, it sounds cruel, but it means when they can't look after themselves at home, or they can't stay in residential homes. It was like they were just waiting to die. It shouldn't have been like that. A trip to the pantomime, and some kids from the local school to sing carols, and they called it therapy.

Anyway, first morning. They give you a check overall, and your name badge, stick a frilly bit of a hat on your head and call you a care worker. I was so frightened. I'd never seen a naked man before, and there was this old man we had to get to the toilet – I saw his willy, and I felt funny, because he was so old and his legs all shrivelled and skinny. Then we had to wipe his bum. I gave the piece of paper to Rose and said, 'You do it.' I couldn't. There was people ringing their buzzer, and it's like, you were in the middle of something and you were called away, and you had to remember not to leave that old lady sitting half-dressed and this other old dear on the commode.

I was just fascinated, looking at [the old people] some of the time. Some of them were very sweet, but others looked at you like they'd never seen anyone young before. Then some of them were senile, they didn't know what they were saying. One kept calling me Barbara, which I found out was her daughter's name. Some of them have been left there by their children, who don't come to see them.

Matron wasn't really a matron. She called herself that, because it gave her authority. Basically, they were doing it on the cheap, charging a lot and giving only basic help. At night, they had people in from an agency, which I don't think is fair, because the old people want to be put to bed by somebody they know.

Sometimes, they asked me to kiss them goodnight. It really got to me. I used to go home and cry. And then I saw somebody die. I was on late duty one night, and this old lady more or less died in my arms. And I didn't panic. I'd thought about it, because I'd never seen death before, except a hamster and when the dog got run over. But the idea of seeing somebody dead, well, partly it intrigued me and partly I was frightened. But when it happened, she died so peacefully; she couldn't get her breath and she just sighed a deep breath and then sank back; then she opened her eyes again, and her head fell sideways, and I knew she was dead. I was holding her hand. That day I think I grew up.

I have definitely got a gift for it. I'm getting some qualifications now. I think eventually I'll do geriatric nursing. But I don't think young people should be put into that situation. Linda tried to stick it out – she didn't want to admit defeat. But the other girl, she couldn't stand the smell, because some of them were incontinent and you had to take these nappy things off them in the morning, and they did stink.

The people are overworked. Matron was nice with them, but she was always trying to find ways of saving money. Like the bulbs in the rooms were very dim, so they couldn't see to read. I made friends with the chef – he wasn't really a chef anymore than I was a care assistant, I think he more or less taught himself to cook. He was only about twenty; but he liked doing it, and sometimes we'd try and give them little treats, find out what things they liked. He was good. He managed on a very limited budget to make some nice food; some had to have everything minced because they couldn't chew.

But I'll never forget that first morning. The nurse – she was an SRN – she sat in the office and drank coffee listening to Atlantic Radio, and she left me to deal with all these old people, without offering even to show me what to do. She was the one I really hated. She was very snooty about being a qualified nurse, and anything else was beneath her dignity.

Later, you learn to cope, you develop your own method of not letting it get to you too much. I don't mean you get hard – only if you don't a little bit, you couldn't do it. I think I had plenty of practice. My Mum used to talk to me about her feelings and her boyfriends, and she kept asking me to call all these men Daddy, then they pissed off. So, I don't know if you know what I mean, I got so I had this shell round me; and I think that helped me to cope with things that other young girls couldn't handle. It's all about survival.

A lot of young women think they want to do caring work, work with people. Only when they get contact with the reality, they run a mile. Old people isn't sweet old ladies sitting there being good girls and giving you a sweetie if you're nice to them. These people are gonna die, they know they are. They feel angry, they feel they've been dumped there by their families, some of them are just not very nice people; some have gone completely into another world. My mate, she works with kids, and she says they're not sweet either – a lot of them have been unwanted, abused, beaten. They're impossible to deal with.

I'll tell you what it does to you. It makes other people of your own age seem very childish. Like boys – I have a boyfriend, and all the things he wants to talk about seem stupid to me. I mean, I like music and dancing, I like to go out, I like a drink. I don't smoke. But I don't wanna sit and listen to him talking about cars and engines and motorbikes and football. Well, I don't mind, but he won't listen to me. When I start to tell him what's happened at work, he says, 'Yeh, sure', but I can see him not listening. And that makes me mad.

I walked out last Friday; we were sitting in the Silver Slipper, it was a nice night. But it was just as if I wasn't there. I thought, If I go, how long will it take before they notice? So I went, and a few minutes later he's running after me, giving me a lot of mouth because I've spoilt his evening. I just burst out crying, and, then he said, 'Tell me, tell me' – he's very soft underneath, but most of the time he doesn't want to know. And I could not tell him I'd had a bad week. Two people had died in a week, and one of them I liked a lot; you could have a joke with her, she used to call me 'Smiley'; and whenever I walked in, you could see her face light up. I'm not boasting or kidding, but I do know how to be decent to people, and to listen to them. You can say I'm big-headed, but I know it's something I've learned how to do. I really felt sad when she died, and I went to her funeral.

I'd like to start my own home one day. But I don't know where I'd get the money from. I won't stay where I am much longer, but you have to be there long enough to prove that you can stick a job, you're serious. The pay is all right because I give my Mum some board, but the rest is mine. It wouldn't be any good if I had a family, but I'm not thinking about that yet.

Sometimes, I think I'm a bit of a freak. I get impatient with my mates. Don't get me wrong – I care as much as they do about having a boyfriend, how I look. I love clothes. But when we go out at night, I often come home and think, What's it all about? Why am I not satisfied? Then next morning I've got to get up and go to work, it's a different world. In fact, because I do shifts, I sometimes can't go out at nights. They say, 'Tricia's moody again.' I don't say anything. A lot of my mates are working – one is a clerical assistant, one works in Wimpy's, one is a trainee hairdresser; only Julie I can talk to, she's the one who works in the children's home.

In some ways, my work day is unbelievably boring. You know, each day you have to start afresh – clean people up, wash them, give them their meal. You know what you're gonna find every morning when you go in. Some days, something will happen. Somebody's relation will give you a box of chocolates, because their mother has said how kind you've been, or somebody who's never given a word of thanks will just squeeze your hand. Little things that can change your day. But it's hard work a lot of the time. But once you've done it, you can't do anything else.

PART 2

Twenty: Grimethorpe – Requiem for a Pit Village

Grimethorpe, June 1993, six weeks after the closure of the pit, which was the reason for existence of a community of about seven thousand people. The story from this little town, caught in the folds of the South Yorkshire coalfield, is of a sense of bereavement, of trauma and of grief. A people schooled for labour have had their purpose ruined. A culture of stoicism has been junked. A vital social function has been abruptly cancelled. How can it not deeply affect those who must learn once more that even pit villages that have half a century of accessible coal beneath them are expendable for reasons that have nothing to do with economics? A terrible violence has been done to the sensibility of the people. They talk of stress, tension, anxiety, a sense of futility . . . On the sick. Invalidity . . . It's those bastards, they say, they have invalidated a whole way of life.

It is perceived by the community as a story of political revenge: for 1974, even for 1945. Who knows, they say, what dark atavisms stir in Tory breasts at the mere mention of miners, those heroes of Labour, those barely human creatures of the early industrial era who toiled in their true element, the earth; whose villages were sooty blots on the landscape, and whose ways were alien and terrifying to the cultivated society that resented its dependency upon them? But out of our oppression and isolation, the miners say, we nevertheless constructed, with pain and effort, a life of dignity and endurance.

One o'clock in the afternoon. In the shabby pub with its scuffed floor and torn leatherette seating, a television, faded to violet monochrome, is showing the defeat of England by Australia in the test match. A miner who lost his job when the pit closed six weeks earlier says, 'This country's finished. They can't play cricket, they can't play football. Sack the fucking lot.'

A male-dominated culture is dying. All that is left is a desperate machismo, no longer even anchored in its social purpose. The chapels and the Co-op, with their commemorative foundation stones, have been boarded up. The chapel is for sale. Only one previous owner. The men drink, bluster and pose. Tattoos and singlets in the chill June wind. The pints follow each other on the spindly round tables . . . 'I left school on Friday and started in the pit on Monday. It took twenty-five years from me. I was told I had a job for life . . .'

When cultures are destroyed, it's always the same. People lose their faith in the life that has sustained them. Some die of grief; others damage themselves, colluding with the power that has vanquished them. The Aborigines, the Indians of the Plains, the Yanomami, the people of the desolated pit villages at the heart of our society: it's only a difference of degree.

What has happened here has been a colonization, by more powerful forces, of a strong, rooted, apparently indestructible culture of labour. It is unbearably poignant: solidarity, community, shared experience of work, a vigilant regard for one another – values destroyed in the cities, clung on to tenaciously in the pit village.

It wasn't all good – sexist, xenophobic – but that isn't the point. And it would be less painful, perhaps, if it were yielding to something more humane, if women really were the inheritors. But they are not. The miners see a money-driven individualism set to rush into the evacuated spaces, just as it has done everywhere else in the world. Survival International should be working here.

Over the village hangs the silvery strato-cumulus of midsummer. The wind ripples the field of unripe barley. The vivid yellow of rapeseed invades the cramped gardens of former pit houses with their empty pigeon pens. High above the village the remains of grey stone farm buildings – dangerous structures, bricked up with breeze blocks by the Council. Empty condom packets tell of sexual encounters not tolerated by the jealous, closed community. The ruined farm on the hilltop, the ruined colliery below: two epochs fallen into decay – country and industry, side by side, and the people trapped between them. No wonder the old man in the threadbare suit who sits on the bench is suffering from dementia: a merciful refuge from a world become incomprehensible.

The long-term effects of unemployment have not yet sunk in. The enhanced redundancy payments gave those working for twenty years almost £20,000. So much cash in hand, spent on home improvements, extensions, carpeting, double-glazing. Phones ring all the time, salespeople helping the ex-miners to part with their money more quickly. For the time being, a new car, a holiday – if it doesn't feel too bad yet, it's because people are still in shock.

A strong sense of something terminal. The men wake up at four o'clock, because their bodies have not yet learned what their minds know – that the boots and helmets and lamps will not be used again. One man's souvenir is a jar of metal alloy discs, each with a number representing a worker. One the worker kept, and its counterpart remained hung on a board above ground, so that in the event of an accident it would be known who was missing, who was lost, who was dead.

On the rose and grey marble war memorial outside the cavernous parish church are engraved the words, 'May their reward equal their sacrifice' – a melancholy epitaph also for the human sacrifices of an undeclared industrial war. Pity the past . . . 'My first wage was 2s 11d. We walked home every night black-bright from the pit . . . My mother took a loan of £10 to take us to Scarborough for a week . . . Premature death. My father died at forty-eight from injuries in the pit . . . You never remembered your grandfather, he was long dead.'

'. . . You feel guilty to the dead and guilty to the future. What is there for the young? Nothing? Rubbish,' say the old men working on their neat gardens, 'they've had it too easy . . .' A generational incomprehension, egged on for profit by a comprehending system that knows big money is to be made out of promoting discord . . . 'They go up to that farm, glue-sniffers, everything. They find tubes of Evastick. Pity they don't find their bodies as well . . .' A resentment of victims by victims. Those whose children are still young fear for their fate: 'I don't want them to finish up stealing, joy-riding, sniffing.'

'. . . Once we had work, now we're lucky to get jobs . . . Cleaning at the bookmaker's – I still wake up at four o'clock' – for £40 a week . . . Caretaker at the school . . . Care assistant in an old people's home for £2.50 an hour . . . Security at £2 . . . Free driving lessons so you can drive away somewhere else to look for work that isn't there.

Role reversals. Women are the breadwinners, although that's about all they do win. Depths of bitterness must be choked back by the men . . . 'My day? I get up and do the washing, hang it on the line, get the kids to school, do some shopping, get the tea for when she gets home . . . The government talks about training, education. What for? We had the skills, and they've gone. Train them to expect less, to do less, to ask for less. That's what it means. They don't know where the fucking jobs are coming from any more than we do . . .'

Anger and bitterness. They cried on the day the pit closed. It was like a death. They remember every detail: 'May 7, 2.20 in the afternoon. I felt gutted. Choked up. I came home and cried to my wife. We wept together. I cuddled my mate, I'm not ashamed . . .' So much bottled up, the tension and hope of the last months. And then the betrayal. Again. Such a story of betrayal. The Labour leadership, the Notts miners, the government, Heseltine. It is an old scenario, written long ago, that they are condemned to play out over and over.

A culture that now has so few sources of renewal. 'It was built on our labour. That was it. We had nothing but our solidarity. Yet it was more than that. You were each other's eyes and ears. I miss them, the men I worked with. It's like they were dead. They've gone their separate ways . . .'

Technological change. Another old story. It used to be called 'progress'. Now we're not so sure. The pit was built in the 1890s, it closed a year or two off its centenary. What a day that would have been . . . 'They performed a ceremony, laid a wreath in the pit yard on the last day. Not for death of the pit, but for all the men who had worked there, those whose lives it had claimed in one way or another.'

In the cemetery, the sun gleams on the headstones, marble angels and crosses, four generations of miners. On the cemetery gate, a notice says: Christmas Wreaths will be Removed from the Cemetery at the End of March. Before next Christmas, one thing is sure: those who lie here will be joined by others.

Mr Hancock (60s): ex-miner

Coronation Avenue, Grimethorpe. A row of 1950s houses overlooking the newly closed pit. Many of the houses are boarded up. They have been bought from British Coal by a property company for £1,000 each, and are now being refurbished and sold off at between £20,000 and £26,000 each.

Mr Hancock's wife died recently of cancer. During her last illness, he took over the job she had been doing – cleaning at a bookmaker's from 5.30 to 7.30 each morning, for £40 a week.

He started work in 1946 at Frickley Colliery. For the first six weeks he worked at the pit-top, and his first wage was 2s 11d a shift.

I was still in short trousers. I left school on the Friday, and by the Monday I was to start in the pit. I'd been up at eight to go to school, and now I had to get ready to jump out of bed at five. I even did a week at Leeds, but that meant getting up at four, and that was too much.

It was pointless going for an apprenticeship outside of mining, because all other jobs were taken up by councillors' sons; they got the apprenticeships on the railways, in joinery or as electricians. They were the teachers, preachers, police. There were no indentured apprenticeships in the pits.

I went with my father. By the time you were twenty-one you were on top wages. It was still classed as semi-skilled. My father had come up from Staffordshire in the 1930s; we never did know why. That side of the family remained a mystery.

After nationalization in 1948, lads were not allowed to go on nights till they were eighteen. But I was on nights at fourteen. If they were heading a face, there'd be three or four lads on the plough, fourteen-, fifteen-year-olds, shovelling coal off. It was bloody graft. Slave labour. We got used to it. I was ripping by the time I was twenty. 'Ripping' means when the coal is taken from the face, rings are set up, six to eight feet, leaving an overhang which had to be strengthened. You get used to it. In fact, you don't think of anything else. That is your life. I was married at twenty-one.

I left the pit in 1963. My wages then were £18 a week; I wore sweat-rags on my wrists and forehead, filling headings out. I left it to go to an engineering company in Sheffield. I'd always been handy with tools, and I got a job as fitter. In my first week I made £21 in four days, next week £50. When I took the money to my wife, she thought I'd robbed a bank. We were doing jobs at power stations. I had a chance to go to Gateshead for £140 a week, on a contract. I was sending her £100. That was the highest wage apart from Pearson's Steam Turbines. We were working on a power station, and the overtime was fiddled. They'd get a contract for so many pounds to pay so many men, and you made out there was more of you than there was. You'd get stuck in and work like the clappers – there'd be eight men instead of fifteen. You didn't fail to complete the work, because you wanted the money.

I left that job and came back to the pit, because the company had been taken over by Green's Engines of Wakefield, and they wanted their own labour. We were made redundant. I could've gone to Sunderland, but Betty wouldn't. If she had we'd've been out of mining for good. But her family was here, she couldn't go.

[By 1968] . . . mining had changed a bit. It's like riding a bike, you go back to it as though you'd done it only yesterday. I had a good job at Frickley, which was a little pit, a family pit. You were supposed to be trained if you'd been out of the industry more than twelve months, but I was told I could just start Monday. I was ripping on a two-man gate. It was a doddle-job, top-rate money, home early.

The pit takes its toll of everybody in one way or another. I never had a bad accident, but I have back trouble. Most do – it's lifting things too heavy for you – because they had no cranes then. It really is hard. A lot of men have hernias that don't get treated. They suffer with their back and working in water which is freezing, even in summer; you soon get rheumatism, arthritis. It's a way of life. It's not a job like a postman or a market trader. You can tell a man that's never been down a pit; me and the lads, we'd talk about the pit, aspects of pit life . . . you can soon tell anyone who is not familiar with it.

You get used to it. It's like climbing a mountain – it's what you do because it's there. You get up for work and go out thinking, What a beautiful day, must I do this? – then you get changed and you're with your mates, you're joking with them. The time used to fly at work – get with your mates in a team, help one another. Go home, have a bath and supper, then out for a couple of pints. There's great humour down the pit. A lot of stories. Jimmy Lancs – he's a lad from Lancashire – has this dog, and it's old and he's having it destroyed. He meets his mate in the street, and he says, 'Where's that going?' 'Have the dog destroyed.' 'Is he mad?' 'Well he's not very pleased.' This man goes to the doctor's, he says, 'My knee's hurting me.' 'Which one?' 'Left one.' 'It's old age.' 'Well the other one doesn't hurt and it's the same age as this one.'

There is a lot of racism among miners. There was a miner in the pub on about Pakis doing our lads out of work. He'd taken his redundancy money, and his wife was doing two jobs. They don't see that the blacks took all the low-paid jobs. They've never worked in the pits. No Asian or black has ever taken a job off us.

In the sixties a lot of men left to go in the car factories. It's always been a close community. During the '84–'85 strike, we stayed solid. That is to say, out of the eighteen hundred employed here at the time, there was a solid core of three hundred; and that determined the feeling of Grimethorpe.

A lot of women left their husbands as a result of the strike. We had a hard time, but nobody lost their house through it. Some women egged their husbands to go back. In Grimethorpe only eleven went through the picket line. Since it closed, 80 per cent of miners don't have a job. A lot of people are sick. Of course they are. It's been a blow to pride. Lack of work kills people. One mate of mine, he'd never had a shift off. Six months on strike, he went to the doctor's – it was his heart. After the strike, he was told he'd never work again. Betty said to me, 'He's ill.' He had a heart operation, and before he went into hospital he said he would die. And he did. A lot of men die of heart attacks, not when they're working, but when they stop. One man was sitting in the back garden with his wife. She went in to make a cup of tea, and when she brought it out to him he was dead. And he'd never had a day's illness in his life.

The Labour Party betrayed us in the strike; only the grass roots stayed with us. When I started in 1946, there were 3,500 working here. It was called the pit with the golden pulleys.

There has been a weakening of solidarity in the village. A lot of people don't even vote. They grumble in the pub, but don't do owt. The trouble is

144

the working class don't want to be told things by the working class. If they're told it by somebody with a cut-glass accent they'll listen.

I'm used to getting up early, and I still do. I've a thousand jobs to do, I'll find work that wants doing. Even when I was separated, she would come down and look at the house and say, 'This wants doing, that wants doing', and I'd do it. Now I put it off. I have an allotment with my son. I've the garden to do, decorating the house.

I took redundancy. I'd had asthma, and I went to the doctor, and he advised me to pack up. I felt as though my life had come to a close. I'd been put out to pasture. I still get free coal tonnage; those who stopped over fifty years old get it, those under fifty don't. They can't even do coal-picking any more. They've been chased off; they got prosecuted for taking a few lumps of coal.

The Coalite works which is next door to the pit is still going; but even they have made some people redundant. Coalite uses what was formerly waste product from the mines. In fact, they used to buy up quarries to bury the stuff. Now they're opening the quarries again to dig it out. Coalite produces tar, and chemicals. It makes toluene, which is a solvent, a weedkiller. It was actually the base of Agent Orange that was used in Vietnam, supplied by Coalite, 245-T. In fact, nobody quite knows what dangers there are in it. There have been a lot of sicknesses attributed to Coalite – heart, asthma, cancer – there's a lot of bowel cancer in this area, some attribute it to the carbonizing plant. Coalite produces oils and tars that go to the perfume industry; they distil it to such a degree of refinement that one barrelful is worth hundreds of thousands of pounds.

When I first started we were ripping all by hand – later they had ripping machines. Work got easier through not shovelling, but there were more girders and moorings to be put up; so although you produced more coal, the work didn't get easier. They took the shovel off you, but machinery and supports were heavy to handle, so you were kept at the same intense level of work. It took four men to lift the girders . . . In a rip, there'd be five men; on a face, twelve or more. On a full face, there was a team of twenty men, at either end of the face. Each could do the other's job. You had to work together. Then I was on a heading machine which had cost £200,000. Of course, it's safer now. I wouldn't mind my grandchildren doing it now; but then it's gone. Just as it's getting reasonably safe, it's finished.

The safety rules were broken by the men themselves, because they wanted the money. Then as soon as someone was hurt, they jumped on you. Until then, they closed their eyes to it. Lies were made up at accidents so it didn't look as if rules were being breached. But Grimey had a good safety record.

They're dismantling the pit now. Contractors are dragging the gate out. They're asset-stripping. A lot of the miners are working with the contractors, helping to demolish what gave them their livelihood. They can't help it, they have no choice.

There are thirteen square miles of land owned by the pit. At one time, everybody had allotments, but now that houses have bigger gardens they don't use them so much. Pit villages traditionally had no gardens, so they had allotments to eke out the wages with their own produce.

Women always worked round here – in the mills in Barnsley, also at the pit-top. They now do cleaning jobs. They can be paid as little at £1.87 an hour at Barnsley. There's security work: Group Four are offering £2.25 an hour for a twelve-hour shift at the pit.

There are no apprenticeships now. I don't know what the young will do. There's only training, bricklaying, welding; but there's no jobs in building either.

My father went to Luton in 1933-4, before he came here. He worked for Skifco Ballbearings, for £1 a week. Miners always used to travel around. They used to be like gypsies. You could move easily at that time. You could move into a house at another pit for a few pence a shift more. A lot moved to escape debts. It's only recently that mining communities became more settled – since nationalization. Till then we were industrial nomads.

Ken Hancock (*40s*): *NUM branch delegate*

I left school at fifteen in 1968. I left on the Friday, signed on for work on the Saturday and I was working at the pit on the Monday. There were nowt special about that, that's what happened to everybody.

Pit were only three hundred yards from where I lived, so I was actually working in my own back yard. For the first couple of years, you're basically just training on surface jobs – filling tubs with wood, being a bath attendant and so forth – it's just getting you into the ethic of being at work. The first day at work, you feel you've become a man. You grow three inches, all the way round. And you know all the people at work from growing up. I've just been made redundant with kids I started in junior school with. You've known each other for forty years, you've had forty years of each other's company, or displeasure . . .

And that's the whole argument of a mining community, because they are so different, so unique. Nearest thing I can equate it to is the fishing industries, where they also had to depend on each other, fathers, sons and brothers.

I remember my first job were in the powder-filling magazine. That was where they used to fire the shots to drill and bore underground. We used to have to fill small cartridges of wax paper, about two inches across, six inches long, with dry sand. It were really dusty. I were in that about three month, and I couldn't believe how boring a job could be. So eventually, us fifteen-year-old lads, though we thought we were grown up, we got into the normal ways of throwing them at each other, and we finished up with sand fights.

When I got to be sixteen, I managed to get an apprenticeship – I were an apprentice fitter. That didn't last long. After about eighteen months, there was an altercation with the training officer about a micrometer that had gone missing. We all knew who had thieved it, but we weren't prepared to say. We sorted things out our own way. So I got sent back to the pit from the training school, and I went on to coalface training. Rest of my life I've been a face worker, on three shifts. Never knew nowt else till I got Branch Delegate job just after the strike.

It were a hard life, and I feel ancient now when I talk to some younger men who have only ever been on retreat mining, because we were on the advance mining system. Advance mining was considerably harder, because you have main-gate ripping and tail-gate ripping. That was basically my job underground. I was always a tail-gate ripper. Underground, it's dusty, it's wet and it smells. It smells of hot machine oil, and everybody's excrement, you get that. And just that damp, horrible smell. You know, you go into an old house, a derelict house, and you've got that musty damp smell. All your pit clothes smell of that damp.

Basically it was a dirty, filthy job, and bloody hard. The thing about it is, you're not working in bad conditions with a bit of height. You're working in cramped, crouched conditions, where you've got to try and get yourself in all sorts of positions in order to pull and push. It can be damned awkward. But that's what mining's all about.

I've no regrets that I worked down the pit, but I wouldn't want my son to go underground. I wouldn't want him to because of the filth, the muck, the danger. You don't see many old miners. And there's not many young, fit miners either. After twenty years, you're developing your aches and your creaks. Everybody I know round here has got a bad chest, and on pension day – well, it's a big hill in the village, but there's not many of them can clear it. They're not in a fit state when they come to retire.

But we fought to keep the mines open because in a mining community such as this is, there's no other form of employment. I would go back underground tomorrow if I could. It nearly broke my heart, closing the pit. Because I am a miner, although I haven't got a job to go to. And I know this country needs coal, it doesn't need cheap foreign crap. Mining's my life. It's my livelihood. Why do people go out to sea? Why do steeplejacks go to the top of buildings?

I don't suppose anybody wants their kids to go sweeping the streets. But if it's employment, if it's keeping a roof over their heads so that kid can keep his family, then they have to do it. We can't all have glamorous jobs. It's all this village has known.

What people have got to understand is that everything depended on the pit. We had communities, where the union and the Coal Board provided the schools, the hospices – they provided for the general welfare of people, they provided the entertainment at the Welfare Club, and parks, football facilities, cricket. That were your community. There were good benefits, from the cradle to the grave. When you were born, there were grants, even back in the 1920s, and it continued through all your life. Like these houses, we got our house because I were a miner. I paid my rent to British Coal. They were fairly subsidized houses – not over-subsidized – but subsidized. There's your fuel from the pit. So basically, you've not got much more to find.

Of course things have changed. People are more intent now on wanting to go abroad for their holidays, and they want to go to these nice theme pubs and theme parks instead of going to the Welfare. But you can't alter that, you can't alter people from changing. People have got to develop, and things are always different.

I've always enjoyed being a miner. I'm not saying I particularly enjoyed it on a Monday morning, when I'd been out on a Sunday night and I had to get up at five for work at six. But overall, I enjoyed it. Basically, what I enjoyed was the comradeship. I was working with men I'd always known. You had to watch for each other's backs. There were no petty squabbles, you couldn't afford to have petty squabbles. If you'd had a hell of a bust-up the night before with somebody, you couldn't afford to take that underground. Because you were too busy watching for your own safety, and watching for your mate's safety. And miners have a terrible humour. When someone was injured, first thing you'd do was have a joke, and get them laughing – daft as it seems.

It's a man's world. There's no use trying to get round it, it's a bloody macho, sexist world. But people have to understand why that is. You work hard and you play hard. With that comes hard people with hard humour. I don't think miners are any different from other people. It's just that we're enclaved somewhat in a mining community.

When I was getting more involved in the union, the undermanager at the time was cajoling me, saying I would make a good deputy – I'd only be twenty-three or twenty-four at the time. He said, 'Within twelve months you could be an over-man, and then you could go for your undermanager's ticket.' And I said, 'Oh yes, but I suppose when I've stopped with my union activity and gone to be a deputy, that's where my career will stop for the rest of my life. Basically, what you want to do is get rid of me, away from the men, and keep me quiet.' Anybody who knows me will tell you I've never been quiet as such, certainly not in the political environment. So needless to say, I stopped where I was, and got some of the men to put me up for Branch Committee.

The miners' strike, it were wonderful – daft as it sounds. It were £15.33 pence a week to start with, then it dropped, because the government deemed we'd already had £15 strike pay. I mean, our union couldn't afford to pay £15 strike pay. What a year to go on strike – best summer we'd ever had. Everything was dead ripe for the Coal Board. In retrospect, it were probably the worst time ever to go on strike. But then, we didn't pick the battleground, and we didn't pick the time. They said they were closing our collieries, and we reacted against that threat.

I thought we were going to win. In fact, eight months into the strike, I think we had won. But the Tories at that time, they got to a position where they weren't going to let us win. They would have bankrupted this country before they'd've let the miners win. They always saw the miners as a threat. It might sound a bit conceited, being a miner, but I've always seen the miners as the vanguard of the trade union movement. Owt that's ever happened, we've been there, we've been involved.

I've been involved with print workers, ambulance drivers, the seamen's strike, hospitals, teachers, railways – you name it. If they came down to Grimethorpe and put a picket on here, and asked for our support, we didn't go to work. Because the trade union edict is that you don't cross picket lines. That's the be-all and end-all. We've put more wealth into this country than any fat-arsed Tory bastard has ever done in his life. And then they train their police to subdue us. And there's nowt changed since the 1700s or the 1800s. As far as some of them are concerned, it's still master and serf.

What they've done to the coal-miners over the last ten months is barbaric. It cannot be justified in any economic, or moral, or logical sense whatsoever. They've paid no thought to individuals and to their families. They've got such bitterness against us, and then they don't expect us to be bitter. They've no thought for our communities – not just mining communities, it's not just our jobs, it's a domino effect. The railway workers – there'll be no coal to load; the coal power station, the one over at Doncaster, they've just announced the closure of that. There's other affected organizations – I understand Plessey are making redundancies down South, because they're not selling the computer equipment into the mines. They've done it in such a barbaric way. It's so different from in Germany, where they've built factories and provided new jobs. But they haven't done that. They've closed down whole villages.

What people have got to bear in mind is that it's not just now it's happening. There were a pit closed three weeks ago, there were a pit prior to that six month ago, and in a nine-mile radius from here I know of twenty-three pits that's closed. Now they were all mining communities, and the infrastructure of mining communities is that there's no good roads to them. No one's going to come and build a factory in Grimethorpe.

I think the spirit of the village will die. In ten years if you come back, there'll be a lot more empty houses, or boarded-up houses, and them that's not boarded up will be owned by these housing associations. People are moving out, people are going to try and get out one way or another, though I don't know what prospects of work there are. There's nowt. I can't think of anywhere. Even now there's people travelling twenty or thirty miles. And they're not long-term jobs, just six-month contracts. The vast majority of the men that have gone out have gone back with mining contractors. I know some lads that have gone to Easington in the North-East – you're talking 100, 120 miles a day. Now what they're having to do is to stop up there five days and come home at weekend. Inevitably that leads to families breaking up, because people are not used to commuting. You go to work, you come home.

. . I think you'll see the businesses start closing up, like your small shops on the High Street. Every shop that's closed and boarded up now has only done so since the '84–'85 strike. Before that there was never an empty shop, and the money used to circulate in the community. Now it's not going to be there. It's bleak, the future's bleak.

This country's going to be one massive theme park. You can either be hot-dog sellers or taxi-drivers. It's a terrible prospect, but I can't see anything more realistic being done.

What's happened in this country is that you've lost your industrial baselands. You've lost your steelworks, your dock labour schemes – you've even lost your docks and your shipbuilding. You've come away from industrial workers to white-collar workers. Now that's not saying that white-collar workers are less militant or less unionized, but inevitably, they don't live in communities. Shipyards were shipyard communities, steelworks were steel communities – Sheffield, Rotherham. Now you haven't got them any more, ever since you started closing everything down.

So people tend to move inwards. That's what I've found for a lot of years. If you can't find nowt to attack, and you get so fed up, and sick, and tired. So people have inevitably moved on to other jobs. They see themselves as being a bit more secure. They see themselves as not being a dock labourer – 'I'm now an insurance clerk' – or not a miner – 'I drive a taxi, I'm self employed.' People have turned inwards, and they've started blaming. But they don't blame the Tories for everything that went wrong – they blame the Labour Party, and they blame the unions.

It's a dirty word, 'working-class'. Partly because under the Tory government, young people haven't had any experience of work. If they haven't had parents who've been involved in the industrial working classes, they think it's archaic. I went down to speak at the LSE about six months ago. One silly young bugger with a very nice accent said, 'You don't look like a miner. You've got no tattoos.' So I said, 'You've got to remember it's 1993, and we up in Yorkshire, in these islands, we live in the real world too. We like nice cars, we like nice homes, some of us possess televisions, and we've even got to microwaves.'

People are ashamed of being working-class. I don't know what's so dirty about it. I accept there's upper-class twits, so they can accept that there's lower-class twats. I'm working-class. I've worked for my living, my Dad worked for a living, my grandfather worked for a living. I'm not ashamed I've got a Yorkshire accent, and I'm not ashamed that I were a collier, so why should I have to hide the fact that I'm proud to be working-class?

What's happened to the younger generation is that the Tories have never allowed them to have work. The Tory philosophy is that you look after Number One, and in the great enterprise boom of the 1980s they were told, 'Go out and get your own jobs, go out and get your own homes.' I know decent lads and lassies who got married that have sold their houses in this village because they wanted to live on a nice estate. But your environment is what you make it anyway. If the Queen started putting scrap cars in front of Buckingham Palace, it would be just like any gypsy encampment.

The Tory government policy that people look after Number One has got through to a generation that has never known nowt else. It's been shoved into them that that's the way forward. It's as simple as that.

Gail Hancock (*30s*): *pub cleaner*

I'm just a cleaner at the local pub at the end of the street. It's a little job I got when my little girl started nursery. I had worked before, I'd worked as a barmaid previous to the strike.

I get up at half past seven and get Matthew up for school. He goes off at eight, and then I've got Charlotte, who's six. I feed her and prepare her for school. Basically, we pile everything into the sink ready for when I come home, there's not much time. I'm not an organized person of a morning – in fact I'm not a morning person at all.

I work three days a week. I work with my friend down the street, so I have company. But basically I'm on my own. It's just two hours' cleaning – I can do it on remote control now, you just go round automatically. I put my music on, just go round and wash my tables, and mop the floor, and occasionally have a moan or two to myself if they've thrown the stuff all over, or what have you.

Half past eleven, back home, quick bacon butty, cup of tea, and then the usual cleaning round, as normal housewives do, picking up after my son. Then that's it till about half past three or four, when Ken appears or the kids come home from school. Pretty normal. Just come home and plan what the lunch is, get as much done as I can before the kids come home, and then start again when they've had their tea, because it never looks no different. Housework seems like a worthless job. You're constantly doing the same thing. Its mundane, but it's life, isn't it?

It's not particularly hard work at the pub, unless they've had a good celebration. It's a grotty job from that aspect, but I've adapted to that now. It's a sort of everyday thing. It's not a particular job I'd choose to do, but it were convenient. It's my own money, it's my independence if you like. I know it sounds ridiculous when you talk about cleaning pubs and what have you, but it were my little strike against Ken. Because he'd always left it so I couldn't find no alternative but a few hours' work in the morning, when the kids weren't here. He just came home one night and I announced I'd got a job at the end of the street. 'You haven't . . . You're not . . .'

But basically I've never had a very interesting job. When I left school I went into the sewing factories in Barnsley, but I got bored with that. Then I worked as a waitress for a season down Torquay – chambermaiding, waitressing, bar work – and then came back to the sewing factories, which was very very hard, to go back from having a split-time job like that, and it sort of being fun, to coming back to the monotony of being fastened up when the sun were out, and you were in this factory eight while five. But I knew if I did it again I'd never come back inland, I'd spend all my time wandering round the coasts, and that weren't on.

It were real good fun. I grew up when I was away. My Mum's very parochial, and I live further away than any other of my three sisters. It were looked on that I were abandoning the family, because I wanted to go off and be independent . . . I was seventeen, it gave me a yearning . . . I'm a frustrated seaside landlady. [Laughs.] I'd still like to have a start at it. I worked at it for twelve months, and we did everything. I felt I'd got the know-how. I thought when I came back, I could do that. I could make a good crack at it. And then again, with the bar work, I can smile at people when really I want to say, 'Go home.' You know, put a face on.

If you don't go out to work, you tend to sit in, and then your conversation when you do go out is all about kiddies. I never thought I'd miss work when I were having Matthew, but then I found that I were waiting for Ken to come in. He were on three shifts at the time, and when he'd been on afters and were coming home for his dinner, he just wanted to have his dinner, read a paper, have a cup of tea, and then he were ready for me. But by the time he were coming home on afters at eight o'clock at night, I were really raring to go, I wanted somebody to talk to. And it were a little relief, going to work behind a bar. I think you need a break. I think it's important to be at home for the kids. But on the other hand, it's important for you to do sommat, and have that little bit of independence. Even if it's just pub-cleaning, it's there, I'm out. Even if I'm on my own, I get to know the gossip when the regulars start coming in as I'm going out.

When Ken got involved in the union, it were not just his choice – it were out of his hands. Them old union men had their eye on him. They knew they were coming to the end of their time, and they were moulding Ken to move in – because Ken didn't need the union, he knew his rules anyway, because his mother were a trade unionist and he were like-minded. Before he went and complained, he knew what he was talking about. He were the prime candidate. The ex-Branch Secretary said to me, 'I've trained him to be the Secretary, he can do that job.' But Ken had a choice of two positions to go for, and he went for the Delegate's job. They used to call Ken 'the fearless fighter'.

I'm not having it that any mother wants her son to work down the mine, even with today's technology. And if we'd been living in years gone by, I certainly wouldn't have wanted him underground. But even with these new conditions, there are terrible things. A young chap at twenty-seven, all them injuries he got . . . I know you've got that in factories, but it's just not on the cards at all for Matthew, as far as I'm concerned. We've geared Matthew to going to college, and with this redundancy happening it's given us a blow, because even when they're going to college and university you have to have funding to back them.

Matthew's twelve now. He knows he's working-class. I believe if he were asked, he would know that . . . We gear him up to not leaving school and rushing on to the dole queue, to further his education, and to look for higher things, and on the same hand, we do say to him, 'Don't forget your roots.' We shove him up, but to work for the benefit . . . I'd love him to be a solicitor and earn stacks of money, but I wouldn't want him to be a solicitor that only works for money. I think he knows.

Kevin (*late 30s*): *ex-miner*

A comfortably untidy house on the edge of the estate of former Coal Board houses; wild grass in the front, back yard with Alsatian dog. In the living-room, on the wall, a painting of a vast swan cradling a naked man in the fold of its wing, and a naked woman in the foreground, on a terrace. Kevin is a burly figure, with fair hair, and an apparent sedateness that belies an inner turbulence.

I started work at fifteen, but not in the colliery. My father promised that no son of his would work in the pit. Many fathers said that, because they had seen so many mining injuries that they dreaded their son might go through the same thing. The pit killed my father, through injuries and illness. He was just forty-eight when he died.

I had a job in Barnsley, labouring in a plastics factory. I stayed there seven years. I had the chance to leave Barnsley, but I'd tasted working life, drinking pints with my mates, and I enjoyed it. I couldn't wrench myself away. I went in a year from a raw fifteen-year-old to top-level chargehand – just below management.

Just before I got married, I was discussing the wedding arrangements with my father, when he died in my arms.

After he died, I got a job in the pit anyway. It looked like a job for life. I had a medical and passed for underground. I took redundancy from where I was working in 1980, and got £192. Just as I was about to start at the pit, there was a pay dispute, and they decided they were taking no new recruits. The pit's books were closed until the dispute was over. I went to the Coalite company next door as a stop-gap. Then to Grimey, where I spent four years underground. After that, a year on strike. Three months after the strike I had an accident. I was in hospital eighteen weeks. It was an underground haulage accident. I was dragged with an illegal coupling in a tram – a belt-sling on the underside of the tram, I got caught in it. I was on crutches for twelve months. I had keyhole surgery three times, and later, a plastic kneecap. The accident was in July 1985. After that, I worked on the surface. I never had a good wage; even underground, haulage pay, it wasn't much with a wife and three children. I had to take out a second mortgage.

I got 75 per cent compensation. People think you have a lot of money if you get compensation, as though you're lucky to be injured, and they get jealous. It was always my ambition to earn £10,000 in a year. I did; and the year after, £11,200. But with a family of six that wasn't brilliant. For the last tax year, it fell below £10,000.

... I invested £9,000 [compensation money], and it was a bad investment. I took advice from a financial consultant ... I spent £10,000 in six weeks. If I've got it I'll spend it. I believe that my family should live good. My lifestyle is not through earnings, but through injury; I claimed against future loss of earnings. As well as that I qualify for about £20,000 redundancy pay. I'll buy a camcorder, a new microwave, a fast-text Japanese TV. I manage on what I'm getting, together with a bit out of the bank. I don't want cars and luxury holidays. I'm cautious. People will bilk off you if you let them.

I've applied for several jobs. Some firms are not setting on redundant miners because they want to give jobs to those who've never worked. I can't drive, I'm unskilled and disabled. I can get some training from British Coal, auditing and computing, if I get a letter from a firm offering me a job afterwards. They don't actually have to give me a job, they just need to say they intend to. I've been on the finance committee of the Working Men's Club, and I've done voluntary work with the children's fund and club.

I can foresee difficult times for the family, for the district, for the whole country. It scares me, what this government has done to people's lives here. I feel for the kids. There's no order in the village now, the kids are roaming around, fifteen-year-olds, doing nowt. They're on some ET scheme – I call it Extra-Tenner scheme, because that's what they get. It's no life for them.

I'm sick myself. I have depression. I can't sleep at night. I sit up watching TV all night, go to bed at two o'clock, then I'm awake at five, just as I was when I was working.

My wife got a job four months ago after two redundancies. It was temporary at first, but now she's been made permanent – in the clothing industry. The only jobs now are for women and girls, ironing and sewing in the garment industry.

My day. I start in the morning, get the kids to school. Then down to Kwiksave to do some shopping. After that, buy a paper and come home. Then I pick up the cricket or the news on TV. Then I do some baskets of washing, prepare the kids' dinner for twelve o'clock. They used to take packed lunches, but they like to come home. Take advantage of my good cooking. Then I dry the clothes, help my daughter with her little girl. She's just moved into a house of her own. All she has is a toaster and a three-piece suite, so she needs a lot of help. I wash and dry the baby clothes in the tumble-drier. My mates ask me to come out for a pint – I say I can't, I have to do the washing. I can find plenty to do. When my daughter is settled in her new house, maybe it'll be easier. I'll do some do-it-yourself around the house. Re-carpeting, painting. I'm crap at it; but like they say, you've got to shag with the tool you've got.

I find housework demoralizing. I can do it, I always could, because my father had many illnesses and injuries; I'm used to it. My mother used to work as far away as York when I was a kid; she'd be out of the house from six in the morning till six at night, so I learned. Sometimes I feel I'm on holiday from work. I go up and down. This is what the government has done to people.

We're sat above sixty-three million tons of coal, enough for my lifetime and my lad's lifetime. Closing the pits has nothing to do with economics, it's retribution for 1984. We are the last pit in the Barnsley area. The pit made £7 million profit in two and a half years; only 30 per cent went to the power station, the rest to Monkton coking plant, Coalite, high-grade coal, some to Blue Circle Cement. We have the potential for a market other than the power stations. But British Coal are stripping bare the pit underground. It would need £60 million to replace what they're taking out of there. A private investor could make it work, but they won't do it. We clung to the hope that we'd finish on the Friday and then start again with a new owner on the Monday. It is a productive and profitable pit. That would make sense. It is depressing, seeing the waste of a national resource. That 'dash for gas' doesn't make sense. Once closed, it'll be too expensive to sink new shafts. I spent an unlucky thirteen years in Grimey.

We tried to keep the pit open. We came up with some good ideas for Grimey; we hit on every cost-saving idea. But it didn't mean a thing because British Coal manager is on forty grand a year – is he going to take any notice of some crippled bastard on the pit-top?

It was almost our centenary. Nearly a hundred years of profitability. I'm very proud of what I've done. I'm patriotic. I'm proud to be a miner . . . wherever I go I talk to people. I say to them, 'I'm a miner.' People say, 'Oh you must be on about £400 a week.' I used to carry my wage slip with me. Once Barnsley was playing at Wimbledon, a snotty-nosed lot down there. I went into a pub. They thought I was on at least £250 a week. I showed them – for forty hours I earned £86 that week.

Being a miner, it's part of your life. Like being a farmer, a fisherman, an oil-rig worker. You have your own kind of life. It's our environment. It's bred into us. We don't know any different.

It's all very hard work in the mine. Some is less hard than others, but equally important. There are jobs on the face which other people wouldn't do for a million pounds a year, where you strip to your underpants, wearing knee-pads, with the heat and the dust, and coal spewing all around you. Those who do that job ought to be at the top of the tree as far as rewards are concerned. Between 1973 and '75, miners were the best-paid workers in the country. Now they are forty-fifth in the pay league.

The conditions are horrific. Every day. There are no toilets, you just pull your pants down and drop your guts where you can. You can't wash your hands at snap-time – you spit on them to clean them, wipe them on your vest. You have to eat with filthy hands. The coalface may be two or three miles from the pit bottom. The last seam I worked was three thousand metres because there were no man-riding paddies. But you were happy to be doing what you were doing. People from the South wouldn't last five minutes. I've seen visitors, they've been horrified by the conditions just for a visit, let alone all the time. Even so, it's brilliant now compared to fifty years ago.

When I first started, I kept hitting my head on the rings; you soon learn. When I was a kid, there were bad accidents underground. They brought the people out black-bright and injured. In the sixties, some paddy ropes broke, and there were bad injuries. It was part of life in the pit community. As a kid I saw my father working on the pit-top in the slurry ponds; driving a JVC, a noisy machine like a fairground engine – the noise was deafening. I would have liked to be able to take my lad down the pit to look around, so he understood; but that can't happen now.

Now it's gone, it wouldn't matter if they levelled Grimethorpe. It'll never be the same. I feel like the community has had its arms and legs cut off. We all stuck together during the miners' strike. They were the greatest twelve months of my life. You were fighting for your beliefs, for your community. It wasn't a question of self-indulgence, it wasn't greed or avarice. We were fighting for our lads' jobs, to keep the community together.

I think this money, £300 million, that is supposed to be invested in the area to generate new work is just a propaganda exercise. They have a job shop in the pityard – we call it joke shop, because that's what it is. What's the use, training people to be brickies when there's no building going on? All this money that is going into redundancy pay, sick pay, invalidity benefit, dole – it could all have been put into a pit subsidy. After nationalization, three thousand worked there. There wasn't the same desperation to make profit. Nobody will ever know what a shame it has all been.

My father's people all came from Grimethorpe. My grandfather had come from Cleveland. There are fourteen brothers and sisters. Most live on the old estate – it's problem-torn now, with lots of problem families from other areas being moved in. They're not Grimeys. Grimeys don't turn bad. We stuck together. There has been a loss of solidarity nationally. There is a North–South divide as well. I'd rather be on this side of it. There is a lot to divide people now. There's four new houses at the bottom of this road. A miner bought one two years ago for £43,000. The price has now dropped to £29,000, so there's people living next door who paid £14,000 difference.

I bought this house for £2,625 in 1980; the electric bills were higher than the mortgage. They were pit houses. It's worth about £25,000 now. I don't want to leave it though. I wouldn't leave Barnsley. In thirteen years I've only missed half a dozen home matches, and about twenty away matches. I was Barnsley Supporters' Club Supporter of the Year for two years running, and then I lost it the third year to my son. I'm proud of Grimey, of Barnsley, of England. I've two ambitions – to see Barnsley at Wembley and to see it join the Premier League. I'll never forget my roots.

You feel you had something to offer. It seems now we have no choice but to sit back and waste the years away. My father wanted me to have something he didn't have. But what he had was good – the miners were close-knit. They could hurt you though. They can be cruel. There is a one-upmanship, fun and games that could reduce an outsider to tears. Like once, there was this miner whose wife had run away with the milkman. Somebody made an announcement over the underground Tannoy system: 'How many pints today?' They were quite hard: you trap your hand under a girder – if you squeal, they'll say, 'Oh shut up.' But then, when there was a serious accident or death, they organized collections, they had charity concerts. When it came down to it, people stuck together.

Management are also losing jobs now. I think they could've done more for us. We fought and fought, and now I think we've had the fight kicked out of us. And you can't understand why. The whole Barnsley coalfield must contain 250 million tons of coal. It's so saddening. It's like being in another world. People are making decisions at your expense; you feel you can do nothing to influence it.

Last October, when there was such a wave of public sympathy for the miners, we should have had every union out on strike. People were really on our side; we didn't capitalize on it enough.

I'm not militant, I'm not a Communist, but Scargill has been the finest union leader in the world. All he said in 1984 was branded as poppycock. Yet everything he said has come true, and more besides. I'm sorry about those who didn't support him, who thought he was exaggerating. They don't know what they've done. They've ruined the mining communities, they've ruined the unions. We took a ballot in 1980 which agreed to strike if there was any threat to the community; not just a work-based undertaking, but which understood that the community and the work were the same thing.

I was always brought up never, never to cross a picket line. Thatcher did for the unions by threatening the leaders and their funds – that effectively took away the rights of the unions.

What the police did to us during the strike for twelve months, I would never have believed it could happen in this country. If the strike had not been called off when it was, it would have been like Northern Ireland in the coalfields. Violence creates violence, and we were on the receiving end of a great deal of it. The local police didn't want to get involved. So they shipped in the big boys, who are rougher, especially the Met and West Mercia. They thrived on violence, coppers with steel-capped boots who never hesitated to put them in. I was a big activist in the strike. At that time there were five of us in the family. My wife got the family allowance, I had £24 a week from the DHSS, even though, technically, I was entitled to £39 a week. We were 'deemed' by the DHSS to be getting £15 a week strike pay, so they deducted it.

I was arrested at Orgreave. The lorries were due to arrive at nine, and there were thousands of pickets. There were snatch squads of police standing by to make indiscriminate arrests; they were in effect taking prisoners. There was a line of police and behind them, horses; and behind them, another line of coppers. The pickets shoved and were repelled, it was a kind of battle of the giants. We took them by surprise once or twice. We gave another shove, and I said to the men, 'Take note of the coppers at the back of the horses. If they come, grab them, rough them up enough to get them out.'

From behind somewhere, somebody threw a brick – one of the Militant or SWP members, not a pitman. Then the snatch squad moved. I said, 'Get ready lads'. The line opened up in front of me and I was left alone. The snatch squad got me. I was frog-marched across the road. I thought, I can see what's going to happen – I thought they would throw me down the bank. They took me up, and I tripped a copper up on the way. He dragged me down with him. I thought I was winning. But at the bottom there were about thirty of them waiting. They dragged me off to the portable nick. But there were some cameramen then – I was splashed all over TV. I had been arrested with my hands in my pocket. I admit I'd done illegal things during the strike, but on that day, nothing.

The evidence in court was unbelievable. One copper said I had been arrested from the front, just as I was about to throw a stone; two others said I was arrested from the side as I was about to throw an earth clod. When I went to court, I knew my fate because I'd heard the previous cases. I knew I had no chance. Even so, I tore their evidence to pieces. I spoke precisely, and told exactly what happened, whereas they had been rambling and couldn't tell the truth. My witnesses corroborated everything. The magistrate said, 'We've heard evidence from the defendant, the police did not corroborate their own evidence. The witnesses were of previous good character, but they have let themselves down in court today by lying. I find you guilty.' I was gutted. I couldn't believe it.

We announced an appeal, which was due to be heard at Doncaster. But when I heard who the judge was to be, I recognized him as an indiscriminate gaoler. He was locking up everybody in sight. I dropped the appeal and was fined £250. I was getting £24 a week, and they demanded I pay £10 a week.

I respected the police before the strike, but in the end I finished up hating the system. I have so much hate for those who have damaged working people. I'm bitter, I'm angry. I'm very disappointed. I really feel for the kids' future. My daughter – that's her picture on there – wanted to do modelling. We made a portfolio of her pictures, but she got pregnant at sixteen . . . Her fellow has no work. My first was born out of wedlock, but at least I had a job then.

It's bad enough at thirty-five to feel you'll never work again, but for the kids it's worse. You can see what'll happen to a lot of the youngsters. I don't want to see them finish up stealing, joy-riding. I like to think I've brought my kids up properly. I've given them what I can; they've had holidays, any trip going at school, because I was let down so many times when I was a kid. My Dad once took a £10 loan to take us to Scarborough for a week.

I stopped till the end of Grimey. I'll never forget the last day. Two-twenty p.m. on 7th May. I closed the door, went to see Personnel. I felt gutted, choked up. He said, 'Bad time isn't it . . .' I've spoken on TV, melted one or two hearts, because I'm a basic sort of kid, I can say it like it is. I signed my job away. I took voluntary redundancy, except that it was compulsory. There's nothing voluntary about it. When I did it, I was shaking . . . It was like when my father died in my arms . . . How can I describe it? – it's like having one of your kids on a life-support machine, and having to switch it off.

On the last day, my wife came with the youngest to meet me from the pit. I became more emotional, my wife gave me a cuddle. The women at the women's pit camp gave a cheer as we went out. Then I went and got drunk. That Sunday night I was on duty at the Club. I came home after a few pints, and I got my work clothes ready for Monday morning. I was looking for my pit-boots, I picked them up; then suddenly realized what I was doing. I threw them down and wept uncontrollably. And I've been like it since.

I'm up and down. I get very depressed, then cheer up a bit. I went to the doctor for a self-certification note. He said it's affecting everyone. Some people who've got jobs, other people who are happy-go-lucky types, they can take it; they see a couple of years' enjoyment with the money, then they'll think about it later. The doctor gave me these tablets. They didn't work. He gave me some more. Then another lot. You're not supposed to take them with alcohol. I have a few lagers; I still can't sleep. I have this tension, then these fits of weeping, shaking. The important thing is to keep yourself occupied. It isn't the money – that can't save you.

We had pride in our work, we made a contribution to the world, we had a place, a proper purpose. Gone. Now I'm a housewife.

The job shop is useless. I've no skills, I can't drive. Caretaker at school. Care assistant in old people's home, wiping their arses at £2.50 an hour. They've employed counsellors at the pit to advise you. It's just PR, to show they care. It's just a waste of money, propaganda.

I had my moment of glory on headline news, the day I was arrested at Orgreave ... The kids were here and they saw me. They ran into the kitchen where my wife was getting dinner ready and said, 'Mummy, Daddy's on TV.' She said, 'Get out, I'm getting the dinner.' It was on the midday and evening news. When I came out of Rotherham nick that night, I went down the Club. The bingo game stopped. Everybody stood up and clapped me. I get goose-pimples just thinking about it.

The strike had its moments. People supported us from all over the country, with money and food. We killed rabbits and nicked spuds from the fields. Somebody even nicked a cow, strung it up and cut it and shared it around ... That wasn't a bad time.

Twenty-one: Is there an Underclass?

Mass unemployment has made a dramatic reappearance in the past twenty years. In the earlier years of the century, unemployment seemed to be a transient phase – after all, the traditional industries remained, and there was always potentially work to go back to in textiles, shipbuilding, steel and coal. But now, economists are more pessimistic: unemployment is seen as 'structural' rather than cyclical, although with the rise and fall of economic activity, obviously, the cycle remains. In the advanced economies now, the ratio of capital investment to labour is very high: it costs hundreds of thousand of dollars to create one job.

It is partly the existence of a pool of long-term unemployed that has led to discussion around the emergence of an 'underclass'. This debate is made more difficult by the fact that many of the long-term jobless also appear to be the products of unhappy backgrounds – so the argument becomes one about damaged individuals who are unemployable, rather than about the structural problem of insufficient work. The truth is that long-term unemployment is most likely to affect the weakest and most vulnerable people.

Currently, there are officially about 2,500,000 people unemployed and claiming benefit. Others have simply fallen out of the market completely; their failure to claim benefit does not necessarily mean they are employed in some way or other, but it does mean that they tend to be beyond the reach of the agencies of the state, and they cannot easily be counted.

It is commonly asserted that workers should 'price themselves into jobs', but the fall in wages of the least well paid may well have the opposite effect – driving people into illegality, the black economy. Within the last fifteen years the growing inequality in earnings has been marked, and the gap between the highest- and lowest-paid workers in Britain is now larger than at any time this century. According to the report *What Has Happened to Wages?*, published by the Institute of Fiscal Studies in June 1994, between 1978 and 1992 the real hourly rate of the poorest 10 per cent did not change at all, while those in the middle range saw their wages grow by 35 per cent, and the highest 10 per cent experienced salary increases of over 50 per cent. Whether growing inequality serves as an incentive to the poor to work may be doubted.

In the early industrial period, certain towns and cities in Britain became synonymous with one particular product or activity; indeed, the very reason for the existence of many communities was their industrial function. The decline of these staple, sustaining occupations has left many places, and their people, in a state of shock – a phenomenon as strange and unfamiliar as their rapid development a century and a half ago.

Middlesbrough: *the breakdown of work in the 1980s*

An estate on the outskirts of Middlesbrough on Teesside. The area consists of a neighbourhood built in the thirties, to take people from the docks area and around the steelworks. It was further developed in the sixties, and then in the late seventies. Here, the male unemployment rate is around 45 per cent – the highest since the 1930s.

Wednesday is giro day for most people on the estate. This turns the midweek evening into a substitute weekend: time for a drink and meeting with friends, without the anxiety of whether you'll be able to pay for the round of drinks when it is your turn. On Tuesdays, the day before pay-out, when things get really tough, that's when those who have something left over, or people who had their giro earlier in the week, offer a sub to neighbours and friends. Rab and Eddie don't mention money. Rab rubs his nose with a forefinger crooked if he wants to borrow a fiver; if Eddie can lend him one, he returns the sign. If not, he shakes his head: a kind of freemasonry of poverty.

On giro day itself, there are seven or eight people sitting around the table in the pub. Time to pay back: the fiver comes out and does the round of all those sitting there. It seems no one can remember who it belonged to in the first place, so it goes on a round of drinks for everyone. 'I've found a fiver.' 'It's mine.' 'How do you know it's yours?' 'Mine is blue and has the Queen's head on it.'

On Wednesdays, then, a moment of relaxation. The pubs are conspicuous buildings, on the corners of estates – sometimes the only building that remains from the nineteenth century. Pubs are places of comfort and escape: hit songs of yesterday on the sound system – Frankie Laine, 'Ghost Riders in the Sky', Rosemary Clooney, 'This Old House', Satchmo singing 'Mack the Knife'.

163

Steve has just come back from the Falklands. In his late twenties, a muscular man with copper-coloured hair. He was on a twelve-month contract, as labourer and docker at Port Stanley, unloading goods and materials for the construction companies working on the airport. His contract was for £10,000 a year. He has come back after only three months, because he could not stand the isolation and boredom. He had to pay his own fare home because he had broken the contract. 'It's a village on a rock. You wonder what all the fuss was about, let alone fight a war over the bloody place. I was keen at the time. I really thought it was the greatest thing this country had done in my lifetime while the war was on. But when you go and see it, Jesus.' He passes round his photographs: the stores, Bluff Cove, Tumbledown Mountain, the Hotel.

They're just shacks. The sunsets are beautiful and the wildlife is great, but apart from that, nothing. The novelty of being there wears off after about a week, and then depression sets in. There's nothing but work, sleep and drink. You get pissed out of your head every night. That's when guys do stupid things. There were six deaths in the space of the three months I was there. Two lads killed themselves – one cut his throat and the other hanged himself. Four others died: one tried to jump between two ships when he was pissed, and was drowned, another got speared by a forklift truck which somebody drunk was driving. You can't even fuck the sheep.

Steve would never have gone if he had not spent two years unemployed in Middlesbrough. 'I'd been in Germany before. That was bad enough, but at least you can go out into the city and enjoy yourself. The terrifying thing about the Falklands is that it throws you back on yourself, your own resources – something you're not used to. Even if you've got the money, there's nothing to spend it on.'

A man in a flat cap says, 'Fucking Falklands. When it first come on TV, they did a survey. Eighty per cent of the people in this country thought the islands were off the west coast of Scotland. Didn't stop silly buggers from egging Thatcher on to fight for 'em.' Steve says:

There was one lad, his mother and father were killed in a car crash in England, and it took thirteen days before he could come home, because there were no flights. The only way to get sent home free was to be repatriated for misconduct. So on the day before the plane was coming in, blokes used to have fights, set them up, so they'd get sent home. There'd be about sixteen people, all scrapping on a night. You had to do it seriously, so it looked bad enough to get reprimanded and sent home . . . There were some articles in the *Sun* and the *Mirror* which said we were having orgies and taking drugs. Were we hell. I had to ring my girlfriend, she said, 'What the heck is going on out there?' What they were saying about us was all a load of lies. The truth was it was boring. There was danger – they still haven't found all the mines the Argies laid, and some of those are still being found the hard way. And the Argies keep on probing – you hear the jets taking off in the night, but you get used to that. I'm going to Algeria next week on a contract. At least it's a bit nearer home. I wouldn't want to leave Middlesbrough. I was born and brought up here. But when you have no choice, you have to take work wherever you can find it.

By contrast, Tuesday night is quite dead. Soon after ten-thirty, even on a warm summer night, the streets are empty, the dog has been walked on the green, the pubs are empty. Tuesday-night supper is a few chips and a couple of sausages. There is no sauce; the sugar ran out several days ago. Salt is the only condiment in the house. The plates are metal; the furniture is wearing thin – you can't stop the baby from playing, and things deteriorate fast when kids are around. You can feel the place getting shabbier, and you know you'll not be able to do anything about it. Television has become a necessity. You don't watch it all the time, but it's on even in the afternoon – nothing serious or challenging, just an aid to getting through time.

I got an interview for a job. It made my week. I thought, Great. Only then I found out they were interviewing everybody who applied. There was to be a second interview, and then the finalists would go to a third. It was like bloody Miss World. And it was only an office job.

People resent the portrayal of Middlesbrough as a no-hope place, full of deadbeats and derelicts.

They think we're all sat on our arses waiting for sommat to turn up, living between the next hand-out and whatever falls off the back of a lorry. They did a TV programme about us. What a load of cobblers. This lad who lives near me was on the programme saying, 'We all burgle off each other, everybody's ripping everybody else off.' Next morning, he had the police on his doorstep. His Mam and Dad said, 'He's been misquoted.' But he said it in his own words, so how could they misquote him? People don't know how to stick up for each other.

It is easy enough to see Middlesbrough as a sad, even despairing place; and it would do nobody a service to minimize the effects of poverty and insecurity. But human life is not the sum of a weekly income; nor do the majority of people make no effort to find work. Indeed, some of their efforts have been heroic, even when they have failed. Brian was apprenticed at Smith's Dock, a shipyard due to close at the end of 1986.

I was apprentice five years. I'm a boiler-maker. I enjoyed my time at work. Oh yes, enjoyed it. I felt I was doing something worthwhile, something I knew how to do. I'm not a carpenter, not a decorator, I'm a boiler-maker. That five years was my security: it was a trade in my fingers for life. I can sit in the flat where I live now, and see the place being run down. How do you think it makes me feel? I remember on my first day, they sent me for a bucket of steam, like all the apprentices. I learned all I know from the blokes who worked there. It was your life – it wasn't just work, it was friendships, relationships and feelings.

Brian was made redundant in 1980. He went to live with his father in Wakefield, where he worked in an engineering company until that company also closed two years later.

I got on my bike, like they say you should. While I was in Wakefield, the Yorkshire Ripper murder investigation was going on. I was picked up by the police, and they quizzed me for over two hours. Because he was supposed to have a Geordie accent. I said, 'I'm not a Geordie, I'm from Middlesbrough.' They were looking for anybody with a Newcastle accent. They said, 'What are you doing down here?' I said, 'I've come down here to work, because work packed up in fucking Middlesbrough.' In the end, they make you feel you don't know whether you're telling the truth or lies. You wonder if you're quite sane when they've finished with you.

Brian returned to Middlesbrough, and lived with his mother in her flat. He was still without work, and they started to get on each other's nerves. He was given a single person's flat in a reconditioned block of 1960s dwellings that had been refurbished: blocks of maisonettes partly demolished and landscaped, with intercom and security cameras so that you can see on your TV screen who is knocking at your door. It's like a symbol of community dissolution: people have become strangers to each other.

I still visit my mother every day, run her messages for her. Then I come down to the pub in the middle of the day, have a pint, make it last. I wake up at five in the morning, so by the time the pub is open half my day is over. I stay here till three, have a bite to eat, get my head down in the afternoon, wake up at six, have a wash, look at the paper, come back down here about half seven, make another pint last while ten. Then I go to bed at eleven. Only I'm not tired, so I wake up at five again.

Brian, not yet fifty, doubts he'll work again, even though he says that from the day he was born he was made for work. He is slightly stooped, looking older than his age: people formed for shipyards and steelworks, whose physical strength was the only commodity required by the market, are being told to retrain, re-educate themselves, adapt to the changed times. This is seen by many not as an opportunity, but as compounding the insult of 'redundancy'.

It's all very well for those who've never had to wonder what they're going to do with their time – politicians, bureaucrats, people who are never going to lose their work – telling us we have to change. Life isn't like that. Your character is formed when you're a kid. We were told – we didn't need to be told, it was in the air you breathe, like the smoke from the chimneys – that work was our destiny.

A sense of waste hangs over these places, where there is no longer any getting up for work in the morning, the curtains remain closed until eleven or twelve, and the lights burn until it is light on these bright summer mornings. People speak of becoming disoriented, the body mechanisms disrupted; of nightmares, dreams, disturbed patterns of existence; of an industrial discipline, for the inculcation of which no effort had been spared, so casually discarded. And this isn't the only sense of waste in the old working-class communities – the abilities and intelligence of people have always been neglected or repressed: 'You didn't think of a career,' people say, 'all you were bothered with was the money you needed to survive. It wasn't about having a good time, it was about survival. We never had the luxury of doing what you found fulfilling, let alone cultivating our minds.'

But the minds and the understanding of the people get cultivated just the same: the humour and endurance of those born to labour are always one of the great consolations, in even the bleakest material circumstances. Yet it remains a paradox, of which many are aware, that both work and the absence of it deny people in different ways. 'When I go up to the school and hear the teachers talk about developing each child's potential, as though there was going to be a wonderful future waiting for my kids, I can't believe it. I don't know if they believe it or not, or if they're just paid to say it.'

This town was called by Gladstone 'the infant Hercules': a Victorian boom town built on iron ore, with its docks, and the remaining evidence that it was a place oriented towards the Continent – the German church, the

Swedish seamen's mission and the Danish Vice-consulate. The nineteenth-century redbrick warehouses and factories, eaten away by ancient acid and grime, are now 'To Let' and invaded by fireweed. It is difficult to believe that it was still an object of migration and hope to those who came from more derelict areas in the 1960s and 70s.

Rab came from Paisley in 1974. He jokes: 'I was going to Musselburgh, but I fell asleep on the train and woke up in Middlesbrough.' He worked at Warner's, then at British Steel, at the rolling mill; later in Smith's Dock, then back to British Steel, on continuous casting.

I finished up with an industrial cleaners at £1.70 an hour. That was after the rot had set in. I'm forty-nine now and my chest has gone. I've chronic bronchitis. I've a free bus pass, and that's your badge of being a senior citizen. At forty-nine. I've sixteen years of work left in me, but I doubt I'll do many of them.

Rab is a smart man, in sports coat, tie, grey flannels; he has receding hair, a gingery moustache; and great humour and intelligence.

There must be light work I could do. I'd run the Social Security offices on a different basis for a start. I uprooted myself from Paisley. Do you think that was a pleasure? I left behind my wife and three children, because there was nowhere down here for them to live. I was told there was a five-year waiting list for a house. You know what happens – you can't keep up a marriage by remote control. It broke up. I came here essentially for money. That's what the world turns on. We're all capitalists at heart. You must have a top dog: if there were no bosses, somebody would become one pretty soon. There's no society – Aztecs, Eskimos, tribal societies – that doesn't have a head; and they are always the richest people. In the same way, there's always a bell-wether in a flock of sheep; if one cow gets up and moves, the rest will follow. People say, 'But we're not animals.' You can argue about that. It's an insult to animals, the behaviour of people in this century to one another.

I'm a working man, or perhaps I should say I was a working man. Wilson said, 'You need half a million unemployed' in the sixties. I volunteered, and lived to regret it. I was apprenticed as a green sand moulder in an iron foundry, but I left after fifteen months. I made the classic blunder – I left a job as an apprentice on miniscule wages to go to a higher-paid, dead-end job. I was sixteen or seventeen: I saw my earnings go up from £2 to £5 – a 150 per cent rise. I went labouring on a building site for 3s 8d an hour.

You always remember your first week's wage. You remember how any money seems a lot, when you've never earned before, but how little it really is when you have to start living off it. That is the basic truth on which all government schemes have been built. You can persuade kids to price themselves into jobs when they're living at home and being subsidized by their parents. It's only when they come to start a family, look for somewhere to live, that they find they've been conned. The baby boom of the 1960s is just reaching that stage now. There's gonna be a lot of angry young people. There is nothing like having to fight for the kids and realizing you've been conned, for making people angry.

But in my case, the household needed my money. If we'd been better off, I'd've been able to continue my trade. That's how you finished up unskilled. I'm unskilled but I'm far from stupid. What makes you bitter is having to leave home. Of course it hurts you. Then you lose your wife and kids through enforced separation. I'd've had to wait five years for a house. I wasn't going to bring them down here to live in digs.

I've been in bed all day today. Lying in bed, reading. I'm lucky, I can occupy myself. I got up at half past seven this evening. Mind you, I was out last night till three with a woman-friend. But that's how it gets you. Tomorrow morning I shall be up at five. There's no rhyme or reason to your life. They say we have to learn to be more flexible for the new jobs that are coming. What could be more flexible than that? Getting up and going to bed at virtually the same time on two successive days. But still they don't want me. There's a Russian proverb which says, 'A pessimist says things are always bad, will stay bad and may get worse; an optimist says that things were bad in the past, bad in the present, but can't get any worse.'

One of the other men at the table counters with a quote from Oscar Wilde: 'An optimist says this is the best of all possible worlds, and a pessimist believes it.' Rab says he would like to think he is not a pessimist, in spite of all the evidence that supports such a view.

The trouble is, people in power say we must increase productivity; everybody says, 'Great, true'. But what they really mean is that more people must be put out of work. They use language to say one thing and mean the opposite. The information we get, it's of no use in helping us make decisions.

'When I started work,' says Dave, 'it was at Kilmarnock bus station. I had to sign the Official Secrets Act. That was to promise you wouldn't tell anybody the times of the fucking buses.' Rab also had to sign the Official Secrets Act when he worked in the shipyard, in a firm subcontracting to

Yarrow's on Ministry of Defence work. He says, 'The biggest official secret is that there's nothing we've got that they don't know.'

Rab takes part in quizzes that are run in the pubs. For twenty-five pence, you can do general knowledge or specialist quizzes.

You can win your beer money, a few quid for extras. You can go to a different quiz every night. Some are specialized – pop music, cinema, history, football, politics. But for the most part, I shut myself off and read. I don't like doing it, but when there's no money, what's the point in fretting about it? I can read, but there's a lot of people who can't settle to it.

Teesside now, it's like Paisley when I left it twelve years ago. There were so many things they used to make in Paisley – Robertson's jam, McRae and Drew who did all the seating for the motor industry. They moved down to Coventry. There was Coates' thread, the Anchor and Thread Mill. You can still buy the products, only they're not made where they used to be. The companies might close down in Britain, but they're still alive and kicking somewhere in the world. The thread company went to Elizabeth, in New Jersey I think it is. A lot of people went there from Paisley. And the shipyard built the best dredgers in the world . . . Not any more. I'm too old to uproot and migrate all over again.

What emerges from these communities is not the stereotype story of stability and continuity in Britain. Quite the reverse – they are full of memories of migration and upheaval, departures and farewells to loved ones: the ship to New Zealand, the letters from Canada, the move down South, the walk to London – and the contemporary version, the girl back from London after six weeks living rough – the postcards from Riyadh, the phone calls from Australia, the young runaways: the desire to migrate as a form of escape. Rab returns to the theme of migration:

The day I came to Middlesbrough it was a Saturday afternoon, Scotland beat England 2–nil that day. I got off the train. The first bloke I saw, I said to him, 'Where can I get a job straight away?' He said, 'There's ICI, British Steel.' 'Will I be able to start Monday?' 'I shouldn't think so – you'll have to fill forms in.' That was no good to me, I had to start straight away. I started at Warner's as a crane-driver. I went there Monday first thing. That's what migration is all about: you have to start because you haven't got enough to last you beyond the weekend. I worked on a Scotch derrick, a Montower crane. Then a job as a structural painter at Lackenby's, then to Smith's Dock shipyard. I hadn't been here for two weeks when I bumped into Wally Reeves: he'd been here fifteen years, and had lived round the corner from me in Paisley. I went into a pub, and there was Jimmy Kendry, whose house I used to go into as a kid. He'd come here thirty years ago. I didn't know either of them was here.

Don't let them tell you our history has all been great and glorious. Nobody knows the resentment that's underneath all the upheavals, the pain of partings, leaving people you might never see again. There's nothing civilized about it. It's primitive and it's barbaric. It's up to the individual to set right everything that is wrong in the system.

I'm in this bed-and-breakfast place: a functional kitchen, second-hand furniture, very basic. Forty pounds a week. Since I'm on invalidity, that leaves £25 for everything else, all other meals and all the luxuries the unemployed live on. I put 50p on the horses. Occasionally, I win. Once I got £120; but usually, if I win, it's the price of a couple of pints of beer . . . What I could do really well is lead the Tory party. The skill I have in losing money, I could get the jobless figures down to one and a half million in a month – I'd lose two million of them easily. They've changed the way they count them ten times, and still they can't get below three and a quarter million.

The change from work to unemployment has other effects. For instance, they say, 'You used to see more of your mates than you did your wife.' There was a kind of sexual apartheid in the division of labour between men and women. Many are now thrown together in one another's company, and find they have little to say to each other.

The men cast a critical eye on the casual labour that is on offer.

You can go strawberry-picking for a few weeks. They don't pay much and it's back-breaking. If you don't declare it, somebody'll bubble you to the DHSS. Last September, we were picking potatoes, £8 a day. That was no privilege. The field was raided by DHSS officials, to see who was claiming dole. Raiding a field. Can you imagine it? – people running in all directions, dropping potatoes everywhere. I don't think anyone was daft enough to let themselves get caught. But imagine, stooping to surround a potato field – they did it like they were commandos, planning a military operation. It was no pleasure working there: you had to sit in a bath for two hours afterwards, trying to ease your back. Poor buggers, trying to get a few extras for the kiddies. Is that England? We used to think we lived in a decent society.

Says one middle-aged man: I've never been on the dole. I'm working now for the British Beef Company. My two sons are working, my wife works at the Bingo Hall. I bought my house fifteen years ago for £2,000. But that doesn't turn me into a Tory.

There was one lad running a taxi service while he was on the dole. Somebody spragged on him to the Social. He gets a call one morning: 'Could I have a cab at seven o'clock?' He turns up. It's the social. 'Hello Mr So-and-so. Shall we have a little discussion about the matter of your benefit?'

I always think of what George Orwell wrote in *Down and Out in Paris and London*. Whatever he went through, when he wanted to think of somebody worse off than himself, he said he always thought of the bloke unemployed in Middlesbrough. It was always Middlesbrough. Is this the worst thing that can happen to a human being?

I left Scotland because I couldna get work. Being a Catholic didn't help. My name is McLoughlin, that's a Catholic name. The minute I went into a place and they said, 'Fill in a form', I knew that was it. On your application form, as soon as they asked you what school you'd been to, if it was St Something-or-other, in West Scotland, you immediately knew that was a Catholic school. I got so sick of it. I went to one place where they were advertising for workers. They said, 'Will you fill in a form.' I screwed the form up, threw it in the basket and said, 'Forget it. I'm a Catholic.' I got to the door. He called me back. 'Wait a minute. This is a Catholic firm. You can start tomorrow.' I said, 'No thanks, that makes you as bad as the other side.' I wouldn't take it on principle. As a matter of fact, when I was a child I went to a special school, a school for handicapped children, because I always had a problem with my chest. But that didn't stop them employing me for thirty-five years of heavy manual labour. I always say that was my second handicap. My first was being born a Catholic in that part of Scotland.

I worked at one time, delivering for a company. There was this Protestant Orangeman, he did his rounds with another bloke, and they always finished up at his house for dinner every Friday. On this particular Friday, his mate wasn't there, and I worked with him. I could tell he was nervous. He didn't really want me to come to his house at dinner-time, but there was really no way round it. I said, 'That's OK.' When we got to the house, he showed me into the front room. I heard him and his missis having this whispered argument in the kitchen. She comes in and says to me, 'I'm afraid I haven't got any fish ... but you're welcome to stay.' I said, 'That's all right.' She said, 'But it's Friday.' I said, 'I know.' She said, 'But aren't you a Catholic?' I said, 'I am, but I've got a Protestant stomach, and it's protesting that it's hungry.' She laughed. She said she had been in a panic; but it was all right.

When the conversation lightens, the undertow of racism, sexism, anti-gay sentiment comes out: everything but the maleness of a male culture has gone. There are jokes about getting it up, the size of somebody's prick. 'What did the cannibal say when he saw a missionary on a bicycle?' 'Here comes meals on wheels.' 'Have you ever been abroad?' 'No, it's just the way I walk.'

'It's not the town I used to know. You could leave work at dinner-time and start somewhere else in the afternoon for an extra penny an hour.' 'This town was built for work. That's why it's here. It's not a fucking holiday resort, is it?'

I went for a job I was sent to by the Jobcentre. It was a filthy job in a foundry, disgusting hole, like something out of Dickens. I took one look at it, and made myself obnoxious as I could, so I wouldn't get it. They offered it to me. I went to the DHSS, for a grant for boots and jeans so that I could start. I'd no clothes to work in. There was an entitlement at that time – to, I think it was £7 for jeans and boots. They refused me. 'You had one last year.' They were Tuf boots, only guaranteed for six months – working in hot metal, they were ruined. Nothing. I went to the library, and read up all the Social Security Acts, all the Amendments. I pored over them. In the afternoon, I went back for a redecoration grant, a clothing grant for my wife and the kids, clothing for myself. 'Oh you won't get that.' 'It's not your job to tell me what I'm entitled to.' They sent somebody down. 'Weren't you here this morning?' 'This is a different matter.' I showed him my claim, quoted the Act and the Section and the Amendment. A few minutes later, he said, 'There'll be a giro in the post tomorrow.' Ninety-four pounds. You only have to show them you know the rules. But why should you? I'm lucky, I can make sense of the jargon; but nine out of ten people can't.

John has recently retired. His brother lives in New Zealand.

He left Middlesbrough in the fifties, because even then it seemed the prospects were not brilliant. I've just been to see him. It's beautiful. They got somebody to paint a picture of the view from the window of the room where I slept – mountains, grass, water. He'd never come back here. When he went, it was a big wrench, but he wouldn't change it. You think you can't pull up your roots, but you can. You can if you're still young; they grow again.

The youngsters are different from us. They don't have the servility to authority that we had; that's good. But we expected to get a job. They don't. I was brought up in a rough part of town. In that neighbourhood, if you locked your door, you were considered a snob, or you were doing something you shouldn't. There used to be these back-arch bookmakers. If the coppers came, they'd dash through the houses. They could get four or five streets away in a matter of seconds, just nipping through the houses. It was nothing to see somebody running through your kitchen. The only thing ever stopped them was if they came to a locked door.

I can remember all the neighbours in the street where I was a kid. I can remember all their names, what work they did, and what their family circumstances were. At the time of the means test, if a lad lived at home his father was expected to take money off them, as if they were working. He lost benefit. So as soon as the means-test man set foot in the street, all the lads'd take a tent and go camping. Stay away for a day or two. Nobody ever did what they do now – write anonymous letters to the Social, grassing on their neighbours.

When I left school I was fourteen, and I went to work in a foundry. I was sacked for not joining the union, I'd just started work, and these two lads came up to me as I was going home. 'Are you in the union?' I didn't know what the union was. 'It'll cost you a penny a week.' 'I'm not paying a penny. You and the union can go and jump off the transporter.' I was sacked on the Friday. I was fourteen – I didn't even know what it was. And I've been one of the staunchest union men you could imagine.

My father was in the steelworks, worked there all his life. When he left, he got ten shillings pension from the union – from the company, nothing. I went to work with him. He was straightener of rails, and I was a gagger. When they cast the rails, they weren't straight, of course. They had to be evened out by hand. I had to sit and signal to my father to wield this small hammer, to the right or left, up or down, to even out the lengths of steel.

When I first started, it was slave labour. I was overawed when I first went into the foundry. It was filthy, noisy, there were no toilets – you had to go out on the riverbank. I was small, so they put me cleaning locos; I had to get inside the boilers to clean them. But I enjoyed it. I'd go home filthy. My mother said, 'What've you been doing?' I enjoyed my work life. I never expected anything different. If you get fair pay, you feel you've given something of yourself. There is a satisfaction in it. I was dipping components in paint at one time, the fumes were overpowering. Then to wash it off, I had to use kerosene – both deadly substances in those enclosed, hot, fiery conditions – there was always danger of explosions, fire, fumes, damage to the lungs. But it didn't bother you. This is my home. Middlesbrough, to me, tells me who I am. It's not distinguished. You wouldn't stay here for health reasons. Middlesbrough, it's the accent, the people. It's home.

I left school on the Friday, and started as a labourer with a building contractor on the Saturday. Then I went into a foundry, and I was in the Forces at seventeen and a half. I stayed there for nearly twenty years. I was in Borneo, Malaya, Cyprus, Northern Ireland.

[He shows the tattoos on his arms, one from each place he has visited.] I was in Malaya when they were fighting for independence. But I was born and bred in Middlesbrough. I always came back here, wherever I'd been, all over the world. But I didn't think I'd ever see it as it is today. I'm proud of the place, but not of what's been done to it. People have taken a pasting. If you mention the word 'holiday', it's like swearing at them. Will my lads be given the chance to earn a living? Is that asking too much? I worked as supervisor on the Youth Training Scheme. I was expected to teach kids to use a grass-cutter or a hammer. Those things are second nature to people up here. That isn't giving a kid skills. When they finish the govvy schemes, the employers don't want to know. The youngsters still don't have the knowledge. Apprenticeship is the only way to teach kids, show them on the job. There's no substitute for learning through work, through practice.

My lad's started with Wimpy's the builders, as a brickie. I said to him, 'Don't think of anything else. That's your backbone. Once you've got a trade, show you're worthy of it. Learn from the tradesmen.' When I was born, God said, 'This is an ugly bugger, we'll give him a bit of common sense to make up for his looks.' My father was a master pipe-fitter. I learned from him. I've proved myself, I can turn my hand to most things.

I went for a job, they wanted to class me as unskilled. All right. They were putting these pumps in the pump-house. They got a master fitter. He couldn't get it in. They even broke a pump, trying to get it in before they put the roof on. I sat on the ledge, laughing my head off. The site engineer said, 'Why's he laughing?' He called me up. I got in the bucket and the crane took me up. 'Why you laughing?' I got more sense in my backside, I can do it. He offers me £50 if I can do it without breaking the pump. I tell the crane driver, 'Right, I'm the boss. You do as I say.' I got two scaffolding planks and a tin of grease; got the pump at an angle, greased these planks, slid it down on to the jacks. It took me twenty-five minutes.

These people who have their cards saying they're brickies or fitters or anything else, don't you believe it. I said to a bloke who was moaning he hadn't got a trade, I said, 'What do you want to be?' He said, 'I'm a brickie.' I said, 'Right, give us ten quid. I'll give it you back.' He gave me a tenner. I went to a club out of town, and I said, 'Will you give us a brickie's card for £10?' I took the card to him. 'Now you're a qualified brickie.' I took it back and got the ten pounds back. Oh you can get an MOT certificate, a clean licence will cost you £25, with logbook and everything. You can get any qualification you want. It's only a piece of paper after all. How do people survive? Of course some will play the system. It's a bloody unfair system, everybody knows that; whatever you want – fitter, painter, welder, scaffolder, anything, if you pay for it, you can get it. People have to survive.

It's always been the same. Don't talk to me about the good old days. I was in a lumber camp in Suffolk in the thirties, owned by a match company. Four shillings a week. Then I worked on the runway at Mildenhall airbase. So the Yanks could come and occupy it. If I'd known what it was going to be used for, I'd've made craters in the middle . . . I went on the tramp. Round the farms. Knock on the door in August, harvest-time. Little kid comes to the door. 'Dad, there's a tramp at the door.' 'That's not a tramp, that's a worker wants a job with the harvest.' I go back a bit later in the year. Same kid answers the door. 'Dad, there's a workman at the door.' 'That's not a workman, it's a tramp.'

Is that right, Mrs Thatcher's having a street party for the unemployed? She's using the M1.

Migrations of hope, destinations of despair

Iris Blandford (*mid-50s*): *cleaner*

Most Afro-Caribbean migrants to Britain came to work during the last periods of labour shortages in the 1950s and 1960s. Many worked in the public sector services – transport, hospitals, general labour. Many were actively recruited in the Caribbean, and were scarcely prepared for the levels of discrimination that they met, not so much in employment at first, but certainly in housing. Later, as unemployment became more widespread, non-whites were more likely to lose their jobs than whites; and while there is now a strong emerging black middle class in Britain, there is also a generation of young people who have grown up

*to unemployment, marginalization and exclusion. The promise and hope with
which many migrants travelled thirty or forty years ago have turned to
bitterness, as times have become harder, structural unemployment becomes more
and more intractable and, with it, the existence of racism less covert.*

*When Iris Blandford considers now the poverty that she fled in Jamaica
nearly thirty years ago, she says that it was her destiny to meet another form
of it half-way across the world. What is more, she says she has seen her three
daughters lose even that hope that filled her and her husband when they
arrived on a liner in Southampton in 1964. She has seen a loosening of the ties
of kinship, the hardening of racist hostility that cramps and limits their lives.
She has known continuing exile, but from a home-place which it is no longer
easy for her to define.*

We came to work. And work was what we did. We didn't do nothing but
work. It killed my husband. He worked on construction, he helped build
the development in the docks of London. He built luxury flats, while we
lived on one of the most worst estates in Hackney. When we came on the
ship, he said as we came into Southampton, 'Oh look at all the factories,
we'll have work for all of us.' Only they were houses.

At that time, I left my two daughters at home. I was going to send for
them when we got settled, but I never did, and then they changed all the
rules, and the girls grew up and they had their own lives there. They didn't
know us, or my husband, so they stayed there. Better for them they did.

My husband worked in just about everything. He worked in ice-cream
factory, he was a waiter in a hotel, but the money was better on building, so
he worked as a labourer. Oh, he worked. He went off at six-thirty when it
was dark and he came home when it was dark. We said we would earn as
much money as we could to get our own house, to go back home, but it
never happen. Everything was so expensive, and by the time we had four
children, all the money kept going out just to stand still. At home, when
you were hungry, you just reach on the tree for the fruit you want, but
here, everything you have to buy. It is all money.

I had to work too. When he got ill, he couldn't carry on working. He
had a heart attack when he was forty-seven, and after that, he never really
worked. We thought, By the time the children grow and they get work,
then we'll be able to buy somewhere to live. But it was not to be. I can
see him in the hospital, worrying what happen to us if he gone. We said,
'You will get better', but he shake his head and he got a look in his eyes
that say, I'm looking on the other side of life – like he could see something
we couldn't.

I worked cleaning. I got up at half past five to go to the City. I clean one place till nine o'clock, then I come home and make the meal for the children, do shopping and clean the home, and then at five I go back to the City and work from six till eight, and then when I come home it's ten o'clock or ten-thirty. I'm getting £60 a week.

We feel disappointed. Not bitter. My husband one day, a police car stop and they pick him up and take him to the police station for no reason, they say he spat at the police car. It was wrong. He always say the police have a hard job to do. But they beat him and frighten him. He complain. He is a very innocent man. And he got an apology from them. He said he satisfied.

We thought we knew what is England when we come. But we didn't know a thing. We see how it all change, all the disappointment come. You think your children go do better than you, they have all the chances at school, but the teachers aren't interested, they don't learn. They leave school and then there is nothing for them to do.

My oldest daughter is married to a Nigerian. She don't even understand the language. Tell me if I wrong. They could be talking about you and you not know what they saying. When I first come to England, I stayed in an African house, and one day the woman have her monthly while she was coming home from work, and she break the pay packet before she gets home to buy some cloth. When she get home, he beat her. She say, 'What you want me to do, walk the street with it running down my leg?' It not that she get married I don't like, but she never tell me. But when I'm just she mother, I'm the last to know.

My boy is Gary. He was living with Marie and the baby. One day she say to him, 'Give me eighty pound, I see something in the West End I want to get for the baby birthday.' So he give her the money, and he goes to work in a fruit and vegetable stall. And when he comes back, he find she used the money to get married to somebody else. What kind of a world is it? Who could you trust these days? You can't trust no man, no woman, you can't trust no children. You live with a man, after one month he could change, after twenty years he could change. The time get too serious now. Life getting harder. Last week, a woman jump out of the window and kill sheself. One day, an old white woman fall down in the street. I go to help her. She starts screaming at me, 'Leave me be, leave me be.' Next time, they can fall in the street, I let them stay there.

Melissa is my second daughter. She has got a council maisonette for she and she two daughters.

They got the property on medical grounds – Melissa has a hole in her heart. Her younger daughter has sickle-cell anaemia. Melissa's boyfriend, father of the younger child, doesn't live with her. Melissa says:

178

I get £58 a week, and £15.75 for the children. On Monday morning, I get my money, pay £8 rent, and something off the arrears, £10 electricity, food – and I'm not kidding, by Monday night I haven't got a pot to piss in. I've had to pawn my jewellery. He doesn't give me any money. He puts himself first. He's a skilled worker in the jewellery trade. He was going to take us to the United States. He sold his house here and went, he went like a big shot, bought himself a house in Florida, but he didn't go through the proper channels to get a visa. So he can't stay. He's got to sell. When he came back, he went straight into a three-day week. He tells me he'll give me money when the five-day week comes back. I know how Princess Di feels, poor cow, she had a selfish sod like I have. You have to be hard. I've got to be like stone, I can't let it get to me for the sake of the kids.

'Beatrice is my other daughter,' continues Iris. 'Karim, her boyfriend, was deported when little Karim the baby, was just six weeks old.' 'Missing fathers,' says Beatrice. 'The government sent this one missing.' She is an ancillary worker in a London teaching hospital. She has been on nights for the past six months, because this way she can be sure that baby Karim is sleeping before she goes. There are other advantages too – she can do overtime, and comes home with up to £150 a week.

Karim has seen his son only once, and then he was in prison. He was arrested after a wounding outside a pub when Beatrice was pregnant. He was found to be an 'overstayer': he had come for a holiday with relatives from Turkey three years earlier, and had stayed on. He had worked: there are always jobs in restaurants, kebab houses, particularly for those whose illegal status encourages them to accept rock-bottom wages.

Beatrice went to Turkey to see him. She had never been outside of London before. She is sure she loves Karim, and thinks he feels the same. They speak on the phone every few days. That is to say, she makes the calls. 'And I've just paid a phone bill of £250 to prove it.' Beatrice was worried about whether she would be accepted by his family. 'I don't know how they feel about black people. There isn't too many of them in Turkey.' That was why they met in Istanbul for a few days before going to the little country town where the family lives. She wouldn't take the baby. She has read in the papers about tug-of-love babies, whose parents dispute custody across national boundaries. In the event, the family were kind to her; but she and Karim discovered they didn't love each other after all. He said, 'I'm only twenty-one, I've got my life to lead. I'm too young for that kind of responsibility.' Beatrice says, 'A woman is never too young for responsibility.'

Iris comes home from the small evangelical church where she goes each evening. She looks in at the sleeping children, takes off the straw hat trimmed with linen daisies, and closes her eyes. The flat is in a small 1960s block, on an estate where nobody would think of buying, even if they could afford it. The security door-phone installed two years ago is not working, and the door stands permanently open. The kids gather in the echoing stairwell to get out of the wind. There was a fire in the rubbish chute last week, and the inside wall is black from smoke.

When Iris looks at her grandchildren, she says she sees another generation destined to poverty from their birth. It is not that there is any lack of material comforts in the flat. There is a big fleecy elephant, an electric-blue panda. On the wall, a hand-painted text declares that Christ is the unseen guest at every meal – although most of these are now take-aways, consumed in the street. There are pots of plastic flowers, glasses, bowls, ornaments, paintings; a CD player, an ice-container in the form of a pineapple, a gypsy waggon, a digital clock, a china horse, a smoked-glass coffee table, a leather suite, a gilt mirror, records and clothes; children's toys – a telephone, bricks, animals, dolls. It isn't a poverty of possessions, even though things lose their value so quickly. It is a poverty of power – they have so little control over the shape and direction of the society that shelters them. What can you do? Nobody listens. Nobody cares.

The idea that young women have children simply to get rehoused is a further insult to them. Raising a child is their only function in a society which has failed to furnish them with other skills. They have children in order to provide themselves with a meaning in life. Iris:

We came to work, and the work vanish. We came to run away from poverty, but poverty must love us very much because it didn't let us go. We found it waiting here for us all the time.

Coming out of the underclass: **Elaine Griffin** *(30s), Eastbourne*

If there is an 'underclass', this should not be regarded as a homogeneous group of people who are permanently excluded from the mainstream: people fall in and out of poverty, as they always have done, according to the family cycle. Young unattached adults are better off than those who marry and have a young family; then when children reach working age, their parents become better off again, only to sink back into poverty in old age. Similarly, there are people who desperately seek to improve themselves, make heroic efforts to rise out of adversity, just as there are others who become poor because they are vulnerable, unstable, make unhappy relationships, become addicted to alcohol or drugs.

*One thing that emerges clearly within recent years, since the setting up of
the Welfare State, is that work does not have the salience it once did in
people's lives. The security we have – however fragile and modest it may be –
means that people give their humanity priority over their labour; when they
speak of their lives, they talk about their pain and their hopes, their unhappiness
and their relationships, before they talk about their work. And if work does
play a lesser role in the lives of the majority of the people now, it would be
difficult to argue that quality of life should not take precedence over the
necessity to labour in order to survive. Of course, for most people, work
remains the source of livelihood, but when asked to define themselves, to express
an identity, that identity is increasingly not articulated to function, to labour.*

*The testimony of Elaine Griffin suggests more pressing needs in life than the
search for work. Even though she has been care assistant, shopworker, barmaid,
cleaner, these activities all take second place to the struggle to overcome a
desperately disturbed and unhappy childhood. It is interesting to compare
what Elaine says with Ada Carey (see page 6), born nearly sixty years earlier
into a similar social class.*

*A house on an estate behind the South Downs, which Elaine and her husband
bought recently from the Council. The old downstairs bathroom has been ripped
out, and the kitchen has been modernized. The house is lived-in and comfortable.
Doug Griffin has made a separate room at the top of the house for the
children, which is reached by a ladder. The whole house has been renewed – a
symbol, says Elaine, of her own life. 'We used to have to ring up the Council
and plead with them to come and do repairs. Now we ring up a builder and
they call you madam; you look round to see who they're talking to.'*

Elaine was born in Dublin.

I always remember my mother as being ill. She often seemed to be in bed.
I later found out she had cancer, and she died of it when I was ten. My
father would be drunk almost every night. When he came in in a fighting
mood, our mother had us on the floor, saying the rosary. From time to
time, my mother's husband came from England to visit, and then my father
would move out. [My mother's husband] had left her, and had settled near
Lincoln; he had another woman, with whom he had three children.

My mother was always accusing my father, going on at him to provoke
him. He used to say to her, 'Not in front of the child.' 'She isn't yours.'
'Yes she is.' Then they would ask me who I loved the best. I always said,
'The Virgin Mary'. He used to sit me in his lap, and he hadn't shaved, and
I used to feel the stubble on his face, and I could smell the drink off him.
It frightened me. I still shudder when I think of it.

There were eleven of us, not all of them his . . . My father used to go out every day, driving lorries. He used to bring back things for us: any luxuries we saw came from the lorries he drove. Meat was a luxury for us: then he'd cook a big pot of stew – it was lovely, and it lasted for days. I always went to the shops for my mother; and I always asked for money for sweets, but I never got any. One day, I had threepence in my mouth when I was coming home from the shops, and I swallowed it. I was terrified of what she'd say. I told her I'd put it in the poor box, because they needed it more than we did. I tried to make myself sick. I tried everything to get that threepence, but I couldn't.

When I think of it, anything good that came to that house went to her. She'd buy two ounces of butter or fresh bread for herself. If she wanted anything, she generally got it. She used to sell broken seaside rock. She bought it wholesale, broke it into pieces, bagged it up, and sold it for a penny or twopence a bag. She drank also. We never saw any of the money she made from selling rock. She never bought us clothes. With her, it was either drink or prayers. Only they never drank together, always separately. I saw her one night, coming home from the pub, and she was singing. I thought, Oh, she must be better.

One day, I was playing in the front garden, jumping across the path. I fell and screamed, and the next thing I remember was waking up in hospital with a broken collar-bone. My father was with me then, I don't know where my mother was. I think she loved us though. My sister later told me I was spoilt, but that isn't how it felt to me then.

In Dublin, our house had a big living-room downstairs, which later had mother's bed in it; there was an upstairs bathroom and toilet, but the bath was always full of jam-jars, we never used it. I used to sleep with my mother and father when I was small. It was very frightening when they made love, if that's the right word for it. They used to ask me if I was awake, but I never dared say anything, because if I said yes, they'd punish me. So I just lay there, petrified, while they did what they had to do. I always assumed it was hurting her, whatever it was. I assumed that, because my brother Paul used to do it to me, and it always hurt. But because my mother never said anything, neither did I. I thought that was what men and boys were allowed to do. I think I assumed that if my mother went through it and didn't protest, it must be all right. I mean, the level at which you accept it is quite amazing if you're a woman. I was only a little girl when Paul started on me, but I already knew that it was a secret that had to be kept. I saw a psychiatrist last year, when I had a sort of breakdown. I always imagined it had all finished when I was about four, but I discovered it had gone on until I was ten, until I went to England.

My father calls me up from Dublin sometimes. He's drunk, and he says, 'You should be here with me, not over there in England.' I'm supposed to be the faithful daughter, all he did for me. Well, I think he could have fought for me a bit harder. Once mother died, they were all too busy.

I was the youngest of the eleven. In fact, the next one up, Paul, was eight years older than I am. Rita, the next sister, said mother had fourteen, but three died. The twins are the oldest – they are in their fifties now – Benny and Shay. Then Maura, Peter, Joe, Noel, Pepsi – his real name was James; he was a little retarded, and one day he was looking up at a big balloon advertising Pepsi, and the name stuck with him. Shay I remember: he modelled himself on Elvis, and used to stand looking at himself in front of the mirror; I've no other memory of him. I can't remember Benny at all. Maura's boyfriend used to come to the house. He'd say to me, 'Come on, gi's a kiss for sixpence.' Mother used to take it from me and say she was saving it, but needless to say, I never saw it again. Maura's boyfriend went to the Congo, where there was a war on. We had this shiny radiogram, and we wrote up asking for a request for him when he was in the Congo, and one day it came through. We thought it was wonderful, getting a mention on the radio. Maura got pregnant to get out of the house. She never married her boyfriend though. I met her last year for the first time in twenty-two years; her son is now married, and his wife has a baby of her own. When mother died, Maura came home. I can see her standing at the bottom of the bed where my mother lay, saying she was sorry. I didn't know what she was sorry for.

Most of them came to England to live with Mr May, my mother's husband. I hated him. He died only recently. Life was better in England: they came back only when mother was dying. Only Rita, Pepsi and Paul stayed in Ireland. They were somebody else's kids, not Mr May's, nor my father's . . . I knew I wasn't [Mr May's] child, and he didn't like me. I felt different. They all had their own Dad, they could go away to England to see him. Mine was either drunk or not there. Yet he loved [my mother], my Dad. She's the only one he ever loved, he said, even though she treated him badly. I don't know if she loved her kids. When Mr May went, she took it out on them, and on my Dad. Both she and Mr May came from farming families, and the families objected to the marriage.

When I look back on it, I used to hate it when Mr May came. I said to him, 'I hate you, why don't you go away?' When she died, he told me it was my fault she was dead. They had a wake, and because I was the baby, it was all as if it had nothing to do with me. I had to go to a neighbour, out of the way; I felt I was being pushed aside. The day before she was buried, I saw her. She looked beautiful. She was forty-seven, and she looked so pretty. I'd always been afraid of seeing anyone dead. Mr May put his arm round me; my mother's brother said to him, 'Don't you ruin her life like you ruined her mother's.'

There was a punch-up at the graveside between my brother and a cousin. They couldn't even let her rest in peace. As we drove away, my brother Peter said to me, 'You're coming to England.' I always had this fantasy about England. To me, you walked across a bridge to get to it. It was a house – just one house, belonging to Mr May – and it was all surrounded by water. There was no one else there. My brother Peter and his wife said they would have me there. My father, Peter, his wife, Rita and I all went on the boat to England. But I couldn't get on with Peter's wife. She wasn't kind to me. She made me eat fish, which I hated, and she stood over me while I ate it. She found I had fleas in my hair. The doctor gave her some stuff to clean it, and she poured the whole bottle over my head, burning my scalp. I was ten.

Peter and Doris lived in Southall. The boat trip was magical; and I remember going by train to Hayes. There was a bridge, just as I imagined, but it was a railway bridge; and you had to cross it to get to my brother's house. The first thing that struck me was how clean it was. People dressed properly in England – they had shoes to their feet. We never had shoes. It was so exciting. 17B Villiers Road; and it had an upstairs.

I do remember one lovely Christmas at Southall before everything went bad. I'd had two big bags of presents. I'd never had a Christmas like it. Once, in Ireland, I'd had a doll's pram for Christmas. I'd sneaked in and looked at it before Christmas. Then my mother took a wheel off it and said to me, 'Look, it's broken. It'll have to go to the mender's.' Well, she pawned it, and I never saw it again.

After a little while at Peter's, Rita came to visit, and Peter said, 'I can't have her here. Doris has left, and won't come back until she is out of the house.' He worked on the railway, so he couldn't look after me. They took me to Lincoln, to Mr May and Maura, who had a baby by then. Mr May looked at me and said, 'You're like your mother.' Mr May's children were all perfect. I started school in Lincoln, and I hadn't been there many days before they gave me the strap for beating a boy. I went mad and hit him. I went home; the school had informed them what had happened. They said it was impossible – they couldn't keep me there. I wasn't wanted. So Paul took me back to Southall. We got to Peter's house. He opened the door and said, 'You can take her back, Doris doesn't want her here.' 'I can't take her back.' 'You'll have to.' I remember all this conversation, and just felt wretched that I wasn't wanted, and there was no place for me. Paul took me back to Southall station; and there he tried it on with me again, interfering with me, handling me, molesting me. I said to Paul, 'I don't like it.' He said, 'Well I can't take you back to Lincoln.' He left me on the station and just went away.

I knew that I was being virtually abandoned. I found my way back over the bridge to Peter's house. He said, 'Well, you can stay here tonight, then tomorrow I'll contact the Welfare.' They came the next day, and got me into a home. The day before I went into the home, Rita took me to see mother's brother in Middlesex. He said, 'I'll come and see you. I'll phone you.' I waited seven years for that call. It never came. He made a promise, and I was desperate for something to cling to. I waited for him to phone. I didn't forget. All those years.

It was natural that I should go into a Catholic home, so I came to St Ann's in Brighton. On the first day in the home, a nun sent me to get some towels. I'd only been there half an hour, I didn't know where they were kept. I went back to her and said, 'I'm sorry, I can't find the towels.' I was given a beating for that. There was a group of us girls, we used to set aside a penny a month, save up and buy sweets, have a party with what we'd saved. [The home] was quite good at times, but the underlying feeling was very punishing; I suppose I thought I deserved it. I was still only ten. My mother had died in the September.

I was molested by both Pepsi and Paul when I was a child. One day, Pepsi was caught doing it, and was given a beating. I just thought that he was beaten because he wasn't quite right in the head. That would explain why Paul wasn't punished. He used to behave towards me in a very possessive way. If I was out playing, he wouldn't let any boys play with me – he would go for them, start a fight. It was as though he was sticking up for me, but he was the one I needed protection from. When I contacted my family again, I thought I'd go and see him, but my husband said no. Rita says he's ever so nice, but Doug couldn't bear the thought of it. I'd like to know if he is still like he was then ... I'd also like to ask him why ... 'Why did you treat me like that?'

In the convent, we were told that if you held a boy's hand, you got pregnant. I believed that until I was giving birth to my first child. When they told me I was having a baby, I told them I hadn't got anywhere it could come out of. I didn't even know if I'd been raped. The bloke hadn't held my hand, therefore I knew I couldn't be pregnant ... I was six months before it was confirmed I was pregnant. You have a split in your mind – you believed what they told you at the convent, yet at the same time you know what's happening to your own body – but you don't put the two things together. They coexist, separately. Even the Welfare found it difficult to believe that in the 1960s the convent was still teaching us such crazy things, and that they treated us in such a way. I was once hosed down in the snow because I had said a bad word. And when it was your time of the month, you had to go and ask the nuns for whatever you needed. That was their way of keeping a check on you. It was horrible.

Once, when I ran away, we were picked up by the police. We were examined by them, and they asked, 'Did anyone do this to you, did anyone do that to you?' Well, those were the things my brother had been doing to me for years: it was only then that it occurred to me that what he had been doing was wrong. I was thirteen, fourteen, then.

At sixteen, I went to foster-parents. At that time, the Welfare used to judge whether people would be good foster-parents according to how wealthy they were. The people had a girl, the step-daughter of the father, and of course, she was brilliant, perfect; she could do no wrong. I was a failure – how could I be anything else? I ran away from there.

I used to go ice-skating when I was in the home. I met a young chap there who asked me if I wanted to go and live with him at his mother's house. I asked the Welfare if I could go. They said no. He disappeared out of my life then. I wasn't allowed to go ice-skating alone after that, I had to be chaperoned. In the home, everything was regimented: the TV went on and off at a certain time – it didn't matter if you were in the middle of a programme.

I started work in a big store, Littlewoods, on the counters. I met a young lad, brother of a workmate. We ran away together, but we were caught the next day, and I was told that if I didn't behave, I'd be put away. One nun wanted to take me back to Ireland with her – Sister Kathleen – she seemed to care, and I felt she understood me. But the cruellest thing in the home was that they told me my father had died. I knew he had not. Why would they say that to me? So that we shouldn't think we had been rejected? I don't know.

We had to help in the kitchens, washing up for all the kids. You were privileged in being allowed to stay there, so you had to work. There was an old man, said to be a millionaire, who had donated a lot of money to the home. Little girls had to go out with him. When it was my turn, he wanted to kiss me. I said, 'No, I don't kiss.' I was given a beating for that. One girl who was petrified by him had to go to the pictures with him. We had to do it, to please the nuns, to keep in with him. He'd been such a source of finance to the home, they couldn't afford to get on the wrong side of him.

Then I went to foster-parents in Hove. They were two old ladies and were very nice. Unfortunately, by that time I thought, Sod it, nobody gives a damn, why should I? – everything I do is wrong. The old ladies couldn't cope with me. I'd had so much, I took advantage. They tried, it wasn't their fault. I feel sorry for them now.

I fell pregnant. The boy didn't want to know. I sat on the bus, crying. I went to his house. 'Please. I'm gonna have a baby.' He took me to bed, then told me to piss off. They took me into hospital, and I lost that baby.

I went to another couple. There was a stepfather who was only a few years older than I was. It was thought that being younger, they might be able to help me. I was put on the pill. Nothing was explained to me. I had to leave there, because husband and wife split up. I was eighteen. The Welfare made sure I was on the pill, then launched me into the world; I was no longer their responsibility. Then it was a case of if anyone showed me any affection, I'd stay with them. I thought it was love. I slept with people, I slept rough. Some nights I slept in the toilet, and I'd wake up in the morning so bloody cold . . . I went to the Temple Bar pub up Western Road, where you could meet lots of foreigners, rich young people learning English. They'd buy you a drink, introduce you to drugs.

I was fat and dirty at the time – at least, that's how I saw myself. There was a black girl who used to go to the pub, she was so pretty. One day, she got hold of me and said, 'Right, that's it.' She took me home with her, put me in the bath, tidied me up, fed me and got me a job in the Temple Bar pub. She did me a great favour.

I worked there for some time, and met a bloke I liked. He talked of marriage; what I didn't know was that he was sleeping with another bloke at the same time as he was sleeping with me. We got a flat together on the sea-front, but he never paid the rent, so we got kicked out of there. I was with him when I met Shane's [Elaine's son's] dad. I finished with him, and felt I was a failure all over again. I was all over the place. One night, Shane's father had had too much to drink, and he beat me up in the street. He had me by the arm, and he made me go to his place. It was horrible. I didn't realize he'd raped me. I woke up in the middle of the night, and found his friend had his hands all over me. I screamed, and ran out of the flat into the pelting rain.

Then I knew I was pregnant. I said to myself, Oh God, I'm having a baby. My body was saying to me, 'You're pregnant', while the Catholic part was saying, 'You can't be, you haven't held his hand.' I told my mates. They couldn't believe it. It became a joke – 'She didn't even hold his hand.'

I went to work in an old people's home on the sea-front. I had to get jobs where I could live in. There was an Irish woman I couldn't get on with. Then when the doctor confirmed that I was pregnant, she seemed to feel sorry for me. She said, 'You poor cow', and she got me a beautiful shawl. I've still got it. She bought me some shoes. The only thing wrong, some bleeder nicked my wages on the day I was leaving. The old people's home looked all right on the surface, but when you came home at night you could hear the cockroaches scuttling away over the lino.

I had to leave when the baby was due, to go to Gorton House, mother and baby home. It was a charity run by the diocese of Chichester for single parents, unwed mothers, whatever they called them.

Once Shane was born, oh he was lovely! I knew the minute I saw him that I loved him. The social worker was a cow. She wanted to take him off me. She was like that with a lot of the women: one of them smashed her door in one day. I was determined to keep him – the only thing that was mine, that nobody else had any right to. Doug adopted him just this year. That was one of the hardest decisions. The funny thing was, Shane was just waiting for Doug to say he would adopt him. We were hesitating, not quite knowing how he'd feel; and when he was adopted he came out of the court, going round telling everyone, 'I'm adopted, I'm adopted!'

While I was in the mother and baby home, I was going out with a foreign guy who loved Shane, but Shane didn't take to him. I said to myself, Whatever my child decides, he's the one. And Shane went to Doug right from the start. I met Doug while I was in the home. He was going with a woman who was in there, and he said to me one night, 'Wouldn't it be fun if you and I pretended to be going out together, just to wind her up?' So I sat on his lap, and at the end of it I said, 'Don't I get a kiss for it?' And he gave me a kiss, and my stomach went all light. It wasn't that he's beautiful – he's the plainest sod you could meet. I said to my friend, 'I want to marry him.' She said, 'But you don't like English blokes.' I said, 'He just kissed me.' She said, 'You stupid cow, I should think you've had enough kisses in your life.'

Doug was unemployed. He sold his guitar to the matron of the home and bought an engagement ring. I'd got a flat, but I moved in with him. We were married in the August. I never loved him. I told him it was just for company. It was hard work, living on the Social money. The flat got dirty. I didn't give a damn . . . One day, I'm gonna take my kids to Disneyland, and Doug and me are going to spend a couple of nights together in a good hotel, where we can order what we want. I don't ask for the moon: that's my ambition.

I didn't love him then, but I do now. He understands me. The psychiatrist told me the way I was treating Doug was the way my mother used to treat my Dad. I put Dad on a pedestal; and the psychiatrist said I was testing Doug, to see if he lived up to that ideal.

I had a breakdown when Lee, that's our child, was two. My childhood caused it. What triggered it off I don't know, but it had to come out. And then last year, I went through a bad stage . . . I'd built a fantasy about my childhood and my family, and when my sister appeared on the scene, she shattered it. She came out with things I knew were true, but I'd buried them. She was determined to break the view of the world I had.

I felt protective towards Shane, but I know I can't protect him. I've got to let him grow up. This year he's twelve. I allow him to go swimming. He has some horrible experiences – some kids said to him, 'What is it, blackie, come here to wash yourself?' Lee and Shane fight together, but as soon as they're outside, Lee jumps to defend him. I even put Shane on the at-risk register last year. I used to think I hated him whenever I felt angry. All that anger – it came from resentment at the way I was treated. I was on tablets, anti-depressants, and I was drinking sherry by the bottle. Since I've got off them, things are better. Life is better altogether. I feel I've come through, I'm a different person. For as long as I was denying what had happened to me, and I couldn't admit that my brothers had been molesting me, I hadn't been able to say that I'd been treated rotten, without consideration or love. I was trying to hide it. That's when you get desperate, take to drink or tablets.

I tell myself now I mustn't let the past win, I must let the future win. You have no confidence when you've been through such experiences. I've tried to build confidence into my children. Shane is mouthy, but it's through nerves. Lee can be aggressive. Whenever things are going well, I get frightened, I feel I don't deserve the happiness I've got. All the kids in the neighbourhood come knocking on this door. I love playing with my kids; it's like the childhood I never had. I'm discovering it through them. I'm reliving my past, but the way I would have liked it. When they say they're going fishing, I say, 'Right, I'll come.' They say, 'Oh Mum.'

I've been with Doug twelve years now. I find it hard to accept that I am loved. When you've never known it, you can never be sure. Doug had a tough time as a kid, too. When I met him, he used to stutter, but he's gained confidence. His stepfather used to beat him. He was kicked out of home. Now Doug is working, he has a job on the building. We've bought our house. I keep feeling I've no right to be happy, even though I know I have – everybody has really.

PART 3

Twenty-two: Work and the Working Class

Work

What is the relationship between people's work, the materials with which they work, and their apprehension of the world? Those whose function it has been to take what have been seen as 'raw materials' from nature – the diggers of coal, iron ore, clay, lime, the cutters of wood and those who sowed and harvested the crops – these we would expect to have a different kind of knowledge about the world from those who worked with these materials and shaped them into articles of manufacture – steel, pottery, boots, textiles.

Those who strove with nature gained a first-hand appreciation of the intractability of nature's laws: they did not, for instance, sow seeds in October, nor did they lightly take risks with unstable rock formations in taking coal from the earth. A structure beyond that of mere employers imposed itself upon their labour, and effective work depended upon a recognition of physical limits. Their work anchored them to the resource base in a way that had a kind of continuity with agricultural labour. It is a commonplace in the testimony of mining villages that work underground led to a lively appreciation of the consoling powers of nature, the sweetness of the air, the long walks over the mountains, the cultivation of the allotments, even the pigeons in the backyard – those symbolic messengers of freedoms the workers never had.

Of course, workers in manufacturing industry also took delight in similar recreations beyond the workplace. But their awareness of the world was somewhat different. Theirs was a preoccupation with a product, to the making of which their labour was indispensable. For some, like carpenters, blacksmiths, artisans, coopers, handloom weavers, cobblers, even ship-builders, this meant a continuing closeness to the material on which they worked directly. For others, it involved increasing interaction with machinery, to which ambiguous attitudes emerged – there was hatred for the implacable taskmaster which drove them and their labour, but at the same time affection often grew for the instruments with which they made such useful and serviceable necessities. There was no absolute break with those working more immediately upon natural resources – after all, they, too, knew where leather, wool and wood came from. But new rhythms came to dominate their lives, disarticulated from the more familiar tempo of the seasons. A new knowledge came to them of their growing loss of control over both the conditions of their work and the instruments of their labour. Their lives were circumscribed more and more by the world of the manufactory. Surviving became more thoroughly dependent upon the weekly wage, and the opportunities for making shift beyond it shrank. It was in these factories that the sensibilities of a new working class were forged.

Over time more sophisticated machinery performed more repetitive and routine tasks, so that people were constantly disemployed and, sometimes, reabsorbed into more complicated manufacturing processes. At times machinofacture threatened permanent unemployment, but a new generation was repeatedly accommodated within a growing division of labour. Whatever mitigations organized labour could impose upon it, the terms and conditions of labour became ever more inflexible, passed beyond the control of the workers. The increased monetary rewards for labour to some extent masked and made more acceptable the growing depowerment in the workplace, so that by the time so-called 'de-industrialization' took place there was little that workers felt able to do, except to form committees to resist a closure that had become inevitable.

These were continuous and overlapping processes. Epochs had no fixed term – they merged one into another. Some sense of this movement may be gained from the crude employment statistics: in the 1790s, twice as many people were engaged in agriculture as in manufacture; by the 1840s, this proportion had been reversed. Similarly, in the 1930s, twice as many people were working in manufacture as in the service sector. By the 1990s, this proportion has, likewise, been more than reversed.

Service industries have been seen by many workers as a liberation from dirty and dangerous manufacturing occupations. Many expressed their pride in saving their own children from a lifetime in the industry which they themselves served, even though that industry might have been on the brink of extinction at the time. It seemed a step up in the world to see their children go off to work in a bank, an insurance office, in a hotel, in shops and hairdressing salons, in schools and hospitals and leisure centres. It looked as though choice of occupation would give everyone an opportunity to do what best suited his or her temperament. These were now 'real jobs'; it was manufacture that had become marginal: the market was being supplied from elsewhere.

Whatever the precise changes in the next stage of industrialization, it is certain that the further detachment of people from the resource base will continue. The open secret of the industrial system is its internal need for self-expansion; and its strength lies in the irreversibility of all that has happened. Those who speak of the de-industrialization of Britain misunderstand. What is happening is a more intensive industrialization of those areas of human experience hitherto regarded as beyond its reach. Similarly, the greening of industry may also prove to be an impossible task. Recycling, a more rational use of energy sources, the development of new technologies that will clean up the effects of the old, are doubtless desirable; but in order to achieve these laudable aims, industrialization must be further intensified. This means it must move into new areas, invent new products, fresh services, novel experiences, other ways of answering human need which might have hitherto been closed to the penetration of the market economy. Since the only obstacle to the industrial system is people's continuing capacity to provide for themselves and each other outside of it, we may be sure that such hindrances will be swept aside as relentlessly as the ways in which people once grew their own food, or cared for each other. To imagine that this system can change its own inner dynamic, in order to throw up solutions to those intractable problems it has dumped upon us, is to expect it to deliver the one product it does not know how to make. In this connection, growth, no matter how green, may share the maligancy of all that preceded it.

Thus those who have evoked happy pictures of a workforce dispersed in high-tech cottages, each individual attached to her or his interactive computer terminal, engaged upon globally productive labour within the autonomy of the home environment, may seriously have underestimated the levels of stress, isolation and despair which such disaggregated labour may impose. The odds are that this ecologically sound activity may require such intensive and expensive consolations that the need for these will only send industrial development soaring to undreamed-of heights. No matter how sweet the roses blooming around the cottage door, no matter how fresh the clear air breathed in the absence of traffic jams on newly emptied roads, no matter how sharp the definition of distant interlocutors on videophone screens, what will be the condition of the human relationships within the claustrophobic confinement of the solar-panelled walls? When at our present, primitive, already archaic stage of industrialization one in four households is a single person living alone, who can say what family structures will support this bucolic vision of a universal exurbia, where individuals can at last express their true nature? To what remote shores will they travel in order to find relief from the inadmissible dissatisfactions that still haunt this hopeful dream?

Similarly, with an infinitely flexible labour force, individuals will be released from oppressive workplaces, in order to negotiate their own individual contracts, to work at times that suit them in activities which are freely chosen. Unburdened by specific skills that tie them to one single industrial process, liberated from the need to understand the function they perform in the division of labour – the elective journeymen and women of the electronic metropolis – what will they actually be doing? Will they be waiting anxiously for the fax or telephone call summoning them to a brief interval of labour in an enterprise which has already let them go in order to be able to employ them at lower rates of pay under inferior conditions? Will they be endlessly retraining, going on courses, receiving the necessary inputs to make them employable once more, hoping that others will be willing to invest in them as human capital, adding value to the wasting asset of their superseded skills? How will they prove themselves worthy of being developed, so that they may acquire that competitive edge which means the difference between contract renewal and termination? Who can say what such people will need to buy in, in order to be able to manage their lives? Whatever they require will surely only deepen their dependency upon a growing industrialization and its exotic produce.

The direction we have taken now becomes clear. The experience of work in the twentieth century has been essentially a slow, uneven, yet unmistakable movement away from direct contact with materiality.

If we are looking for explanations for the extraordinary changes in recent popular consciousness and sensibility, one crucial factor may be found in this dematerialization of work. For the materiality – or otherwise – of work has important consequences for people's sense of how the world is. The making and production of, even the involvement in, material necessities shapes those who are the makers. The removal of such labour is bound to have equally far-reaching effects on their consciousness as on their daily lives. What happens when these activities, these skills, these capacities, are struck from the hands and cleared from the heads of the people? What does it mean to be no longer anchored in the experience of labouring with material things?

This central question has been too easily elided by the concern to release people from dirty, dangerous, noisome manufacture. The fact that the conditions in which people were compelled to work were frequently appalling does not mean that the work they did, the labour of their hands, was itself necessarily demeaning or unworthy. In the struggle for 'a better deal for the workers', the significance of the work they did was rarely an issue. Looking back, it may be seen that if the worth of the work and of what it produced had been adequately recognized, and if this labour had been given the prominence accorded to pay and conditions of work, we might have seen a very different labour movement and, consequently, be living in a very different kind of society. Perhaps if the workers had known, if they had really believed in their own labour and in their contribution to what was useful and needful to people, they would have resisted the assault upon it and been less prepared to permit the virtual wiping out of the boot and shoe industry, the textile industry, the steelmaking industry, the coal industry.

For it is not as though we have outgrown the human need for shoes, clothing, steel or energy. Quite the contrary: we consume greater quantities of all these things than ever before. It is simply that others now make them for us. Does this make us more free, or more dependent? Does it mean that the people who currently provide us with these necessities are doing work that is less valuable than our own? One thing we do know: the conditions in which they labour are every bit as bad as those which we once knew. And what do we think will happen when they decide that they, too, would like to be free from such labour? Who will be the next working class?

Flexibility has been presented to the workers of the West as the supreme virtue in an industrial system committed to ceaseless change. But flexibility shades readily into malleability, manipulability, suggestibility even. What has happened to those forms of knowledge and kinds of skill acquired in a more 'material' industrial era? Clearly they must have disappeared: otherwise, we would not hear the insistent demand that workers 'adapt', 'retrain', 'acquire new skills', 'get retooled', be 'topped up', 'upgrade their proficiencies', 're-equip themselves'. Where, in their own direct experience, do people now find the capacity even to begin to understand the nature of the society they live in? How do they learn to resist a version of the world that is not their own, but is presented to them by those whose task in the division of labour is to form opinions, to create a climate, to give a lead? It has become almost traditional for the Labour Party to blame the popular press and the media for planting damaging and unseemly ideas into people's heads. It might be asked what alternative view of this world the party of labour now finds itself able to articulate. It sometimes seems as though the spaces in the great industrial cities once occupied by a former working class have their counterpart in the inner spaces which were once home to another kind of consciousness.

What has also become clear is that just as there are no neutral accounts of the working class, so there are no objective accounts of work and its social significance. It would seem that all versions of labour are saturated with ideology. The Right has discussed labour as a factor of production, as a problem of labour costs and discipline. But even the Left, which has sought to come closer to the lived experience of labour, has been profoundly influenced by the sulphurous denunciations of Marx. Their representation of work is always as oppressive, exploitative, relentless, dehumanizing, repetitive, meaningless, alienated. And yet, when people talk about what they actually did in the workplace, work often turns out to be, as well as some or even all of these things, also satisfying, enjoyable, challenging, significant; and, for many, the source of the strongest sense of belonging and comradeship. If this latter seems an unfamiliar picture of work, it is because those on the Left have been constrained to find evidence that the experience of labour was indeed tending in the direction that Marx had foreseen; that the unbearable conditions they perceived were indeed driving the proletariat to the limits of endurance, beyond which they would surely rise up and play out their revolutionary role.

At the end of his section on the factory in volume 1 of *Capital*, there is a characteristic passage where Marx comments:

We shall here merely allude to the material conditions under which factory labour is carried on. Every organ of sense is injured in an equal degree by artificial elevation of the temperature, by the dust-laden atmosphere, by the deafening noise, not mention danger to life and limb among the thickly crowded machinery, which, with the regularity of the seasons, issues its list of the killed and wounded in the industrial battle. Economy of the social means of production, matured and forced as in a hothouse by the factory system, is turned, in the hands of capital, into systematic robbery of what is necessary for the life of the workman while he is at work, robbery of space, light, air, and of protection to his person against the dangerous and unwholesome accompaniments of the productive process.

In the light of these fulminations, how difficult for the concerned observer to perceive anything else within the walls of the manufactory. Even when the technology changes and the conditions of labour are transformed beyond all recognition, accounts of work still bear the impress of these inexpungeable evocations. How the voice of Marx echoes in this contemporary description of catering workers in the London of the 1980s:

The physical conditions are appalling, the level of job-related disability is high. Much of catering involves sheer physical pain – if the labour disappeared, you'd call it torture. The equipment is not designed to make the work easier for women; you're standing all day, you have extremes of hot and cold, you suffer from constant cuts and scalds and burns which don't get a chance to heal. You have to contort yourself to reach up, to reach down; you suffer from back pain, rheumatism from cold water; and if your hands have been for two hours in orange juice while you prepare fruit salad, the acid makes your skin sore; you get varicose veins and stiff necks ... It is violence, selling yourself and splitting your real self from what you do ... This service is impersonal, it's dehumanizing, you can't transcend it as an individual ... It is more stark in industrialized services, there isn't the pretence that sometimes conceals the exploitation in personal relationships and marriages. You can't buy your way out of capitalism.

While there is no doubt that this articulates the real pain of low-paid women workers in catering, there is something forced and not fully authentic in the language employed: the vehemence of Marx is silencing something of the experience. The companionship and the solidarity of women, the complexity of the human relationships that exist in spite of the cash nexus, the humour that expresses creative disaffection – all this is suppressed for the sake of maintaining a grimness which alone can guarantee the survival of the ideology. Because the labour process was believed to be the prime locus of that exploitation which would ultimately lead to a transformed society, any mitigation or diminution of that oppression simply could not be admitted, for fear that the ideology might crumble and the future transformation be jeopardized.

Of course, equally tendentious accounts of work have emanated from those who saw in the industrial system a fulfilment of the purposes of Providence: accounts are no less grotesque which told of the happy atmosphere in a spacious and airy manufactory, where juveniles sang as their nimble fingers plied the shuttle or drew the thread – occupying hands for which the Devil would surely have found less innocent labour. Similarly, how distorted are those views of the present division of labour which see 'real jobs' or 'meaningful work' in such savourless errands as dashing through the city streets carrying hot pizzas in imitation leather bags on the back of motorcycles, or carefully vacuum-cleaning the grass in front of five-star hotels, or tape-recording salacious stories for telephone chat-lines. If there is violence inflicted upon people through the labour process today, it is likely to be through the overwhelming inutility of what they are compelled to do rather than through the breaking of bones and bodies, as in the early industrial era.

Such partial accounts of work do not begin in the nineteenth century, but draw on a long Christian tradition which offers other interpretations of the meaning of labour. In the Christian tradition work is service, a living-out of prayer. Work is a calling, a 'vocation' in its original sense. Work is an enhancement of the given: we labour with what we have, whether these are material or spiritual attributes; and on the Day of Judgement we will be required to account for the use to which we have put our gifts. Nevertheless, work is also a curse, proclaimed by the voice of God in the Garden of Eden. 'By the sweat of thy brow shalt thou live.'

At an earlier period, industrial society made ample use of the Christian rhetoric of labour and sacrifice. The warning of St Paul, that 'If a man will not work, he shall not eat', was widely deployed to impose industrial discipline upon people who had previously known only the discipline of the seasons, and to whom the admonition 'As you sow so shall you reap' had had a more literal resonance. At the same time, the Christian deferral of rewards until hereafter assumed even greater plausibility, given the considerable degree of suffering to which large numbers of the labouring poor were then subjected.

It sometimes seems that in more recent times industrial society has promised the lifting of the curse of work. This has achieved nothing less than an opening up of the path back to paradise and, simultaneously, the descent of the after-life into the heart of the here and now. It has required only minimal reshapings of the Christian story to realize this state of double blessedness. These rewards, however, have not been severed from the satisfactory completion of certain duties, labours, services. If we no longer have to toil in mill and mine, we are still under the compulsion to sell our labour in a shifting and volatile market-place, a market-place which also then furnishes us with the attributes of this particular form of beatitude. In other words, what has been called the consumer society still depends upon a complex division of labour, a division which has become more diffuse, more opaque and more intricate as it has become more global. The conditions for the liberation – even the salvation – of the working class in one country can be understood only when we grasp the function of that local working class in a far wider patterning of labour.

Has the working class simply been changed, or has it disappeared? The answer is a disappointing Both and Neither. The nature of the manual work performed in, say, Britain continues to be altered by accelerating technological development; on the other hand, menial, repetitive, ill rewarded, laborious, stressful work has not disappeared for the majority of the people. What does seem to have disappeared is the ability of those people to name themselves as a class constituted by their form of working, or to identify each other as being shaped by similar social and economic forces.

The working class that dug the coal and built the ships and wove the cloth and created the pottery and fished the seas has certainly all but disappeared. And yet, coal is dug, ships are built, cloth is woven, pottery is made, the seas are fished. Who does this work, if not a working class? So has class become merely a matter of geography? Or, perhaps, of race?

Whatever the future configurations of a global working class might be, it is hard to resist the sense of the ending of a whole epoch of class history in Britain. It is a poignant story. The working class in one country does appear to have been laid to rest. And rest from labour was above all what the working class sought for itself, although perhaps not in the way that this has come to pass. This was the hope that was carried in the promises of liberation, promises which working-class parents made to their children, promises proclaimed in socialist visions of the world that was to come. But this easing of toil which they longed for was never confused with that other familiar release from labour, the squandering of their energies in unemployment and worklessness. Nor is the liberation they hoped for necessarily recognizable within the alienated and strangely oppressive forms of leisure which money can and, it sometimes seems, must, buy.

'Work was our life,' say the disemployed miners. Does this mean that without work there is no life? When the workers of an earlier industrial period were told that rest from labour could only come with death, is this what they meant? *Laborare est orare* was engraved upon the pediment of many a town hall erected to celebrate the function of a town or city in the national division of labour. How shall we pray without work? And what would they inscribe on their civic pediments now?

To people overburdened with work, its ending on any terms must seem like paradise. That such work was exploitative as well as essential makes liberation from it a strange blessing; and a wider sense of justice might lead us to ask who, then, is to perform the necessary labour that has been lifted from our shoulders?

Of course, a mystique of non-work has always existed in the world. Some human beings have always been excused the need to work on the grounds of their exalted rank and birth, their inherited powers, or their closeness to heaven, from which they derived their authority. This exemption from labour bestowed upon them a capacity to reflect upon the deeper meanings of human life, even to exemplify its more playful and aesthetic aspects. To them were entrusted the higher purposes: they were the stewards of the earth, in their hands reposed a civilizing mission, in their impenetrable avocations lay the destiny of humankind.

Such an ideal also informed the aspirations of a rising bourgeoisie, who longed to see their sons and daughters delivered from the burdens of business and money-making, so that they might pursue the gentler activities of overseeing their newly acquired country estates; and for their daughters, the acquisition of such accomplishments as the speaking of French and the ability to acquit themselves with distinction at the piano. Freedom from work meant freedom to take on what classical tradition defined as the responsibilities of leadership.

It was for a somewhat modified version of this privileged and aristocratic model that the thinkers and dreamers of the 1960s reached, when they envisaged a whole society delivered from onerous labour by the further development of advanced technology. Were we not all to become aristocrats of the mind? Mysteriously, the masses were to become inheritors of a formerly elitist tradition. Aristocratic traditions were to be marketed for the people; the best of all that had been thought and said in the world was to become a common possession.

The consumer society is the present inheritor of these distant ideals – somewhat altered, as they have been transferred through time. Thus it is that the lives of most of the Western working class have become modelled on what was formerly regarded as the sacred prerogative of the highest-born. We cannot say whether those called unwittingly into the support and service of this latest manifestation of privilege will be happy to carry the burden indefinitely. Nor can we tell whether the restless freedoms now won by the Western working class will furnish for ever the satisfactions which may have been anticipated. Nor, indeed, whether it will remain sufficient function for a former working class to reconcile the poor people of the world to their permanent exclusion, when they, too, ask why they cannot follow them and live in this same privileged way.

Class

If class is no longer so visible in the public life of our society, where are we to find it? If we were to follow people into their homes, would we, perhaps, find class there?

Probably not. For the attributes of class seem to have been lost in the multiplying symbols by which people now measure their own, and other people's status. Increasingly since the 1950s, the labour market has ceased to be a primary source of identity. It has yielded its dominant position to the consumer market. People are, it is said, no longer what they do, but what they have, what they own. Perhaps this is why, when we look at a crowd of people, it no longer makes sense to ask whether they are working-class or middle-class. All we see is a collection of individuals going about their chosen business, freed from the limitations that bound earlier genera-tions to their place in society. We may feel it a great relief no longer to be forced to use the language of class to describe our relationships with each other.

Has the time now not come when we can gratefully leave class to be a technical term, employed in ever more obscure debates between sociologists and historians and all those whose academic business ties them to the investigation of times past? For who else could have a vested interest in clinging to archaic discourses of class? Only revolutionaries, perhaps, those still wedded to antique prophecies which would have put the working class at the centre of a project of redemption.

We have seen the fate of such visions once they have entered the realm of lived experience. The recent eclipse of the attempt at transformation in the Soviet Union and Eastern Europe seems finally to have laid to rest all debate about the working class. The vanquishing of 'socialism' is felt to have involved the elimination − liquidation, even − of the class on whose radical dissatisfactions it was to have been founded.

The question of whether or not the working class still exists is a far cry from the more troubling one of whether the working class will one day rise up and overthrow the existing order of things. For while such debates raged − and they did until very recently − it was taken for granted that not only did the working class exist, but it was indeed the most important of all the classes in society. Thus we may now have to ask an even more disconcerting question: in spite of the apparent solidity of the imagery of streets, factories and chimneys, did the working class ever exist at all?

It all seems to depend, like so much else, upon definitions and discourses. The working class has always been a contested concept. Sociologists, historians and political theorists have all used the working class for a variety of partly conflicting and partly overlapping purposes. Specialist argument has hinged upon whether the working class is best defined as manual workers, or as the creators of surplus value, or as those who are limited to inferior life chances, or as those who bear a set of alternative values − even an oppositional culture.

Over the past twenty years such debate has become increasingly arcane, as fewer and fewer people recognize themselves, their lives or their concerns in these discussions, which nevertheless have always claimed centrality for themselves. 'Why do you keep going on about class?' people ask. 'Where does it get you?' 'I am who I am and that's it.' 'I like to think of myself as an individual.' 'Why all this harping on the differences between people, when nobody is any better than anybody else?'

Inequalities do continue to trouble people, but they no longer present themselves so clearly as the inequalities of class. People may certainly be angered by discrimination because of race or gender. Much concern is also expressed about the persistence of poverty, particularly when it comes to people sleeping under bridges and in doorways. But for most people such concerns are not central. Most of us see our destiny as a consequence of individual effort, aided or impaired by a bit of luck or a stroke of misfortune. For the most part, we feel that we are, more or less, and barring accident, masters of our own fate. Such individualism is rendered less heroic by the fact that the majority in the two-thirds/one-third society are provided with everything needed for their comfort.

If most people no longer wish to see themselves as working-class, it is because they want to distance themselves from those older experiences of poverty and dispossession. For one thing which linked all the discourses about the working class was that it was a class that was always insecure, with no guarantee that any of its basic needs would be adequately answered within the industrial society that had called it into existence. The working class looked out upon an alien world, a world it had not made, one in which it had been conceded no right to participate except insofar as it functioned as hands, as operatives, as labour. The sensibility of the working class was formed by this basic experience of insecurity and insufficiency. The values it may or may not have borne, the institutions it may or may not have created for itself, the resistances it sometimes managed to establish, are as close as we will ever come to the essential nature of the working class. Its essence was not a culture, nor an historic mission, nor a necessary heroism, nor a given morality; it was an experience. This experience was one of the most cruel disregard for the human person, marked as it was by an exploitation that ruined lives, broke the body and stunted the imagination. It is this collective trauma that has left the traces and scars which some have mistaken for an essence.

In such situations of deprivation and exploitation, it is the only rational response of people without any other recourse to band together, to find ways of mitigating the horrors of their condition. Such collectivism requires little idealism; it is, in fact, true common sense. Those who refused such common sense certainly diminished their already slender chances of survival. Where life expectancy is low (thirty-five in Engels' Manchester), where sickness and malnutrition take their daily toll of the most vulnerable and hunger remains constantly unappeased, life takes on a heightened intensity. Its fragility and preciousness are brought home to us, not simply in the consolations of religion or philosophy, but through the daily materialities of want and loss. The existential and the social are for a moment fused; and it is the afterglow of this intense moment that has lent a continuing lustre to the working class, long after this had been transformed beyond all recognition.

Of course, this experience has not been banished from the world. Wherever people suffer want and insecurity, exploitation and dispossession, we shall expect to hear echoes of the 'classic' working-class experience of

Britain and elsewhere; we shall see similar responses and forms of resistance. Is this perhaps why we have a curious sense of visiting our own past when we visit the exploitative workshops of Seoul or Manila or the townships around Johannesburg, or listen to the testimony of the textile workers in Bombay or the jute workers of Calcutta? If, today, we look round in vain for the working class, is it not so much that we have left the working class as that the working class has left us?

Was the true destiny of the Western working class oblivion? Could it have been otherwise?

Actually, although we now find it almost impossible to talk about the working class, it continues to haunt political discussion, though not directly. Whilst the working class seemed to be the most significant threat to order, continuity and stability in society, class was bound to preoccupy conservatives and reformers alike. This continuing centrality is now hidden as a consequence of those very means whereby the working class was attached to an existing order which it once seemed to call into question. For the price of reconciling the working class to the structures of industrial society has been very high indeed. The cost of this conciliation has produced what we have now come to call 'the ecological crisis'.

The connection between working-class affluence and ecological destruction may not be immediately apparent. Yet the greatest achievement of capitalism has been the peaceable, orderly, piecemeal absorption of those elements in society which were once regarded as hostile and alien. In spite of all the predictions of unrest, violence and revolutionary turmoil, the working class marched with dignity to take up the place it had earned at the heart of a society from which it had once seemed hopelessly estranged. And if this assimilation remained peaceful, it was because no one had to suffer loss in the process. The rich could continue to grow richer even as the working class became less poor. Redistribution was avoided by a vast expansion of the productive power of industrial capitalism. The enmity between capital and labour was laid to rest; they became partners, equally devoted to the creation of more wealth, even though disputes continued to arise about its exact apportioning.

It is this very much augmented productive capacity, which won the working class for capitalism, that now lies at the heart of the present crisis. The violence that had been seemingly avoided was only 'externalized'; that is to say, it was passed on by the economic system, so that it was borne by the natural resource base of the earth. Of course, it seemed until very recently that the treasures of the earth were inexhaustible, that the riches of nature were available for an indefinite pacification of the working class. Water, air, soil, the elements of life – these could be relied upon to absorb all that the system could produce, just as the system itself had appeared to possess an infinite capacity for absorbing the people.

It is therefore to be expected that there should be a tension, even a hostility, between those who strive to protect the planet, and the working class. This is what lies behind taunts that people in the Green movement are middle-class, privileged people who, having enough for themselves, now want to pull up the ladder against the have-nots. The reason for this is clear. The Greens are now the only political movement in the West that seriously calls into question the nature and scope of economic growth. And to call into question economic growth is to threaten the fragile well-being of the working class, and the accommodation it has reached with industrial society. When George Bush said in 1992, before the Rio Summit, that 'the American lifestyle is not up for negotiation', it was to this repressed relationship that he was alluding.

And perhaps the working class is right to be distrustful of the Greens. For the pressures upon the Green movement to become absorbed into capitalist society, even as the working class has been, are enormous. And if this reconciliation can be brought about (a big if), and more rational, less wasteful forms of production set in place, there is no doubt that in the necessary sacrifices the working class would be the first to suffer, unless redistribution became more of a reality than it has ever previously been (an even bigger if). If the working class has learned anything from two centuries of industrial society, it is that industry operates on the principle of 'last in/first out'; and the working class is only too aware of how recently it has been taken in.

Capitalism changed in order to meet the needs, the demands and the threats of its working class; and to do this, it externalized its own inner contradictions. In doing so, it transformed the working class; it radically depleted the resource base of the earth; it visited the poverty lifted from the Western working class upon the poor of the earth; and it rendered unimaginable all alternatives to itself. The peaceful reconciliation of this working class has produced echoes which reverberate with ever increasing violence around the world. This is because the cost of this historic achievement is not a once-for-all payment, but a kind of continuous tribute, a hush-money in perpetuity, to those who have been bought off.

For the price of social peace in the West is now the continuous, uninterrupted, rising disposable income of the people. Ensuring this is the sole policy of all the mainstream political parties. No wonder the working class has been written out of the story: its disappearance is exactly what the story is all about. It takes a great deal of economic growth to ensure that the working class stays hidden – supporting an absconded working class cannot be done on the cheap. The high costs of this enterprise cannot, however, be completely externalized. One consequence of it is the emergence (from where?) of a class recently discovered to be lurking within the classless societies of the West: the underclass.

'The underclass' is an unpleasant word for 'the poor'. The underclass is those left behind when the working class has moved upwards.

For it must be remembered that the working class was never a homogeneous, monolithic social block, but was always fragmented, differentiated. There was, however, amongst all the variations, one overwhelmingly unifying factor – the terror of poverty, of insecurity and loss; and the solidarities and similarities that were exhibited were a response to this intractable fact. And even these solidarities should not be exaggerated: there were always large numbers who allied themselves with the powerful and possessing classes – the deferential, conservative working class.

There is always more than one version of common sense, and alongside the growth of collectivist responses and institutions ran a more individualistic form of deference. This had its origins perhaps in earlier social relationships, whereby the poor saw their best chance in accepting their lowly station and hoping, by means of exemplary behaviour, to attract the favourable opinions and the benevolence of their betters. If you had to be poor, they reasoned, best to be deserving; and this was carried over into the new industrial society by those who had every reason to believe that serving the best interests of their masters would not leave them entirely without resource. It could be argued that their patient endurance was rewarded, although not necessarily within their own lifetime. For that identification of the interests of the working class with its masters has become the dominant perception of the world since the coming of generalized affluence in the 1950s. There is now no disharmony between the interests of rich and poor, united in their common commitment to more.

But with this more complete attachment of the working class to capitalism other, older fissures and fragmentings have become more obvious, particularly those which once divided the 'respectable' working class from the 'rough' working class. These two elements, a cleavage once scarcely visible to the outsider, have gone their different ways. The split has been magnified, as a majority of the working class has gone upward and a minority downward. The majority migrated to the middle class, whilst the minority sank into the underclass. It is this evacuation of a social space once occupied by the working class that has made people pose the question as to whether the working class exists. It has been a kind of mass transhumance, an out-migration, to diverse destinations: like a country overtaken by some cosmic disaster, where the refugees are dispersed to unpredictable destinations.

The preoccupation with an underclass at this time is the rediscovery of that fragment of the working class that was excluded from the more general improvement – the embourgeoisement, as it was grandly called – of a majority in the 1950s, 60s and 70s. Only now, this fragment of the dispossessed has been much augmented by the inclusion within it of the casualties of social breakdown – single parents, the separated and divorced, broken families; many young people, especially the unskilled; some former migrants and their children; large numbers of the many elderly (their increased longevity is a factor here); perhaps most of the chronically sick and disabled. The underclass has become problematic, because what looked like a containable residuum, a rump stranded by the general betterment of the working class, now appears to be a far more intractable section of the people. In a two-thirds/one-third society, that third is not negligible, nor merely a temporarily excluded minority awaiting the better days that will see its automatic absorption into the ranks of the well-to-do.

In the early industrial era the solution to the problem of poverty resided in universal enfranchisement, because, it was reasoned, the poor – then a majority – were unlikely to vote for those who would perpetuate their sufferings. This is why the extension of the franchise was resisted so furiously by the possessing classes. It would not have done for the people to have voted away privilege. It required a portion of privilege, however modest, to be extended to a majority of the people, before they could be expected to see the wisdom of its retention; then the franchise was conceded. A different problem emerges once the poor have passed into minority status; for then, no matter how they use their vote, they are as effectively disfranchised as though it had never been granted in the first place. The poor can now vote for anything they like – the wildest utopianisms, the most bloody of revolutions; it matters not, as long as the newly prosperous majority still identify their interests with those of the rich. The franchise, once resisted as a threat to civilized society, has in this way become the surest guarantor of its preservation.

The 'decline' of the old working class is best understood as a metaphor. It indicates the decay of a specific response to insecurity and poverty in the early industrial era: the eclipse of values of sharing, of solidarity and of collective resistance. These values attached themselves to one historical moment within the evolution, and subsequent modification, of working-class temperament and sensibility. They were never intrinsic. No values are ever intrinsic to one social group or class or nation or race. They were borne, briefly, by the working class. That they have been dissolved is, in part, a consequence of the Welfare State, the object of which was precisely to remove those earlier threats of insecurity and poverty.

It may be that the Welfare State always contained the germ of its own ideological decay. The securities that it offered, 'from cradle to grave', abolished for many the harsh and cruel conditions that had necessitated the old solidarities and forms of mutual defence. Who could have imagined that the old asperities would ever become the focus of strange nostalgias, not only for a ruling class, but also for those who were the intended and actual beneficiaries of the Welfare State? Throughout the 1960s and 70s, much discussion about the working class asserted that they had become 'feather-bedded', 'lazy' ('Nobody wants to do a proper day's work any more'); that their moral fibre had been 'sapped'. 'The trouble with this country is that it's gone soft.' It is a measure of the absorption of the working class into mainstream ideology that they found themselves echoing what had once been middle-class complaints – that the country was full of 'scroungers' and 'layabouts' and 'shirkers', and that what was needed 'to put us back where we belong' was 'a damn good dose of unemployment' or, 'although I hate to say it, another war'. Both of these prescriptions were subsequently realized, although their beneficial effect upon the moral fibre of the nation remains uncertain. It is these 'sub-political' changes that help to explain the ability of the Right to dominate popular debate in the 1980s.

And yet, the values of solidarity remain. What is more, they remain important – vital, even. It is crass to say that they have collapsed, or become redundant, simply because the social forces which gave rise to them in an earlier industrial era have been in abeyance. The tradition of working-class mutuality that was identified with such values may have gone, but that does not mean the values have been superseded. They live on, particularly in the Third World.

The resolution of the problem of the working class within Western society has been achieved, as we have seen, only by having been externalized; that is to say, it has created the ecological crisis and intensified poverty in other parts of the world. As people confront these transferred crises, they discover for themselves the potency of the discarded values. They have no other recourse in a wasting, impoverished and damaged world. The essence of solidarity is a pooling of both human and material resources: who can doubt that such a benign synergy is what is most needed in a world laid waste by the over-exploitation of material resources and the disregard of human capabilities?

Here we may catch a glimpse of the most fundamental reason why it has become so difficult to use the term 'working class'. If it now seems almost impossible to employ it, it is because of developments that have led to what we might call the 'invisibilizing' of the working class. Its disappearing is part of that process of eclipse, loss and elision of those values which cannot figure in a world dedicated to the abuse of both material and human resources. The working class has become the class that dare not speak its name.

If people still admit to being working-class – and surveys suggest they frequently do – it is seldom the heroic working class of Marx that they have in mind. Increasingly, the working class is something that people come from. It is what most people's parents were. The working class is a starting point, from which we can measure the immensity of the distance we have travelled. The working class has been, as it were, evicted from history. This is a particularly vengeful act, given that history is what was, in some accounts, supposed to have vindicated it. This eviction opens up vast possibilities of rewriting the past; the blank pages of history offer ample space for the most fanciful of projections.

In this context, some would see the 'underclass' as the bones, the skeleton, the consumed remains, of the working class. Within two centuries a working class which emerged from, and defined itself against, the lower orders, appears to have lost itself again. But nothing is lost for ever. The voices we have heard are not dead, even though some of them speak from beyond the grave.